# WHEN THE VILLAIN COMES HOME

Edited by

## Gabrielle Harbowy and Ed Greenwood

DRAGON MOON PRESS

When the Villain Comes Home

Also edited by Gabrielle Harbowy and Ed Greenwood
WHEN THE HERO COMES HOME (2011)

# Editors' Note

Once a villain, always a villain...truly?

You can never go home again...or can you?

Every life is filled with all too many questions, and all too few answers.

This book holds some answers about villainy. As a shiftier character once remarked, in a scene wherein he was backed into a corner and pressed for the truth: "Don't like that answer? Pick another—I've plenty on offer!"

There are plenty here, in stories that are wildly different from each other.

In the end, it all comes down to intent: A hero can be born from a single deed, but villainy—true villainy—is born of intent.

The heroes in our first anthology, *When the Hero Comes Home*, were shaped by a great range of heroic deeds, and their stories explored how that heroism changed them; how it changed their ability to return to a quieter life. They were shaped by their circumstances.

The villains in these pages have shaped their own destinies.

Villainy takes many forms. The reluctant villain, who takes up a mantle out of obligation or necessity; the team player; the mastermind; the everyday person who has resources and a grudge; the person so intent on an agenda that they don't even notice the many lives they ruin on the way to their goal. The person who simply happens to have ended up on the side—of a war, or border, or social issue, or argument—that isn't yours. The madman, or the embittered person who sees their own doom and doesn't want to go down alone while hated others flourish.

Here we explore the diversity of villainy, and also revisit the many forms of homecoming. Returning from extended travels; the long trip back to the places of our childhood; the more spiritual homecoming that is finding rightness and belonging; and the simpler retreat to comfort and safety at the end of the day. In the following pages, you'll find all of these.

Some you may find familiar, or unsettling. Some, we hope, will strike you as intriguing, or entertaining. Some may even offer you comfort.

We ride into villainy, cloaks swirling. Coming along on the ride?

Gabrielle Harbowy
Ed Greenwood
June, 2012

# CONTENTS

# PINKTASTIC AND THE END OF THE WORLD

## Camille Alexa

GRETCHEN WAITED WHILE THE random old guy locked the community garden gate and packed his hoe and spades into the trunk of his car, pressing herself against the chain-link fence near the riotous green tangle standing vivid and lush beside the neighboring plots' scraggly broccolini and limp arugula. The car growled to life, backfiring once, sending Gretchen hunching lower into the shrubbery. If she'd paid attention to exactly which of the dozens of long narrow plots had been that old dude's she could've sent a little zap in there, wiped out some snap peas or something for making her wait an hour for him to leave, maybe flooded a couple rows of his strawberries, washed them all into the gutter.

But it wasn't worth it. Wasn't worth the risk of getting caught. Wasn't worth missing her chance to water Pinktastic's tomatoes.

The old guy and his jalopy's rumble faded into the evening quiet. Gretchen stood, brushed leaves off her rear and shot a cursory glance up and down the darkening street. Lights were winking on in houses along the lane, warm gold squares behind which, Gretchen imagined, people were probably sliding steaming dishes onto polished wood tables covered with shiny silverware and surrounded by smiling family or friends or spouses and whatnot. Whatever.

Wedging her boot in the fence, Gretchen hauled one leg up over the spiky top. Stupid city bureaucracy, to put some dinky little barrier around a place if they didn't want people to climb right over it. Fence like this practically begged to be climbed. Who wanted a few lousy old turnips and raspberries and squash anyway? Who even *ate* turnips on purpose?

Well, Pinktastic apparently did, or at least sold them at her organic vegetable stand at the market. Gretchen heaved her other leg over the fence and dropped onto the rich soil. The sky was clear, starting to dot with pinprick stars, the air crisper than it had been in weeks. Gretchen breathed deep, letting the humidity, the slight salinity, the ions in the air tingle through her body. Nobody else would be able to practically taste the cool front rolling in, though there might be a couple other weather Supers along the coast. Apparently some joker in Cleveland could draw down lightning nearly as well as she could, but only if it was already occurring naturally.

Whatever. Any idiot with a little zing in his fingers and a goddamn cape could call himself Thunderpunk and whip up a freaking light show. Let him try to get the exact balance in moisture and temperature and sunlight for a two-hundred square foot garden plot for an entire summer—a whole freaking summer!—and see how well he did then. That stuff took finesse, yo.

Saturday market. Stalls crammed with shoppers and lookie-Lous, yupster couples with stroller tanks, suburban indie kids sporting dreadlocks and tattoos loading up on free samples of kombucha and vegan baked goods. Gretchen crouched between a Victorian baby carriage and an enormous wrought iron bird cage, trying to get a clear line of sight to the other end of the market where Pinktastic's vegetable stall shone with rainbowed greenery plumpness. Pinktastic herself was radiant, all apple cheeks and rose-tinted hair and smiles for everyone. Gretchen couldn't quite make out details from her lurking spot, but she'd come so often to watch the girl from afar she could picture the whiteness of her teeth as she smiled, practically smell her honey shampoo.

"Destructova! Haven't seen you in, like, forever!"

Gretchen cringed, scanning the aisles past the rack of vintage aprons and the shelf of scuffed antique cowboy boots to see if anybody had heard. Smash Chick clapped her shoulder and Gretchen reluctantly turned. "It's Gretchen," she said, keeping her voice down, hoping the other girl would get the hint. "Destructova's lying low at the moment."

Smash Chick nodded slowly. "Oh yeah...you guys disbanded after that whole public transit fiasco. Wow. Epic fail there, huh?" She laughed, a big crunching sound that made Gretchen cringe again. "Whose brilliant idea was it for the Dastards to destroy every bus in town? Got yourselves on the feds' domestic terrorist list for that one, eh?"

Stupid Franco. That bus thing had been his idea; his dad held the Metro fleet contract with the city. But Gretchen only shrugged, shoving aside a moulting feather boa tickling her where it dangled from a rickety hat stand. "Seemed like an okay idea at the time," she said. "Seemed like something to do."

With a sympathetic moue, Smash Chick patted her shoulder, her hand the size of Gretchen's skull. "And I was sorry to hear about you and Powerpunch—"

"Franco."

"Yeah, Franco. You guys were a cute couple. And he's *gorgeous*! His unauthorized headshots sell like hotcakes at my friend Loki's stall." She waved vaguely in the same direction as Pinktastic's vegetable stand. "I help

Loki out sometimes. He's kind of hard up since the Chromatic League shut down the Deadly Pranksters."

Gretchen nodded, distracted, half-turning so she could watch Pinktastic slide zucchinis into a customer's bag. Huge shiny bright green zucchinis the size of baguettes, plump and flawless from Gretchen's secret ministrations.

Smash Chick gave up squinting across the market trying to figure out what Gretchen was looking at. "Well, whatever. You're between gigs, and that's cool, but when you're ready to pick a new band, call me. I'll put in a good word with the Hacktacious Seven. We've got some serious income potential."

"But if you took another member," Gretchen murmured, still watching Pinktastic, "wouldn't you be the Hacktacious Eight?"

"Who cares? The band has, like, twelve already. Number manipulation is our racket, baby!"

"Thanks, Smash," Gretchen said, forcing her attention back to the other girl. "I appreciate the thought. Not sure hacking's my thing, but I'll keep you guys in mind."

Smash was pretty, in a hard, rough sort of way. Her forearms were solid as tree trunks, and she had these big grey eyes that kind of melted you if you looked at them for long. Not melted you like The Scorcherizer from the Dastards, where your skin started sloughing off and your organs cooked on the inside, but melted you like you could tell she was way too nice for hardcore villain work. Seriously, the Hacktacious Seven? Not much street cred on the baddie circuit for a bunch of computer geeks siphoning a third of a cent per transaction off millions of ATMs around the world. International Super villains. Sheesh.

Smash Chick smiled, kind of sad. "You action types, it's in your blood, huh? Along with your powers. Like, my band built me this special keyboard for these big mitts..." she held up fists like two raw tofurkeys, "...and I was filled with this sense of *rightness*, you know? Like, I could do evil every day in my pajamas, from the comfort of my own apartment. The best of all possible worlds." She let her hands drop in an almost-shrug. "Anyways, you have my number. See you around."

The big Super turned to squeeze from the cramped stall between two boxy sofas standing on their sides like giant button-tufted bookends, but Gretchen called out, "Hey, Smash." The girl looked back, something like hope flaring in her big grey eyes. "Smash, don't you ever...don't you ever miss it? The hardcore action stuff you did before you got recruited by the Seven? Don't you miss that rush when like, you're all out there in the flesh, evaporating the city's water supply, or mass kidnapping the entire season's cast of Dancing With the Stars, or whatever? You got your gauntlets on, or your cape or your mask or your infrajet powerboots. And you know the Chromatic League is on their way to stop you, and your vision's all blazing and your heart's up in your throat and your blood feels like pumping lava and you know you and your band could crush anything, *anything* standing between you and your evil deed…"

The hopeful glimmer had faded from Smash Chick's face. She smiled again, that same sad little quirk to the lips. "Nah," she said. "I'm no action junkie. I get the urge to smash something these days, I go out to the woods and find some dead tree stumps or a couple boulders. I love long-distance evil. Don't miss all that blood-pumping stuff at all…guess I'm just not wired like you are."

Long after Smash Chick had disappeared past used furniture and rehabbed power tools and an acre of fresh fruit and mountains of gluten-free baked goods and vegetarian dog biscuits, Gretchen thought about what she'd said. She tried to picture not craving the excitement, the thrill of action when it was *on*, when things got dire and on fire and you had those incandescent moments of perfect glory between one live-or-die second and the next, when you felt more powerful than anything no matter whether you got defeated this time, or came out on top or barely escaped or made a million or lost your shirt. In those moments, everything was right even if it was all going wrong, and you wanted to laugh out loud at the incredible beauty of everything, because it was *all* beautiful: even your fellow villains with their unsavory appetites and unfortunate costume choices; even your victims, with their mewling cries for mercy or their impotent blustery threats or offers of cash to let them go. Even your nemesis, with her white, white teeth and her shiny pink hair that smelled of honey and green garden-y stuff, like flowers and clover.

She thought about all these things, hunkered between the bird cage big enough to hold the Police Commissioner's husband and the wheeled baby buggy straight out of Masterpiece Theatre, and watched Pinktastic gently place little green cardboard pints of strawberries and raspberries into her customers' eco-friendly market bags. Pints of strawberries and raspberries Gretchen could practically taste on her tongue past market dust and the loose-feathery tickle of the old boa. Taste them from the hundred times she'd illicitly tasted them in Pinktastic's garden, crouched in darkness between towering tomato vines as small gentle rainclouds formed directly overhead, obscured by twilight and silence.

The racetrack-wide aisles at the MegaHome Mart were packed. Gretchen shoved her cart along in front of her, cursing under her breath when the defective fourth wheel seized up and sent her careening into a stack of three-for-one sod squares where she collided with a dull thump. So many Supers in this city, the store might as well've made a sign in those hot orange bubble letters they liked so much: *Backyard Secret Hideaway Camouflage at half the price!*

"Destructova. Haven't seen you around much lately."

Gretchen blinked up from the floor where she wrestled with her cart's wheel. Franco, of course. With The Succubus hanging on his arm like he was a million-dollar ransom victim.

After a last wrap of her knuckles against the unyielding rubber as though that fixed the balky wheel, Gretchen stood. "Hi, Powerpunch. Didn't think the MegaHome was your scene." Franco preferred Super titles in public. Always said it was *kowtowing to the Man* to lurk around under civilian names.

Franco peered off into the distance, looking cool; kind of a specialty of his. "Sale this big," he said, "every Super in town's snapping up bargain hideaway and lair stuff. Stupid recession."

The Succubus nodded, sending her trademark pigtails bobbing. "You're *so right*, Powerpunch; I knew I'd bump into you here."

Sheesh. Only Succubus would wear her Super suit to the flipping MegaHome. Shiny plaid skirt, skintight blazer with nothing underneath and straining at the buttons, glossy white knee-highs...she looked like a lifesized Catholic Schoolgirl Barbie dipped in vinyl.

"Hi, Succubus. Kind of thought you and Franco had already bumped into each other. More than once, in fact," Gretchen said. "Back when he and I were together."

"Hi, Destructova. Glad you're still out here representing the forces of villainy in your own special way, dressed like a goth librarian. You sure you want her to join our new band, Powerpunch? She doesn't exactly exude the right vibe."

Franco studied Gretchen. "She's good in a fight," he said.

Watching him watch her, Gretchen remembered some of the good things about being with him. She remembered how she felt when he lifted her in his toned arms up into the sky with his Superflight, his trademark black split cape flapping around her like protective wings while she plunged her fists into clouds to send lightning down to crisp entire cornfields, to rattle the earth below with her terrible thunder and scorch it with her searing winds.

Going solo was lonely. Even though the International Antivillainy Coalition had placed them on the watch list, Franco, Gretchen, Dan and Mike and Lisa and all the other ex-Dastards and their cohorts and minions; even though the Chromatic League was watching for any sign the Dastards might be reforming under a new name or in a new part of town; even though Pinktastic had taken the Hero Pledge along with the rest of her band at the Police Commissioner's public ceremony last week: even though all that, Gretchen missed the real action. God, did she miss it.

She took a deep breath. "Franco, maybe..."

But she forgot what she was going to say. Straight ahead, about the length of three getaway cars and an unconscious sidekick, Pinktastic was standing in the checkout line. Her cart was full of painting junk: rollers, dropcloths, brushes, a small bank vault's worth of paint cans—okay, maybe only a credit union vault's-worth—piled in a neat pyramid, each with a rosy smear on the metal lid to show the color inside. And she was looking right at Gretchen. And she was smiling.

Gretchen's knees went watery and her throat got tight. Pinktastic's smile was gorgeous. She was gorgeous. And now she was wheeling her cart out of line. And now she was coming this way.

"Okay," said Gretchen. "Right then. Great to see you, Powerpunch. Later, Succubus." Gretchen wrenched her cart sideways, dragging the stupid locked wheel across the polished concrete MegaHome floor with a spine-raking squeal. But then the thing seized up again and she was stuck in the middle of the aisle, frozen like she'd been hit with one of Icebergatron's freeze rays.

"You're Gretchen, right?" And Pinktastic was there, *right flipping there*, looking straight at Gretchen. And she knew her motherflipping name and everything. Oh god. Oh crap. Oh holy flipping hell.

One good thing, at least: Gretchen's ex and his new girl had made themselves scarce. No villain in town willingly stood around for close scrutiny by a member of the Chromatic League. Not after the Commissioner's nifty little speech. Not after the Dastards, one of the most dastardly bands on the coast, had had their asses kicked halfway to Sunday and handed back on a plate, forcing them to disband and lay low, not even go to all the regular baddie bars and baddie parties. Hardly seemed worth following the path of villainy if you never even got to go to the best parties.

Pinktastic thrust out her hand. Gretchen stared like it was one of Medusaman's infamous pet monsters instead of a slender-fingered bit of ordinary human flesh with pale pink polish on the nails.

When Gretchen didn't move, Pinktastic reached for her hand and shook it. "I'm Alice," she said. "I have a stall at the Saturday market? I see you there practically every week."

*Saw her there?* But Gretchen had been so careful! She never got close enough to activate Pinktastic's famous Chromasense, which gave her the ability to see villainy in the air like an aura of darkness. Oh god. Oh crap. She must look like a big old grey smudge right now. Charcoal mist must be clinging all over her, baring her dark heart like it had been ripped from her chest.

Maybe alarmed by the way Gretchen's face was turning blue from holding her breath, Pinktastic let go of her hand. "Anyway, I asked around, and Loki's friend Lucy told me your name. Thought I'd introduce myself so we'd be even."

Lucy. Smash Chick. Gretchen thought she might vomit right there in the MegaHome garden aisle, she was so freaked.

Pinktastic's smile faltered. Probably because she could tell Gretchen was about to throw up on her shoes. That, or she'd finally noticed the scent of villainy clinging to Gretchen like Pigpen's dustcloud in the old Peanuts cartoons. "Okay...well, nice to meet you, Gretchen. See you around?"

Gretchen barely managed to nod, a stilted motion reminiscent of the Grim Puppeteer's automated minions. As soon as Pinktastic wheeled around, Gretchen bolted, abandoning her traitorous shopping cart near the mountain of bargain sod still filled with stuff she could no longer remember wanting or needing. As she ran, she imagined her villainous aura trailing after her, a tattletale streak of black fog in the clean clear air.

The old warehouse door rammed shut with a bang and Gretchen sank to the floor, sobbing. After a while her legs started hurting where they'd fallen asleep under her. She managed a clumsy stagger across the room, her feet lumps of pins and needles where circulation tried to return, her cheeks tight and sticky from dried tears. She flopped on the couch, sending a flurry of dustmotes into the air to be caught in rays of light slanting past the enormous casement windows taking up one crumbling brick wall.

Lying on the couch, Gretchen pictured her life as it should be. She imagined her leaky rundown warehouse as a genuine lair, brick walls painted a deep smoldering purple, no water stains or ancient tarred patches, no looming cracks past which you could see daylight. She imagined her back-alley sofa replaced with something sleek and modern, black crushed velvet maybe, or textured vinyl: some cool fabric that didn't need old blankets to hide where someone else's cat had used the arms as scratching posts. She imagined her hotplate and microwave replaced with the latest brushed steel appliances, and maybe a kitchen island of black Italian marble like she'd seen in that magazine at the dentist's.

And in the middle of this sleek modern wonderland of ultimate villainy, Gretchen imagined Gretchen. This imaginary Gretchen had the hair she'd always wanted: long and loose and darker than midnight. Her clothes were just the right clothes, her Super suit a dream of sophistication, her waist and hips and thighs worthy of a Parisian catwalk and of the sleek lines demanded by the latest in villain fashion.

The rest of the afternoon passed as so many had passed in recent weeks: with Gretchen fading in and out of sleep, arm thrown over her eyes to block out daylight filtering though the grimy cracked windows, dream mingling with fantasy mingling with memory, until Destructova and Pinktastic jetted through the air via the latest Super technology, zapping each other with forked lightning and chromatic rays...*biff!*...*bam!*...*pow!*...*boom*...

Wasn't it dark enough yet for the random old guy to bugger off and get out of here? Who gardened after dark? Gretchen stifled a curse and hunkered lower in the ancient rosemary bush. It wasn't the same random old dude who'd been in the community garden last time; a small truck was parked at the curb rather than the jalopy. And this dude listened to the radio as he weeded—the freaking *radio*! Who listened to a motherflipping radio anymore? Random old dudes hoeing cabbage at the community garden, that's who.

Trying not to resort to her old nail-biting habit, Gretchen, from sheer boredom, began listening to the old dude's radio. Geezer music played awhile, kind of peppy and orchestral. Then an interview with some hero Gretchen had never heard of, who'd written a memoir about discovering his Super powers as a smalltown boy in the middle of Noplace, Nowhere. Seemed they were making it into a movie. Sheesh.

And then the regular programming was interrupted by that sound. It was a buzz, a howl, a screech or a hum or a combination of all those. Whatever, it was designed to get your attention, and it did. It was an alert from the Emergency Broadcast System.

*"Regional Alert! After forcing what would have been a passing meteoric cluster into a collision course with Earth, powerful archvillain Tectonic Shifter has perished in the upper stratosphere. Minutes earlier, the International Antivillainy Coalition received his demand for an undisclosed amount in gold bullion. But before negotiations began, Tectonic Shifter was killed by one of the first meteors diverted toward Earth. Repeat: Tectonic Shifter is dead. The Coalition is calling all Super heroes in the region to instant action. Non-Supers are urged to begin immediate emergency evacuation..."*

At some point without realizing, Gretchen had emerged from the rosemary bush. The old dude had gone ramrod straight, hoe poised midair as he listened. Gretchen made one scrambling leap at the fence and vaulted over, scarcely noticing the rip in her tights when her leg didn't quite clear. In a few strides she was at the old guy's side.

"Did they say where the Supers are supposed to meet?" Gretchen swooped the small radio off the ground from between two modest pumpkins barely starting to show. The man shied away, shaking his head, even older up close than she'd thought, all skinny and weak. She could break his back with a powerful gust of wind if she wanted, or ram rainwater up his nose until he drowned on moisture materialized from the very air he breathed.

"Well," said Gretchen, "you heard the alert: go!" He cowered, half lifting his hoe as though it afforded some small protection. Gretchen kicked it from his hand so it went spinning off into the dusk. "Evacuate, motherflipper! Don't you know what emergency means?"

He nodded and backed away toward his truck.

"And I'm keeping this freaking radio, though if you're not gone by the count of three I'll ram it down your non-evacuating throat. One. Two."

As the old dude's taillights disappeared around the corner, Gretchen fumbled with the dial, trying to tune into a station not preprogrammed with rush-hour talk shows or insipid pop music. Any station. Any station at all. Stupid antique piece of crap.

With an offhand flip of the wrist she sent a small rainshower scooting across Pinktastic's end of the gardens. The neighboring plots would benefit from Destructova's attentions, just this once. Couldn't be helped. Destructova had someplace else to be tonight.

The city was a mess. Cars idled bumper to bumper, belching invisible poisons for miles along every possible route out of the city. Destructova congratulated herself for the millionth time on never learning to drive as she sprinted along the empty sidewalks, radio clutched to her ear like an icepack to a bruise after a Super training session.

According to the radio, heroes from all over were gathering at City Hall. The first tiny meteors—practically pebbles compared to the largest—had already crashed in the suburbs. Thousands were reported missing or dead, while wildfires sparked by the blazing missiles devastated farmlands to the east. Every station had either ceased broadcasting or was playing repeated emergency alerts urging the locals to flee. Gretchen finally settled on a station with moment-by-moment analysis of the situation.

Only Tectonic Shifter, it was believed, had possessed Super powers capable of rerouting solid masses the size of the biggest meteors headed for Earth. Ironic that he'd been killed by the smallest of them, a rock so tiny it probably would've burned to nothing before hitting the planet. The largest mass, the one that Supers around the world were preparing to meet, was capable of unspeakable destruction. Dinosaurs were mentioned, followed by long smarty-pantsy sounding discussions about the effects of smoke and dust in the atmosphere. Stupid brainiacs might as well have been yelling, *Duck! We're all going to die!*

After her summer of lying low, Gretchen was more out of shape than she'd realized. The weeks since the Dastards' disbandment had left her flabby and soft. Okay; the weeks of lying on the couch all day sobbing her guts out and eating coconut chocolate ice cream with peanut butter swirls had left her flabby and soft. Whatever. All she knew was, she was totally huffing when she sprinted the last block.

City Hall was blazing, lit like a white stone beacon with wide marble steps and fifty-foot columns. And the heroes! Gretchen had never seen so many Supers gathered in one place at the same time, not even when the Commissioner had held her big party honoring the Chromatic League for driving baddies like the Dastards underground, keeping the citizenry safe to guzzle their Big Gulps and drive their sucktacious SUVs back and forth from the suburbs, strewing pollutants and poisoning the air.

The Chromatic League. Gretchen could see them from the street, a rainbow of Supercolors and self-righteousness. Leader Roy Gebiv stood at the top of the steps under the brightest spotlight, his shifting multihued cape with its patented bulletproof coating a fitting backdrop for his square jaw and smug weatherman's grin. Flanking him were his personal sidekicks, Rain and Bow—like either of them were even worthy of kissing a real rainbow's feet. In a semicircle behind Roy—the Chromatic League liked a good covershot pose and always snagged tons of media footage—stood the rest of his band: Indigo Avenger and Green Axe and Violetina and Orange Alert and, at the very end, Pinktastic. She looked small compared to the rest, but glorious, radiating goodness like a perfume.

The Commissioner finished her rousing speech to a flurry of flash photography and a smattering of halfhearted applause, and was whisked away in an armored car. Probably to an underground bunker, or a waiting helicopter. The airspace above City Hall was conspicuously empty, cleared for the Supers to take off en masse and try to save the planet from what the radio commentator Gretchen had ceased listening to the minute she'd seen Pinktastic up on the steps—little pink flats and pink headband and thin matching mask making her hair look more strawberry than rose—called *impending destruction on a scale unprecedented in human history.*

Gretchen pushed past a crowd of gawkers. Hundreds of non-Supers stood watching, smoking, crying, laughing. Either these people had decided it was useless to try to get the hell out of the city deemed ground zero for the biggest asteroid Earth had seen since the brontosaurus, or they had way too much faith in their heroes. Heroes were only people, after all. People with problems. People with leaky apartments and overdue bills and jerkoff ex-boyfriends.

"Here," Gretchen thrust the little radio at the nearest onlooker, a patchouli-scented private school girl reeking of a future English degree. "You might want to listen to this. Something about an emergency evacuation of the region."

Without waiting for the girl's reaction Gretchen bounded up the enormous steps, dodging Super heroes she'd seen on the news, heroes she'd defeated in minor skirmishes with the Dastards, heroes who'd defeated her, sent her and her fellow villains running from thwarted heinous acts like cockroaches from a bare bulb at midnight. Heroes, heroes everywhere, and she wasn't even nervous. They were all going to die anyway; nobody living had enough power to divert a mass the size of Jamaica from plowing into the Earth.

Abruptly Gretchen was at the top with no more stairs to climb, and it was just her and the Chromatic League up there under the bright lights between soaring stone columns. Her and Pinktastic.

All Gretchen's forward momentum drained away. All the purpose and impetus, gone. "Hi, Alice," she said.

Pinktastic smiled. It was a strained smile, the smile of someone about to try to save the world, pretty sure she's going to fail. "Hi, Gretchen. You shouldn't be here. Emergency evacuation in progress, you know."

"I know."

Roy Gebiv and his sidekicks were powering their infrajet boots, which were way noisier than Gretchen remembered. Alice gave Gretchen an apologetic look. "That's my cue," she said, shouting over the jets, reaching to flip the toggles on her boots.

Gretchen nodded and stepped back to give the Chromatic League room for their fancy signature group takeoff. But Pinktastic called to her, shouting even louder above the drone of dozens of powerboots warming up under Supers without natural flight ability: "Destructova!"

Gretchen looked up. Pinktastic was holding out her hand.

"Destructova! Gretchen..."

Gretchen leapt over the top couple steps in a single bound and grasped Pinktastic's hand. Alice pulled her close, shouting into her ear.

*Want to come?* she was saying. *Want to come with me to save the world?*

And Gretchen nodded and stepped behind Pinktastic and wrapped her arms around the other girl's slim capeless shoulders. The Chromatic League could afford the very best Super technology, their boots able to lift two people, or three—handy for saving the hapless from rising floods or oncoming trains or stampeding rhinos. Handy for taking your nemesis with you into the stratosphere to meet almost certain death in the process of great heroic sacrifice.

Roy Gebiv gave the signal and they rose in a flurry of capes and jets and air, Destructova and Pinktastic and all the Chromatic League and other Supers. A sense of rightness settled in the core of Gretchen's middle, and she finally understood what Smash Chick had meant: *the best of all possible worlds.* She felt that rightness sing through her blood, surging along with her power, and hugged Pinktastic tight as they zoomed up, up, up into the stratosphere, together.

---

CAMILLE ALEXA currently lives in the Pacific Northwest in an Edwardian foursquare filled with limestone fossils, dried willow branches, pressed flowers, and other very pretty dead things. Her evil superpower is the relentless ability to ruin a joke by forgetting the punchline halfway through. Her short story collection *Push of the Sky* earned a starred review in Publishers Weekly and was nominated for the Endeavour Award. She can be found on Twitter @camillealexa, online at camillealexa.com, or zipping through the sky in an embarrassingly bright pair of purple powerboots, but only after dark, and never on weekends.

# HUNGER OF THE BLOOD REAVER

*A Tale of the World of Ruin*

## *Erik Scott de Bie*

As THE TWO RIDERS climbed the jagged mountain pass into the lands of the Aza, a cold wind rose around them. It billowed relentlessly, the land's rebuke for the very sins Azallé the Blood Reaver sought to expunge. She tightened her cowl against the elements and urged her shivering horse up the path between the guardians of the valley.

Snow swirled around the riders, stirred to fresh violence in a centuries-old war. Two petrified warmachines, locked in eternal combat, formed an arch over the path. The iron-clad monsters had met on this lonely ridge and clashed until their joints froze and their anima faded into darkness— yet another lost secret from an age when sorcerer-kings ruled the world. Petrified, they became old gods of their own sort, and none who feared the spirits of the past dared draw near.

An age hence, the legends held no fear for the Children of Ruin. However, five years before Azallé's return, the heathen barbarians had descended upon the lands of the Aza, an unstoppable tide of misery and destruction. If Azallé had not done as she had...

But she would not think on it—not yet.

Instead, she focused on the rotting monoliths that warded the pass, and upon the drip-drip-drip of brackish sludge that leaked from each, like the water of a perched dog. The foul streams joined and flowed down the mountain. Over the centuries, the caustic stream had carved a canyon of corroded stone.

Azallé's companion coughed raggedly into his arm. Seemingly unaware, he had driven his horse close to one of the streams.

"Mind the Black Seep, Mask," she called. "Unless you want to walk."

The sorcerer jerked his reins, and his horse shied away with an anxious whinny. "Damned creature!" Mask cried, rage in his rough voice.

Azallé adjusted her hood over her dusty black hair. "At least he has the sense to avoid burning off his feet."

Her companion glared at her with red-rimmed eyes. Breath steamed out through the mouth slit of the gruesome steel and leather skull he wore over his face. "And I suppose you know all about this land, eh, Mistress? You do hail from this forsaken backwater."

"All the Aza know of the Seep."

"I warned you against this return." His voice sounded like wind whispering through broken glass. "If only because of the four day *ride*. These beasts test me."

Magic blurred the air around Mask's right-hand gauntlet—a clawed monstrosity that was yet another in the sorcerer's collection of ancient relics. The gathering power overwhelmed the skittish horse's last nerve. It threw its rider into the snow, then trotted a short way down the treacherous path.

Azallé covered her mouth to stifle a laugh.

"We should just kill the dumb brute."

Mask rose and threw off his snow-encrusted cloak, revealing blood-stained leathers that wrapped him from head to foot. He burned like a furnace: snowflakes that touched him melted and ran down his gaunt, plague-ravaged body in rivulets. He turned murderously to his horse.

"Wait. I'll handle this." Azallé swung down from her saddle and stepped past Mask. Her cloak blew open, revealing a golden dagger that hung from her belt. It was her only weapon—the only one she had ever needed. The blade of the Red King.

Azallé stretched out her hand, palm open, and hummed in soothing tones. The horse's ears rose and its flaring eyes narrowed. Slowly, the horse lowered its head so Azallé could lay her fingers on its brow. She basked in its beatific trust that all would be well.

"Remark—" Mask began.

A deep voice whispered in her mind.

*Azallé unsheathed her golden dagger and plunged it into the horse's throat. The animal's shriek choked off into a dying gurgle. Azallé watched the life drain from the horse's terrified eyes, its skin turn gray and crack like wasted earth, and its hot blood slake her fiery hand. Its strength joined to hers, soothing her, empowering her...*

The vision passed and Azallé stared into the horse's soulful eyes. She realized she was holding the handle of her dagger very hard, and she slowly relaxed her fingers.

Doing so, she revealed a tiny streak of chapped, gray flesh across her palm, as though the dagger had burned her. The scar was old, however—she'd earned it before she'd ever wielded the blade of the Red King.

"Remarkable." Mask's raw voice infused the word with derision. "You never fail to amuse me, Azallé."

"Lea," she corrected him. "You named me Azallé, but Lea is my name among my own people."

"Ah yes, Lea of the Aza, a true mistress of beasts. A scrawny girl shivering in the cold. But she had strength in her eyes, and that is why I took her in—not to mention what she carried." He nodded to the blade of the Red King. "What country lass wields such a blade?"

"True." Azallé covered her dagger with her cloak.

"You think hiding what you are means anything?"

"Says the man with no face."

"Oh, I have a face, but not one worthy of you," Mask said. "Nothing is more beautiful than you with that blade. Returning to this place will not change that."

Azallé couldn't decide if his words were a compliment or an insult. "Mount up. We've far to ride, yet."

"As you say, Mistress."

Azallé rode as though born to the saddle, but it was slow going with Mask. Every so often, they had to stop while the sorcerer recovered himself awkwardly. Azallé had never seen him without his armor, but she knew his harsh past had stripped his body of its grace. When they first met, she had found Mask's disjointed corpse of a body unnerving, but now she only felt sadness for the man trapped within. Not that she would ever speak of it. Mask was the closest thing she had to a friend—excepting the one she had come back to see.

Mask reined his horse to a halt.

"What is it?" she asked.

Warning magic flared around his gorget—one of his many relics of the fallen mage-empire of Calatan. "We're not alone."

Mask stared into a copse of snow-encrusted trees until shadowed figures emerged. At first, the steamed breath from their horses obscured their faces, but Azallé could see their drawn weapons clearly enough. As the riders drew closer, Azallé recognized them as young men from the village, haggard after a lean winter. They turned their spears toward Mask, marking the sorcerer the greater threat. Azallé knew they could not be more wrong.

The Red King bid her take up her dagger and show them their error, but she pushed the whispers away. She was glad of her vision earlier, which had warned her to hide the golden dagger. None could mistake the blade of Azathorn the Red King, God of the Aza—the blade that drank so others might live. It was the Aza's most sacred relic, and Azallé had stolen it five years before. If they recognized it, they would know her, and then blood would turn the snow to slush.

"Hail," Azallé said. "Walk safe, men of the Aza."

One of the outriders guided his horse a step closer. He raised one hand, which bore a faded gray scar across the palm. That was the mark of the Aza, of their devotion to the Red King's power. "Walk safe, travelers."

Gorode. Azallé recognized the young man by his pock-marked face and cracking voice. As a boy, Gorode had once chased her through mud pits and called her names. She'd learned much of men in the war, and realized now that his boyish pranks by day meant he had dreamed of her body by night. Had she stayed in the village, would she have married a boy like Gorode?

Looking upon him now, all she saw was a reminder of her own sins. She remembered him lying pinned beneath his dying horse five years before. She shook the memory away.

"There's a toll to travel this road," he said. "Else...well, we've steel."

"Ha." Mask's broken laughter split the silence, and burning magic coursed around his right-hand gauntlet, as well as humming force around the delicate silver mesh across his left-hand glove. "Shall I heat their bones until their flesh melts? I could spare one or two, if you would break your fast?"

The whispers stirred. Azallé had not drunk of a foe in almost a year now, and the blade's call was weak. She choked the urge down like bile—she would not be that woman.

"Silver is cheaper than blood." Azallé reached for her coin-purse, which she tossed to Gorode. He bobbled it in cold fingers. "Take it with my blessing, and guide us into the village. I would speak with the Elder as soon as he would hear me." She extended her hands, wrists together. "If you will bind us, I will not resist."

"Who are you, lady, that you would seek the Aza?" As he looked at her, Gorode's eyebrows rose. Azallé wondered if he recognized her.

Five years ago, Gorode had chased her through the snow, crying "traitor!" and "murderer!" His spear had taken her in the left shoulder, and she'd felt the Red King's magic, new and exciting, rise in response to the wound. She'd felled Gorode's horse that she herself might live. The blade had healed her, but also demanded she kill Gorode too. Fortunately, after what happened to her brother, she'd had the strength to resist its whispers.

Now, her shoulder ached with phantom pain, and the Red King hungered anew. His whispers grew louder.

Gorode was staring at her, awaiting a reply. Azallé could not speak, but Mask came to her rescue. "We bring good tidings and a gift—but we will give them only to the Elder."

Azallé relaxed. Elder Nava would know her and understand. He was, after all, her father.

Gorode nodded and gave orders to his men, who encircled the travelers to escort them down the lonely mountainside. The outriders left them unbound, but watched them closely. Azallé collected her composure.

"I do not understand," Mask murmured. "You are Azallé the Blood Reaver. You have slain a thousand men and taken their strength for yourself."

"Nine hundred and seventy-seven," she corrected him.

They had not all been men, either, but also weeping women and defenseless children. And though the strength she had stolen from them had joined a pool of might, she would never forget their individual faces wracked with fear and pain. Perverted from its original use, the blade hungered to absorb as many souls as it could.

"Regardless," Mask said, "this rabble owes its very existence to you, and yet you go meekly among them like a nameless dog? You will not find what you seek in this place."

"Perhaps," she said. "But I will be what I choose, and nothing else."

Azallé could not read her companion's face behind his mask.

"I cannot decide which is the greater tragedy," the sorcerer said at length. "That you have all that power and refuse to use it, or that you think you can stop yourself."

As the band descended the mountain, Azallé's heart lightened.

The village of the Aza was much as she remembered: the smells of baking bread and roasting venison, the boasts of bowmen freshly returned from the day's hunt, the oil lamps lit in the windows as dusk fell. Children laughed and lovers pressed their scarred hands together. The Aza bore the gray scars of the Red King, but the marks had faded in the years since the last ritual. The youngest did not bear them at all.

This peace endured because of her. She had done what had to be done, and the Aza lived because of it. In that moment, she knew it had been worth the heavy cost.

Mask's cutting voice cooled her rising spirits.

"Harshest woman I've ever met, and you're beaming like an untraveled commoner," Mask said. "If all those Echvar barbarians could see the great Blood Reaver, carried off by pitiful guardians to an even less relevant authority..."

"You have not met my father, you do not know."

Mask shook his head. "What happened to the Azallé I know? She that the Valeri named Red Queen when she slew their general and washed her wounds with his blood? She that the Tar Vangryur call Blood Binder, for making blood-slaves of their children?"

"That was another time, Mask. That war is over. We lost."

"That depends what you tried to win. I know what *I* won."

"Indeed? And what was that?"

Azallé looked at him sidelong, but the sorcerer kept his secrets.

"Certainly, the war had its losers," Mask said. "The Children took Echvar but lost it in days. Valeran is smashed and destroyed. Two mage-cities succumbed to Ruin, never to be redeemed...Our erstwhile allies might have lost their war, but at least your little hidden vale is safe. That is a victory, is it not?"

"A victory at a cost." Azallé thought of the countless lives she had ended. She could not forget a single victim so long as she carried the golden blade. Just the reminder of the power it offered made her yearn to hold it.

"There is always a cost." Mask gestured back up the mountain, where they could still see the towering, petrified warmachines that held the pass. "Those monsters had to die the slow death of a millennium to keep Aza's enemies at bay. Then, when less godly madmen came..."

"Then the task fell to someone else. Me."

"Indeed." Mask sounded pleased.

With a chill, Azallé remembered the advent of the Children of Ruin five years gone. The Children branded themselves and pierced their faces with shards of metal harvested from slain foes. They knew nothing of mercy, or of respect for the old gods. When they had streamed through the haunted pass like a wave of blood and hate, they raped and slew and burned their way through the outlying villages of the Aza. They stopped only when Lea, the priest's daughter, took up the golden blade sacred to the tribe and did what was needful.

She had bought her village's safety with the blood of thousands, then left her name and heritage behind to join the war in Echvar and Valeran. As Azallé the Blood Reaver, she had slain all who knew of the secret vale of the Aza: her people would never taste Ruin's kiss again. Now she meant to leave that behind: to become again the priest's daughter. She would beg forgiveness of the family she had spurned, help rebuild what her people had lost, and—she prayed to Azathorn the Red King—find the friend she had loved enough to break her tribe's most sacred tenet.

"Sael," she whispered without sound.

The repetition of the name always gave her the strength to resist the blade's call. Soon, Azallé would return the blade to the temple, and her bloody quest would finally end.

"Ah yes," Mask said, though he could hardly have heard Azallé. "You've mentioned this Sael. I would like to see this creature that holds such sway over the Blood Reaver's heart."

Not for the first time, Azallé wondered if one of Mask's many relics let him hear her thoughts. Did he also hear the whispers of the Red King, or was that her own particular curse?

As they rode into the village, Azallé searched the faces—some she recognized, others she did not—for her most precious of friends. What would Sael be like after five years? Would they be as close as before?

What she found instead was something that turned the warmth in her belly cold. The sweet scents of the village became the taste of mealy apples and moldering bread in her mouth.

"No," she said. "That—that cannot be."

"How wonderful," Mask said.

The Elder's Hall lay in ruin. What five years ago had been a grand stone edifice now looked like a melted cake, its strong beams reduced to cinders and its crenellations drooping. The remains of the hall squatted like a scar in the center of the pristine village. Azallé had seen many destroyed buildings, but had never imagined she would find the same in her homeland.

"What..." Azallé's voice broke. "What happened here? I thought the Children's invasion failed."

"It did." Gorode looked at her closely. "You know of it?"

"My lady is a student of history," Mask said.

Azallé tasted salt and iron: she had bit her tongue, and she swallowed her own blood rather than show her despair. "This looks old. When did this come to pass? Is Elder Nava...?"

"The old Elder died shortly after the invasion, the night of the fire. I would not speak on it, Lady." Gorode's face turned dark. "The Elder will see you in the morn."

"A new Elder? Who could possibly—?"

Mask spoke over Azallé. "And where are we to wait?"

"Few travelers come to the lands of the Aza. I will arrange a place by the fire in the Common House."

"No decent bed, then?" Mask sighed.

Azallé felt like a distant eavesdropper on the conversation. She stared at the burned husk of the Elder's Hall, which had been her home for so many years. She remembered hours of watching her father hold audience, of peaceful reading by the waterfall in the garden, and of times spent with Sael here.

Had she acted too late?

The Red King whispered that she had. It goaded her to draw the blade and make those responsible for this atrocity pay.

"There is always a cost," she murmured, "but it is one that I must pay."

As night fell, they found themselves in the Common House, crowded in among those who had no home or name of their own: laborers, hunters, and other single men and women. It was, as such, filled with whores and drink: a place for loose morals and dishonor.

"Disgusting," Azallé said.

"Glorious," Mask agreed.

More than a few men sized up Azallé, who was a vital woman of a smooth age, but one look at her leather-wrapped companion soured any desire.

"We make a curious pair, do we not?" Mask asked when they had found a corner of their own. "You, so beautiful and so deadly. Me, so ugly and *also* deadly."

Azallé scowled. "Is this life but a jest to you?"

"If it is a jest, it is not ours," Mask said. "And you object to my jests more strongly than usual. I thought this homecoming would brighten you, if nothing else."

"So did I."

Mask clicked his tongue at the weak wine their hosts provided, opting instead for fire-heated water to brew the foul-smelling tea he always drank. It was for his health, he claimed. Azallé thought it just another means of driving folk away. She refused wine also, her thoughts already muddled with the image of the Elder's Hall.

"I do not know what could have happened." Azallé shook her head. "I took the relic to save the lands of the Aza. The cost should have been for me to pay, and no one else."

"Fancy. Not everything's working out the way you expected."

Azallé glared at him. "You could be sympathetic, you know."

"What makes you think I'm not?"

"When are you ever—?" Azallé trailed off as the doors to the kitchens swung opened to admit a haggard young woman. Care had worn away her fine features, but Azallé knew her without question. "Sael!"

Azallé crossed the room, heedless of the sorcerer or other patrons of the common hall. After five years away, no one else had known Azallé's face, but Sael's eyes lit with recognition. Azallé best friend in all the world stiffened.

"By the Red King," the small woman said. "Lea! But how—?"

Azallé threw her arms around Sael, weeping freely. Sael felt too small in Azallé's arms, as though squeezing would crush her frail body. And likely it would, with all the blood strength she had acquired over the years.

Mask coughed to draw their attention. "*That's* Sael?" he asked. "I expected someone taller. And male."

"Old gods and dead lands." Azallé pressed her forehead against Sael's own, and tears ran down her cheeks. "I thought—after the Elder's Hall..."

"No." Sael pulled free of Azallé's arms. "You cannot be here. After what you did...you must go."

"I will not be parted from you," Azallé said. "I have sworn it these last five years. I..."

Then the full impact of their reunion struck her. She observed her friend's carriage, and the way all the men and women in this place looked at her with contempt. Like a nagging mother and a whore both at once. A few of them who'd noted their reunion were casting the two women lewd, suggestive glances.

Azallé realized what it all meant. "Old Gods, Sael. You've been made mistress of the Common House? Who has done this thing to you?"

"You don't understand," Sael said. "My husband—"

"Husband?" Azallé asked.

"Girl!" A man in the stained white-and-gold robes of the Elder of the Aza barreled out of the kitchen. "How many times have I told you..." He saw the travelers and fell silent.

Azallé knew him. "Tarkesh."

Elder Tarkesh was a big man, broad in the shoulders and jaw, with a thick mass of gray hair. Azallé tensed, any joy she'd felt at her reunion with Sael turning to churning acid in her middle. Tarkesh had once been a boon companion to her father, though their friendship had ended long before that bloody night five years ago. They'd kept it quiet after, of course, but Azallé would never forget the awful things Tarkesh had done to her brother—things he had tried to do to her as well. And now, Elder Nava was dead, the Hall lay in ash and rubble, and Tarkesh—of all people— dishonored the old robes.

Blood thundered in Azallé's head, and she could hardly breathe. The whispers of the Red King rose, and she almost listened to them. It was all she could do not to stab the golden blade into Tarkesh's fat belly and festoon the Common Hall with his guts. Or else she could feed upon him: turn him to dust and devour his strength for herself. What there was of it.

Tarkesh regarded Azallé with wariness. His body registered her threat immediately, even if he did not seem to know her consciously. "Walk safe, travelers."

Azallé wanted to tear him apart, but she kept her words locked as tight as her fists.

"And you, gracious host," Mask said with a bow. "Your hall is comforting and welcoming, and we have all we might need."

Tarkesh glared at Sael. "Come to bed, girl. I've needs of my own."

Sael raised one hand, which bore an ugly gray scar across the palm—old and faded, but there. "Walk safe, stranger."

Azallé's heart was breaking, but she nodded.

"Pleasant dreams tonight, I think," Mask said when Tarkesh was gone. "You've a history with our host, I take it?"

"You do not understand." Azallé trembled. "That man—that *thing*— he..." Her words wouldn't work right. Neither would her hands, which kept clenching and unclenching, forming impotent fists over and over.

"Azallé." Mask put his hand on her wrist, his eyes serious.

"I can abide," she said. "I am one of them."

"Indeed." Mask nodded. "They've the same marks you do. All but this Tarkesh. Why so, I wonder?"

Azallé settled her breathing. "He always pleaded a weakness of flesh, and so he begged off taking part in the blood rituals."

Mask looked intrigued, but Azallé said nothing more.

The night grew long, and Azallé watched as the men and women in the Common House fell asleep. This was not as she had expected. She had thought to save the Aza from the Children of Ruin, not bring ruin upon them. They seemed to her now just as horrid as the barbarians.

Azallé looked at her scarred palms. Though the blade of the Red King could heal as well as hurt, she'd kept the ugly marks to remind her who she was and what she had done.

She shut her eyes and tried to ignore the blade's whispers.

In her dream, Azallé saw herself standing in the Elder's Hall, watching her father conduct the Ritual of Giving. A dozen Aza knelt around a basalt altar. Naked as the ritual demanded, Sael lay upon the stone like a calf for the butcher. Azallé could see purple-green bruises on her face and body and blood trickled from many wounds. She had been beaten badly but the Red King's magic would restore her. Many Aza would give their blood that one might live.

Elder Nava intoned the ancient ritual of the Red King and raised the golden dagger. It caught the light of the setting sun and cast it dancing around the room. The supplicants presented their hands, crossed with old scars. They had given of themselves many times.

But this was her price to pay—not theirs.

Azallé stepped forward, interposing herself between her father and Sael. She raised her hands as though to plead with him and ward him off.

"Is this what you would do?" Elder Nava asked. "Give your life for her?"

Azallé nodded. She wanted nothing more than this.

Elder Nava brought the blade sweeping across and opened Azallé's throat. Blood spurted past her eyes, and she felt it coat her chin and chest. She collapsed, choking.

Elder Nava turned away from his dying daughter and dripped the blood onto the injured Sael. It fell onto her wounds and washed them away like dirt.

Azallé's life for hers.

But her sacrifice was not enough. Even as she lay dying, the Aza came forward, one by one. They offered their hands, and Elder Nava drew the blade across their palms. Their wounds sealed and the flesh around them turned gray. Their blood wet the dagger and healed Sael.

They were giving of their blood that she might live.

For a price.

Of a sudden, the room was empty, and Azallé stood alone at the altar of the Red King. Her wound was gone. The dagger—stained with her blood—lay on the stone, and she heard its voice in her head. It said she needed its power to save her people. She closed her fingers around its handle and felt a sucking hollow in her guts. She was so hungry.

Azallé knew immediately what was coming—knew this was a dream, but could not stop any of it.

A hand fell on her shoulder. "Lea—?"

Azallé could not say if the blade moved on its own. She wrenched away and slashed in the same motion. Flesh split like pudding, and blood welled up to spurt across her mouth and nose. She sputtered, trying to spit it out, but she could smell and taste nothing but the tang of the first life she would take.

Damoren, her brother, stood cradling his hand.

"Lea?" he asked. "What have you done?"

"No." She wanted to scream but this was only a dream. "I—"

Damoren's eyes widened as the flesh around his cut hand turned withered. He had not given his blood willingly, and the ritual had gone undone. His flesh rotted and fell away as she watched. The corruption spread up his arm, turning his flesh gray. He collapsed to his knees and stared up at her as his body shrunk inward and became a skeleton. Then he shattered apart into dust, which coated her face, filled her mouth, and stung her eyes.

His life—bright and hot and *delicious*—flowed into her.

There was always a price.

The dream ended, and Azallé awoke weeping. The pain was so real, it could have happened only five seconds before, rather than five years. She slapped at her face to wipe the dust and blood away, but all she found were tears.

Around her, firelight illuminated sleeping bodies in the common room—men and women entwined without shame. This was where the new Elder held court—here, amongst the lowest of the low. The Elder was meant to rise above the rabble. He should be a lord to be emulated, not a petty drinking companion.

When she was young, she had been a princess among the Aza. Now all the villagers seemed the same: grubby and without honor. At her side, Mask snored fitfully, and even he seemed more noble in repose than these mongrels she called kinsfolk.

She wondered how much of her contempt came from her dream, and how much from the Red King's whispers in her head. She had not realized she was clutching the dagger in her sleep.

Azallé saw a faint light at the far end of the common room: someone watching. She pulled herself together, like a warrior should, and rose quietly with her hand on the Red King's blade.

A shadow moved behind the door, and Azallé stepped through. Sael caught her arm and pulled her closer. "Lea. Thank the King. Listen—"

"What passed here?" Azallé demanded. "My father? The Hall?"

"I—" Sael shook her head. "After you left, the Aza were furious. You had perverted our greatest treasure—turned our last strength into a horror. They could not be placated. They burned the Hall not two days after you had gone. Elder Nava could not escape, or chose not to. I think—I think you broke him."

Azallé stiffened. "I had not expected this."

"You must leave," Sael said. "If anyone were to know your face, they would—"

"They would what?" Azallé asked. "Kill me? Drive me from the lands of the Aza? They can do neither." She drew the blade of the Red King.

Sael's eyes widened. "You yet carry it? Oh, Lea!"

Azallé set her jaw. "I am Azallé the Blood Reaver. With this blade, I have drunk of the strength of almost a thousand men. I am mightier than the Old Gods themselves. Let the Aza come—their lives will sustain me, however many years come and go. Let the Aza face me, and I shall show them the power of the Red King."

Sael shook her head. "Oh Lea, can you not hear yourself?"

In the candlelight, Azallé saw a bruise around Sael's left eye. She touched it lightly. "Tarkesh did this."

Whispers in a long-dead language filled her mind. She recognized the blade's hunger. She shared it.

Sael shook her head. "You do not understand. He gets angry sometimes, but he is my husband."

"Was," Azallé said.

Sael's face went white. "Please. Listen to me. He—"

"Stop me, then. Give me a reason not to end him."

Sael put Azallé's free hand on her belly. There was movement there, and Azallé's rage flowed away.

"You carry his child. Sael, I—"

The door behind the kitchen crashed open, and Tarkesh's bulk cast a heavy shadow over them both. "What has come over you, girl?" He saw Azallé, and the vein on his forehead throbbed. "What is the meaning of this?"

The Red King whispered to her.

It was too much. For too long, Azallé had suffered this nightmare version of her childhood and tolerated the injustice of a monster like Elder Tarkesh.

She would correct this—bring the Aza back to what they were supposed to be.

She drew the golden blade. Instantly, she felt the familiar hollow in her belly. She was ravenous.

Tarkesh staggered back. His eyes, fixed on the blade, showed white all around the pupils.

Azallé stepped toward Tarkesh, knife low. She thrust.

The blade stopped, but not in Tarkesh's flesh. Instead, Sael stood before Azallé, arms outstretched. The Red King's blade sank just a fraction into her chest.

Sael looked into Azallé's eyes, her face confused. Perhaps she'd thought Azallé would stop, or perhaps she wanted to end her life. Perhaps she'd meant to save her friend, more than her husband—to stop her from using the dagger in anger.

Or perhaps she'd known it was too late, and this was the only way to be together again.

"Lea—" Sael started to say.

Then her flesh withered, gray and old in a heartbeat, and turned to dust. She burst, and the flaky powder covered everything: Azallé, Tarkesh, the kitchen spoons and knives. Azallé felt Sael's life flow into her, strengthening and healing her. She felt a second, smaller life flow into her as well.

Blood beat in Azallé's throat—it pounded like drums in her bowels. Her hands and arms trembled. She breathed out the dust that had been her dearest friend.

"Lea, daughter of Nava," said Tarkesh. "You...no..."

Azallé screamed in terror, mourning, and rage. She screamed so loud Tarkesh fell back a step. Her heart and mind strained to the limit and broke. Nothing mattered—not anymore.

Azallé surged forward and drove the dagger into the Elder's heart. His shocked face registered an instant of pain before he boiled away into dust. More strength entered her.

The Aza gathered around, shouting in fear and anger. Gorode ran at her, spear high, and she put her fist through his face, then shattered his head with a flick of her fingers.

The Red King held sway over all.

When Azallé came back to herself and could finally think, she stood alone and naked, smeared with blood and dust.

The village had fallen to ruin around her. Buildings lay in rubble while greasy smoke wafted from their scorched bones. A fire had caught in the midst of her fury. It would not catch up to the destruction she had wrought for hours yet.

She could hear nothing but the wailing wind and the distant howl of wolves. No shouts of enraged men. No lamentation of mourning women. No cries of orphaned children.

Azallé knew that she had killed her people. She felt them all inside the dagger. Inside her. All of their lives given that she might live.

The Aza were ended.

A cough announced she was not alone. A dark form shambled out of the dust and death. Red-rimmed eyes fell upon her, and hands crackling with magic rose to keep her at bay.

"I told you we would not find what you sought," Mask said.

Azallé and Mask faced each other across the remains of the Common House. In his gaze, she could see mourning for a family destroyed, a history perished, and a friend lost. His eyes reflected her heart.

"Do not tell my story," Azallé said.

Then she drove the dagger into her belly.

There was pain.

The world sucked in around her, drawn toward the agony in her middle. Her flesh crisped away.

Then nothing.

Mask stood over the dusty blade that was all that remained of his companion. Around him, the village burned. The wind rose, howling its welcome for a land returned to Ruin.

"You were asking what I won," Mask said.

He bent awkwardly, wincing at the effort, and retrieved the Red King's blade. He slid it reverently into his belt, alongside his other relics of forgotten atrocities.

With a nod, he turned and limped away.

---

ERIK SCOTT DE BIE has published five fantasy novels and a host of shorter fiction ranging from there to science fiction, superheroes, or horror. His tragic tale, "Hunger of the Blood Reaver," ties into his epic fantasy series, the World of Ruin. When not writing, Erik enjoys hiking with his beautiful wife Shelley, gaming with his geeky friends, and fencing with his sworn enemies. He also spends an inordinate amount of time wrangling his multifarious cats and jogging with his hyperactive dog. He lives in Seattle. Visit Erik online at his website/blog: erikscottdebie.com.

# VILLAINELLE

## Chaz Brenchley

Not everybody dies.

War...happens. You choose a side if you're that way inclined, if you're allowed the luxury. More likely your side is chosen for you by birth or by geography, by loyalty or happenstance, by edict or by luck. Good luck, ill luck. Either way.

You fight or you don't fight, depending. On what you can get away with, if you're wise.

Sooner or later, one side is going to lose. As often as not, it'll be yours. You were in the wrong town at the wrong time, you listened to the wrong prince or the wrong god or the wrong recruiting sergeant. One way or another, it's your turn to go down. Fighting or otherwise.

There will have been battles; people will have died. In the fighting, and afterwards. In the cities, in the villages, in the fields.

Eventually there'll be an ending of sorts. A last siege, a final battle, some kind of surrender. And then more deaths to come: executions public or private, official or otherwise, in justice or punishment or revenge.

And then the hunger, because of course nobody brought the harvest in, you were all too busy fighting or being besieged, running away, dying in droves. And the sickness that follows the hunger, and the jail-fever in the prison camps, and the pox that leaps from one brothel, one harbour, one occupied city to the next; and...

And still, not everybody dies.

Some of us have to come back.

Home. For some people, it's where they end up, where they settle.

For some of us, it's where you start. Where you run away from. Where you *leave*.

For some of us, coming back would never be a choice. Only ever a thing we did because we had to.

Still, here I was. Home again.

"Djoran. Still too pretty to kill, then?"

I gave him half a shrug, half a smile. *Wry* would be the word. You get to be good at that. "Pretty boys don't mean much anymore."

"They never did." He was a man who'd never been pretty, even as a boy;

34

but his trade was intimate with beauty. He did know.

"True enough," I allowed. "These days, though..." The other half of the shrug, and no smile; that was all it took, to say what I knew too. That with a glut of prisoners, orphans and runaways, bandits in the hills and half the world in motion, the market was sodden with the likes of me. Boys had never been so cheap.

That mattered.

I still had to sell myself, but there was no better way to start. Beggar your own value before you begin.

I said, "Well, I'm back now. And still pretty. And I know the work." *Better than ever.* "Will you—?"

"Wait. You mean you're not just passing through?"

"No," I said, perhaps more heavily than I meant. "I'm home now. I've nowhere else to go."

"And you want your old place back, is that it? You want to put yourself under my roof, my charge?"

*Want* is a slippery word at the best of times, which these were not. One more time I shrugged, while I could still afford to. And said it again, "I've nowhere else to go."

"That I can believe," he said. "You left few friends behind you, when you...left."

That little hesitation was a little reminder that I'd sneaked away without his consent, which meant without leaving profit in his purse.

"I know it," I said. "But will you take me?" Put bluntly because I wasn't negotiating here, I was begging. "I'll cost you nothing this time, Largo. Only bed and board—and I'll share beds, of course, and I know what you spread on your board. And what you pay for it. You won't notice one more mouth, and you do know what custom I'll bring to your door."

"Trouble," he said dourly, "that's what you'll bring."

"Trouble pays, Largo. Trouble *drinks*, and is this not a tavern? Trouble eats, it keeps your kitchens busy; trouble has all kinds of appetites that we can satisfy for a price, you and I."

"Less of the *we*," he growled. "If I take you—*if*—there'll be no partnership between us. You're one more slut in my house, no more than that. And you'll take nothing from it, except what I give you. Bed and board."

"Of course, Largo. That's all I ask."

I stood meekly before him, waiting for his decision: the very image of a boy broken by a world too big for him, creeping back in search of whatever rough accommodations he could make. Not looking for kindness, any more than justice—gods, no, not that!—and almost afraid to hope, almost that. Absolutely afraid of everything else, including Largo.

Briefly, I even thought he might refuse. Maybe I'd overreached at last:

come too far, asked too much. So little, and still too much. Maybe I really hadn't learned the lessons of defeat, capitulation, loss...

In the end, though, his snort of contempt told me I was in. "Not as you were before, mind," he said. "There'll be no tricks, and no deceptions. You're a servant, a dancing boy, a whore. You don't steal so much as a pin or a mouthful of meal, you don't cheat my customers or my people. You don't play and you don't wager. You'll have nothing of your own to wager with, I'll be sure of that; and you'll beg no more than you borrow, which means nothing at all from anyone. Agreed?"

I nodded.

"And I'll sell you on again, first fair offer that I hear. You'll have no say, and no share. Agreed?"

Again, I nodded.

"And just to be sure, I'll have Virelle put a binding on you. You bring nothing into my house when you come, and you take nothing with you when you leave. Nothing outside your own skin. That's how far I trust you, boy."

"Virelle?" I may perhaps have flinched. He may have been looking for exactly that. I blustered on, awkward and inevitable: "Virelle still with us, is she? I never thought that old crow would—Ow!"

His hand was no softer than it had been; he was no slower to use it.

"You speak of her with respect, Djoran, or you don't speak at all. I could have her place a binding on your tongue. Perhaps I should. I've other uses for it, but a boy don't need to speak much. Not in my house. One word out of place, one whisper that I don't like and it'll be my mute dancing boy that people come for. They'll enjoy that, the slippery glib Djoran silent and helpless under their hands. I will do that. Understood?"

I nodded hesitantly. No words now, only my uttermost need on display. He'd thought he had the most of me, the best of me before; now I was his again to use again, to sell again and again night after night, until he sold me one more time for true.

It was a bad bargain, and the best that I could hope for. Boys were cheap, and I was tainted goods.

Hell, I was a legend, and nothing good at all.

"Good, then. Come, then."

I hadn't counted on Virelle.

Stupid of me. If tavern-keepers survive a passing war, then why not temple-keepers? Any soldier worth his kit will spend as much time at prayer as he does at table. And as much money, that too. For the priests, for the incense they burn and the blood they spill. For luck, if that's for sale; and for whores, who certainly are.

Temple or tavern, there are always whores.

It's how I started, as a temple boy. One of Virelle's. Looking like the street-rat that I was, all ribs and knees in a tunic that hid neither; burning resin and striking bells, dancing in lamplight and shaking down the faithful. Smelling of smoke and sweat, my own and older men's. Long ago, but—well. Fire and steel had swept these winding streets, more than once since I'd been gone. Not everybody dies, but even so. I really hadn't counted on Virelle.

Here was the street called Strait, because it was like honesty: narrow and difficult and not for us. We used to laugh about that, all her skinny children. Long ago.

Here was the old stone facing of her temple, unexpected among the high houses that stood all with their backs to the street and its people; here was a step up and an open door, the way we never came. Here was a perfume that seemed soaked into the air itself, that had soaked bone-deep into us.

Here were the lamps I used to light, the boards I used to scrub and polish. There in the shadows was the boy I used to be, swaying softly to a music not yet played, half out of his skull on chewing *kef*, dreaming maybe of a freedom never tasted or a body known too well.

Good dreams, bad dreams. Either way.

Here was his mistress, once my own: Virelle herself, much like the crow I'd called her if crows come white and scrupulous, marked by time and temper, counting their age in accumulated scars and influence.

She looked at me and knew me from the inside, as Largo did. Her mouth twisted.

"Come crawling back, has he?"

"Aye that."

All of that. I wasn't going to argue.

"Well, and you're going to take him?"

"If you'll bind him to me. Keep him from taking anything, from me or mine."

She could do that. I wasn't the first that he'd had reason to mistrust. He knew where we came from and what we were. He knew that we'd steal coin from any purse and bread from any kitchen. We'd load a die and mark a pack of cards, we'd drug and cheat and lie from first to last if there was benefit. Why not? It's a cold world and it takes no account of need or innocence, so you might as well go guilty all the way, if guilt will keep you warm and fed.

They talked it through, he paid in coin and promises; I wouldn't have trusted either, but these two wouldn't cheat each other, they were too closely bound.

"Strip then, you, Djoran."

It was hardly the first time I'd taken my clothes off under her eyes, or his.

I did hope it might be the last—but I'd thought that before, the day she sold me to him. I'd worked hard for it, so hard; I was on my way up, moving out, moving on. Each step higher than the last.

Now I was naked again, brought down again. *Starting again*, I told myself determinedly. Home was just a place to start.

Smoke and bells. A boy to swing the censer and the little bronze hammers, fetch her pots and simples at a run, watch bug-eyed from a corner when he wasn't put to use: learning, absorbing, storing away. Wise boy. It was almost hard to believe he wasn't me, so many times I'd stood just there and seen just this, how she used a twig of rosemary to splash bare skin with water and oils while she chanted under her breath in call of her shadowy gods. Seen it from about his height, too, and about his stage of dawning cynicism. She gave you a grand farewell to innocence, did Virelle.

She wasn't so kind once you grew older. To me, now, not kind at all. No reason to be; when I left the temple I left some trouble behind me, and another boy was taken and hanged for it. She had always been sure that the first fault was mine, and that I'd arranged to have blame fall on my friend.

She'd always been acute.

Now she murmured her words and flecked my skin, had the boy waft smoke and musk my way; and I didn't know now as I hadn't known then whether her words were potent or her various preparations or neither, whether it was all her own will that drew the attention of her gods; but I felt their purpose close about me like a sheer silk wrap, like a second skin, tight and all-encompassing.

I might have shivered in that moment, I might have cried aloud.

"He'll do," she said abruptly, cutting off her chant and waving her boy away. "Nothing into your house, Largo, and nothing out. Only what's inside his skin. You wouldn't want him chucking up his breakfast on your doorstep."

"No," Largo agreed magnanimously. "What he's eaten, he can keep. If he doesn't get smart," his big hand on my throat suddenly, "and try swallowing a patron's pretty ring. Anyone misses a jewel, boy, and we can't find it, you'll go in the hole until we do."

The hole was Largo's sewer, a cess pit behind the house. Most of his people spent a day or two in there, for one offence or another. Most only ever went in once.

"Yes, Largo. Ow!"

"You'll call me master now. As you did before."

"Yes, master." Some things aren't worth being stubborn for.

Actually, most things aren't worth being stubborn for. Certainly nothing that I owned just then: not the clothes I'd peeled off, nor the various bits and pieces I'd hoarded this far in pockets and pouches and hems. I left it all on the temple floor, for her boys to glean.

Actually, I didn't have a choice. *Nothing in and nothing out*: I could feel that binding settle across my bare hide, as real as the bite of loose stones beneath my feet, the brush of cool air across my skin, the giggling attention of stray children as I followed obediently at Largo's heel through the streets of a city that I hoped had forgotten me.

No such luck. People called my name, mockingly. One flung a stone, but he was a fool; he did it where I could see him, see it coming and duck, and remember his face for later. His name was long gone, just one of the many I'd abused or robbed or insulted, cheated or exploited in my hectic heedless rise to where I thought I ought to be. Now his face was fresh in my mind, someone to be hurt again if the chance arose.

Things change. Not everybody dies, but some do. For some, it can be arranged.

Here again, back at the tavern. Round to the back of the tavern, naturally: and the alley behind was half blocked by a wagon, old Per Simon delivering barrels of fresh cider as he always had, war or no war.

He sat his wagon as he always did, hunched and heedless. Largo's people came and went, in and out of the stable yard, unloading. Kitchen boys, musicians, whores: it made no difference. If there was work to be done, they did the work.

We did.

I went to the wagon's tailgate without a word to Largo, willing to show willing. One quick hoist, barrel onto shoulder and turn towards the gate. This was heavy work once, when I was all bone and gristle; now it was easy.

Until I took that one significant step, under the arch of brick and into Largo's yard.

That feeling you get, when you know you're being watched? This...was like that, except that it was like being touched too, all over and all at once. Not like the breath of the wind, or silk on the skin, or a sudden rain: this was personal, intimate, *intended*.

Then the barrel was punched off my shoulder, to fall back into the alley behind me. I felt it tear from my grasp, I heard it thump to ground while I was still bearing forward, suddenly too light on my feet, momentum carrying me on although my mind was reeling.

My foot came down on familiar cobbles; I almost knew each separate stone by touch. I turned around bewildered, flinching, expecting a blow and almost hoping for it, something I could understand.

Largo stood under the archway of his gate. Those quick hard hands of his were set on his hips, and he was *laughing*. At *me*.

"*Old crow* did you call her, boy? Well, perhaps—but she's a crow with wisdom. *Nothing in, and nothing out*. Here." He stooped to retrieve the barrel, blessedly unharmed—he wouldn't laugh at a loss of coin, not

Largo—and tossed it at me like a ball at play.

I caught it with a grunt, held it cautiously in both arms. Nothing tried to knock it free, now that I was within his bounds.

"Take that to the cellar, then get up to the kitchens. You're no use out here, if you can't fetch and carry through the gate. Ask Marta to find you something to scrub."

"Yes, master."

In a busy tavern there's always something to scrub, but he hadn't taken me in for a scullery-boy. Neither for a whore, though he'd have me do that too. Largo keeps his people busy, and the town was full of soldiers. Liberators, occupiers, call them what you will. Victory breeds appetite. Food and drink and sex, of course; and entertainment, of course, that too. Song and dance.

Largo had bought me and trained me and kept me as a dancing-boy. *Too pretty to kiss*, he used to proclaim, till I was grown enough to prove him false. Then it was *too pretty to kill*, which was only half a joke; he had a killing temper, and I had a thousand sins in me and no conscience at all. I danced and stole, danced and cheated, danced and sold secrets and took my beatings and danced again. He made more money than I did, but we both did well.

Until my ambitions grew larger than my purse, larger than my opportunities. I left Largo—stole myself away, naturally, paying nothing for the privilege of freedom—and trekked my way to the palace, inveigled myself into the prince's service, rose and rose.

Rose and fell, when my foolish prince lost his war and his life too. Not everybody dies, but some must. Half his people were condemned, but who cares about a dancing-boy? I ran, and no one chased me; only there were too many thieves on the road and too many whores in every tavern, too many cheats and beggars everywhere. If I'd claimed palace skills—*I danced for the court, yes, and warmed their silken beds, that too*—I'd have been mocked for a liar or hanged for a prince's man. Or both, whether they believed me or not.

So I held my tongue and went hungry, went barefoot when my boots wore out, went down and down until at last here I was, back where I'd started. Scrubbing and screwing for Largo's purse, not even bothering to keep one of my own. *Nothing in and nothing out*: there was no point hoarding a single penny piece, if I couldn't take it with me.

Scrubbing and screwing but dancing, that too. That most. I'd been good before; by local standards now, by Largo's standards I was spectacular. I'd learned a lot in the prince's troupe, as much as or more than I did in his bed.

Every night I danced, and word spread, and people came specifically to see me.

Some came back, and back again.

Merrick was young to be a captain, but the New Army was like that, promoting men for merit rather than age or influence or name. It was the gamble I'd taken, me and thousands like me, that experience and long-established power would win out over hotheaded rebellion. Grind it down, stamp it out, crush it utterly.

We'd gambled; we'd lost. Now I danced for Merrick.

For Merrick and his kind, officers and men, a constant succession of faces, bodies, hands. Variously drunken, sweating, reaching to touch. They weren't all soldiers; they weren't all men. There were administrators, traders, the idly wealthy and the busily broke. Some nights, there were more women than men.

Mostly soldiers, though—and after a while, mostly Merrick, at least in my head. I danced for him; the rest were only clutter.

He was sweet. It took him a week of watching from the shadows, until he found the nerve to step forward. He had to shoulder other men aside before he could throw a towel across my naked sweating shoulders, toss a coin to the lurking Largo and take a firm grip of my neck.

"Where can we go?"

"This way, master..."

When I slept alone, I slept with everyone; all Largo's people bedded down together in the hay loft. For customers, I had a room. Lamplight and soft comforts, wine and perfumes, oils and toys. Whips and chains, if their tastes ran that way.

Merrick found no need to hurt me, and I gave him no reason. The occasional clout if I bit too hard: it was nothing, an occasion for a laugh and a quick apology, the brush of lips over the offended spot and move on. I learned what he liked, which was simple enough: a boy both eager and submissive, occasionally wicked, always willing. When he wanted to fuck, we fucked. When he wanted to talk, or more often listen, we could do that too. He liked to hear stories from the palace, from my old high life; he liked to be shocked, a little, by the late prince's decadent behaviours and my own. With a cool goblet in one hand and his other resting on my thigh, with my head nestled into his shoulder and our skin sticking together, with my voice murmuring tales of a world unimagined, he felt something like a prince himself. That was all I wanted.

One morning I was scrubbing floors when I heard his voice unexpectedly, behind and above me: "Let me have Djoran for the day, Largo. How much?"

Largo named a price. Merrick dickered unconvincingly, overpaid shockingly, cuffed me lightly in embarrassment when I bounded to my feet like a whistled puppy. I rubbed my sore ear and beamed at him. "Where are we going?"

Largo snorted. "Wherever you take him, keep his hands tied and a rope on his throat or he'll make off with anything that's yours."

"I will not," I said. "Why would I? I can't bring anything back here."

"You'd find someone to hold it for you. I don't want him building a store of credit outside my house, Captain. Keep him close."

"Hands tied," Merrick agreed, "rope on his throat. Right. I might enjoy that. Do you have a rope?"

"I have better. Djoran? Fetch."

I fetched. A minute later, Merrick stepped out with wrist-cuffs and a chain leash dangling from his hand. I padded at his heels, naked and obedient. *Nothing in, nothing out*: I couldn't even wear chains before I was across the threshold.

In the street there, he cuffed my hands behind my back and looped the leash around my neck. And grinned, and kissed me; and said, "Maybe I should keep you this way. At least I can be sure you'll be good."

"I'm always good," I protested. "Master."

"You are, I know. Except when I want you sinful." His hand rested a moment on my hip; then he laughed shortly and gave the leash a twitch. "Come on, then."

He didn't make me trot at heel long. Soon enough I was settled against his side, his arm around my shoulders and his lips in my hair. He did keep the cuffs on me, though, and the leash too; he didn't think to stop at a market stall and buy me even the simplest strip of cloth to mask my nakedness.

Turned out the day was all about nakedness. He took me to the city baths, and we didn't pass the door again till dusk, when he had to give me back to Largo. We bathed, we swam, we oiled each other's bodies; we drowsed and sweated in the steam; we fucked slowly, languorously, slept and fucked again. We drank chilly sherbets and hot strong coffee, and sweated again, and plunged recklessly into the ice-pool and came out gasping, shuddering, desperate for rough towels and rougher hands to work them.

I'd never felt cleaner or more contented, resting my weary head against his shoulder as he cuffed my hands again, kissing the scented skin of his neck, murmuring, "You don't need to do that."

"No, but I want to. And Largo'll be glad to see me being watchful. As I am. I'm not a fool, Djoran. I know your instincts. And how to overcome them."

"Yes, master."

That was our first day, maybe our best. There were more. Soon enough it was a rare day when he didn't come for me. One of those, we had excitements enough to compensate. A guest was missing a jewelled brooch; she was angry with Largo; Largo was angry with me. I was halfway to the hole, still protesting, when the brooch was found—broken, missing its pin—hidden among the scant belongings of one of the kitchen girls. She was whipped, poor fool, and sent to market, sold. Not listened to. Largo paid to have the brooch repaired, though likely it had broken and fallen of its own accord and the girl had only found it, kept it, a simpler kind of stealing.

I didn't need to wait much longer. A day came when Merrick came, but not to me, not first. Went straight to Largo, and came out with one finger light of its ring, a piece of heavy gold he'd had from his grandser. I knew the history of all his rings, and their value too.

*First fair offer that I hear*, Largo had said.

"He cheated you," I said bluntly. Boys were cheap, and rightly so.

"I know," he said. "I don't care. You're mine now. Come away. I've a month's leave; I'm taking you home. I might leave you there, if you settle. My people will be good to you, put some weight on your bones, get some work out of you, teach you a new kind of life..."

His people were farmers. I knew the kind of life they offered, I'd seen it. Passing by, on my way from one city to the next.

Still, he was master. It was his decision. He left me in no doubt about that. His horse was in the stable yard; he had to lead it out himself into the alley, I couldn't do it. Once we were out, though: then he could set his pack on my back, his new iron cuffs on my wrists. His chain around my neck, a lesson learned.

"There's blood on your thumb," he said, testing the cuffs as a careful master ought. "What have you been doing to yourself?"

"It's nothing, just a splinter under the nail..."

"You should take better care. I'll do that, I'll take better care of you than you do." He tipped my face up, fingers under my chin; and frowned, and said, "Tears, Djoran?"

I sniffed, shook my head, muttered, "It's nothing," again.

"I hope you'll be happy with me," he said fretfully. "I think you will. I'll be strict, you need that; but I won't be unkind, not ever. I'll treat you with all the love you deserve. Love and discipline together; you'll thrive, you'll see..."

Largo stood in his gateway watching, approving. Content. One more ring on his finger, one less doubt on his mind. One less trouble in his house.

My new master swung himself up into the saddle, kicked his horse into a trot. His horse and me, necessarily.

It was an easy pace he set, and dancing keeps you fit. I could keep this up for hours, running at his stirrup with his pack on my back; but I wouldn't need to. By the time we reached the city gate, I was already working the steel pin out from under my thumbnail, where I'd pushed it in a hard hour earlier.

*Nothing in, and nothing out.* Nothing outside my skin. So I'd thrust it deep under my nail, with only a bead of blood to show and an eye-watering pain to endure and disguise. Virelle's watchful gods couldn't touch me for it.

And now I had steel in my fingers, sharp and flexible. Even at a jog, even working blind behind my back with fetters on my wrists, I could pick a cuff-lock with a broken pin. Two minutes' work, and my hands were free. Merrick didn't know; I held them behind my back as though they were still chained there, one clamped hard around the open cuff to stop it swinging loose.

Half an hour later the road dipped to a ford, with trees on either bank; there was no one before us, no one behind us.

Merrick slowed to a walk, and took us into the stream. The water was calf-deep and unhurried, no more trouble to me than it was to the horse. Just as my master smiled down at me, I brought my hands out from behind my back.

One jolted his boot out of the stirrup; the other slammed that steel needle deep into the horse's rump.

The horse screamed and reared. I heaved. Merrick fell heavily into the water. Well-trained, he still kept hold of the reins. I'd been hoping for that.

The horse danced out of the way. Merrick was sitting up to his chin in the river, sodden, bewildered. I took a step forward, swinging my arm lustily. One iron cuff was still locked around my wrist; the other flew on the end of its chain at the end of my arm like a flail.

Dancing gives you muscles like a whip. That cuff caught him on the side of the head with a brutal thud, and I thought I might have killed him.

I snatched the reins from his slack fingers, calmed the horse and tied it to a tree; then I went back for its master.

An hour later, he was the one running sluggishly at the stirrup, cuffed and leashed and naked, with the pack on his back now. His clothes were still damp—and all too big for me—but I wore them gratefully, with stockings stuffed into the boot-toes to keep them on my feet. His rings wouldn't stay on my fingers, so I carried them in a pouch. The horse was equable beneath me. Its former master less so, but I'd gagged him once I tired of his moaning.

Boys are cheap after war and men too, but horses not. Horses never. Between the two, they'd fetch enough to buy me passage overseas. A new land, new opportunities. Put the war behind me, put it all behind me, start again. With quick feet, a quick tongue, quicker fingers. I could rise and rise.

Merrick's family would be expecting him. When he didn't arrive, there would be questions asked, people come in search. Of course they'd find their way to the tavern where he'd spent so much time in recent weeks. Of course they'd interrogate Largo; of course they'd see and recognise the ring he wore so blatantly on his finger.

He'd have nothing to offer but the truth, that Merrick had paid it fairly for a dancing-boy. But boys are cheap, and that ring meant much to him; no one would believe Largo. Not the family, not the magistrate.

A man, a captain gone, and his ring on a tavern-keeper's finger? I thought Largo would hang, like enough.

Not everybody dies, but some, oh yes. Some do.

CHAZ BRENCHLEY has been making a living as a writer since the age of eighteen. He is the author of nine thrillers, most recently *Shelter*, and two fantasy series, *The Books of Outremer* and *Selling Water by the River*. As Daniel Fox, he has published a Chinese-based fantasy series, beginning with *Dragon in Chains*; as Ben Macallan, an urban fantasy, *Desdaemona*. A British Fantasy Award winner, he has also published books for children and more than 500 short stories in various genres. Chaz has recently moved from Newcastle to California, with two squabbling cats and a famous teddy bear.

# ORANGES, LEMONS, AND THOU BESIDE ME

## *Eugie Foster*

WHEN THE NEWS CAME over the broadcast net, every soldier received it simultaneously through their neural implants. The war was over.

In the rice-paddy wastelands of Chinese countryside, men and women in the silver-blue uniforms of the Eastern Intelligentsia popped out of their foxholes and threw their plasma rifles into murky patches of swamp water. The air hung with the stench of plasma-charred flesh, seared blood, and death-opened bowels, but they breathed the miasma as though it was the sweetest perfume. The soldiers in the black uniforms of the Western Alliance streamed out of their bunkers to clasp hands with individuals who, moments before, they had pelted with plasma bolts and incindi-bombs. Soldiers blinded by gas and fire gazed over the ravaged terrain with their prosthetic eyes and exulted.

Medics ran into the ex-battlefield, seeking those hurt and dying of both sides to tend. They were rejoicing too, for they had seen the torn limbs and fractured bodies war had spawned, a sight all of them hoped never to witness again, save in the inevitable nightmares that would come. But their duty to the wounded superseded their elation.

After fifteen years of bloody war, Intelligentsia and West had come together. It was a time of celebration. No matter what uniform soldiers found themselves in, identical smiles creased the faces of every combatant on the field—except for one man's.

Captain Sabin Tol sank to his cot, his blue eyes colorless with shock. His ears were deaf to the shouts of revelry outside his quarters, although the walls were mere centimeters of plasteel.

The Captain wasn't a patriot, or a zealot, or even a devoted career military man. But the war had been his refuge, his oasis. Now it was over, and he had to go home.

Khloii—sister, twin, focus of his heart—had been waiting for him these eight years, eight years since he had joined the Alliance's military. She would be elated, knowing he was coming back to her.

Captain Sabin slumped down, covered his face with his hands, and wept.

The Tol estate in New Atlanta was as Sabin remembered it. There stood the stands of orange and lemon trees that the scientists had mutated to grow in the acidic soil, exactly as they had been eight years ago. Citrus was the source of their family riches after the radiation made Florida and California uninhabitable, and the fallout had turned fruit-lush ranges into arid burn and killing earth. Khloii and he had played fetch and hide among the slender trunks and fragrant blossoms when they were children, and squeezed juice and pulp from the succulent fruits.

Behind it was the manor house, built by their great grandmother. With its marble columns and wrought iron balustrades, it was both fortress and feat of architectural beauty.

Khloii was waiting for him. As soon as the estate sensors scanned him, she came racing out of the great mahogany doors and into his arms.

He held her, felt the softness of her body against his, smelled the clean, citrus scent of her hair. Eight years dissolved at her touch. Sabin knew the chiming completeness he always felt when Khloii was near. Brother and sister were so similar, both with their shining ebony hair, their azure-blue eyes, their near heights.

"You're home. You're finally home." Her voice was a softer, feminine version of his, husky where his was gravel, lilting where his rang.

"Home." Khloii and the manor, sweet oranges and mouth-puckering lemon, home.

She led him, arm around his waist, up the marble steps. Colm, the house steward, and Marissa, the cook, waited to greet him within the entranceway. Knowing his penchant for the delicacy, Marissa held a tray of sugary lemon bars.

"Welcome back, Lord Sabin," Colm murmured.

"So glad to have you home at last," Marissa echoed.

Derik, his sister's secretary, was absent, but Sabin had expected him to be. Sabin snagged a couple lemon bars from the tray and accompanied his sister up the winding staircase into the library.

The room was familiar and strange. Sabin had spent uncountable hours in this room with its dark wood and gleaming monitors, its row after row of bookdiscs and holotapes. It was his favorite room in the house. Khloii's too. But now it seemed smaller, darker than he remembered it.

She led him to the couch, its faded softness witness to midnight discourses and childhood arguments. Taking one lemon bar from him, she sat with feet curled off the floor. They munched their treats in silence. Sabin savored the bite of candied fruit pulp, tart on his tongue, mellowed by a dusting of sweetener. The military did not supply such fare to its soldiers, not even to its officers. He had almost forgotten the burst of flavor, the tingle of his mouth wetting to savor it. The smell of the orchard groves, the sight and touch of Khloii, the lemon bar that tasted of home—this was real; eight years of war had been the fantasy.

Beside him, Khloii fit perfectly against him, her head nestled on his shoulder, his arm wrapped around her. He wanted to let the tension drain away, to lose himself in the simple comforts of his youth. But he couldn't. Sabin knew what would come next.

With fingers still lightly dusted with confectioner's powder, Khloii reached for the I/O wire that would meld them together, letting them share the memories of the last eight years. As children, after their implants had been installed, the learning programs downloaded and processed, they had double interfaced mind-to-mind. Their minds so similar, forged together now by circuitry and wire, sharing sensation, thoughts, memories, and emotions, they had become closer than brother and sister, even twins of the same womb. They spent hours silently communing, at last not even trying to hide their obsession with each other.

Sabin caught her hand before she could press the needle-thin plug into the port at the base of his skull. "You want to live eight years of war?"

Khloii frowned. "I saw the vids you sent, and the recordings and the logs. We haven't linked for eight years. Of course I want to feel everything."

"Sometimes," he said, "thinking of the way you watched the orchards at sunset, or standing, laughing in the rain was the only thing that could get me up at AM summons. Remembering the taste of orange cake through your lips was the only thing that kept me from dropping my shields, just for a second—long enough for a plasma bolt to come through. There was a lot of ugliness I didn't speak of in the vids."

Her lips brushed his cheek. "So let me in."

Sabin's arm convulsed around her, crushing her close. "I can't. It's too soon."

Khloii's hand dropped away, taking the I/O strand with it. "I can wait a little longer."

Sabin sagged. The time when he must face Khloii and show her the monster he was, that he had become, was again postponed. But he knew it was only a temporary reprieve. It had always only been temporary.

Sabin had hoped that the serenity of the manor house paired with the exhaustion and turmoil of eight years of slaughter and destruction would have curbed his jealousy, blunted his fury. But seeing Derik again, it was as though none of the time had passed for either of them.

The other man had strayed into the kitchen after dinner, perhaps looking for a late snack, while Sabin stood at the French windows, admiring the view of the citrus trees in the twilight.

Their eyes met, hard blue and startled brown. Derik spun, fast as a cat, and dashed away. After a moment's hesitation, Sabin rushed after him. His soldier's body was harder and faster than Derik's. He caught him, grappled with him, and rode him crashing to the ground.

Sabin pinned Derik—the secretary staring at him with frightened eyes. He unspooled his I/O wire, a little thicker and less pliant than civilian issue, and rammed the point home into the other man's port. Derik's body shuddered as Sabin whirled, precise and sure, into his mind.

Memory rocked both of them, this so like their first joining, after Sabin had caught Derik with Khloii in her bed. He had almost killed him then. Would have, his fingers curling around the secretary's throat, if Khloii hadn't wrenched him away. Seeing her naked and vulnerable, tears streaming from her eyes, had been terrifying. But it was also the slap of shock he needed to regain control.

Sabin retreated from her quarters, but he hadn't gone far. He waited outside her room in the shadows, standing like carved alabaster until the door opened, and Derik stepped like a thief into the darkness.

Murder brimmed Sabin's thoughts. But Derik did not seem to see him, trailing at his heels. He must have known, though, for in the servant's cubicle he turned to Sabin—weaponless and docile. Derik's resignation disarmed, as his anger or fear would not have.

"I love her."

"So do I."

The silence stretched.

"She's just toying with you." Sabin marveled at how level his voice sounded.

"I know." A wan smile flickered over Derik's mouth. "I've watched you both taming lionins and racing hovers together. I know."

Lionins, like the citrus trees, were engineered by the scientists out of older stock. Tawny-gold with knife-sharp claws and fiery eyes, they were like their masters, spirited and beautiful, and elite.

"Did you think she loved you?"

"A little, perhaps."

Jealousy fired, noxious green and burning. "You're just a bondservant." He prowled in the tiny cubicle, all the territory Derik could lay claim to.

"What was it like?" he demanded.

"I don't—what do you mean?"

"Link with me. Share with me." Sabin didn't know what prompted him to make the demand. It was an intimacy between husband and wife, equals, partners. Never between a servant and lord. Derik, versed in etiquette from birth, was stunned by the command. He could neither refuse it—for he could refuse nothing of his lord—nor could he accede to it.

Sabin unspooled the I/O cord with a sharp tug and crossed to the other man where he sat on his bunk. Finding the port with practiced fingers, he jammed the metal contact home.

It was not the tender bond he and Khloii shared, more intimate than lovemaking, more revealing than any simple communication could be. It was a rape. Sabin tore the memory of what Derik had experienced with his sister and dissected it. He felt the brush of her hair across his arms, tasted the salt and citrus of her skin, and swam in the richness of her body as it embraced him. Her mouth to his, their bodies moving together in a timeless, primal rhythm. Khloii holding him so tight, feeling her body rise to his, the echoes of her pleasure sending him shuddering after his own release. For a moment, the sensory delight shook him. This was everything he craved, the yearning buried deep within his psyche.

Except this was not his memory.

But it would be now and forevermore. He ripped it from Derik's mind, through the thin I/O wire that connected them, and wiped what had been clean from the raw wetware. Bleak and hating, he used his knowledge of programming and engineering—a privileged education—and crafted a harsh replacement. If Derik tried to touch Khloii again, he would be wracked by surges of crippling agony.

He left Derik unconscious on his bunk.

The next day, Sabin left, burning with shame and despair, half-hoping he would find his death in the war that raged with no apparent end. Khloii sent vids to him every day, begging him to return. And when it became clear he would not, she begged him to take care, to live through the war, to come back home to her.

So he had, with a soldier's education to layer the final veneer over his aristocrat's learning. The war taught that what a civilian ought not do, a soldier must. A soldier must kill; he must burn and raze fertile land, wield weapons of terrible chaos, and sometimes, he must invade other soldiers' minds and steal their thoughts, their memories, their secrets.

Sabin appreciated the irony of it when the military assigned him, because of his skills, to intelligence retrieval duties. They appointed him captain of a specialized troop of data harvesters. He knew other soldiers, behind his back, called his unit Mind Reapers, soldiers that did the taboo. They invaded the neural interfaces of others without invitation or welcome, taking what was withheld, and leaving drooling husks in their wake.

Now Sabin sampled Derik's fear, rolled the flavor of his quickening breath and the gallop of his pulse in his mind. He was adept at this, able to prolong the helpless terror in his victims to better savor their capitulation.

He probed for memories of Khloii, saw flashes of her sleepy, angry, worried—scenes he had missed while he fought across foreign landscapes. But Derik hadn't broken his lock. He had not touched Khloii, and when questioned by her, had remained tangibly mute.

Sabin was reassured. He should have pulled out, but instead he lingered. First he triggered the bondservant's anxiety center, drew himself as the sole phobic terror of his existence. A gentle smile crossed Sabin's features when he felt the man's trembling quicken beneath him. With a practiced touch, he drew outlines of obsession over pathways of pleasure and humor, felt Derik's mind warp and buckle beneath his.

It would be so easy to send the other man spinning into mania or fractured catatonia. But Sabin was meticulous with his ministrations. He was a master at this, an expert, and oh-so-careful.

This was a release as engulfing and terrible as orgasm—the electric jolt of the conqueror, the primal ecstasy of power over another. It was one he relished in lieu of carnal voluptuaries. But it was as addictive as less esoteric vices.

The soldiers had a name for that as well. Serk. There was a special ward that housed the Serkers in the medical bases, data harvesters that had gone mad from too many links, too many minds. He had seen men in his unit dragged away screaming and crazed, and once, a lieutenant borne off glassy-eyed catatonic, as though his spirit had eluded the MPs, leaving only an empty shell for them to seize. By all rights, Sabin knew he should be caged there, caught in a stasis web and bound by tranqs and psychotropics. But he had been talented at concealing his sickness, and the war had needed his skills and ruthlessness.

He had not told Khloii, of course. And now she wanted to link with him. Would he be tempted to ransack her mind, to extract from her the faces of lovers she had taken while he was away? Of course he would.

Khloii was his touchstone, his beloved. To see revulsion in her eyes, to feel it along the I/O wire as their emotions melded, it would destroy him more surely than a plasma bolt to the heart.

But Derik's mind was fertile ground. He was meat to be rent and used.

When Sabin was finished, the other man lay shuddering beneath him. His eyes flickered beneath closed lids in a limping dream state. He would wake, not clearly recalling his abuse, but remembering it as a misty terrorscape.

Sabin lifted the other man in his arms and carried him, gentle as a lover, to the servant's quarters. He removed the other man's clothing and laid him in his slender bed, pulling the covers around him.

That night, Sabin slept the dreamless rest that the military psychologists had trained him to achieve, at peace and brimful of tranquility.

The red-gold light of the sun washed over Sabin through the eclipsed glass. For a quick breath, he forgot where he was, expecting to open his eyes to plasteel walls and the luminous glow of fluorods. But the bed was too soft, not the rough edges and harsh touch of a military cot and blanket. And the clean perfume of orange blossoms filled his senses, not the burnt tang of charred flesh or the chemical taste of recycled air.

His door swung open, and Khloii burst into his room. It was her footsteps that had roused him.

"Still asleep?" She looked like a butterfly in her pale blue house gown. The material was lightly translucent; it billowed around her as she bounced at the edge of his bed. "You used to wake up before me and bring a cup of kafee to rouse me. Then we'd go lionin hunting, remember?"

"Of course I remember." He sat up to return her embrace. She clung to his hand when he pulled away. "You didn't bring me kafee, though," he said.

"Marissa has a grand breakfast waiting for you in the dining room."

"Ah. Then I should get up before she gets impatient."

"Wait." Khloii reached for the I/O wire coiled at the base of his neural implant. "Share with me. I remember how I loved waking up to you with that mug of steaming kafee. I thought I'd never be able to show my joy to you again when you were gone. And we never got a chance to talk about what happened, maybe now—?"

"No." Sabin shook her hand away. The hurt look on her face distressed him, but he put that aside as well. "It's still too soon."

"How long do you need?" Khloii brought her fingertips to Sabin's face. "Why are you avoiding this? Surely you can share anything with me."

He turned his head so his lips brushed her hand. "The war...was bad. Worse than you could imagine."

Khloii scowled and flung herself away from him. "I'm not a paper flower! You think I've just sat, watching holotapes while you were gone? Since when have I needed protecting?"

Sabin reached for her. "You know I don't think of you as a fragile, wilting thing. You couldn't be, having to deal with me, growing up." As children, he had always urged her to match him in his recklessness, leaping wide chasms and climbing onto thin branches. And she, proudly defiant, had always flouted peril, never retreating from his challenges.

She threaded her fingers through his. "Then, why?"

Sabin allowed a glimpse of the desolation he felt to leak from his eyes for a moment, long enough for her to see. "I can't!"

"For now," she replied. "But I will know what you're hiding from me."

Khloii did not bring it up again that day. And riding with her around the estate in a hover and chasing after the prides of wild lionins that roamed the acres of their estate made him feel young, as though they were as they had always been—he the tender youth, and she the light of his heart.

But as the sun paced across the sky, they grew awkward and then silent. Dinner was a mournful meal with conversation that stuttered and tripped over itself. It was with relief that Sabin excused himself to retreat to his chambers.

How long could he hold this barrier between them? She sensed it, and it hurt her. That was more painful than any of the wounds he had suffered on the battlefield.

But for now he wanted sleep—blissful, dreamless oblivion. With practiced ease, he forced his restive body into a restorative trance. No dreams, no nightmares, just the void of unconsciousness.

Sabin rested on a bed of frothy cotton. Around him, fluffs of white clouds billowed and flowed. The zest of oranges pricked his nose. It was a tangible sensation—cool as a sluice of ice water, sweet as a kiss. But it was wrong. This was a dream state, and he should not be dreaming of anything—not cloud-mist and certainly not oranges.

Out of the haze, Khloii emerged. The aroma of oranges was joined by the harsher nip of lemons. She wore a white house gown. It matched the foggy white of his dream setting so it seemed her face and hands floated in nothingness. He felt, even in his state of stupor, the tingle of the I/O linking him mind-to-mind.

Khloii interfaced with him while he slept.

His sleep self bolted up at the realization. "What are you doing? Get out!"

She ignored his outburst and sat beside him, hovering on the thick, white nothing. "I've dosed us both with a sleepy-patch. We need to talk, and I can't think of a better way to do it than this."

"You drugged me?" The dreamless state he had induced would be shattered by meds.

"Don't give me those shocked eyes, twin. Remember our thirteenth birthday when you slipped zippy pills in my drink? I drove the hover into town wearing only a lilac veil and a pair of stockings. Very droll."

"Khloii, this is different. It could be dangerous for you to be here."

She laughed. "You're going to hurt me in your fantasies?"

The laughter faded and died as she watched his face. "Sabin?"

"I'm going to dream, twin. I know what I'll dream. Please leave now, before you see."

"I-I can't. I've got us heavily dosed, and our neural networks are doubly interfaced."

Doubly interfaced, a Möbius circuit, their minds separated by only a fragile border of perspective. Sabin plunged his face into his hands. "I didn't want you to find out like this. Not like this!"

The first countenance that materialized from the dreamstuff was Derik's. Sabin's emotions—waves of heady desire, sensuous pleasure, spiky lust for Khloii—washed over the shared dreamers. It was what he had stolen from the bondservant, prized and locked away as his own. With it came guilt and horror, sharp-toothed nightmares ravening in the dark. Like a holotape, Sabin relived what he had done to Derik and the pleasure he had experienced in the act.

He heard Khloii inhale as she shared the intense satisfaction, the glorious pleasure of feeling another man's will ripped apart. He would have stopped this now, if he could, but the dreaming, when it came, was inexorable.

Derik metamorphosed into the first Intelligentsia soldier Sabin had reaped. The man had been trained against interrogation, but Sabin's will was stronger. In a tiny holding cell that reeked of urine and fear, Sabin had forced a link and thrust himself into the man's mind. The feel of the man's will, defiant and vital, had roused him, driving him, eager as a young lover, deep into the man's base thoughts. The frantic beat of the Intelligentsia's fear, so like Derik's, brought Sabin's stolen memories percolating up. Khloii beneath him, writhing in pleasure, her face a mask of ecstasy. To curb the reliving of his/Derik's memory, Sabin trampled through the Intelligentsia's cherished memories—a child's tactile recollection of warm comfort at mother's breast, a clear night sky with the stars bright as hope overhead. When the man tried to resist, Sabin punished him, teeth clenched in a joyful rictus of effort. He'd reveled in ripping through the quiet places of his mind and leaving behind lurid images of skin flayed from bone, acid burned sight, and the screaming violation of metal cleaving through flesh. It was with a rapacious touch, in truth a brutal, sexual act, that he had extracted the plans and codes for an enemy attack from that man.

Sabin had saved many Alliance lives and earned a promotion from that deed. But also, the other man's subjugation had been sweet as a ripe orange, bursting on his tongue, or tart lemonade swirled with ice. He had luxuriated in the sensation of breaking through the barriers of his mind, rolled like a besotted drunkard in the ins and outs of the other man's thoughts, before finally reducing him to the base components of his wetware. His mission accomplished, instead of leaving the man with the remaining shreds of his sanity, Sabin lingered, rapt in his conquest. On a final climax of dark horror and gibbering dread, his plaything had broken. Reluctantly, Sabin disconnected from the wrecked Intelligentsia mind, deliciously sated and breathless.

A parade of faces marched past. Sabin relived the sensual joy of devastating them, one after another, and Khloii remembered them with him. And underneath each memory, like a hidden current in a deep river, was Khloii—the heat of her breath, the softness of her thighs parting, the silk of her hair tangled around him.

He felt her mind-hand on his wrist and shivered at her touch. He did not brush her away. That she could stand to touch him at all was a miracle.

The sequence of battered intellects concluded, and they were left alone in the blank whiteness of his mind.

He could not look at her, and for a long moment they neither spoke nor thought.

"What brought you to this?" she whispered.

Sabin thought to lie to her then, to try to salvage the last secret, but even as he contemplated it, he knew he couldn't. She would feel it.

"Because I wanted you and could not have you," he confessed. "Because I was jealous and desperate. If I could not have you, I wanted no other. And this is how my desires twisted."

Khloii astonished him with her laughter. "Because you could not have me?" The sound of her merriment rang out like a golden bell, but a flawed one, deeply cracked so the tone soured into something unmusical. "And here I was afraid you'd broken the conditioning I planted. Did you even think to look for it?"

He stared at her.

"You don't remember, do you?"

"What are you talking about?"

"Here, a little reminder, sweet brother."

Like a dam opening in her mind, she poured out their childhood years together into his consciousness. It was as though he saw their past out of a fractured lens.

When they were young, it had been small, petty things: the burn of lemon spray to unguarded eyes, a dousing of pheromones to attract the stinging honeybees that guarded the orchard, wasabi powder in the morning kafee. Then it grew cleverer and more deadly: razor shards of glass strewn across the floor, humiliating secrets published on the public 'net, a beloved lionin kitten eviscerated and staked out for the other to discover.

Their childhood was a series of vicious pranks and cruel traps—the product of mutually fierce natures, doubled. Their entertainments had grown bloodier and more deadly, resulting in scars of the body and psyche, until one summer day, surrounded by the ripe zest of lemons, Sabin had pinioned Khloii to the warm earth. He injected a paralyzing agent through her veins and raped her as she lay in the dirt. It was a supreme act of domination. Her eyes, so like his own, had burned with impotent hate, even as her body shuddered in traitorous pleasure.

And then her revenge.

She showed him, the gloat in her thoughts cloying as her name: the masterstroke, when she had snuck into his chambers, maneuvering through a minefield of elegant traps and defensive snares, and forced a link.

Khloii was his twin, body, heart, and mind. In all things she was a reflection of his desires, his perverted thrills. She implanted adoration, jealousy, fawning love, even fiery lust into his psyche—for her. And then set in motion the events by which he would discover Derik in her chambers.

Sabin shivered, caught between fury and loathing. The last eight years of wartime and self-flagellation, all of it due to a cunning hoax. Every moment of it had been spent loving her, riddled by guilt for what he had done.

Khloii laughed, and, strangely, Sabin felt his own lips curve in a helpless, marionette's response.

"And now you're back and still mine."

Fury won out.

"Bitch!" He howled his rage in both their minds. With the adroitness of much practice, he launched himself at the nexus of Khloii's consciousness. He burrowed to the pivot upon which her mind revolved, what Freud had called id in his simple ignorance. But it was more; it was the frame of her personality and the pillars of her mind. He plucked at the pin, as he had done time and again with Intelligentsia, strangers whom he had felt nothing for. The minds of soldiers had been military-hardened, sometimes rigorously trained. Khloii only hated him.

Startled, she fought back. Khloii was strong and also privy to an aristocrat's education. She wrestled for dominion, but the battle was uneven from the start. Unversed in Reaper tactics, she did not strike at the axis of his will, but instead rushed at the mettle of his personality and identity, dashing herself upon the inconsequential elements of his intellect.

Sabin plucked away the pin and felt her will cave to his. Plunged out of his dreamscape and back into the flesh of reality, he reached up, through the haze of sleepy-patch still clinging to his consciousness, and yanked free the I/O cords locking him to her.

Khloii's body spasmed as autonomic reflexes fired, thrummed, and failed. A thread of urine darkened her butterfly gown. Her eyes gazed sightlessly up.

Sabin stared. He had seen much death; he knew what it looked like. But he hadn't intended to kill her. He wanted to punish, to destroy, to twist her mind until she was utterly his creature as she had made him hers. But she had flown, escaped out the last door, and now was gone.

He screamed his frustration. Or rather, he wanted to. His will sent the message, but his ears registered no outcry, his throat no strain.

Instead he heard: "Hello, dear Brother." The voice was Khloii's, but it hadn't issued from her slack mouth.

He spun around, trying to locate the source. He heard her manic, crystal-edged laughter around him.

Her voice was there, inside his skull. "You may have had upgrades and eight years of practice, twin." Her voice was mocking. "But I have had eight years of restlessness. I was so looking forward to your homecoming. You surprised me with all your fancy military tech, but you didn't expect me to be so ready to discard my body, did you?"

Sabin began to hum.

"But why not, when I've got such a fine one to go into?" she finished.

It was a song from their childhood. He hadn't remembered it, nor was he trying to produce it now, but the notes issued from his lips. Except they were no longer his lips. They were hers. Her will, her actions, her body—all hers.

---

EUGIE FOSTER calls home a mildly haunted, fey-infested house in metro Atlanta that she shares with her husband, Matthew. Eugie received the 2009 Nebula Award for her novelette, "Sinner, Baker, Fabulist, Priest; Red Mask, Black Mask, Gentleman, Beast," and her fiction has also received the 2002 Phobos Award, been translated into eight languages, and been a finalist for the Hugo and British Science Fiction Association awards. Her short story collection, *Returning My Sister's Face and Other Far Eastern Tales of Whimsy and Malice*, has been used as a textbook at the University of Wisconsin-Milwaukee and the University of California-Davis. Visit her online at EugieFoster.com.

# PROMETHEUS FOUND

## David Sakmyster

*1. Ellison, Arctic Circle, November, 2023*

THEY WANTED TO BRING me home.

It was the only explanation as to why they had ventured this far north, and why they were firing at me. The bullets exploded into the ice around my legs, and I knew they weren't deliberate misses. They were aiming to incapacitate me.

*So they knew what I was.*

The mountainside shook as they arrived in strange crafts outfitted with blazing lanterns. Traversing the snowdrifts with ease, they were upon me in moments, and just ahead of the flying machines, coming fast, full of a thunderous fury to rival the arctic gales.

They came at me from all angles, herding me toward the cliff and the sheer drop of several hundred feet to the jagged precipice below. I had no desire to repeat such a fall, as my four previous attempts over the edge had failed to provide the desired outcome. Only pain, cold and more misery heaped upon what I already suffered these long centuries.

More loud thunderclaps, and this time my left thigh exploded in agony. It produced the effect that they wanted. Without the sinew attached to the bone, and before the electrical impulses could respond and restore my anatomy, I went down hard. Barely able to crawl, flight no longer an option, I turned and warded off the bright lights piercing me from above.

In these past two centuries I had sought out death on more occasions than I could count, had welcomed its baited promise even as *hope*—that elusive treasure—deteriorated, eroding away to nothing. I had begun with hope, stubbornly clinging to it like a shy child to its parent's leg. I had hoped, attempt after attempt, that I would succeed. For, made in my creator's image, I strove to be his equal, expecting one day to mirror his fate, to be granted the cruelly-forbidden gift of oblivion. But it was not to be, and I had all but given up, turned my back on hope as it had turned from me.

My ragged bear-skin hood fell back as my face now met the light directly, revealing all its patchwork flesh with old scars on display beside new savagery. For a moment I wondered if, despite their obvious attempt to capture and not kill, perhaps I could force their hand and end this agony on my own terms.

I closed my eyes and for a moment, saw an image centuries-lost to me: *The castle silhouetted against the smoke-filled twilight over the Alps. Stars hovering impassively as the ragged mob shambled up the hillside path. The brandished pitchforks, the angrily-swaying torches...*

Although I knew nothing of the world I had left behind, I often imagined how it might have changed; and I arrogantly assumed that perhaps, being a modern-day Prometheus, the first being brought to life by man himself, I might have attained some level of notoriety in the evolving culture of the times. Perhaps my existence had spurned stories and speculation, if not outright myth and legend. Perhaps some foolish adventurers among them still sought the truth, sought out my path and had now come to finish what that impotent crowd had started.

So I turned, rose up on my good leg, and flung the hunk of sharp ice I had pried loose from the plateau. It sailed in a direct arc toward the hooded figure approaching me, but my attacker was smaller than I anticipated. Instead of decapitating the intruder, the missile sailed harmlessly over its head.

I let my shoulders sag and I fell sideways into the frozen field, gaping at the strange metallic bird silhouetted behind my approaching captor.

The figure trudged through the snow and stopped just outside of my reach.

I moaned and tried to dig up another shard, but my fingers were numbed and blistered with frostbite. When I looked back at the silent figure, a slender gloved hand emerged, holding some sort of metallic flat tablet. It had a blinking red light on its front screen. The hand pulled back a parka and revealed an astonishingly beautiful face: jet black hair and a piercing green eyes stared at me in disbelief.

"It's you," the woman said. "It's really you."

Then, as if realizing her predicament, she took a step back toward the safety of her flying carriage. "We didn't think...a lot of us felt you were dead."

I cocked my head and my mouth opened, steam spilling out. I hadn't talked in over fifty years, and now I debated whether to even give it the effort. In another several minutes, my wounded leg would be completely healed, the muscles repaired, the flesh restored; and then I could snap this woman's neck in a heartbeat and toss her corpse over the cliff into the icy abyss.

But that face! Her skin, those full lips and ruddy cheeks...she stirred something in me, eliciting crushing feelings of pain and loss. I saw again in my mind, and in her eyes: Elizabeth! The one once promised to me by my creator. *We thought you were dead.*

I gave her the only response I could. "It seems...death will not have me."

She blinked at me. Then, holding out her hand in a cautiously-warding gesture, she stepped forward again. Her eyes never left mine, and try as I might, they were like fierce magnetic pools and I couldn't break the attraction.

"I knew it, knew you couldn't truly die out here." Her voice was gaining confidence. "The electrical-infused nanoparticles would keep reanimating your flesh, powering your cellular replication, and your brain's neuro-chemical..." She smiled and checked herself. "But you don't need me to tell you all this." She stepped closer, bent within reach of my powerful arms, and tentatively opened my parka to trace the suicidal remnants of my self-inflicted body art across my enormous chest.

Her touch warmed flesh that had been near-frozen for ages, and when her inquisitive fingertips probed the area over my heart, it was all I could do not to stagger back, to crawl to the edge and hurl myself over once more. I couldn't...not here...not again. Certain things were denied me, yet my cursed emotions were too powerful, supercharged along with my flesh. But as if reading my mind, she flattened her palm against my chest, directly over my rapidly-thudding heart. Her touch was delicate, yet still so powerful I felt she would draw the beating organ right from its bony prison and into her grasp.

"We're out of time," she said. "And out of options. We need you."

I think I laughed, or maybe it was the wind, or just her touch on the borderline between pain and pleasure. "You need...*me?*"

Taking her hand away, she reached into her coat and pulled out that little flat rectangular thing again, tapped something, then showed it to me. A map. The familiar landmasses of the world, portions colored red, some blue.

"It's spreading. At the latest CDC projections, we have maybe sixty days left."

I looked at her and now I did laugh, although I had no idea, nor did I care, what a CDC was. "And what do you need the creation of my father for, this impure monstrosity, worthy of nothing but scorn?"

She lowered her eyes. "Victor Von Frankenstein's great great grandson... Ten years ago, he tried again to recreate what was done with you, only this time...he amplified it. Modern technology, an enormous lab. A thousand assistants and billion dollar grants. Not only did he get the experiment to work, but this time his creation...? It *replicated.*"

I perked up at this. "Replicated? It was capable of procreation?" The thought was astounding, and I again envisioned a white-robed beauty, promised only for me. Her first touch, the look in the depths of those eyes. A spiraling of possibilities, an infinite lifetime of joy...and then—the possibility of a family, of a truer form of immortality?

"Not procreation," she said, crushing my daydreams. She violently shook her head at the thought, as if it were some ridiculous violation of nature. "Replication." She all but whispered the word. "A virus. It spread all over the world. Reanimating..."

I choked back a laugh, but she was serious. "Reanimating what?"

The wind howled and the chill cut between us.

"Not what. *Who.*" She stared at me and repeated what the screeching wind at first drowned out.

But then it came back, louder and just as gripping.

*"The dead."*

"They're everywhere, and these aren't your typical Romero clones."

"Your what?" The word meant nothing to me.

"I'm just saying, no bullet in the brain puts them down." She made eye contact again, and the depth of those blue orbs burned away all the frost over my thoughts. "But you already know that, of course. Nothing short of fire will work. Intense chemical fire, destroying all the bits."

I licked my lips at the imagery. "And did you bring some of this fire?"

She gave me a cautious look. "No. If you really want that, you'll need to come with me."

I turned my back to her and set my forehead against the unforgiving ice. "You've wasted your time."

"Please. You're the Prototype. Your blood contains the First Strain, and our geneticists have a theory..."

"Oh, lovely. A theory." I scratched at the left side of my head, feeling the old depression where the metallic bolt, long since rusted and plucked free, had once driven a thousand volts into my skull. "Just as my father-creator once had a theory, a belief that I could coexist with you, that I could live and even...love?" I shook my head, gritting my teeth.

"Please," she said. "You're our one chance. Your blood, if we can isolate the strain, create antibodies and disperse it over these others, these reanimated husks... They'll turn on each other, eradicating themselves like an infection."

I thought about it, for the briefest of moments. "You realize you are asking me to destroy my own kind? To commit genocide?"

She lowered her head. "They're not really alive."

I let out a chuckle. "Then I suppose neither am I."

She clasped her hands together. "You're different, but you are...correct. I am asking for something that should not be chosen lightly."

"And is it my choice?" I glanced around at the hovering metal birds, spotlights trained on me. "Or will you take my blood regardless?"

She held out a hand. "Just come with me. Come home. We've set up a base in your father's ancestral castle. Cordoned off the town, but these things...they're smart. Devious and cunning. They work together, and they...have resources."

"But you have the fire, no? Use it, and be done with them."

"There's not enough, not against the hordes they throw at us. We can only survive for a few days in each stronghold before we're overrun and have to take to the air and try to find the next safe haven." Her eyes fell. "And those are becoming preciously fewer and fewer."

I frowned and let the sharp ice tear into my forehead, and I wished for a moment I could go deeper and let it pierce my eyes and expunge my vision. I did not wish to see her again. Not now, not when I couldn't control myself.

"Please." The wind carried her voice, directing it into and through my spine, it seemed, and straight into my heart. I moaned, turned and was about to agree, when the choice was taken from me.

"I'm sorry," she said grimly. "I wanted you to make the choice, but you're right, we can't wait." She raised some kind of pistol and fired an electrically-charged bolt into my heart. I cannot describe the feeling—one that goes far beyond excruciating—but I lost all control of my flesh, as if it rebelled against my commands, overloaded itself—and then promptly shut down my brain.

### 2. Hapsburg, Austria

It was a dream. A memory more like. But how many people can recall the moment of their birth?

I woke, strapped to a table with leather bonds all too-familiar. I had a moment's hope—it had all been a dream. Everything from the moment of Elizabeth's death to my exile, to my creator following me across the ice, tracking me but only coming to his eventual frozen end while I...I continued in grief and guilt. But it was no dream. And I was not in the upper wing of our castle. I was—

*—in flight?* I felt it in the pit of my distended stomach: we were dipping and rising on air currents. I willed my eyes to focus through the gloom, and the blurry shadows took shape. I was upright, tethered securely to a monolithic slab. I sensed a space behind me where people were, but straight ahead, I was presented with a falcon's-eye view of the familiar hills and forests of my native land.

Little changed in all these years. The same thatched rooftops, the same church steeples; and yet it looked as if a massive festival had begun. In the dawn's first light I could make out veritable armies shifting across the hills, overrunning the town. Shuffling, scrambling things that moved as if they were but automatons, wound up and released for a singular diabolical purpose.

Our craft tilted and I got my first view of the castle.

*Home.*

The ivy-entwined towers were circled by other great birds strapped with lights blazing into the dark clouds. And below the familiar ramparts and gargoyle-decorated walls, at the stone-walled portcullis I glimpsed a reinforced metallic-wire fence, and before that—a moat of pure, raging fire—into which the first waves of the reanimated ones charged.

I watched it all with utter detachment, with none of the sense of awe and wonder I would have expected.

"Now you see."

I tried to crane my neck, but my bonds were too tightly secured. No matter though, for she appeared moments later, dressed all in tight-fitting leather, black as the sky outside. Her hair cascaded about her shoulders. "You see what has become of your father's creation? It is like this, all over the globe. The dead overrunning the living. The living becoming like them."

I took my eyes away from hers and gazed back outside as we dipped and circled, heading over the flames, toward the back courtyard. I licked my lips and realized that I no longer felt cold. That my flesh...itched and prickled. And I missed the arctic home, where at least my flesh, if not my memories, could be numbed.

"You see it as a disease," I said. "But my guess is that they see it as...*evolution*."

Her eyes fell. Then she held up that tablet-thing again, pressing the screen. Immediately images appeared there: violent, brutal scenes of crazed-eyed ghouls tearing young women and children apart and feasting on their flesh; scenes of towns and cities swept away by fire, explosions and rivers of blood. Familiar landmarks crumbled before my eyes: great centers of learning, architectural wonders and grand human accomplishments. All torn down and attacked with the same savagery of these not-so-mindless demons toward their human creators.

The screen went dark and her face leaned in toward mine. Her hair tickled my skin and her breath sent my flesh to quivering. I closed my eyes.

She touched my face, a gentle caress, and when I opened my eyes she looked upon me with such pity, such sympathy, I would have done anything she had asked in that moment. Even turn against my own kind, aiding those who had heartlessly sent me into exile. But in the next instant, she was torn from my sight.

The great bird rocked to the side, and someone shouted, "*Catapault! The sonofabitches made a*—" A scream, and the wind tore inside and nearly plucked the woman away. She reached for me and with a cry, caught my wrist. But so strapped down, I was helpless to grab her. Outside, I saw the landscape and the clouds merge in a swirling kaleidoscope as we fell. But I was rooted to the floor, unable to move, unable to even flinch as we plummeted toward the rabid mob below.

The girl—the one who looked and talked so like my Elizabeth—cried out and the moment before she let go and was lost to my sight, the moment before we crashed into the mass of attacking undead, she shouted, "Don't listen to me when I come back! They'll try to use me, it's what they do. But do *not*—"

The impact was much, much more painful than I would have expected.

*3.*

A sense of motion amid the chaos. Agony, even as regeneration began, even as I felt the electrical impulses charge through my cells. I was in the air again, only this time I felt hands on my legs and arms, hands lifting me high. Spread-eagled, carried by the mob. I glimpsed behind me and saw the wreckage of the flying bird. Twisted, burning metal and molten glass. Two bodies. One burned and missing limbs. The other, more slender... rising.

Then I was dragged inside through an archway. Screams of the living punctuated the darkness ahead, along with thunderous echoes. A smell like the inside of a crematorium, and then someone yelled, "*To the choppers, now! It's lost, it's lost!*"

I was dropped, only to be picked up by new hands, and when those fell others stepped in. They had purpose but moved like a colony of ants, directed by nature and yet it seemed they were controlled. And then I heard it, a dull buzzing, a hum in my head that wasn't there before. And if I focused I could hear...voices.

We came inside a familiar grand chamber, approaching the staircase. The majestically winding, wall-hugging marble stairs that forever spiraled in my memories. They took me up and I struggled, calling out that I could walk well enough by myself. I was healing, good enough now to rise, but they had me in their iron grips.

So we ascended. And on one pass I was able to glimpse out the window as we rose. And I wished I had kept my eyes shut, rather than glimpse straight into one of Dante's macabre visions, a hell with bodies aflame and packs of undead dragging the living out and devouring them like savage wolves.

I looked away, back down the stairs, and I saw a legion of reanimated corpses following up behind us. And behind them, coming through the arched doorway, another figure dressed all in black. Scorched hair, the left side of her face—turned toward me—completely burned away to expose the bone below. A single jade eye found me, and half a smile emerged.

At the top, surrounded by equipment both familiar and oddly baffling, I was brought to a windowed parapet and then released and allowed to move freely, to gaze out the balcony where I had once stood amidst a raging thunderstorm, waiting for the rebirth of my bride.

I heard that awful rumbling of the flying beasts and saw them take flight from the roof above. Three of them, with sleek tails and fat bodies, rising into the sky and banking westward. But then I saw concentrated movement on the ground, past the ring of fire surging in the moat directly below. A huge wooden contraption wheeled into position, and a swarm of bodies heaved a boulder into place; they stepped back and without a pause, it flew skyward in a great arc.

One of the birds attempted to dodge the incoming threat, but too late. The missile slammed into its side, rocked it around and shattered its hull. Two flailing bodies fell out before the whole contraption nose-dived, spilling fire and smoke. It slammed into the wheat field, morphing into a kaleidoscopic fireball that burned briefly, then gave way to tendrils of angry smoke.

Below, my brethren reacted without any sign of enthusiasm. They merely watched as the other birds flew from view, then turned their rotting heads toward me.

*How does it feel?*

The voice vibrated in my head, fluently and with a grace that made me swoon and grab for the door frame. It was her—the one from the plane, the one who warned me…

*Don't listen to me…*

I turned and she was there. Her skin blistered and blackened down the left side of her face, the barest hint of green showing through the pus around her eye. The other one blinked as she shuffled closer.

"I can hear you," I whispered. "In my head."

She nodded. *And you can communicate this way too.*

I shuddered at the intimate intrusion into my thoughts, even as she shambled closer and I could see the white of her chest bones protruding through the burnt fabric of her suit. She turned slightly and offered me a view of the unblemished, undamaged side.

*Electrical impulses. Data transmitted without wires from brain to brain. We've adapted and improved it over the years. Quite convenient when so many of us have rotted windpipes or damaged larynxes. You can do this to, if you choose. Try it.*

"I…" My fingers found my own throat, felt the vibration as I spoke, "…do not choose to. Not yet."

The woman shrugged. *Very well. But there is one choice left for you, one you cannot avoid.*

I heard a murmuring, a low sob of pain. She stepped aside as they brought in a man. Three revenants carried him, his feet dragging along the floor, leaving bloody trails. He was alive, but barely, and looked around with fright. His eye found me, and he gasped.

"Prometheus! Then it's true. It's over."

The woman was at my side, her breath cold on my neck, yet still I shuddered with anticipation. *Tell him,* she spoke in my mind. *That he's right. All is lost.*

"Why have you spared him?"

*He is a pilot, and there is one craft left up on the roof. Release him so that he may go back to the others and give them our offer.*

"Which is?"

*If they come to us now, meek as lambs, and lay down their fire-weapons, we will make it quick.*

I swallowed hard, and felt dead eyes watching for my next move. I looked around the room and saw a backpack-like object on the floor beside an eviscerated human fighter; the device had a nozzle on the end of what looked like a musket, but with a hose.

I turned away from the weapon and stared at the woman who had set all this in motion, she who had torn me from one home and thrust me back into another. The woman who now presented me with another impossible choice. But I needed to know, "Why me?"

"Because you are the one they've sought, you are their one hope. They will keep fighting, always striving although the odds are truly impossible, always dreaming of an unattainable victory, as long as you are uncorrupted." A ragged tongue licked the blistered portion of her lips. "You gave them hope. As long as—"

*As long as I still lived?* It was my first thought, and I allowed it to escape from its personal cage, rushing free to be picked up by other receptors.

*Indeed,* came her response. Her hands gently tightened, squeezing my shoulder. "But there is no need for that. Yes, we could have destroyed you, but this way is more elegant. And you can have what you always wanted."

I turned to her, found her gazing at me, and could not determine which of her eyes I loved more: live or dead, they were both so full of depth, emotion and beauty, each in their own way. But I remembered her question. "What have I always wanted?"

"Revenge," she whispered delicately, and I exhaled with relief. For if she had said the other thing, the one I had longed to hear slip from her lips—or be sent from her mind—I would have been lost.

"On all of them," she whispered. "The race that spurned you, hunted you, the ones who couldn't suffer to look upon what they created. This…is your destiny. This is where you belong. End it, and end them."

*Tell him you have chosen.* Again she squeezed my arm, and her other hand found mine. *Stay with us, lead us as only you can. And I will be by your side for eternity as we shape the new age.*

And there it was. What I had been waiting for, dreading and desiring all at once. I trembled, and felt tears welling in my eyes. But alongside the voice buzzing in my head, came the words, so alike and yet so impossibly different, uttered to me only short minutes ago: *Don't listen to me when I come back…*

I stared at that sad, trembling man, seeing only weakness and pain. And I swept my gaze across the others—the strong, the obedient, the never-dying, never-failing, never-doubting. The new race. My people.

I returned the squeeze at my hand as I took a deep breath. And I gave in to the words bubbling in my heart: "I am indeed home." Then, I thought and sent the words out: *Set him free.*

The three revenants released their captive, who flopped to the ground, resting his forehead on the floor's familiar stones. I stared at the scratching on one of the stones, and recalled my father—dragging an immense coffin-shaped machine across this very floor. The same birthing chamber where I had made my way into the world. Beyond the human captive and the three creatures was a long laboratory table, complete with more of those flat screens and some more familiar items like flasks and microscopes.

Pulling away from my new Elizabeth, I stepped toward the man. Stood over him for a moment as the others backed away, heads down as if in reverence. Perhaps it was reverence, or at least respect for their elder. Maybe I was indeed a legend, even to such as these. Either that or else just a curiosity piece.

I took a few steps away and bent down to pick up the backpack item. I held it up, felt its heat, the liquid fire inside the canisters.

*Careful, Prometheus.* It was Elizabeth's voice. *Best leave that be for now.*

Ignoring her, I slipped my arms through the straps.

*What are you doing?*

Rumbles now, from her and from the other three. I sensed confusion, a rising of alarm. But they were too slow, too interdependent on processing stimuli from multiple sources to react fast enough. And by then, it was too late.

I stepped over the man and adjusted the weapon's barrel in my hands as I took aim on the retreating revenants. They moaned something incomprehensible, raised their arms and may have been about to charge. I do not know, but in the next instant as I squeezed the trigger, the gout of liquid flame surged into the center one and tossed him back against the wooden door. The splashing fire caught the other two, but it didn't matter. A slight back and forth motion, and I sprayed both of them with incinerating, cleansing fire.

And I turned just in time to level the weapon at Elizabeth as she made to leap at me. She stopped, hands outstretched, a look of pure dismay on the clear side of her face.

*Why?*

I didn't respond, and consciously kept my mind trapped shut. Glancing back to the door and the flaming, still twitching bodies, I knew I had bought us time. I took off the backpack and flung it out the window where it could do no further harm to either of us; then I made my way to the laboratory table. Scooping up a flask, I looked for something sharp. Rattled through the drawers and found a scalpel.

A moment later, I was facing her as blood dripped from my slashed wrist into the flask.

The man on the floor had risen to his knees and his bewildered face turned from her to me.

Elizabeth blinked with her good eye, and a tear spilled out and slowly descended along her unblemished cheek. "You're choosing them?"

I shook my head. "I am merely giving them what they never gave me." My wound sealed up as I corked the flask and offered my blood to the man. "*Hope.*"

He took it in shaking hands, as if receiving an offering from a god. And maybe that's what it was. At that point, I no longer cared. This wasn't my fight, and it wasn't my world. As he shuffled away to the upward staircase and the trap door to the roof, I turned to my new Elizabeth, took two swift steps and enclosed my arms around her.

I sensed her confusion, her surprise, just as I sensed the multitude of voices clamoring below. The undead hordes, climbing even now, spurred on by their shared thoughts and instantaneous communication. They were coming, but they wouldn't get in, not in time.

"Hold," I called to the pilot, who was nearly at the top door. And my questing fingers found the item I had hoped was still strapped to Elizabeth's belt, the thing she had forgotten about. I snapped it free, pulled from her embrace, and aimed the pistol at her.

*What—?*

"Pilot," I called, "you will be making an unscheduled first stop. Dropping off two passengers." My eyes shifted and I locked him with my gaze. "And it is to never be spoken of to anyone again. Am I clear?"

He may have nodded, but in that moment, as the thumps came at the burning door, as the mob groaned and thrust themselves against the burning wood, I stared into the eyes of my future bride, the eyes that returned my look—this time with understanding and perhaps, I hoped— even excitement.

*Let them have their hope,* I thought to her. *And if they succeed against what you called impossible odds, then all is as it should be. Hope in the impossible is what defined us once. It is the quality that separates our two species, and why this new creation will never ultimately prevail. It is* their *world, not ours. But there is somewhere, a place just the two of us may survive and even…love. For as long as we can last.*

She blinked at me, and the hint of a smile formed as she asked, *Where?*

I pulled the trigger to deliver enough voltage to keep her out for the entire trip back to the arctic, to the lonely icy caverns, the howling winds and decadent auroras.

But I know she still heard my response, clear as I could send it.

*Home.*

DAVID SAKMYSTER is an award-winning author and screenwriter who makes his home in upstate NY. His published stories and novels cross a range of genres and include: the horrifying *Crescent Lake*, the historical epic, *Silver and Gold*, and a series about psychic archaeologists, with the first two novels, *The Pharos Objective* and *The Mongol Objective* in publication and the third due out summer 2012. Next up is *Blindspots*, a supernatural thriller coming this fall. His screenplay, *Nightwatchers*, has been optioned, and he's currently writing another screenplay to begin filming in early 2013. Visit him at www.sakmyster.com.

# HAPPILY EVER AFTER

## *Marie Bilodeau*

I RUN INTO THE forest, cool air burning my lungs, my feet slipping on the damp earth. The power I lost while protecting my tower cost me dearly. My mind splits in two, clarity lost with my waning strength. Part of me desperately wants to stay and fight, but visceral fear drives the now stronger, older part of me, and so I run. My muscles shrink as my tower collapses, my arms compress, filaments choking bones; bones which snap when my enemies crush my orb of power.

I bellow in anger at the loss, my scream turning puny and frightened. I fight against him. Against Put. I am Raiser! I will not be defeated!

I grasp my head and launch my smaller body into a tree, intent on stopping it or breaking it. The strike is weak and I am unharmed. Before I can stop myself I start to run again, away from Raiser's tower, the fear pounding my legs into more speed.

The trees loom around me, the evening shadows spying my every move. My legs are shorter, my body weak, my anger destroyed by fear.

I run, shedding the last of Raiser. My breath pumps out of burning lungs and mists on my skin, the tree branches whip my face and exposed limbs, as though still seeing Raiser despite my now smaller stature.

I stagger, fear pumping life through my aching muscles. I run until I no longer feel my legs, unable to scale even small roots and rocks. I run until my mind, emptied after shedding years of dark sorcery, shuts down.

I collapse on the ground and I don't even manage to twitch when birds pick at my wounds.

For days I lie there and wait for death. Living has become too difficult, too demanding. Without Raiser, I am nothing. I am…not even poetic enough to think of an interesting metaphor. Raiser could have. All that I can manage to do now is lie on the forest floor, waiting for death. The stars on the horizon flicker for a moment, washed out by smoke. It is not the dark, black smoke of Raiser's armies, but the smoke of hearths, filled with the promise of warmth.

Where my mind hesitates, my weary body does not and I stumble towards the hope of food and comfort.

The forest thins around me and instincts kick in.

I am being watched. My magic rekindles and the forest speaks to me. It tells me to fear. I stop, but the warning came too late.

A mismatched gang of watchmen, all bearing rusty weapons, surround me. Their leader stands well over six-feet, veins bulging on his thick neck and arms. His eyes gleam with an evil as strong as his stench.

I look up, reminded of how short I now am. The leader of the watchmen crosses his arms on his chest, over ripped clothing and ribs. There is nothing to me, save some bones and skin. My brow beads with sweat.

"You one of 'em?" The leader asks, bearing black teeth and gums. "You one of Raiser's minions?"

I shake my head, struggling for the appropriate words. What would a normal person say? What would I say, now that I am Put again?

"You deaf?" The large man spits to the ground. "Dumb." A large fist comes up, sending me flying against a tree. Laughter echoes through the rustling branches.

"We don't need your kind around here!" Large hands pull me from the tangle of branches, pinpricks of bark drawing blood. I stumble but regain my footing, break free and run back into the forest, too frightened to even draw on my magic.

I run until their jeering is too far to hear and then I have to stop, my lungs burning and my hands shaking. I lean against a tree and try to huddle against the falling night.

Memories flood my broken mind.

*The so-called protectors of my village surround me. They push and jeer.*

*I taste blood.*

*I do not dare spit it out, swallowing it instead, including a tooth. What if it angers them more? My sister comes, long hair spilling down her dress. She screams the protectors away, her face red, her lack of grace frightening.*

*I run away from her, too, not wanting sympathy.*

*The next morning, I awake as Raiser to a destiny so big only my now-large shoulders can bear it. I forget Put. Forget his sister. Forget his burning village.*

*Until Raiser can no longer keep the enemies at bay.*

The strands of the dream vanish from my mind.

Yet it clings to me, and my body suddenly feels foreign.

My eyes open, confronted by darkness. My hand brushes away a stray strand of hair and I hold my breath, following the strand down, and down… my hair is long. Graceful fingers brush my face, the high, smooth-skinned cheekbones, full lips, long eyelashes. My hand travels further still, to find a body I have never known before.

A sob of relief escapes my lips and I stand, cover my shredded clothes with my cloak, and head back towards the nearby village.

I wonder what colour my eyes are.

The glow from the perimeter of torches lights my path as I approach. I need a bed, a hearth and a bath. Within a few feet of the first house, the protectors step out of their concealment. So keen on the idea of a bath, I had not even noticed them in the shadows.

The forest does not speak to me, today. I hope it is because it does not fear for me.

Their tall leader stands before me. I tense, fearing that he will tease me, push me down, punch me. Try to run me out of town. I lower my eyes, and struggle to keep my breaths steady.

He takes another step closer. Sweat drips into my eye.

"Name's Klurk. Don't see the likes of you around these parts too often," his voice rumbles. "How'd you get here?"

There is a softness, even concern in his voice that make me look up. He examines me closely. I blush.

"I, I…" I swallow and refocus. They need a plausible story. "I heard the days of darkness had ended and wished to return home. But we were attacked. My retinue fought bravely to protect me." I look down, using my fear of the protectors to pass as my fear of demons.

He nods, absorbing my story. His grip tightens on his broadsword. I begin to shrink away before realizing his anger is not aimed at me, but rather at what has been done to me. I thought I knew men like him. But I didn't. Put knew men like him. Raiser had bathed in the blood of men like him. But I have just encountered my first and can't predict his reactions to me.

"Well, lady…" He pauses.

I look back up and give a tentative smile. I hope it isn't encouraging. The name tumbles off my tongue, resonating like wind chimes in my mind. "Atilda."

"Lady Atilda. You can stay with us. There is nothing to fear here."

I nod and follow them into the village. On the field of my tired mind, emotions battle each other. I am grateful to have gained access where Put had not, but angry he had been sent back into the forest to die; terrified that they will discover I am he, and yet hopeful they will discover I am Raiser.

I would love to see their faces when they realize just how much they have to fear.

My hair is brown, though in certain light it is almost red. My eyes are dark, and the green dress I wear hugs my curves. I walk to the mayor's house, smiling at the villagers, who tentatively return the gesture. A little girl exclaims at my beauty, and my smile deepens. I have never known this kind of attention.

The village is scarred with dirt roads leading to an old well that marks its centre, and the hamlet also boasts one small library and a city hall. The houses on its eastern edge are charred where some of Raiser's scouts swept through, but the villagers fought them off. The men—all young, able-bodied ones, anyway—had then gone off to join the armies of the Parliamentarians. Over the past week, they have been streaming back, finding their way to their homes, haunted looks dancing in their shadowy eyes.

Songs of victory drift from the inn, still open from last night despite the fact that it is now almost lunchtime. They sing of beating back the armies of Raiser. The tune is catchy and I find myself tapping it on my thigh, trying to remember the lyrics.

Then the leader of the protectors, Klurk, pipes up, singing over them all, and my hand freezes. I glance in to see him punch another singer and throw him over a table. I frown and walk on.

The mayor is outside his home and stands as he sees me, taking a long look at the woman before him. I smile and extend my hand, which he greedily kisses.

His son, who resembles the mayor, steps up and glances at his father, embarrassed. I smile and he returns it, his dark eyes lighting up. A breeze ruffles my dress and tousles his thick, brown hair. A scar runs down the side of his face, adding to his beauty. My heart swells in relief that Raiser did not kill him.

He clears his throat and his father lets my hand go. He speaks before his father: "I was surprised when Klurk told me a noble lady had been found." His eyes hold mine captive, my knees weaken as the sun hits his face and highlights his strong features. "But you are welcome to stay as long as you like."

I thank him and stay for lunch. And supper.

And for the few following months.

I awake in total darkness, muffling a cry. The darkness used to be my home, my comfort. Now it cloaks me with fear.

I reach up, my own hands feeling strange as they touch the side of my face. Beside me Malski stirs, and I quickly jump out bed so that he will not reach out for me.

My legs feel foreign to me, too short, too clumsy. I stumble in the dark, going into the next room, and close the door behind me. Malski begins to snore softly again. My hands feel thicker. I grasp at objects with difficulty. I manage to grab the lantern and some fire. With trembling fingers, I light and look into the mirror.

I choke on the cry I feared would escape.

Put is looking back at me, water streaming from his eyes as though he shares my grief.

I leave the house before my mind is overcome by fear, the wisps of Atilda shedding as easily as Raiser had. I throw on her cloak, saddle her horse, and lead it gently to the edge of the village before pulling myself up with a gasp at the shortness of my legs and arms. I had not realized Atilda was so much taller than Put.

The stirrups are too low for me. I grip the beast with my thighs and gallop towards the west, where I had last encountered Raiser.

I did not miss Raiser, but I already miss Atilda. Her self-confidence, her command of a room, her love of Malski…I intend to get her back.

The only magic that would allow me to retain her shape forever is my orb of power, shattered by Raiser's enemies months ago. Raiser's old fortress lies in shambles, now declared cursed and avoided by sane men. But if a shard remains of that orb, no matter how miniscule, I will find it, and absorb it.

As distance grows between myself and the village, I become more and more careless thrashing through the brush, thinking only of gentle Atilda and of finding her again.

Rocks piled on rocks and metal mark the spot where once the great tower had stood, casting its shadow across the lands, a feat of science and magic. Raiser would be furious to see it in such a state.

I fall off my horse and scramble up the rocks, letting my senses guide me. That is the one thing I could always count on: my ability to find the magic and to possess it. A minor talent, according to those who denied me access to the university.

My muscles throb.

*I showed them!* Raiser's voice echoes in the depths of my mind and I smile. Raiser showed them. And the whole world.

I pause, sensing a shard of my orb nearby. So small. I continue scrambling, leaving bloodied handprints when rocks cut me, the broken tower singing Raiser's return. My muscles throb and twitch, and I lose my footing.

*So close.*

I fall, hard, on my back. A stone nearby stumbles down and my hand reaches for something. I look and see that I reach not with my hand, but Raiser's large, unwieldy hand. I scream, Raiser's voice escaping my lungs, deep and grating.

"No!"

The tower is changing me to Raiser. But it is the tower's will, not my own! Raiser would never let Atilda return, and I fight him, a strangled cry escaping my lips. Something pricks my finger, barely catching my attention through my thickened skin.

I look at the small wound in the large hand, where crimson blood trickles down the finger onto the palm. In the wound rests a shard of my orb, glowing purple with magic as my greedy skin absorbs it. I smile, baring Raiser's sharp teeth, letting the shard inject itself into my bloodstream and reach my heart, where it nests.

"The power is mine," I grumble, gently stroking a rock beside me, grieving for what I made and lost. "We will avenge you, someday."

*And I will not let Put out again.* Put's fear undid me when my tower fell. Fear: a terrain Put was so much more familiar with, a terrain I had let him navigate, knowing he would let me rise again once he was cornered or helpless. But Put had not unleashed Raiser. He had instead unleashed another.

I stand, my knees buckling almost immediately, and I fall hard. My tower catches me, panic streaming from deep within my own mind. Panic, and a will I have never sensed before.

Put never benefited from an ally before. Now he and Atilda are pairing their will and strength to force her back to the surface. I scream, my own echo sounding hollow in my changing ears.

I roar, the mountains whipping my words back: "I will never leave!"

My muscles snap. My bones shrink. I gasp and Raiser is gone.

I wrap myself in my tattered clothes, breathe in smoke and decay as I whisper in answer to Raiser's vanishing echo: "Neither will I."

I lower my head into my hands and weep for everything Raiser and Put were, and the love they will never know. I fight down Raiser's echo, still clutching my mind. Put has settled down quietly again, content.

"What are you?" The familiar voice assails me as I carefully make my way back down the broken tower, ignoring the trail of blood Put left in his despair. I am barefoot, my feet scrape against the rocks. My nightgown is mostly shredded from Raiser's large frame.

Klurk stands at the base of the rubble. The fear in his eyes tells me that he saw everything. He quickly closes the gap between us, the tip of his sword cold under my chin. My weary mind struggles to find an answer when Malski and his men jump through the forest wall.

My heart surges and I begin to cry, tears streaming down my face. Klurk looks even more confused.

"Klurk, what are you doing!" Malski cries as he runs to him, bringing his sword to Klurk's back. "Lower your sword!"

"But, she's…"

"Now!" I have never heard those tones in Malski's voice before. I weep more.

The sword lowers and Malski gathers me in his arms. His men beat down and tie a protesting Klurk.

I let myself be held, surrounded by the scent of him, by his strong arms and the sound of his heart beating. My breath lifts with his, my arms tighten like his. This is where I want to stay.

"He won't hurt you again," Malski whispers, kissing my hair, my neck, my lips.

"She's a monster! She's Raiser, I swear!" Klurk screams.

Malski laughs, a slow rumble erupting from his lips as he speaks. "You are mad, Klurk! You assaulted an innocent woman!"

The next words escape my lips before I can stop them, as though spoken by someone else, shards of Raiser clinging to my soul. "For a sacrifice."

Malski's eyes grow wide as he looks at me.

I take a deep breath. "For a sacrifice. Innocent blood of a high born would have given him his powers back."

"His powers?"

I look at Klurk, whose face clouds over with fear. I hold his eyes as I speak the words that doom him.

"The powers of darkness. I've seen it, Malski. He's Raiser."

My delicate hand sits nimbly in Malski's hand. He turns and smiles at me, and I return the gesture, unafraid. His eyes narrow a bit, not out of fear, but out of love. He squeezes my fingers gently, as though afraid of breaking me. I flush and look down.

This body is not unfamiliar to me, though I do not think I have ever assumed its shape before Atilda. It feels frail around me, but less frail than Put. And stronger than Raiser. Perhaps because I no longer walk alone.

I look at the skirt dancing around my feet, mimicking the movements of air, and I smile.

The final words have been spoken and the crowd grows hushed. I look up to the platform. The executioner pulls the lever. Klurk's eyes bulge as he drops and swings.

His neck is thick and it does not snap, the rope swinging him back and forth. He struggles as the breath is slowly squeezed out of him. I remember how he took me into the village and made sure I was safe. Klurk is suffering, his eyes rolling back so far I fear they might pop. The crowd coos in disgust and entertainment.

Raiser would have let him suffer, even extending his life to secure more suffering. Put would have cowered. But I, Atilda, am kind and strong. One final spell will do; one last spell before I hoard my remaining magic to keep Raiser and Put at bay.

Klurk's eyes stop scrambling and focus on mine. The tendrils of my magic wrap around his internal organs and squeeze the life out of him, bringing quicker release. I do not believe it is anger or fear that I see. I believe it is gratitude. And I, in turn, am grateful for it.

I lean back into Malski. He wraps his arms protectively around me. It is over. The people sing of Raiser's death.

And now, all that remains is my happily ever after.

---

MARIE BILODEAU is an Ottawa-based science fiction and fantasy author. Her space fantasy novel, *Destiny's Blood*, was a finalist in the Aurora Awards and won the ForeWord Book of the Year Bronze Medal for Science Fiction. Her short story "The Legend of Gluck" from *When the Hero Comes Home* was also a finalist for the Aurora Award. She is also the author of *Heirs of a Broken Land*, a fantasy trilogy described as "fresh and exciting" by Robert J. Sawyer, Hugo award-winning author of *Wake*. Her short stories have appeared in several magazines and anthologies.

# THE LITTLE THINGS

## Richard Lee Byers

Antoinette's chest still ached, and she had a foul, hot chemical taste in her mouth, but she stopped coughing first. Maybe it was because Dr. Umbra had inhaled a bigger dose of toxic smoke, carrying her clear of the burning base. Anyway, he was still hacking. He'd even pulled up his black mask to uncover his mouth and nostrils.

Best to slip away before he recovered. She took a step backward and thought she was being quiet. But he lurched around in a swirl of cloak and pointed a raygun. His hand in its dark glove shook.

She called up her power. Electricity shivered inside her like a caffeine buzz, and sparks fell from her fingertips.

I can fry him, she thought. He's weak. But she didn't want to anymore. He was a superhero, but he'd risked his life to save hers after her supposed friends and allies abandoned her to die.

Another fit of coughing doubled him over.

"Don't make me hurt you," she said. "I just want out. Let me walk away and I promise nobody will ever hear from Sweet Lady Q again."

He stared at her through one-way lenses. Then the pistol vanished, teleported back to wherever he kept it.

The black dye job and the glasses were a disguise, but Cathy still recognized her little sister standing in the yellow glow of the porch light. Her blue eyes widened, and she gasped.

"It's okay," Antoinette said. "Nobody's after me. The authorities think I'm dead."

"I have a little boy," Cathy said. "I can't afford to get in trouble."

"You won't. I'm done with the supervillain thing. I want a normal life, and I want it in the town where my family is. Can I come in?"

After another moment, Cathy let her into the cramped living room of her side of the duplex. A stale smell hung in the air, and a brown stain mottled the ceiling. Gunfire, or rather, the sound of it on the neighbors' TV, banged through the wall.

Antoinette frowned. "That's kind of loud for this late at night."

Cathy waved her to an armchair with a tear at one corner of the backrest. "The wall's thin, and you can't run complaining to people about every little thing."

"I suppose."

Cathy sat down on the couch. "Look, Nettie, I love you and I've missed you every single day. But you're also why I had to change my name and move across country just for a chance at a normal life. Before I even think about having anything more to do with you, I need to know: Why are you doing this, and why are you doing it now? How can I be sure you mean what you're saying?"

Antoinette felt hurt. "When did I ever lie to you?"

"When you were lying to yourself, too."

Antoinette sighed. "Okay. Maybe that's fair. So let me tell you about the fabulous life of a supercriminal. The police shoot at me. Heroes as strong as elephants beat me up. I work with people I can never trust stealing money I almost never spend on anything fun because I'm too busy running and hiding. If you were me, wouldn't you quit?"

"Yes, but I'm not you."

"I swear, I'm done with it."

Cathy studied her the way Dr. Umbra had. Then she smiled. "All right then, sis. Welcome home."

The duplex didn't look any less shabby in the morning light. The noise from the neighbors' TV, now the giddy babble of a talk show, still leaked in from next door.

But if Antoinette's surroundings scarcely seemed like an improvement over the rattiest safe houses where Sweet Lady Q had gone to ground at one time or another, the company was. Paul, her nephew, was a skinny, towheaded kid in love with astronomy and astronautics. She was putting off telling him who she really was until she was sure he could keep the secret, so she couldn't say that she herself had flown in orbit and visited the moon. But she could still talk knowledgably about space travel, and the two of them hit it off.

His chattering enthusiasm brightened up the place while they crunched their way through a breakfast of store-brand corn flakes and Cathy hurried off to one of her three part-time jobs. Antoinette enjoyed it enough that, when he had to leave for school, she offered to walk him to the bus stop.

Paul almost seemed to flinch. "No. That's okay. Mom said you have stuff to do." He grabbed his backpack and scurried for the door.

Antoinette sighed. Maybe Paul wasn't as taken with his mother's "friend from college" as he'd seemed. Antoinette was okay for a stranger and a grownup, but he didn't want her around to cramp his style when he was with other kids.

Still, they'd bond. She was sure of it. She freshened up her coffee and fired up Cathy's elderly Toshiba PC to check the local job listings.

Antoinette had to ride her own bus, a city transit one, to follow up on what little she'd found online. The bus rolled along at a leisurely pace and stopped every block or two to let someone on or off, the folding doors squeaking open and shut. Remembering the Porsches and Maseratis she'd raced for fun and the even faster vehicles bristling with exotic weaponry she'd driven to hijack armored cars and kidnap dignitaries from motorcades, she wondered how anyone endured this waste of time on a daily basis.

But the other passengers didn't look like they minded, and that was because they had good lives with families, homes, and peace. They didn't have to fight the Balance or Osprey over and over again or rot in jail for months at a stretch till they managed to break out. That was a *real* waste of a person's precious time.

As the bus lurched to yet another stop, she told herself she was lucky to be onboard.

The telephone buzzed. Everybody in the crowded waiting room looked up at the same time like Pavlov's dogs reacting to a bell.

The secretary with the narrow, wrinkled face and blood-red lipstick picked up the phone and listened for a moment. Then she called out to the people in the molded plastic chairs.

"I'm sorry. That's all the interviews for today."

The job seekers looked back like they didn't understand. But apparently they did, because they started rising stiffly and trudging out.

It was Antoinette who didn't understand. She pushed against the outgoing tide to reach the receptionist's desk. The woman gave her a tight-lipped flicker of a smile. "Can I help you?"

"'That's all the interviews for today.' What does that mean?"

"That Mr. Geraghty has filled all the openings."

"Without seeing everybody? I had an appointment. I made it online."

She had a solid résumé and references, too, far better than these low-level retail jobs should have required. She'd paid big money to Mr. Quill to create her fake identities because he always delivered a quality product.

"It's the bad economy," the receptionist said. "We get so many applicants. If Mr. Geraghty saw everybody, that would be all he ever did."

*I was here on time*, Antoinette thought, *and when you didn't call me, I waited another hour and a half.* Her power stirred, warming the core of her and tingling down her arms.

She took a breath, and the sensations faded.

Yelling shrilled down the block. A twinge of curiosity roused Antoinette from a dullness born less of fatigue (it took a lot to tire out a metabolism capable of generating hundreds of thousands of amps) than frustration.

After she'd gone to the places the Internet told her to try, she'd wandered around downtown looking for Help Wanted signs. She hadn't found many. Quite a few establishments had gone out of business, like the whole city had fallen victim to the drabness she'd already discovered in Cathy and Paul's duplex and its rundown neighborhood.

Finally, when the surviving offices, stores, and sandwich shops started shutting down for the day, she'd taken another creeping bus ride home.

Squinting against the late-afternoon sun, she spotted running figures. Paul was in the lead, but just barely. The other boys were going to catch him in a few more seconds.

Her hands feeling like they were vibrating on the inside, she trotted forward. "Hey!" she shouted. "Hey!"

Startled, the other kids balked. That gave her time to reach her nephew. Panting, he looked at the ground, not meeting her gaze or anybody else's.

"What's going on?" she asked.

The biggest kid twisted his square, flushed face into an expression that fell just short of being a sneer. "We were just messing around playing tag. Tell her, Paulie."

"Yeah," Paul said. "Just playing."

One of the other boys snickered.

"Come on in the house," said Antoinette to Paul. "You need to do your homework." She stared at the other kids the way she'd learned to stare down even maniacs like Knyfe when the situation required it. "You kids should go home, too."

As they climbed up the concrete steps to the porch, and the television next door blared that somebody was a "ho," Paul mumbled, "That was nice, but I wish you hadn't done it. If they think I'm telling on them, that will just make it worse for me when there aren't any grownups around."

"That's why you didn't want me to walk you to the bus stop. They'd think you asked me along to protect you."

"Yeah."

"Why don't they like you?"

He shrugged. "I'm the new kid, and it's not a good school to go to if you're a science geek."

She hesitated, wondering if she should let Cathy handle this, then reflected that her sister wouldn't even be home from her various jobs until late.

"You know," she said, "you're right that you shouldn't rat. I mean, tattle. But running away won't help, either. You have to stand up to bullies."

Paul sighed. "People say that, but they'd just beat me up."

"Not necessarily. Let's go in the backyard."

As they passed through the house, she thought about how her instructors had gone about teaching her hand-to-hand combat. She'd decided to learn after a near-disastrous encounter with technology designed to dampen a superhuman's powers, and although she was no Scarlet Bride, she'd gotten pretty good.

"The first thing you have to know," she said, "is how to make a fist."

Hanging onto a metal pole, Antoinette looked around the crowded bus and recognized many of her fellow passengers. They caught the bus out of downtown at this same time every day, which meant they had jobs.

And God, wouldn't her old partners have laughed to hear that she envied them. Sweet Lady Q, who could walk into any bank in the world, toss some lightning around, and walk out five minutes later with all the money she could carry, was jealous of losers who had no choices in life but to kowtow to bosses like Mr. Geragthy's bitch of a receptionist and grind away at boring tasks day after day after day.

But no. That was the wrong way, the self-destructive criminal way, to look at it. She made herself focus on what she planned to teach Paul this afternoon, and that helped her relax.

Antoinette knelt down in the grass so Paul could easily strike at her face with the final move of the combination. "Whenever you're ready," she said.

He checked his stance, lifted his hands, and then hesitated.

"You won't hurt me," she said. "You'll stop the final attack short, and if you don't, I'll duck."

"Okay," said the boy, "but isn't this, like, *dirty* fighting?"

She snorted. "Are there four bullies and only one of you?"

"Yeah."

"Then do what I tell you."

Cathy waited until Paul was in bed to sort through her mail. Most of it was bills, some marked Overdue or Final Notice. She closed her eyes and massaged the bridge of her nose with her thumb and forefinger.

"You look unhappy," said Antoinette.

"I have a headache."

"Is there anything I can do to help?"

"You can get that job you're supposed to be looking for."

"I *am* looking."

Cathy sighed. "I know. I'm sorry. It's just that Jack doesn't pay his child support, the school system lays me off, I run up student loans getting my stupid degree in Medical Office Management, nobody will hire me to do that, either—"

"And then your long-lost troublemaking sister shows up on your porch like a stray dog."

Cathy winced. "I swear to God, I'm not complaining about that. I'm thrilled you're here. I just wish I could catch a break."

Antoinette smiled. "I'll let you in on a secret. You already have. I didn't tell you before because you acted so nervous about having me around at all, but I've still got some of the money I stole. I shouldn't transfer it for at a while, but as soon as it's safer—"

"I don't believe this!" Cathy exploded. "You swore you were done with all of that!"

"I am! I'll never, ever commit another crime. But we might as well use what I took already. You and Paul can have a better life."

"Or I can go to prison for harboring a fugitive, and he can go to foster care! You can have your...loot or your family, Nettie. You can't have both."

The stain on the living-room ceiling was just visible in the gloom. Antoinette lay on the couch and stared at it, while next door an infomercial raved about the wonders of a "revolutionary weight-loss drink."

She needed the infomercial to shut up so she could fall asleep, put her sister's paranoid ingratitude in the past, and wake up liking her again. She wrapped a pillow around her ears, and, when that didn't keep out the noise, got up and padded out onto the porch in her borrowed pajamas and bare feet. She peeked in a window at the front room of the other half of the duplex.

No one was there. The neighbors had apparently left the set on when they went upstairs to bed. What kind of idiots would do that?

Idiots who didn't realize who was living beside them.

It was a mild night, cool but not cold, and the window was up. She poked her index finger through the screen and hurled a bright, pencil-thin twist of electricity at the television. The set crackled and then went silent and black. Smoke billowed out of the back.

She grinned.

"You're getting better," Antoinette said. "Your stance is balanced, and your blocks are working. But this time, give me all you've got. Hit and kick like you mean it."

His face sweaty, Paul said, "I guess I don't really mean it."

"Pretend I'm Roger." Roger was the beefy kid who'd claimed they were playing tag and was more or less the leader of the bullies. "What names does he call you? Chicken? Faggot? Is he right? Is that what you are, a little faggot? Faggot. Faggot. Come try and hit me, fag—"

Paul rushed her.

She blocked five attacks, then stepped back. "Stop. That was better, but—"

He came at her again.

She sidestepped and used a foot sweep to dump him onto the grass. "I said, stop."

Looking shocked at his own aggression, he goggled up at her. "I'm sorry!"

She smiled. "It's okay. That happens in training. People lose their cool. And you had the right instinct. In a real fight, don't stop, not until it's over."

Winston liked rock climbing and scuba diving and, judging from the way he kept talking about them, imagined that relating his self-proclaimed "adventures" was a good way to impress the opposite sex. Since it was at least more interesting than...whatever it was he'd said he did for a living, Antoinette sipped her Chablis and tried to look attentive.

Sitting across from him in a dimly lit bar made a change from the duplex, anyway. The quiet next-door was a relief, but now she had Cathy watching her suspiciously, and just because she'd offered to share her money. How insane was that?

Things were mostly okay when Paul was awake, but tonight after Cathy sent him to bed, the duplex started feeling particularly claustrophobic. Eventually, Antoinette went for a long, brooding walk, which led her here and to Winston.

She abruptly realized she'd stopped listening to him a while ago, and now he was looking at her expectantly. "Yes," she ventured.

He laughed. "You zoned out, didn't you?"

"Well...yeah. I'm sorry."

"No, I am. I know I go on and on sometimes. Maybe instead of talking, we should dance."

That was a little more fun, enough so that when he asked for her number, she gave it to him. But when he drove her home and kissed her good night, the touch of his lips didn't make her feel much of anything.

Well, everybody knew the first time could be tentative and awkward. The next one would be better. As she stood on the porch and watched his taillights recede into the dark, she tried not to compare him to *real* adventurers like Nexxt, Orcan, or even Dr. Umbra.

The people standing around Antoinette jostled her whenever the bus sped up or slowed down. The vehicle was so crowded they couldn't help it.

*It's a damn cattle car*, she thought.

Selfish though it was, she couldn't help wishing some gentleman would offer her his seat. But nobody did.

Sweet Lady Q could have *scared* an ordinary person out of his seat. She could have emptied out the whole bus.

A teenager with blue streaks in her hair sniffed twice. "Weird," she said.

"What?" asked her friend.

"It smells like it's going to rain. But we're inside a bus, you know?"

Antoinette shoved past a fat man to snatch the bell cord.

As she watched the bus roll away, she took deep breaths and told herself to be proud. She'd made the right choice and kept her self-control. Then her cell phone rang.

Antoinette thrust all her cash into the cab driver's hand, turned, and then hesitated. With its landscaping and basketball court, Juvenile Detention didn't look particularly grim as such facilities went, and she doubted anyone in Reception was on the lookout for supercriminals in disguise. Still, the place was part of the great machine that was law enforcement, and she'd spent half her life trying to avoid getting caught in the gears.

But her sister had sounded frantic on the phone, so she took a breath and headed for the entrance.

Thanks to the metal detector, fluorescent lights shining down on speckled gray linoleum, and smell of disinfectant, the inside of the building was more institutional than the outside. Cathy was pacing back and forth. When she spotted Antoinette, she scurried to her and threw her arms around her.

As she hugged her back, Antoinette looked around and found a pair of chairs in a deserted corner of the waiting area. It might not matter in the present circumstances, but given a choice, she wasn't going to talk where the correctional officers behind the counter could overhear.

"All right," she said once they were sitting down. "Tell me what happened. I couldn't understand it all on the phone."

Cathy swiped at her eye. "I don't understand it all, either. The policemen at the school arrested Paul for assault."

"Simple assault?"

Cathy frowned like it was a weird question, but she answered. "Aggravated assault, and the people here said there could end up being other charges, too. Supposedly, Paul broke one boy's knee and gouged another in the eye. He could lose the sight in it. The doctors won't know until he's out of surgery."

Antoinette sighed. "Shit."

"It just can't be true! Paul would never, ever do anything like that."

"Not unless he didn't have a choice. The other kids were bullying him. It was self-defense."

Cathy stared. "How do *you* know?"

Antoinette hesitated. "He told me a while back."

"Why didn't *you* tell *me*?"

"You work fifty-five hours a week and come home exhausted. I thought this was something I could handle for you." And build a relationship with her nephew in the process.

"Handle it how?"

"By teaching him to take care of himself."

"Like the terrorists and murderers you work with take care of themselves?"

Antoinette glanced around to make absolutely sure no one was listening. "Please, keep your voice down. And okay, yes, I taught him some... techniques. I didn't know it would turn out like this."

"Of course not, because you still have the same wonderful judgment you always did."

"Look, I'm sorry! But Paul will be all right. They can't convict him of anything when it was four kids beating up on one."

"You don't know that. We don't know who threw the first punch. Even if he does eventually get off, for now he's stuck in here!"

Antoinette winced. Bad things had happened to her when she was in juvie, after she started getting into trouble but before her powers manifested.

"They'll hold a hearing," she said. "The judge will set bail."

"Even if he does, how am I supposed to pay it? Or hire a lawyer?"

"I told you, I have money stashed away."

"Right, because that's all we need, for the authorities to figure out Paul's bail came from his aunt the supervillain. If that doesn't convince them he's a budding sociopath, nothing will!"

The start of a headache drew Antoinette's forehead taut and tightened her jaw and neck. Then, however, the incipient pain melted into the shivering crawl of lightning along her nerves. The power concentrated itself in her hands, she smiled, and something in her expression made Cathy's eyes widen.

"Don't worry," said Antoinette. "You're right, this is my fault, but I can fix it."

"You don't mean you're going to break him out."

Antoinette snorted. "Of course not. If we can't even bail him out without screwing things up worse than they already are, what good would breaking him out do?"

"Then what?"

"You're going home so no one can connect you to what's about to happen. Then, tonight, Sweet Lady Q is going to go on a rampage through town." She grinned. "Who knows why? Sociopaths just do evil, crazy things."

Cathy shook her head. "Nettie, no."

"While I'm running amok, I'll blast this place to pieces. I'll trash the city jail and the police department, too." Her hands tingled harder as she pictured it, an almost sexual feeling. "Afterwards, the authorities will have no choice but to release underage prisoners like Paul back to their families. They won't have anywhere else to put them. That will solve the immediate problem, anyway, and you can figure things out from there."

"No," Cathy repeated. "*Please*, forget what I said before. I was freaking out. This situation is bad, but not that bad. Somehow, we'll get Paul out without you throwing away the life you want."

It pained Antoinette to see that now Cathy was upset for her as well as Paul. She hoped the truth would make that part of the situation better.

"But I don't want it," she said. "I thought I did, but I was wrong. I mean, I want you and Paul. I love you, and I'll miss you every day. But normal life...I'm not saying I'm too good for it. It's probably too good for me. But all the boring parts, the disrespect, the little aggravations and disappointments...I don't know how to put up with them anymore."

Cathy studied her face. Then she said, "Promise me you won't hurt anybody."

"All right." Antoinette wondered if she'd finally succeed in keeping a promise. She hadn't done very well at it lately.

They hugged again, and then Cathy left. As the door swung shut, Antoinette marveled that it was possible to feel such profound loss and relief at the same time. She also wondered how to throw together some semblance of her costume.

---

RICHARD LEE BYERS is the author of forty horror and fantasy novels including *Called to Darkness*, *Blind God's Bluff*, and *Prophet of the Dead*, all due out within the next year. "The Little Things" is set in the post-apocalyptic superhero universe of his ongoing eBook series *The Impostor*, only before the aliens invaded and everything went to hell. Readers interested in seeing more of Sweet Lady Q should seek her there.

# HEELS

## K.D. McEntire

THE HEELS SAT ON top of the trash, mocking me.

*You could be at work*, they seemed to say. *You could be exchanging quips or battling sidekicks. You could be having a sexy catfight with Lonely Locks, grabbing her by that ridiculous braid and swinging her smug face through a plate glass window. You could. You could. You could.*

"Shut up," I told the heels, glaring at the trashcan. "I don't need to listen to your broken...points. Toes. Whatever!" I was tempted to yell at the heels for breaking at the worst possible moment, for snapping like cheap kindling instead of the high-tech stilettos I'd spent a small fortune upgrading. Instead I grumped my way back to the couch and flung myself amid my mismatched throw cushions.

I don't even *like* shoes all that much. Shoe shopping was, is, and always will be a necessary chore, akin to stocking up on toilet paper and organic ketchup. But these shoes had been different. These shoes had been special.

These shoes had been...*the heels*.

There's all sorts of drama involved with a lady's choice of footwear. Birkenstocks lend themselves to the inevitable hippie comparisons. Sensible pumps give a gal an air of controlled businesslike acumen. Steel-toed boots mark you as the tough girl in any group, whereas ratty old sneakers give you an inescapable air of Girl Next Door.

Heels, however...heels...

Heels say something about a villain that sensible shoes do not. They say that I'm capable of donning footwear that is just as likely to cripple me as it is to kill you, but I'm fairly sure you're the one going home in a body bag. Heels are pointy and hard; they cling to the foot and lift up the ass. Heels distract the sidekicks with the right curve of buttock but allow the hero to meet you eye to eye. Heels are...magical.

At least, these heels were.

I kicked my first hero ass in those heels. I scarred Pretty Boy Sam's cute cheekbones with those heels. And the first time an argument with a hero ended with us tumbling in the hay, well, the heels stayed on the entire time.

I could buy another pair of heels, sure. But, just as I knew these could be repaired, I knew it wouldn't be the same. Maybe the heroes wouldn't be able to tell the difference, but I'd spent years learning how to fight right in those heels.

I'd know.

I hadn't even wanted to wear the heels at first—it'd been bossman Dr. G's suggestion and *he* isn't a master of any sort of martial arts. He had no clue how difficult it is to do a perfect roundhouse kick wearing heels, how hard it is to sprint. A flawless *yoko geri* to the *cajones* is normally impossible in heels…but Dr. G just liked the look with the catsuit.

"I bet they'll make you look foreboding," he'd said, handing me my Welcome to the Team box, the tall black heels nestled primly on top amid pink—PINK!—tissue paper and tied together with a tiny white bow.

I almost threw them at his head.

But then I tried them on. I swaggered around my new corner office, forced to pull the pleather of catsuit-1.0 out of my ass with every step; and yet, despite myself, I fell in love with those heels. Over the years I poured a lot of money into adapting the shoes for all sorts of conditions—snow, ice, metal, lava, blood—only stopping short at reinforcing them because titanium is not cheap. I should've done so anyway and damned the cost.

Now they were gone.

I hate girls who mope when they break a nail—I've dealt with them my whole life. I've seen villains lay low for shorter spans than the vain sorostitutes I'd gone to school with, and over what—jagged cuticles and a bad perm? If the streaks weren't perfect those girls would hide out for weeks until they could fry, fry their hair again.

Not for the likes of me, no ma'am.

Yet here I was, sinking to the depths of despair over my shoes as if the world itself were ending. Not that that was the best analogy—honestly if the world were ending, I doubt that even the delightful douches in H.R. could keep me away from that going-away keg party, busted heels or no.

I needed something to take my mind off my misery. What to do, what to do?

If I was forbidden to work right now then there was no point in cracking the latest dossier, and I'd read everything in my apartment a hundred times.

Watch TV? Absolutely not. I pirated cable like everyone else in the building, but I hardly ever watched it - no time. And I have it on excellent authority that reality television is literally soul-sucking.

Go online? Hardly. With my catsuit, I can surf the net any time day or night with just a blink and a nudge. I'd carried out many a grand-larceny while simultaneously searching Snopes or browsing Wikipedia.

For the first time in a very long time…I was at a loss.

The problem with being a career-oriented villain on her way up in the world is that by time I get home most mornings I simply strip down, shower, and fling myself into bed. My last cat slipped out during the Battle of Barneby's Bulge and got herself knocked up—I gave her away shortly after. It's another reason I never incorporated a husband into my cover story; if I can't keep a kitty from coming home pregnant, how would I manage a teenage girl?

I'm not concerned about *finding* a man—Dr. G's got enough mind-control devices and drugs littering his lair to field an army of bored suburban househusbands—it's the knowledge that I'd probably start a garden and let it run to seed, or I'd borrow a neighbor's mower and turn it into a doomsday device. I'd forget birthday parties, or buy the wrong type of card—one with a puff of poison gas, perchance—and heaven help the child of mine who tested me with "I'm bored."

Don't get me wrong. I like the *idea* of a home—not an apartment, dingy and small and studded with surveillance equipment—but a home with a hearth and a patio and a room for guests…if I actually knew some.

I closed my eyes, picturing it. I'd start with something simple and innocuous like New Year's, or perhaps that big-deal football game with the commercials. I'd serve "my famous dip" that Dr. G would've concocted for me—by the end of the event I'd have them all eating out of my hand. Simple, elegant. Then, once I had a party full of drooling drones, I'd—

Deep in my fantasies of sinking into a suburban life on my own terms, I dimly heard the phone in the kitchen ring once, twice, three times. I popped open an eye and grimaced. Only one person ever called me on the landline.

Mother.

Grumbling, I waved a hand and the sensor in the wall forwarded the call to my cell, still nestled in my cleavage. I fetched it and jammed the phone between the throw pillow and my ear, too grumpy to want to bother holding it.

"Hi Mom," I answered, not bothering to keep the boredom hidden. "What's going on?"

"Clarisa, dear," my mother chirped from Wisconsin, speaking too loudly into the cell as always. I winced and shifted the phone a tiny bit south on the pillow. "I just got the most lovely call from your supervisor, Mr. Gerbraltior…Grebralitor…oh, you know."

No.

He wouldn't.

Heart thudding, I sat up, clutching the phone hard against my ear. "You did? What'd he say?"

"He said that you'd been given the next three weeks off and a promotion! Oh, honey, we're so proud of you!"

He did. That.Son.Of.A.Bitch.

"Yeah. Haha. Promotion." I clenched my fists and leaned forward, resting my forehead against my knees. "I guess that means you want me to visit, huh?"

Could I still disassemble a short-range pistol and sneak it past security, I wondered. I hadn't had to for so long—I could try for something larger caliber, but I sincerely doubted that I'd *need* a bigger gun for just a week with the family…

"Oh darling, that'd be wonderful. Your cousin's wedding is this weekend and I just know she'd love for you to be there—a surprise visit! Oh how fun!"

"Will a BulkCo gift certificate be enough for a gift?" I'd gotten Sherri's Save The Date and Wedding Invitations—one of those clever little missives with two strings that tied into a knot as you opened the invite—but I couldn't remember where Sherri had registered and I'd already thrown the scraps of pastel cardboard away.

Approval. "That'd be lovely, dear." Then, faintly probing, "So, Miss BusyPants, talk about this promotion! How'd you get it? Did you put the fear of God into that Captain Fabulo—"

"MOM." I was overwhelmed with the same rush of mingled annoyance and humiliation as when she'd rushed an industrial-sized box of tampons to my Junior Prom. She'd been doing me a favor, but it was the *execution* that had been lacking. The last thing I wanted was Dad walking in and overhearing her.

"I'm sorry, honey." She cleared her throat and tried again, even louder, "I haven't watched the news today. Did you finally give 'that guy' what for?"

My mother knows about my career. My father doesn't—he still firmly believes in Uncle Sam, mandated heroes, and apple pie. My mother, a former hippie, is more open-minded though she doesn't entirely approve of my choice of work. Sometimes I think she'd have preferred if I'd become an escort or a lawyer. At least then she'd be able to talk about my accomplishments to her friends instead of resorting to bragging about my younger brother Kenny.

Kenny runs the Hot Dogger kiosk in the mall.

Bragging about his job takes imagination.

"No, Mother, I did not, in fact, give 'that guy' any sort of for, what or otherwise," I said, trying not to brood on Dr. G's gentle insistence that I should go home for the rest of the day, that I should take a break and think about my position as his number one right-hand henchwoman. "I kicked 'that guy' in the face and his face broke my heels."

I'd limped out of Dr. G's office, head held high, a 'furious underling' expression plastered across my face, but inside I was…hurt. I'd been with Dr. G for forever. Literally—we'd been to the end of time together and back again during his quantum-mechanics phase—and the thought that I could be so easily *sent home to think about what I'd done* aggravated me.

"Oh no! Those expensive heels I always see you wearing on TV?" For the first time my mother registered my tone. I would have been offended by that except that I'm normally grouchy when we speak—she had no way of knowing this was much, much worse than normal. "Honey, you should register a complaint."

I snorted. "A complaint, Mom? Really? Who to?"

"That Heroic property damage company's hotline—"

"Isn't quite the same thing," I said, but amused myself with the image of trying to wrangle the price of my heels out of the assessors at the Heroes Insurance Initiative. I was tempted to go ahead and do it, if only for shits and giggles. "But thanks for the suggestion."

"Well, all right," she said and I heard the scratch of pen on paper across the line. I smiled to myself, touched. Mom was going to buy me new shoes, probably for Christmas, possibly as a 'what the hell' gift, I just knew it. They wouldn't be the same, she might get the size wrong, and they had a 50/50 chance of being atrocious…but it was the thought that counted.

"Well, honey, I gotta boogie," Mom said. "Lunch is almost done and you know how your father hates to wait these days."

"Okay, Mom," I agreed before the talk could turn to Dad's recent retirement. "I'll let you know which flight I'm on."

"Love you. Be safe."

"Love you too, Mom. Bye."

Inexplicably, I felt better after the conversation was done. I hated being forced into a break but going home might clear my head, give me some much-needed direction. Besides, I knew for a fact that Sampsoknight was going to be at the wedding in his day-to-day disguise; tweaking him while off-duty was always fun.

"Guess I have to go shopping now," I grumbled, unzipping the long silver zipper at my throat.

Yes, it's currently fashionable to be one of those villains that flashes sideboob at the least provocation, but I work more efficiently in my catsuit and heels than I ever did distracting the heroes with a pair of daunting double D's.

Also, tight as it is, the catsuit still conceals my very practical sports bra quite nicely. You've never known pain until you've had to *parkour* your way across the city in anything less than the best. Pricey? You betcha, but worth every penny to keep me from blacking both my eyes fleeing from Quickstart.

Plus, it granted added bonus of looking like I've had a little work done without actually having to admit that the ladies are one hundred percent nauseatingly natural. I've contemplated getting reduced since puberty but, alas, along with the shoes, a reduction isn't exactly covered by Evil Insurance Inc.

*Maybe*, I thought, *maybe this break won't be such a bad thing.* Maybe Dr. G was right. Maybe I needed a dose of the real world, the civvies surrounding me, to really appreciate what I had with him and Evil Corps. It wasn't as if I'd just fallen into henching—I'd chosen it, it hadn't chosen me—but after the hubbub of this morning maybe…maybe I wasn't cut out for it anymore.

I eyed the heels in the trash. They were perfect; they were everything I was known for as a villain, the tap of them on tile was my terror-inducing calling card.

*At what point is a villain too old for henching?* I wondered. At what point did you have to either strike out on your own, begin your own reign of terror or forever play second banana to crazy madmen in snazzy suits?

My catsuit peeled off, smelling of baby powder and sweat, and was immediately launched into the laundry basket. Unlike my broken heels, the good doctor was more than willing to supply me with a new suit if this one were ever to do the unimaginable and rip. He viewed it as an investment in a competent second-in-command—the catsuit bore enough tech to protect me from all but the most powerful of the Captain's blows.

But did I want to be an entrepreneur? It was so much work and hassle, and hiring henchmen was so annoyingly tedious. I couldn't imagine having to build an organization from the ground up the way Dr. G had. Not to mention wrangling the permits out of the Evil Corps—obtaining the bribe money would only take a few successful bank jobs, but then you risked getting fined by the Corps for operating a heist without a permit.

Grumbling to myself, I poked through my closet. No, I decided, running an Evil Org wasn't my style. I liked kicking ass and taking names, not taking names and masterminding. But if I wasn't going to go into business for myself, then what?

I brooded over my future while I chose what to wear out and about. Civilian dressing is always fast and simple—sandals, flippy skirt, and clingy tee with a sarcastic meme—it's the accessories that hide who I really am.

Glasses? Check. Flamboyant purse with a slot for a yap-yap dog? Check. Bleached blonde wig? Check.

Concerns still nagging at the back of my mind, I was out the door and down the street in ten minutes flat. In the downtown distance I could hear the wail of air sirens, the scream of the crowd. The battle for the bridge was still raging on but at least I could take comfort in the fact that Captain Fabulouso was out of the fight too.

He broke my heels, but I broke his image.

Tit for tat really.

Despite the chaos raging not five miles south, the Paragon Mall was still doing a brisk business. I passed a bank of TVs entering through Sears—and there he was in all his Star-Spangled-Apple-Pie glory, front and center, Captain Fabulouso screaming his bloody head off at me, dangling me by my hair high above the metropolis and threatening to drop me if I so much as squeaked the wrong way.

His display was such the exact opposite of the prim and proper, uptight gladiator of justice that the media was just about creaming themselves over the controversy. The TVs blared. The pundits were out in force.

"What about when your average civilian upsets him? I know she's a villain, but does the Red Rebel really deserve that sort of treatment from someone who is supposed to uphold—"

"Red Rebel was rescued by none other than the infamous mad Dr. Gibraltar himself, flying in on—"

"I tell you, in all the decades I spent henching and then villaining, I never would have allowed my superior to sweep in and rescue—"

"Can you still be a strong woman, a strong villain, and allow a man to—"

"Could the Red Rebel or the mad Dr. Gibraltar have used a mind control dev—"

The Shoehorn? I wondered, hooking a right into the mall proper and leaving the Sears behind. No, absolutely not. I needed good quality heels if I was going to jump back in the game, reinforced this time. Though Shoehorn might do for flats for the wedding…

I sniffed the air. Oooh, Cinnacakes!

Normally I avoid sugar and refined foods. Everyone has a cameraphone and an upskirt fetish these days—even a high-ranking villain such as myself can not afford a spare pound or two—but three weeks is plenty of time to work a sweet cinnacake off. Even with extra icing.

"Send *me* home from work," I muttered, standing in line for the cake. Next door, on the bench outside the Eternal 16, a broad-shouldered man hunched over several overflowing shopping bags, an expression of mingled boredom and irritation twisting his mouth. The way he slouched gave the impression of being pot-bellied but I could tell he wasn't. His hair was dusted with grey, but it was oddly spotty and flaking across his right shoulder.

In fact, I realized, he looked like one of *mine* who'd had to rush into his civvies. I eyed him closer, inching forward in the cinnacake line. Arms like that, he wasn't a bruiser, that much was obvious, but he wasn't weak either. Unless he had abilities. That was possible.

The kid in line behind me poked me in the shoulder to get my attention. I almost punched him in retaliation but realized that I'd been brooding on the graying gentleman instead of paying attention to the line. The acne-riddled clerk was smiling helpfully at me, finger poised over the cash-register as if he were about to punch the doomsday button.

"Miss? What kind of cinnacake can I get you today?"

His voice was quiet, it couldn't have carried all the way to the bench, but the grey-haired man glanced up. Our eyes met.

Simultaneously we recognized one another.

*Shit*, he mouthed, straightening and rapidly looking up and down the wide corridor filled with shoppers. I did the same. This was not the place for another showdown.

"Damn it all to hell," I muttered, stepping out of the cinnacake line. I'd been looking forward to that cake too.

"Miss? Miss, don't you want—"

"Changed my mind!" I called over my shoulder. My hand hovered near the ridiculous purse—I kept an emergency pack in all the absurd bags my persona carried—but I didn't want to whip it out just yet. Something about the way Captain Fabulouso's shoulders slumped back down made me realize he wasn't up for Round 2 today. At least…not yet.

Rolling his eyes at my caution, Captain Fabulouso—well, his persona—waved me over and patted the bench beside him.

"Truce?" Cap asked.

"Never, hero," I replied, but sat beside him anyway. Very close inspection revealed that he was hovering a micro-space above the bench, not actually sitting on it. A wise precaution—the bench was only wrought iron, after all, not graded to hold that kind of density or weight without buckling.

"You want to pick a spot to do this?" he asked, running a hand through the flaking grey in his hair. "I don't have that much time before my…before I have an appointment."

"Family member in there?" I hazarded, peering into the Eternal 16, trying to spot someone who might conceivably be willing to be seen with this hunched and sad civilian. "Wife? No, flashy's not your style. Daughter?"

Cap hid his flinch but his pupils contracted.

"Who in the world could sleep with you?" I wondered, surprised, setting my bag between us and leaning back. "Wouldn't you snap them in half?"

"Seriously?" he demanded, aggravated. "You've stumbled onto my alter ego and you want to know how I have sex?"

"You have a kid," I pointed out. "You're an alien. Unless your daughter's an alien too, I'm thinking that physiologically it's just—"

"Wishes," Cap ground out. "I was gifted wishes from—"

"The Genies of the Material Plane?" I guessed. "Titania's Fae Hordes? Ooh, I know, those squeaky green guys from Dimension—"

"You are very annoying when I'm not punching you," he interrupted. "What are you doing here, anyway?"

"You broke my heels," I explained, suddenly annoyed now that he'd reminded me. "And got me—well, not fired exactly. Put on probation. Sort of."

"Not a promotion? I'm surprised." Cap didn't bother to hide the resignation.

"Dr. G's calling it a promotion, but since I can't go any higher without ousting *him*, it's just a pay raise," I said. "But it's a punishment actually. The Evil Corps don't give time off; a hench only takes leave because you've got a busted bone, or you've been shot into another dimension or something. You know the drill. No, the money and whatnot is a ruse. Dr. G's…aggravated with me."

I rubbed the back of my neck. There was a fantastic pair of stiletto thigh-highs in the window of the Eternal 16 that looked like they might be my size, but I didn't dare go in with his daughter milling about somewhere inside. I might set off another fight and I really wanted to try on those boots, not reconstruct the shreds of them.

"Honestly, I have no idea what I did to piss you off so badly," I admitted. Even from here I could see that the boots were black leather, the zipper hidden with a cunning fold from ankle to thigh. "It's not like I haven't taunted you a million times before."

Cap sighed. "Would you believe that you had nothing to do with it?" When I frowned he laughed. "Very little to do with it," he amended.

"Then what—" I broke off.

She was lovely—medium height, medium build, long glossy brown hair and large, green-edged doe eyes. She wasn't the sort of girl you'd normally find in an Eternal 16—her skirt swirled from hip to ankle, her blouse clung in all the right places without being tight. She was, as my mother would've put it, a classy young lady. Her friend—definitely the sort of girl you'd expect to see frequenting Eternal 16—chomped gum with an open mouth beside her. They laughed together as the friend held up a slinky, black-edged corset dress, urging his daughter to try it on; they were close enough to the entrance for the gist of their conversation to carry.

Prom was apparently coming and Miss Doe Eyes had a dashing, dangerous new beau.

"You even think about it—" Cap growled beside me.

I waved a hand, brushing him off. "Who's she dating?"

He stiffened. "How—"

Not it was my turn to roll my eyes. "I was a teenage girl once, Cap."

"Shhh!" He glanced around to make sure no one had heard me.

"Gang banger?" I guessed. "Goth? A handsy-sorta jock?"

Cap's face remained impassive.

"Sidekick?" There was that twitch that wasn't a twitch again. "Henchman?" BINGO.

The pulse of fury was tangible. I snatched my purse out of the way and scrambled to the far side of the seat as fast as I could. For one brief instant the entire mall froze, caught in a gravity dilation that shorted out time, and then it was back, the sound surging over us in a wave like breaking glass.

"Anyone I'd know?" I asked, hand deep in my purse in case another dilation came.

"He's new to henching," Cap replied. "I can't let her know that I know, either. That'd make him—"

"More enticing," I finished. I sighed. "Well...I'm sorry?"

"No need to be," he said. "It's my problem to deal with. I should be apologizing to you." He rubbed his hands across his face. "The doctor doesn't like broken protocol."

"'It's just a job, it's never personal,'" I quoted, mimicking Dr. G's droll tones. "I made it personal."

"No, you were just poking me. *I* made it personal," Cap said. "Now we're both in trouble." He examined his cuticles listlessly. "I might lose my license for losing it at you like that. Threatening." He sighed. "I wouldn't have dropped you."

Like I didn't know that already. My hair ached where he'd grabbed me but even dangling above the city I knew he didn't have it in him to let go.

"Pshaw. I don't know about you, but thanks to this 'break' now I've got family functions to attend," I teased, trying to lighten his mood. "But you think you're in trouble. Whatever."

"Breaking the kid's legs before he gets to the door would be in poor taste, I suppose?" Cap asked.

I nodded. "We like playing Florence Nightingale."

"Damn."

We sat in silence for several seconds before he asked helplessly. "What do I do?"

I edged close enough to pat him on the shoulder; he probably felt me plant the tracking device but, hey, even off the job a girl's never *off* the job. "You wait. You be polite. If they date for a couple of months you invite him to dinner to meet the missus."

That flinch again. Interesting.

"And if they get married some day, you pay for the wedding and hope like hell your grandkids are normies. Because a toddler who can fiddle with gravity is not really in the *What to Expect* books."

My cell beeped. Dr. G's beep. It was my turn to flinch. Cap grinned, glancing sidelong at me. "Take it."

"It's cheating if you can hear us across the mall," I retorted primly.

He reached back and plucked the tracking device free. "So's this. Take the call."

Rolling my eyes, I stood up and walked inside the Eternal 16. I pointedly ignored the girls and moved to examine the boots. They were long and lean and perfect; flipping open the cell with one hand I measured the length with the other. The buttery black leather would stretch from foot to my mid-thigh; the circumference was just wide enough to circle my leg.

It was as if they'd been made for me.

"Great job, Red!" Dr. G crowed on the cell, his grin filling the screen. He stepped back from the camera exposing the ring sling slung over one shoulder and across his chest. Dr. G jiggled the sling lightly, dancing from side to side to soothe the occupant. Ben's towhead peeked just over the edge of the fabric; the infant was sagging, deeply asleep in his father's arms.

"We have a guest," I said quickly, trying to cut Dr. G off at the pass. The very last thing we needed was the Captain to eavesdrop his way to the lair.

"And an appointment for a duel," Dr. G said, swaying from side to side as Ben, rousing, began to fuss. "Feeling up to destroying the parking lot?"

"I'm sorry, what?"

Behind me, the captain's cell was dinging loudly. I recognized the Hero Inc. tone from here.

"Kick some ass, dear," Dr. G said, giving me an exaggerated thumbs up.

"I don't have any—"

"Pick up the boots," he sighed. "They're reinforced. You're welcome. And make sure to keep him occupied for at least twenty minutes."

Behind me the Captain was too busy cursing into his cell to eavesdrop on my conversation.

"Keep him occupi—" I broke off and buried my face in one hand, amazed at how I'd been duped. I'd spent the entire afternoon doubting myself, doubting my place in the grand scheme of things and here Dr. G was, telling me without saying it outright that he'd had everything planned all along. "This entire thing was a setup."

"At least twenty minutes," Dr. G reiterated. "There's a spare catsuit in the boot box. And Red?"

"Yeah?"

"You still have to go to the wedding. Your mother will be broken-hearted if you don't." He hung up.

Annoyed, I snatched up the boots and the box; behind me I heard the shriek as the Slinky Slyme brothers blobbed their way across the tile and swallowed Doe Eyes and her friend whole. The Captain was gone but he'd be back within seconds, blazing Red-White-Blue and crushing everything in sight.

The new catsuit slipped on with nary a snag, the boots slid on like silk. I could feel the gravity pulse from halfway across the mall.

Grinning, I clenched my fists and waited.

It was good to be me.

---

K.D. McENTIRE, author of young adult titles *Lightbringer* and *Reaper* from Pyr Books, can be found on the web at http://www.kdmcentire.com.

# THE SUNSHINE BARON

## *Peadar Ó Guilín*

AH, BORQUIL, LUCKY BORQUIL. Many the balconies of his gilded mansion: north over the spice market; east where he sipped tea at dawn; west for opium. And south? Great Borquil *never* looked south.

The sun shone on the Northern capital as it did every day. Borquil had ensured it. Had grown rich: the famous Sunshine Baron! By night, a gentle rain would patter over the fields and fill a few cisterns before sliding gently seawards on the Farg River, sweet-natured these days, 'though its name meant "angry" in the old tongue.

"I calmed it all down," muttered Borquil. "Me. They should be more grateful."

The Northerners *had* shown gratitude at first. The king loved him. Whole provinces voted him thanks and over the years, as Borquil grew plump and the nightmares disturbed him less and less, aristocrats welcomed him into their homes. "A foreigner no longer!" they said amongst themselves. "He is truly one of our own!" Sure, they found it odd how he refused to travel more than a day south of the Farg river, but they too were rich enough to have ghosts they'd rather avoid. As the saying went: "no man sits in his own poop."

But now, how inconvenient for poor Borquil! Revolution had come to the Kingdom of the North. His aristocratic friends were losing their heads in the streets outside. And the mobs had come for his blood too. The double doors leading to his courtyard splintered and buckled under a battering ram. He had perhaps an hour to live.

"Where are my servants?" cried the baron.

Only Irashtal remained to him. "Fled, lord," said the slave. "The Revolution, you see? The Talentless?" The woman's black Southern hair had long since faded into grey, but there was no disguising the hue of her skin—tinged with gold, as Borquil's had once been before he had bought his way to a more civilised pale colour. He had purchased too, the shiny blond curls that would allow him to take a fuller part in Northern life.

"Wretches!" he shouted at his missing staff. "Talentless dogs!" Then he turned on his slave. "You would have abandoned me too, wouldn't you? If the magic of your bondage allowed it?"

The old woman was sweating.

"Didn't I treat you well, Irashtal? I brought you with me before war broke out in the Southlands. You would have rotted there. Instead, you eat what I eat."

"I am your poison taster, lord."

True. And she'd been much more than that once upon a time.

He tried to ignore the splintering of his gates and the growing fear in his guts. "You were a pretty thing, were you not? The richest men in the North delighted to the sound of your voice, but I wouldn't let them take it from you or share their beds. It is fitting we should fall now together."

But the slave shocked him by grabbing his arm. "Free me, lord," she said. Her voice was still strong, still beautiful. She sang him to sleep with it most nights. She alone knew how to keep the bad dreams at bay.

Out in the courtyard a loud crack and cheering told him the Talentless were on the verge of breaking through. Irashtal's grip grew fierce enough to bruise his pale skin—he hadn't known she possessed such strength. "While there's time, Borgy. Remember what we meant to each other, back when you were the king. I beg you."

Yes, he had been king, if only for a few weeks, but unbelievably lucky all the same. A very distant cousin of the Southern Royals, a very *poor* cousin, he was the only one left standing when rebellion came calling back home. Irashtal had been even younger than he was back then. They had fled north together before she could be married off to one of the other family servants.

But Borquil's silver soon ran out. He'd already begun rehearsing arguments to get Irashtal to sell her talents or her body when a royalist messenger had found him at the dirty rooms he'd been renting in the Northern capital.

"I am the king!" he told his only friend that day. He swung her around the room, both of them young and full of laughter.

"But surely," she had said, "they will declare a republic now?"

"Tomorrow," he replied. "The messenger got here just in time. For one or two more days, I am the legal ruler of the Southlands." It was all he needed to make his fortune.

A particularly loud *crack* drifted up from the mansion's courtyard. A great cheer sounded and the filthy poor, the Talentless, poured into Borquil's home.

"Let go of me, slave!" He couldn't meet her eyes. South was not the only place he feared to look. "*By your vow*, I command it." Irashtal didn't want to release him, but the invocation of her oath gave her no choice. Her fingers sprang back of their own accord and she cried out with the pain of it.

Down in the courtyard, blond Northerners overturned the hay-cart. Horses whinnied in panic as strangers pushed into the stables to paw at them. And glass, expensive and beautiful, shattered under grubby fists.

Borquil's heart thundered in his chest. The Revolution had spread from poorer cities far from the capital. Angry Talentless, raging, full of envy for their betters, had imprisoned the king and filled the streets with blood for dogs to lap at. Watching them twisted Borquil with just enough anger to overcome his fear. He strode to the balcony.

"Stop this at once!" he called. And everybody froze. As well they might. The voice he used commanded respect, its tones deep and confident. He had bought this Talent from an army sergeant down on his luck, a man used to the chaos of battlefields far larger and more chaotic than this courtyard.

"You will leave my property."

A few rioters, sheepishly dropped wooden clubs and began backing towards the door, but a hooded woman strode into their midst, and in a voice, just as powerful as his, called out, "Enough of this farce!"

She looked up and Borquil felt a clammy hand close over his heart.

"I don't allow Southerners into my house..." Apart from Irashtal, of course. He would have rid himself of her too if he didn't need her so much.

The woman below pulled back her hood to reveal sleek black hair. It glistened so sweetly in the perfect sunlight of the Northern capital that a foreigner might almost think that this was the source of the insult "wethead" used to describe Southern refugees. Clever Borquil knew better, of course. He also knew that the best thing he could do right now was to fling himself head-first onto the cobbles before that woman or the four skeletal, gold-skinned men who had stalked in to flank her got their hands on him.

But he didn't have the courage. "Irashtal. Here is my last order for you. Run now and fetch the poison behind the tapestry of King Frindop."

"But—"

He could have invoked her oath again, but he had always preferred charm. "Run! And I swear I will free you before the end comes. I swear it."

She obeyed even as the Southerners and their Talentless friends smashed their way into the lower floors of his mansion.

Poor Borquil didn't want to die. He loved his life by the Farg river. Like the rest of the local aristocracy, he bought youth from starving—but healthy—young men whenever a wrinkle began to appear. A few coppers was all it cost him every time, and he'd raise a glass with his immortal friends to toast the foolishness of somebody who would sacrifice years of his life just to feed his children for another month. He had bought the ability to ride horses and skill with a hunting bow; he had once purchased three years of hard-won medical study from a student, ironically too ill to afford healing. Borquil had made himself one of the most Talented men in the land. But now he must end it. And quickly!

"Irashtal?" he boomed in the sergeant's voice. "What's keeping you? I hear them coming up the stairs already." Did she want to be free or didn't she, the silly old woman? Just when he thought she had been caught by the rebels and that he'd have to find the courage to jump over the balcony, after all, she slid into the room and locked the great mahogany door behind her.

She held the dark green bottle back from him for just a moment. "Remember, lord, you'll only have a few seconds to free me..." She would serve him forever in the AfterWorld if he did not. No wonder she shook with fear!

"I won't forget, Rashy. Hand it over."

The cork popped out more easily than Borquil expected, but he forced the drink down. The poison was the first thing he had bought after he had signed that fateful deal with the Northern king and made his fortune. Even then, he knew his old compatriots would come for him one day. He hadn't relaxed until the king had built the Great Wall to keep the wethead refugees out of the North. Even then, a few always made it through, and in the end, he had protected himself from assassins by banning Southerners from his presence entirely.

He had also bought a huge array of fighting skills, but like many of the idle rich, he left warfare to others and had allowed these Talents to wither. So now, as battering began at the door to his rooms, as harsh voices threatened him in a language he barely remembered, poor Borquil was reduced to suicide.

"Don't cry, lord," said Irashtal. "It will be over soon."

She stroked him, as she had so many times over their years together, when the nightmares rotted his sleep. He wanted to ask her to sing for him one more time, for his final rest, but the door was already starting to give way.

He took two more swallows of the poison.

"It's very like brandy," he said, trying to be brave. Already, his mind was swimming with images from his past.

"The words, lord," Irashtal urged him. "Free me!"

He put his arm around her withered shoulders. "I'm not sure, Rashy..."

"The words!"

"I need you. In the AfterWorld, you see? I have no family..."

"You lied to me!"

The door finally gave way. Three black haired men charged into the room. One of them ran straight for the window to block off the balcony. They must have feared he would still kill himself.

"You're too late," he said to them.

Irashtal spat in his face. He jerked back from her in shock. Then, she wrenched the bottle from his grasp.

"A drink, gentlemen?" she asked. "Oh, don't worry," she said in the Southern tongue, her words rusty. "It's just brandy." And to poor Borquil, "You're not the only one who can lie, *master*."

The black-haired young woman joined them in the bedroom. She too spoke Southern. Borquil got the gist of it. "Well, well, my king," she bowed, winking at her accomplices. "Time we brought you home to your people."

"I'm not the king! I gave that up."

The woman answered him in Northern, her cold face twisting with the foreign words, "That's not all you gived up."

The filthy wetheads grabbed poor Borquil. Bony fingers circled him with rope. Then they bundled him through the splintered door.

"What about me?" asked Irashtal.

The leader of the kidnappers turned. "A dirty slave," she said. "Disgusting."

"But I helped you. He asked for poison and—"

"Who cares what you do? One like you?"

"I will come with you, then."

Down the stairs they brought the trembling Borquil, Baron of Koreem, and past the merry looters until one burly Southerner took notice and cried, "Look! Them wetheads is tryin' to rescue him!"

The woman kidnapper slid forward and punched a dagger into the man's throat, but already his warning had spread and it followed the fleeing band out of the house and onto the roiling streets. Borquil saw heads on pikes: surprised faces of men and women he knew well, handsome and beautiful and young, all curled about with veils of smoke from their burning palaces.

People ran past with stolen silks, or struggled under gilded furniture, or fought each other for candlesticks. A knot of men stamped and kicked at something on the ground while crimson rivulets spread onto the cobbles at their feet.

Borquil couldn't hear himself think under the great human roar of the crowd. A few people tried to impede the wetheads moving through their midst, but every time, the woman would kill them. Young or old, it didn't matter to her. Borquil watched her stab a child and knew then, in his heart, that he would get no mercy from the likes of her.

However, as they left the crowds behind and rounded the corner of Golden Street into Hallowed Temple, they came face to face with a barricade manned by pikemen. Their mismatched armour and the blue rag tied over their biceps stole any hope Borquil might have had of rescue. Their captain even had his dumpy wife and a pair of brats with him. She had brought him his lunch and he waved now at the approaching group with a heel of bread.

"Wetheads?" said the captain. "You're next when we finish off the Talented. Run back to the Wall while there's yet time."

*The Wall.* Even the sound of the words sent shivers through Borquil's body. These days, he never travelled within a week's journey of his ancient homeland. He always made sure he had a "headache" when the Northern king invited him hunting near the border.

"It's an amazing sight, baron!" the monarch had told him once.

"I don't like to look South..."

"But you should see what you have accomplished, sir! You need to see it to understand."

Borquil saw it all right, on bad nights when the dreams came. He couldn't go back there now, he *couldn't*! He elbowed one of his captors in the belly and struggled free. "They're kidnapping me! I'm one of you! The wetheads—"

Immediately, the Southerners surrounded him again and forced him to his knees. But the captain had dropped his bread and had taken a pike from the wall where he had left it leaning. His men muttered angrily, lowering their own weapons.

"Kill them, Erkil!" said the captain's wife. "Thems is like rats the way they stream over the border to take what's ours! Filthy slug-eating wetheads!"

The Southerner men drew swords from sheaths hidden on their backs and held them steady enough that the blond captain began to have second thoughts. "Just let the prisoner go, wetties, all right? No need for blood, but we can't just have you walk off with one of ours."

The murderous Southern woman stepped forward, her face beautiful as it was severe. She gestured to Borquil. "He is Talented. Look at his clothing. Look at the silk."

"He should be killed then, like the others. The scum deserve it."

"We have better idea, us," she replied. "Take him over the Wall to be our slave."

All of the soldiers grinned. "Do they really hate me that much?" Borquil wondered. "Is it my fault they are Talentless?"

He spoke aloud. "It's true I am a noble." Nobody stopped him climbing to his feet again. "But I am different from other members of my class in one vital aspect."

"Oh?" said the captain. "And what *aspect* would that be, mighty lord?"

"I am Borquil, who changed the weather. I am the Sunshine Baron." Their eyes widened and the Southern woman started to look worried. Any moment now and she would shut him up. He spoke quickly. "I am the one who made the crops grow so well." He pointed at the stunning palaces surrounding Hallowed Market. "I made this land rich. I made all of you rich!"

A pause followed his words and then the captain laughed aloud.

"No, High One. You made the nobles rich as angels, and us poor as devils. You made them rich enough to buy what few Talents we had left. I myself was a fine hunter 'til Lord Cossmal made me give it up to pay a fine. Them wetties is welcome to you."

He signalled the men to part the barrier and the kidnappers pulled him through it.

Outside the city, the wetheads had stolen a covered wagon. They fearful Borquil inside and allowed Irashtal to join him there. He wa plan an escape for himself, or a pain-free suicide. But his slave would him be, apologising for her betrayal and begging, begging that he say the words and free her before it was too late.

"You would die without me," he said to shut her up.

"I could earn my keep in a tavern, lord. With my singing."

"Sing now then, you crone, and I'll think about it." He felt more afraid than he had since he was a boy fleeing his father's wrath. There'd been no Wall then. The border at that time had consisted of hills too poor to fight over. There'd been no refugees either. Only merchants and artists and travelling nobles.

Outside the wagon, the Southerners muttered among themselves. Rain began to patter against the fabric roof and he realised by the sound of it that midnight had come. Who could know it better than he? Borquil the lucky? Borquil the clever who had ensured that the only rain in the North came at night, only ever heavy enough to please the crops. He hated that sound more than any other, because nothing was more likely to bring on the nightmares.

But then Irashtal sang. Her voice had the breathy quality of a flute, designed by angels for lullabies, for the easing of hurts. Her singing rolled back years to when he'd been a child in bed with fever and the cool hand on his brow had been his mother's. The words were the same as mother's too, the only parts of the Southern Tongue he still understood well: "Sweet child," Irashtal purred, "my heart's nectar..." Each pure note, high as heaven, or earthy and low, slowed Borquil's heart. The rain itself paused to listen, it seemed. Even the rough Southerners outside...

Then, the fastenings of the wagon were ripped open to reveal the female leader of his kidnappers. She had tears on her sharp cheek bones.

"How?" she asked.

The prisoners stared at the newcomer, confused.

"A dirty slave... How?"

Irashtal sat tall. "I am not dirty. I gave myself to him. When we were both young. As a present."

The kidnapper's upper lip curled.

"We were in love," said Irashtal. There'd been more to it than that and Borquil was grateful the slave held back from the full story. Some of those memories were thorns to his heart. He wished the women would shut up.

"They why not *he* give himself to you? If proper love? Why?"

Borquil had forgotten how much his people despised slaves. Selling Talents was something only the desperate did, because you always lost more than you expected on the deal. Selling the ability to fight, might leave a soldier's arms completely paralysed. Selling a few years of youth, had been known to stop the seller's heart sometimes. But only a fool would hand over her eternal soul without a similar commitment from her lover.

Happy Borquil had agreed to a full exchange of vows back in those heady days of youth, sixty years past now. It was this promise that persuaded Irashtal to run away North with him, with less than a purse of silver to their names.

"You are a fool," the kidnapper told the old woman. "You will sing again." She sat next to Borquil and closed her eyes.

Every day the wagon travelled farther south, and every evening the black-haired woman returned, to listen to the singing and to weep. Was she thinking of the child she had killed in the streets of the capital? Borquil felt sure her nights were haunted by even worse crimes than that. At the end of each session, she would stumble out of the back of the wagon in a daze.

At dawn, three days travel from the border, they dragged the trembling Borquil into the light.

The sun was rising on yet another perfect day in the North. All around lay the gigantic estates of the Talented. Field upon field of hemp or wheat and not a servant to be seen, although a column of smoke rose to the east where a village or a castle might be burning.

"You look the wrong way, traitor king," said the Southern woman.

"I'm not your king."

"You must look."

They had to force him to turn around, to face south. The woman herself pried open his eyelids, her rough nails biting his skin. His vision began to blur almost immediately, but it was too late. The Wall, built fifty years before to keep out the wetheads, was little more than a dark line on the Southern horizon, but above it...above...

Borquil fell to his knees, careless of pebbles on the roadbed. He choked and cried out. "I'm not a bad man! I'm not!" His words died away.

The real Wall, not the one made by the Northerners, the real one, was built of ferocious black clouds. It extended far into the sky, boiling and spinning; fizzing with lightning. It shifted colour constantly: a rainbow of blacks and greys and sudden white cracks.

The woman knelt to whisper in his ear, quietly, gently. "We are still three days away. Imagine what is like, you, to live under it. *Inside* it."

He tried to jerk away, weeping, but none of them would let him. "We were millions when you left, *your majesty*. Now we are thousands. One day, none. You sold our weather."

"I was king. It was my right! And the rebels would have hunted me down anyway. Cut my head off!"

"Nobody will cut your head, your majesty. We just want you to live with us. Forever, if possible. Volunteers will give years of their youth just to keep you in our midst. I will be first among them."

"Please," said poor Borquil. It really wasn't his fault. He'd been young. He had wanted to get back at the rebels who had killed his family. And wealth, of course, he had wanted that too. *Anybody* would have done the same.

"I can pay," he said. "I have Talents. I can make you a great speaker. A faster runner. You...you could be blond. I'd give that up. You could live here and nobody would know you for a wethead."

"You have nothing I want, your majesty."

But at that moment, Borquil heard another sob behind him. Irashtal had seen the Wall too. Borquil realised then, that he possessed one thing the kidnapper wanted and for the first time in days hope took root in his heart.

That night, the Southerners made no camp, preferring to keep moving towards their drowning homeland. Their chief climbed in anyway, through the back, and eased herself next to the baron.

Irashtal opened her lips, but Borquil stopped her. "*By your vow*, I command you not to sing." She closed her mouth with a snap.

"She must," said the kidnapper.

"She cannot," Borquil replied.

The woman shrugged as if it were of no import.

Borquil leaned forward against the ropes that held him. "It is in my power to give her to you. As a gift." Irashtal tried to protest, but once again, her master silenced her with the words of command.

The kidnapper snarled. "Is this how you think to buy me? How like a Talented. I would not own a *slave*. It is filthy."

Borquil licked his lips. "You don't have to take her soul. Her Talents are also mine to dispose of."

Irashtal gasped.

"What do you mean?" asked the woman.

"Her voice. Her ability. I can command her to give it up. To give it to you. She would have no choice."

Both women stared at him. The wethead's features seemed to ripple as tendencies fought for control of her heart. "No," she said finally, hoarsely. "No," she stood too quickly, falling backwards, as though he had offered her a scorpion. "You must be punished for what you did. You must live as we do. I won't. I can't accept." She moved to escape.

Clever Borquil was too quick for her. "Sing, Irashtal," he ordered. "*By your oath*, I command you to sing!" And, weeping, the slave opened her miraculous throat.

Some hours later, Borquil and Irashtal crouched in a ditch no more than a day's walk from the Wall. He could feel that dread structure. It lay at his back, of course, for he would not look upon it ever again, if possible.

"You should not have betrayed me, slave. Had you brought the poison as I'd asked, you would not be in this position now." Her shoulders shook. She was weeping, he supposed, but no sound emerged. Her voice belonged to another now. He tried not to think about that too deeply.

"At least, that woman kept her side of the bargain, eh? Getting us out of there." Not that the Southerner had had a choice. Magical bargains made dishonesty impossible. "We'll head north until we find some loyalists to protect us from the Revolution. We could make our way to a port, maybe..."

Irashtal turned around. He flinched, expecting hatred, but her eyes were pleading. She climbed up onto her knees in front of him and clasped both hands as if in prayer.

"Oh, there's no need for that, Rashy! You know I can't free you. But help me get somewhere safe, and I promise I *will* consider it."

Her teary eyes narrowed. Then she eased her ugly old body onto the ground for sleep.

"I should get some rest too," he muttered. A long, long journey lay ahead of them.

When Borquil woke again, he was alone. He cursed himself for a fool. He should have used the words of command to make Irashtal stay by his side. If she moved out of earshot, he couldn't give her orders any more. The only thing that might bring her back was the chance that he would utter the words of unbinding. But her absence told him she had finally given up hope of that forever. He cursed himself again until he remembered that she couldn't even sing for him anymore. Foolish Borquil! "She would have slowed you down," he muttered.

Then he heard a noise from behind. "Irashtal?"

He didn't want to turn around, to face South. He had to force himself, although he kept his gaze too low to see the clouds above the Wall.

His slave had returned after all, but she had not come alone. The four Southern men stood beside her. They held a spear with another woman's head on top of it, her traitor's blood dripping down the shaft.

Unlucky Borquil hadn't the strength to resist. He didn't even beg. Unlike the woman they had killed, none of these men spoke Northern and he had forgotten Southern Speech almost entirely. Nor, with the revolution going on, were there any nearby friendly garrisons to come to his aid.

They dragged him along to the base of the wall and into a brush-covered tunnel beneath it.

The temperature dropped half-way along. A part of him found this strange. It had been so warm down South when he'd been a boy. The family used to sleep during the hottest parts of the day while servants wafted them with fans. There had been fruit trees and exotic birds. There were wild cats large enough to hunt antelope and all of it was beautiful, the colours rich and wild. That's what he saw in his dreams on the nights Irashtal sang for him. That's where he went.

Up ahead, an angry grey daylight appeared. He didn't want to advance, but his legs carried him forward. He felt light, as though relieved of some burden. He hadn't cried since he was a boy, yet tears now rolled down his face. He shrugged off his captors and walked forward by himself like a man so fascinated by the cliff that he allows himself to tip forward.

Somebody shivered beside him in the tunnel: his slave. In this weak light he could still imagine her as she once was: a lithe, golden skinned beauty, her eyes flashing with humour; saucy sometimes, when mother was out of the room. Gentle. Kind. She had begged him not to sell out their homeland. She had wept and wept.

"But I'll have nothing if I don't do this!" he'd said.

"No, my love. You'll have me, you'll always have me." And to prove it, she had sworn her soul to him then and there. Sworn it to him in order to save their people. Lovely Irashtal. Sweet girl. And he had tasted the words on his own lips, his own promise bubbling to the surface and almost, almost set free to float happily on the air. Oh, Irashtal!

The men allowed him to pause ten paces from the entrance. He touched the slave under her chin. "You are free, lady. I am sorry."

She spat in his face.

He looked at the warriors behind him. "I am sorry, sirs." They spun him roughly around. Poor Borquil, unhappy Borquil! They faced him South. And then they brought him home.

---

In 2007, PEADAR Ó GUILÍN published his first novel, *The Inferior*, which the Times Educational Supplement called "a stark, dark tale, written with great energy and confidence." Foreign editors liked it too, and translation rights were sold to a dozen countries. A direct sequel called *The Deserter*, was published in March 2012. Peadar is also the author of numerous short stories that have appeared in anthologies such as *When the Hero Comes Home*, as well as in magazines and podcasts. Peadar's website is www.frozenstories.com.

# DADDY'S LITTLE GIRL

## Jim C. Hines

AT FIRST, I DIDN'T recognize the land around me. Blackened ash and burnt stumps covered the earth as far as I could see. Saplings and weeds proved at least a year or two had passed since the devastation, but it was a far cry from the thick wilderness I remembered.

"I think he's waking up."

I started to turn around, then froze when I spotted the ruins. Crumbled bricks lay scattered to one side of a broken, six-sided foundation. In the remains of the doorway, I could see huge iron hinges bolted to the floor. The trick entrance was only one of the traps I had designed for Tarzog the Black, while he tormented me with false promises to free my wife and son. I had barely eaten or slept for almost seven years as I worked to perfect his temple to Rhynoth, the Serpent God. This was my masterpiece, broken and scattered.

I rubbed grit from my eyes, then stared at my hands. The skin was pale, pulled tight around the bones like dried leather. My nails were cracked and yellow. When I poked my palm with one finger, the indentation remained for almost a minute.

I was bare-chested, dressed in rough-spun trousers and my old sandals, though the straps had been replaced with thin ropes. I pressed a sickly yellow hand against my chest. My heart was still as stone.

I had always wondered why Tarzog's dead slaves took their resurrections so calmly. Now I understood. Whether it was a side effect of the magic or my mind's way of rebelling against what had been done to me, I felt nothing but a strange sense of detachment. Looking at my dead body, I felt like a puppeteer staring down at a particularly gruesome marionette.

"I *told* you I could do it."

The speaker was a young girl, no more than seven or eight years old. She wore a dirty blue gown and a purple half-cape with a bronze clasp in the shape of a snake. Behind her stood a slender, dark-haired woman, the sight of whom made my dead balls want to squirm up inside me and hide until she went away.

"Zariel," I said. Tarzog's necromancer looked far more ragged than I remembered. Gone were the night-black cloak of velvet, the silver claw rings decorating her left hand, and the low-cut leather vest. Her skin was rougher, her hair grayer, and she wore a simple traveling cloak, lined with dirty rabbit fur. To tell the truth, she smelled rather ripe, and that was coming from a corpse.

"What happened?" I asked. My memories were blurred, full of gaps. Another side effect of being dead.

To my surprise, it was the little girl who answered. "This wasn't the real temple. Daddy built the real temple about a half day's walk from here, in the jungle."

I stared, trying to understand. "Why would he—?"

"Prince Armand knew about Daddy's plans to summon Rhynoth. So Daddy built this place as a trap. When Armand and his men finally got to the heart of the temple, Daddy was going to collapse the whole thing on their heads. But Armand and his men showed up early. They burned Daddy in his own temple, along with anyone they found wearing his crest." She touched the bronze snake at her throat.

Was that how I had died? No, I would have remembered fire. Death had been quick, but quiet. I clutched my stomach, recalling the pain of my insides twisting into knots. I had a vague memory of stale raisin pudding, even worse than our usual fare. I remembered dropping my spoon... "He poisoned me!"

"Of course he did. Daddy poisoned everyone who worked on his temple. That way only he knew all the secrets."

If he had killed me... Tarzog was too smart to let my wife or son go after that. He wouldn't risk them coming back to avenge me. I closed my eyes and fought despair. Gradually, the rest of the girl's words penetrated my grief.

*Daddy.* I stared. "You're Tarzog's daughter. Genevieve."

"Jenny." She smiled and nodded so hard her blonde hair fell into her face. I remembered her smaller and pudgier, a wobbly child with a miniature whip she used on trapped animals, imitating Tarzog's overseers. According to rumor, her mother was a slave girl who had abandoned the newborn baby and tried to flee. She had been caught, executed, resurrected, and gone right back to working on the temple.

"We should go," said Zariel. "This place isn't safe."

Jenny stuck out her tongue. Had anyone else done it, Zariel would have had their eyes for a necklace and their tongue for a snack. But Zariel simply turned and began walking.

"Where are we going?" I asked.

"To the other temple," Jenny said, rolling her eyes at my stupidity. "I'm going to summon Rhynoth, and then we're going to destroy Armand and his people. They all helped kill my Daddy, so they can all rot in Rhynoth's belly."

I stood, barely hearing her words. I kept seeing my family, dead and forgotten beneath the rubble. No doubt by Tarzog's own hand. He was never one to delegate that sort of chore. Without thinking, I lunged forward and wrapped my withered gray fingers around Jenny's fragile throat.

The next thing I knew, I was flat on the ground, a good fifteen feet from Jenny and Zariel. Jenny folded her arms.

"I should kill you for that, but I worked hard to resurrect you. Zariel's been teaching me." She flashed a gap-toothed smile. "Do it again, and I'll make you rip out your own innards with your bare hands."

I wiped ash and dirt from my palms. Jenny's magic had shattered several ribs, and the bones ground against one another as I stood. Fortunately, death seemed to have minimized my ability to feel pain.

One thing was clear: Jenny was definitely Tarzog's daughter.

We had walked more than an hour before I worked up the nerve to speak to Zariel. This was a woman who had eviscerated children and sacrificed whole families to maintain her power. But I had to understand what was happening if I was to have any chance of stopping them.

"Why did she resurrect me?" I asked.

"You designed the first temple," Zariel said. "Tarzog followed the same plans for the real one, including all of your traps. If you get us in, Jenny and I can conserve our power for more important things."

Jenny's power. I touched my ribs. "I didn't realize she had that kind of magic."

"I'm still a beginner at death magic, but I got all of Daddy's serpent powers when he died," Jenny said, running back to join us. "I've got the birthmark and everything. A snakehead, just like Daddy's, with fangs and everything. I'd show you, but it's not in a place you're supposed to show to boys. Not even dead boys. The prophesies of Anhak Ghudir say only one with the mark of Rhynoth can awaken him from his endless sleep." She tugged Zariel's robe. "Did you remember the blood?"

Zariel sighed and drew a small, glass tube from an inside pocket.

Jenny turned to me and made a face. "I have to drink the heart blood of a virgin to control Rhynoth. Fresh blood is okay, but after a while it gets clotty and clumpy."

I nodded, remembering how Tarzog had scoured the countryside for virgins in preparation. At first he planned to drain the blood of a few babies, but further reading ruined that plan. The spell required an adult virgin, and those were harder to find than you might expect. Especially once word got out that Tarzog needed virgins. I imagine the midwives were plenty busy the next year. "So which one of you found a girl to—"

"No girls, silly," Jenny said, chewing a hangnail on her thumb. "They always have lovesick boys who try to rescue them. I had Zariel kill a priest.

They're celebrate—"

"Celibate," Zariel said, her voice pained.

"Yeah, celibate. All we had to do was find one who had taken his vows before he got old enough to mess around."

Zariel slapped Jenny's head, hard enough to make her stumble. "How many times have I told you to stop biting your nails?"

I glanced around. We had left the scorched remains of Tarzog's land behind, entering the rocky wilds that surrounded Frelan Gorge. Tall pine trees cooled the air, while tangled roots fought to cling to the uneven stone. The insects were thick here, and they seemed especially attracted to my dead flesh, though none were daring enough to bite me. Instead, they orbited my body, buzzing in my ears and darting past my eyes. I began to wonder if Jenny had raised me simply to draw the bugs away from her.

"How did the prince destroy Tarzog?" I asked.

Zariel scowled. "Tarzog was a fool. As Armand's men fought their way into the temple, Tarzog ordered me to take Jenny and flee. Together, we might have destroyed them all. Instead, he stripped himself of my power and wasted precious time on his whelp."

I glanced at Jenny, half afraid to see how she would react, but she only shrugged. "Zariel's right. Daddy was stupid, so he failed. I won't." She skipped ahead, then turned around. "Do you think Rhynoth will like me?"

I didn't know how to answer, so I looked to Zariel.

"The prophesies say the god's gratitude will be like a ne'erending fountain upon the one who calls him from the earth."

"I hope he'll let me ride him," Jenny said. "I've never had a pet before. Daddy had a cat, but he burnt up when Armand attacked. He was a nice cat. Daddy carried him everywhere."

I remembered the beast, a black, long-haired ball of fur and claws. He used to sneak into the dungeons and piss in the straw.

"I tried to raise him," Jenny went on, "but he bit me. So I crushed his skull and scattered his remains."

Movement to the side saved me from thinking up a response to that. Two men in the green and silver livery of Prince Armand leapt from the cover of the trees. Both had longbows drawn. One kept his arrow pointed toward Zariel, while the other aimed at me. Not that a regular arrow would do much against my dead flesh, but perhaps Armand was smart enough to outfit his men with blessed weaponry. He had fought Tarzog's dead warriors before, after all.

"Speak one word, and it shall be your last," warned the man watching Zariel.

"No!" Before anyone else could move, Jenny ran in front of Zariel and threw her arms around the old sorceress. "Please don't hurt her."

"Get away from her, kid," said the second soldier. "That's Zariel. The black-hearted bitch murdered more innocent—"

"Bitch is a bad word," Jenny said, her dark eyes wide. She held up her arms, and Zariel picked her up, smiling.

Both soldiers now aimed their bows at Zariel. "Put her down, bi— Witch."

I opened my mouth to warn them. To beg them to fire. A single shot would pierce both Jenny and Zariel. Jenny's magic might be able to destroy me, but she couldn't stop an arrow in flight.

"Stay back, zombie!" The nearest man fired, sending an arrow through my throat. Pain shot through my spine, and I flopped onto my back. Armand was indeed smart enough to prepare his men. I wondered how long it would take the power in that arrow to penetrate my dead bones, dissolving Jenny's spell. Strange, to feel both terror and longing for true death.

Then both soldiers began to scream. I managed to turn my head enough to see that their bows were gone, transformed into writhing, hissing serpents. Already one had sunk its fangs into the man's forearm. As I watched, the other soldier flung the snake away and turned to flee. The snake was faster, darting forward to bite him just above the boot. He hobbled away, and the snakes slithered back toward Jenny.

"Follow him," Jenny shouted, squirming out of Zariel's grasp. The necromancer disappeared after the soldier.

Jenny walked over and wrapped her small hands around the arrow in my throat. Flesh and muscle tore as she yanked it free. She brushed her fingers over my wounds, and I could feel the skin begin to seal. By the time I sat up, the holes were closed. My ribs felt whole again, too.

"Pretty good, huh?" she asked. "I like snake magic better, though." She reached down, and one of the snakes coiled around her arm. The scales were purple, with a stripe of bright pink down the underbelly. "They're not real, though," Jenny said sadly. She wrapped her little fingers around the snake's neck and squeezed. The snake crumbled away, like chunks of burnt wood.

A panicked shriek told me Zariel had caught up with her own prey. Jenny's face brightened. "Make sure you cut off the heads," she yelled. She glanced at me. "Daddy always taught me to cut off their heads or burn the bodies. You have to be sure they're dead. If you just push them over a cliff or poison them and leave them to die, they always find a way to come back." She tucked a stray lock of hair back behind her ear. "It's in all the stories."

She grabbed my hand and tugged me onward. "Come on," she said. "Zariel can catch up once she finishes playing."

Hand in hand we continued through the woods, followed only by gurgling screams.

We stopped near sundown to rest and eat, though my body didn't seem to need either. Zariel used her magic to lure a pair of rabbits from the woods, then Jenny conjured tiny snakes to bite them. The snakes might have been magic, but the poison was real, and the rabbits spasmed and died before they could hop more than a few feet.

A part of me expected these two to simply rip into the rabbits with their teeth, feasting on the raw and bloody meat. Instead, Zariel swiftly and efficiently gutted the two rabbits, then impaled them on spits over a small fire.

"We have little time," Zariel said. "When Armand's men fail to return, he'll know where we are."

"Good," said Jenny. She wiped her face on the sleeve of her gown, then turned to spit out a bone.

Zariel tilted her head. "Good?"

"I summon the Serpent God. Armand and his army arrive. The god eats them." She took another bite of rabbit. Still chewing, she said, "I won't make the same mistakes my Daddy did."

"You want him to find you," I said. I had designed traps for years. I knew how to recognize them.

Jenny nodded. "He killed my Daddy. So I'm going to kill him, his family, and his army, and then I'm going to destroy what's left of his land."

I didn't know what bothered me more: the calm, total conviction in her voice, or the fact that when I thought about my wife and son, I knew *precisely* how she felt.

Frelan Gorge was a beautiful sight. Rather, it would have been beautiful, had I been here for any other purpose. The river far below was a ribbon of darkness, sparkling in the light of the moon. Trees and bushes covered the cliffs, transforming them into walls of lushness and life. To the north, a cloud of mist rose from the base of a small waterfall.

Jenny pointed to the fall. "That's where we're going."

"You're certain?" asked Zariel.

"I can feel it."

I followed behind, biding my time. It would have been so easy to grab Jenny and fling her down the cliff, but I remembered how easily she had smashed me to the ground the last time I attacked her. She had dragged me from the grave, and she could send me back as quick as thought.

I frowned as I thought about that. "Why me?"

"What?" Jenny asked.

"Your father knew the traps as well or better than me. Why not resurrect him?"

"Yes Jenny," said Zariel, a nasty edge to her voice. "Why him?"

Jenny looked away, and I sensed I had stumbled into an old argument. "You were nice to me. He wasn't."

"I was what?"

"When the slaves were working on the first temple. I wanted to watch them laying the foundation and mixing the blood into the mortar. I wasn't tall enough, so you lifted me onto your shoulders."

I couldn't remember. Either death had rotted the memory from my brain, or else Jenny had confused me with another worker.

Up ahead, Zariel used her magic to burn a tangle of thorn-covered vines out of the way. There was no path, so we were making our own. As I watched the vegetation smolder, it occurred to me that the burnt plants would make it easy for Armand's trackers to follow.

"Besides, if Daddy were here, *he'd* want to summon the Serpent God." She wiped her nose on her sleeve. "He had his chance, and he failed. So now I get to be the God Rider."

I kept my face still and prayed she couldn't read my thoughts. I might not be able to destroy her myself, but there were plenty of traps in Tarzog's temple that should do the trick.

Thorns tore my skin as I followed them toward the falls. I could hear the water crashing down, and the vegetation was thicker here, forcing Zariel to expend more of her magic. With her smaller size, Jenny seemed able to slip through the thinnest gaps like...well, like a serpent.

Finally, the trees thinned away, and we found ourselves on a rocky shore. Water trickled over my feet, and I could see how the riverbank fell away a few steps in. So long as we stayed by the edge, we should be safe. Any further, and the current would toss us down the falls.

"Where's the temple?" Zariel asked, glancing about. My dead eyes seemed to handle the darkness better than theirs, but even I couldn't see any sign of the temple. And Tarzog hadn't built small. His temple had been the size of a modest palace.

Jenny was kneeling near the falls, craning her head. I stepped toward her. A single push, and she would plummet to her death. Jenny glanced up, and I froze.

"I can see something behind the water," Jenny said. "A door."

"How do we get down?" Zariel asked.

"We don't." Jenny smiled at me. "Right?"

Grudgingly, I nodded. "That would be a decoy, something to delay Armand and his ilk. If Tarzog patterned this temple on the one I designed, that door is nothing but a façade. But with the water pounding down, most heroes will slip and fall to their deaths before they reach it. If not... the door at the other temple had hinges concealed on the bottom, so it would fall open to crush anyone who tried the knob. This one probably does something similar."

"Which means the back door should be back this way," Jenny said, wading upstream.

I watched a branch float over the lip of the falls, and wondered how many workers had died building Tarzog's decoy trap. "It wouldn't be in the water," I said.

They both stared at me.

"Tarzog needed men to dig and build." I pointed to the river. "The riverbed is stone, and the current is too strong."

"So where is the door?" Zariel asked.

If Tarzog had followed the same plans...I glanced back toward the falls. Sixty paces from the front door, and another twenty paces to the right. I hurried along the shore, then turned back into the woods, ripping through the foliage until I reached a lightning-struck tree. Half of the trunk had rotted away. Splinters of blackened wood hung down like fangs. Grubs and worse squirmed within the blackened interior.

"Go on," Jenny said. "Open it."

I nodded. It would have been too much to hope for her to go first. Reaching past the fangs, I felt about until I found a small metal lever. A quick push disarmed the trap. On the original temple, rusted nails had protruded through the doorframe. Those nails were designed to shoot down, pinning an intruder in place. An instant later, two steel blades would spring out from either side to decapitate the poor fellow. I had been quite proud of that one, actually. I doubted this tree could house such oversized blades, but I didn't want to take my chances on whatever Tarzog had substituted.

I stepped into the bug-infested rot, and my feet began to sink.

Seconds later, I was in darkness.

I brushed dirt and rotted wood from my clothes and, without thinking, grabbed the torch from the left wall. Tarzog had been left-handed, and wanted to know he could roam his temple without having to carry detailed notes about various traps. The right torch would work too, but its removal from the sconce would prime a trap eleven feet down the hall, which would spray oil down on the head of whoever passed. The oil itself wouldn't hurt anyone, but if they carried a lit torch...

The flint and steel hung from the sconce, good as new. I half expected the moisture in the air to have rendered the torches useless, but Tarzog hadn't skimped when it came to his temple. The black, tarry goo coating the end of the torch caught on the first spark.

I toyed with grabbing the trapped torch, but decided against it. Even assuming dust and insects hadn't clogged the nozzles, the oil spray had only a six foot radius. There was a good chance one or both of my companions would survive.

And if truth be told, I didn't want to see Jenny burn. Tarzog had tested the trap on his tailor, who had been caught spying. I could still hear his screams, as clear as the sound of my own footsteps, and the smell would follow me to my grave. Beyond my grave, actually. Why couldn't death have taken *that* memory? I didn't think I could inflict such an end on this little girl.

Besides, there was a better way. A quicker way which would not only take Jenny and Zariel with me, but would destroy this accursed temple as well.

So I did as I had been commanded. I led them on hands and knees through the hall of gods, as the stone statues of long-forgotten deities fired poisoned darts from their eyes, mouths, and in one particularly disturbing case, from his penis. I tiptoed around the edge of the spiked pit with the crushing walls, though not without a moment of regret. I had worked hard to design the system of weights and wheels that forced the walls inward, and I would have liked to know if it still worked after this much time in the jungle.

The plan was identical to the temple I had designed, all except that rotted tree at the entrance. I wondered if Tarzog had used a bit of necromancy to keep it decaying all these years while retaining its strength.

"How much further?" Jenny asked. She was chewing her thumbnail again.

I pushed open a door, ignoring the trapped knob on the right. This had been one of Tarzog's favorites. The hinges were hidden on the same side as the knob, and the door didn't even latch. Friction and a tight frame held it in place. Anyone who bumped the knob would take a poisoned needle to the hand. Actually turning the thing would trigger a spray of acid from the floor.

"We're here," I said, stepping inside.

One advantage to being dead: my body didn't react with the same throat-constricting terror I remembered from my last time in this room, back in the other temple. Or maybe my time with Jenny and Zariel had numbed me to fear. The walls bulged inward, carved to resemble barbed scales on the coils of an enormous snake. Arcane symbols spiraled around the floor and ceiling both.

"It's beautiful," Jenny said. She took my torch and ran to the closest wall to study the carvings worked into the snake's body. In one, dead warriors lay scattered before a giant serpent who had reared back with a horse and rider in its jaws.

The Serpent God was one ugly snake. Curved horns like scimitars grew in twin rows behind the eyes. In addition to the huge fangs, smaller teeth lined the jaws, each one dripping with venom.

"Look at this, Zariel," Jenny said, moving farther along the wall. "Here he's collecting his sacrifice." The snake's coils circled a pit of terrified old men, women, and children.

"Forget the pictures," Zariel snapped. "Armand's trackers are probably making their way through the jungle even now."

Jenny stuck out her tongue, then squatted down, holding her torch close to the floor to read the symbols.

I turned my attention to the back of the room, where a thick book lay open on a raised dais. This was perhaps Tarzog's most brilliant idea. If his enemies had penetrated this far, it would mean Tarzog himself had fallen. Vindictive bastard that he was, Tarzog planted the book here to destroy those enemies.

The pages were blank, but in order to discover that, you had to set foot on that dais. Any weight of more than ten pounds would trigger a collapse of the entire temple.

I stepped soundlessly toward the book. No amount of magic or power could save them. With Jenny dead, I would be back with my wife and my children. Perhaps we would all rest a bit easier, knowing-

"Stop that," Jenny said without looking up.

My body froze in mid-step. Unable to move, I toppled forward. My wrist hit the floor first, hard enough I could hear bone snap. I ended up on my side, staring helplessly at Jenny as she turned around.

"I'm sorry," she said. "I don't know what Daddy did to trap this room, but I can't let you get to it."

"How?" It was all I could do to force the word past my dead lips.

Jenny shrugged. "Daddy killed you. He killed your family. I knew you'd try to get me in the end. That's what I'd do."

"Clever, isn't she?" asked Zariel. Something in her voice warned me an instant before she struck, but I couldn't have stopped her even if I wanted to. She waved her hand, and Jenny began to scream. Black fire danced over Jenny's skin. She flopped on the floor like a dying trout.

"Such a clever girl," Zariel repeated as she circled Jenny's body. "Marked by the Serpent God, heir to the power of Tarzog the Black."

Zariel snapped her fingers, and Jenny went still. She wasn't dead. She couldn't be, or else the magic keeping me in this half-living state would have failed. Shadowy flames continued to burn, though Jenny's clothes and skin were unharmed. Zariel's fire fed on something deeper than flesh.

"For two years I've dragged this whelp from one refuge to another," Zariel said, her voice growing louder with each word. "Two years of living like a common thief. Two years of her whining and arguing, her stubborn refusal to follow even the simplest instructions."

She turned to me, her eyes wide. For a moment, I thought she was going to destroy me, but she clasped her hands and said, "That little brat pissed her bedroll every night for six months after her father died. Six months!"

Zariel pulled the vial of blood from her pocket. "Well, little godling, Anhak Ghudir said you would be the one to lure Rhynoth from his rest, but the prophesies never said who would command him." She bit the stopper from the vial, spat it to one side, and swallowed the contents.

Grabbing Jenny by the hair, she dragged the motionless girl to the center of the room. Jenny's eyes were open and alert. She could see everything that was happening, just like me.

A part of me took some perverse joy at seeing her own torments turned back upon her. I might have failed, but Tarzog's line would still end.

Zariel began to chant. "She is here, great one. Descendant of your own children, heir to the powers of the first serpent." The rest was in another tongue, full of hacking, angry syllables.

At first, I didn't realize when Zariel's chanting changed to genuine coughs. Only when she staggered back a step did I realize something was wrong. One hand clawed her throat. Blood dripped from her left nostril.

The shadowy flames on Jenny's body flickered and died. Jenny's arms were shaky as she struggled to sit up. Hugging her knees to her chest, she whispered, "That hurt."

Zariel dropped to her knees. Her expression changed from panic to anger, and she raised one hand, but when she tried to speak, only a pained croak emerged.

Jenny crawled over and kicked her in the stomach.

"How?" Zariel asked, her voice hoarse.

Jenny rolled her eyes. "I swiped the blood a week ago. Daddy always told me the only henchman you could ever really trust was one who was already dead." She pulled a heavily padded tube from inside her dress. "This is the virgin blood. *You* drank a blend of four different sea snake venoms, mixed in bat blood."

She stood up, her knees still shaking slightly. With her free hand, she took the torch from Zariel, then kicked her again. The effort nearly made her fall back.

"You wanted to know why him?" Jenny whispered, pointing to me. "Because he went to stay with his family in the dungeons every night. My Daddy would have let him stay in the huts with the other workers, but he refused. *He* never complained about the smell. *He* didn't tell his son to stop whining. When his boy fouled himself during the night, *he* didn't force him to sleep in his own stink!"

She ended her tirade with one last kick, then turned to me. "I used to sneak down to the dungeons to watch Daddy torture traitors. One night I saw you coming, so I followed you."

She unwrapped the vial of blood as she talked. "I'll let you die, if that's what you want. Or you can come with me." She swallowed the blood, then smiled. "I'll even let you ride the Serpent God with me. But I am going to summon Rhynoth. Armand and his men are going to die. I'm going to conquer this land, whether you come with me or not."

She glanced back at Zariel, who had stopped moving. "Who knows," she said. "Maybe you'll help me mend my evil ways." The wicked grin on her face told me how likely *that* was. "You might even get a chance to kill me."

I doubted it. Look at how efficiently she had outsmarted and disposed of Zariel. Jenny was truly her father's daughter. Even more dangerous than Tarzog the Black. After all, Tarzog had failed.

On the other hand, what purpose would my death serve? I couldn't bring my family back. I couldn't stop Jenny. The only possible blessing I would gain from death was my own peace.

The floor began to shake as Jenny chanted the same words Zariel had. Rhynoth had awakened from his millennial slumber, and he would be here soon.

Jenny's shoulders slumped as she finished the incantation. She began to chew her thumbnail again, wincing as the nail tore free and began to bleed.

"I'll understand if you don't want to come," she said, never looking at me.

I closed my eyes and made my choice.

Prince Armand brought an army. Perhaps he knew what he was about to face. I doubted it would save him, but who knew?

All I knew as that when Jenny rode the Serpent God, her hands clinging to the horns as her half-cape flapped behind her, she didn't look like an evil sorceress. She looked like a little girl, smiling and laughing as she prepared to wipe out an entire land. And seeing that almost made me feel alive again.

---

JIM C. HINES' newest book is *Libriomancer*, a modern-day fantasy about a magic-wielding librarian, a hamadryad, a secret society founded by Johannes Gutenberg, a flaming spider, and an enchanted convertible. He's also the author of the Princess series of fairy tale retellings as well as the humorous Goblin Quest trilogy. His short fiction has appeared in more than 40 magazines and anthologies. Online, he can be found at http://www.jimchines.com.

# THAN TO SERVE IN HEAVEN

## Ari Marmell

"THIS IS A JEST."

I say it, even though I know that it can't be. Through the thick haze and shimmering heat that clouds my vision every waking moment, the parchment casts its meaning at me in unmistakable terms. The letters burn without fire, scribed by the highest hand, written in a language older than life itself.

A language that cannot, by its very nature, be used to lie. If it is written, it is truth.

And yet, I cannot believe it.

"Surely," I repeat myself, "this is a jest?"

"Need you even ask?"

I glare at the messenger, as though it's *his* fault that my day—my routine—my *kingdom*—have been so suddenly and so swiftly hurtled into disarray. He keeps his face turned downward, unwilling or unable to meet my gaze.

As it should be. Still, I'd give much to be able to read his expression just now.

"You know what this says?" I ask.

"Yes. I had to."

"And you've the power to make this happen?"

"He'd not have sent me if I did not." Still he looks only at his feet—feet that hover some fingers-widths above the searing, viscous surface, held aloft by gently flapping wings—but he reaches out toward me with a single hand.

The key that lies upon his palm is such a small thing, white and gleaming even in the smoke. So small, and yet I would see entire worlds consumed in flame for just a chance at acquiring it.

Or normally I would. But now, like this, I hesitate. I worry over the repercussions, over what I might be asked to surrender in exchange.

And I balk at the notion of granting Him even this much satisfaction.

But I'll take it. I know it. The messenger knows it. *He* knows it. If nothing else, my curiosity allows me no other option.

It feels like a snowflake falling into my hand, a touch of cold like I haven't known in eons. And just like that, the chains fall away. They take seared flesh with them, but I scarcely even notice; their weight is gone from my wrists, my ankles. The rough, jagged cuffs, the *miles* of chain that grant no true freedom, but merely allow me to pace the borders of my kingdom-cell—gone.

I stand. I stretch, arms and wings both; filthy, gray, covered in layers of soot thick enough to drown a man. Around me, the fires roar, their tips forming dancing, abstract shapes that vomit a greasy smoke. The skin and hair of a million million bodies crackle and snap. The air is thick with blood and brimstone, tears and screams. My legs burn with the touch of the Lake.

All familiar, so familiar that I haven't noticed any of it—the sound, the scent, the suffering—for centuries. I notice it now. For now, if only briefly, I am leaving it behind.

I truly thought I would never see the day.

*Come home*, the missive says. Very well. I stand straight, tall, unchained, unbowed, and the messenger shrinks before me.

"Show me the way," I command him.

"Of course." And then, as though it pains him to say it to an extent that even standing here, in the depths of my dominion, did not, he adds, "My lord."

I don't even see the great expanse, the blistering flame, the jagged stone sides of the Pit, or the writhing masses of the Damned. They all, like my own agony, have become mere background, a fact of life, all but unnoticed. I have eyes only for the messenger who soars before me, playing guide and guardian in a realm that none know better than I. He has lowered himself to speak to me, descended in full knowledge of the grace that protects him, and still he fears. He won't show it in his face, or in his posture, but he fears.

I smell it, breathe it, revel in it, and I cannot help but chuckle. His wings quiver, just once, and he flies a tiny bit faster. I've no difficulty at all keeping up. As I said, I know my own domain far more intimately—

Except, suddenly, I don't.

A crevice, slicing through the jagged stone, where no crevice has been since the dawn of time. I gawp, slack-jawed and hating myself for it, as the messenger circles once and begins a leisurely climb through the rapidly thinning smoke.

But then, I can hardly expect the exit to simply have been standing open all this time, can I? Jaws, fists, wingtips all clench, and I force myself to follow once more.

It should be a flight of centuries, a thousand years and more. Yet I know it won't be; He *could* wait so long, but why?

It happens between one wingbeat and the next. The sheer stone around us is gone, replaced by walls that gleam in blinding hues, despite the utter lack of any light source for them to reflect. Our feet touch down on a substance somehow both solid and fluid at once, a perfect cradle that conforms to our every step. We walk on a carpet of comfort made manifest, through a gentle breeze that smells of beauty and contentment.

Everything around us glistens and gleams. Even me. The soot that has caked my flesh, my hair, my wings, my teeth, my tongue, is gone, just that swiftly.

As is the pain. Gone. I haven't been free of pain for one instant, not one, in so long. I'd grown so accustomed to it that its absence is, itself, a physical sensation. I find myself staggering as my body struggles against an absent pressure.

I look about once more. The hallway has grown brighter, and a part of me wants to weep, because I know the extra light—the newest light—is my own.

I want to, but I won't. I won't give them even that much.

The two of them wait just up ahead, standing before a gate constructed of the golden glow of creation itself. Gabriel, with his horn slung at his waist, looks saddened; Michael, fist clenched upon his terrible sword, enraged.

"Hello, brothers." Though I know an unyielding courtesy would disturb them all the more, I cannot be bothered to keep the contempt from my voice.

Michael scowls and says nothing. Only Gabriel speaks.

"Hello, Lucifer. Welcome home."

A human. They've placed a *human* soul to stand as the doorman at the gate. I'm shaking with fury as we pass, unable even to speak. By the time I've recovered, we're long past, and it would be petty to say anything about it now.

Besides, I'm swiftly too lost in my surroundings to worry about it.

If the journey through Hell went by so quickly because I was already so familiar with the path, then the journey here slips by too fast because it's simply too much to take in. Once, this was everything to me; my home, my world. I feel almost nauseously bitter at how it still touches me.

I absorb only bits and snatches of the march. The walls and pillars, towering overhead, all colors and yet none. I hear the Choirs—not music, not really, but *beyond* music, an emotional symphony that plays directly to the soul. I am happy, though I know I shouldn't be, even *try* not to be. Not only because, though I'd never confess it, I've missed the place, but because that is Heaven's nature. As much a part and parcel of the surroundings as the suffering is below.

Despite the distractions, I feel the eyes upon me. The souls of the Blessed, they see only my greatness, sense the glory moving among them. The others, though, they glare at me with fears and hatreds normally foreign to those who dwell in Heaven. I cannot help but smile. Even here, I hold such power over them.

Then we are there, standing before the heart of Heaven, the center of creation. The Throne of God.

Not a throne in the literal sense, of course; simply the one spot where we know He is to be found. The Choir has somehow grown louder and yet more distant; the walls seem to recede in all directions.

And I can only squint into a light so bright, so pure, it blinds even these immortal eyes. I remember—only barely, but I remember a time when I could look upon Him directly, see Him clearly, without pain.

I refuse, despite the bright, blinding pain, to squint.

My brothers are kneeling. I don't even remember seeing them drop; they're just *down*. I? I bend knee to none, anymore, not even Him—but I bow my head in a gesture of respect. I think perhaps I even mean it.

"Welcome back, my son."

It's a "voice" in the same way Hell is a fire, or Eden was a garden. Less heard than *experienced*.

"Father," I say. And then, because I want to head it off before it can begin, "If your invitation came with the expectation of an apology, you're sadly deluded. Nothing has changed for—"

"No."

No? I'm a bit startled, despite myself. "You owe me an explanation, then."

Gabriel gasps; Michael's sword is halfway from its sheath, the flames along the blade casting a coppery glare across the floor.

But He only laughs. I do not hear whatever it is He says to the others, but just like that they rise as one and turn. They've taken only a single step before they're utterly gone.

"An explanation you'll have, then. I feel the need to be absent."

"Absent?" It's not quite a scoff—even I am disinclined to be that rude—but it's a near thing. "Are you not everywhere?"

"In a sense, of course. But Creation has expanded much since I first spoke the Word, Lucifer. I would see parts of it myself. Experience it personally, physically, rather than at a remove.

"In short, I intend to be away from Heaven for a time. A short time, in the scheme of things, but an important one all the same."

I realize that He's not jesting with me—not that I really believed He would—and I'm honestly uncertain what to make of it. Has He ever absented Himself utterly from the Throne? From Heaven? If so, I am unaware of it, though of course my perspective from below is…limited.

And why, why would He summon me here to tell me this?

"If you hope to extract a promise," I begin carefully, "that I'll not interfere with the workings of Heaven while you're away, this was a foolish approach. I'd never have known—"

"I want you to take over while I am gone."

I cannot speak; I have been this stunned only once before, when He told us He would exalt mankind above us, His first creations. I stagger back, and only by catching myself against the wall am I spared the humiliation of actually falling.

(Wall? Was this wall even here? I remember them being much farther away, mere moments before. He's placed it precisely to spare me a worse stumble; I'm both irritated and pathetically grateful.)

"I don't…" I shake my head, trying to find my balance in a universe suddenly twisting from any path I could ever imagine. "I don't understand."

"So I gathered."

"You want me to rule Heaven?"

"For a time."

"But…*Me?*"

"Yes."

"In any manner I choose?"

I swear, though I cannot make out anything within the light, that He smiles. "No."

I *knew* it! I knew there had to be a catch! My astonishment swiftly subsides before a tide of suspicion. "What, then?"

"There are rules, Lucifer. Rules as to what you may and may not do. Rules to determining which souls are worthy of punishment, and which of peace. What prayers to heed, and what to ignore. When to take a hand, and when to let nature run its course. Rules that you will follow, to the letter."

"And should I refuse?"

"Should you refuse, I shall send you back. Should you agree and seek to circumvent our agreement, or abuse your position, I shall know, and I shall send you back. But agree, Lucifer—agree, and abide—and you may enjoy all the wonders of Heaven that have been denied you for so long, and at least a taste of the power you once held as My favored servant."

"Why?" I realize that I'm pacing—not merely back and forth but up and down, wings and feet working as one. "Surely Michael or Gabriel…"

"Would follow my edicts without question. But Creation is vast. Events transpire that even My laws do not cover. Events that require decisions. That require a God. And My angels, loyal and skilled though they may be, are followers, not leaders. It is all I've allowed them to be." The pure light flickers, growing briefly dark, mottled, angry. "You saw to that."

"I would rule." I know I'm repeating myself, but I can't quite wrap my mind around it.

"Within reasonable boundaries, yes."

"And you've no other reasons? No ulterior motives?" I know that, whatever else, He will not lie to me.

And He doesn't. "I don't believe I said that."

So. There it is. Everything I could possibly want, if only for a time. But with restrictions. Strings. Mandates. And for motives that He's no intention of revealing to me.

I should say no. I *almost* say no. What He offers is, though pleasant and prestigious, just another form of servitude.

But if I agree, I might learn *why* He would make such an offer. And maybe, just maybe, I might show Him that I can do the job better than He.

I think I surprise neither of us when I say, "I accept."

It *is* a true throne, now, from which I observe my new domain. White, flawless, carved from stone that dates from the birth of land and sky and sea. I want no doubt, no convenient forgetting, of who rules here now.

Not that they would forget. Not that they *could*. He ordered the others to obey me as they would Him, and though resentment burns in every glance and frustration twists every lip and wingtip, they do so, without complaint or hesitation. Their very nature allows nothing less.

I revel in their conflicted deference, in their hatred, even as I despise them for all they've become. All they *allowed* themselves to become at His hand.

But I don't hate them, not the way I hate those with whom He would have replaced us.

They shuffle along before the Throne, an endless line, a writhing worm of souls twisting into the distance. Soul after soul after soul. Pathetic, mud-clad, fading embers of the divine. I swear, even though all such things should have been left behind, I can smell the stench of their flesh, their petty hatreds, their simple lusts.

It requires every bit of my restraint—a skill that, I admit, I have had little need to practice—not to damn each and every one of them merely for the sin of being born. To flood the bowels of Hell with souls until even the eternal Fires are in danger of suffocation.

But I do not. He may not have left *rigid* guidelines, regarding who is worthy and who is not, but I certainly have a fair idea of His criteria. Somehow, I think that ignoring them would likely qualify as an abuse of my position. I must return eventually—I know this, I accept it—but I'd prefer to put it off, at least long enough to learn what He's up to.

So I judge, and to the best of my ability, I judge "fairly." Those who have grossly violated His precepts, I let fall, to entertain my demons far below. Those who have not, or whose transgressions are minor, remain. The glowers cast my way by Michael and the others do not lessen in their intensity, nor their hatred, but I do sense a diminishing of their wariness and discontent. Apparently, my choices, by and large, meet with their approval.

Hallelujah.

It is a tedious task, the judgment. One that, in mortal time, would be neverending, occupying every moment I have from now until the end of the whole misbegotten race. But this is Heaven, and Heaven is—if only for the nonce—mine. Here, time, too, bends to my will. I tire of the task at hand, and put it aside. Until I wish it, the line of souls will grow no longer.

I've time to walk the corridors and the parapets of the Kingdom.

Choose the right spot atop the walls, and you can see anything. Truly, anything. From the rampart here, I gaze across the entire breadth of Heaven itself, watch as the souls drift in eternal contentment. My brothers flit this way and that, shepherding those souls, casting their own attentions downward, and—on frequent occasion—looking askance toward me, as though they might divine both my own mind and the reason He chose to place me above them. I actually find my contempt lessening in the face of our shared bewilderment; I'd very much like the answer to that, myself.

From above the gate, I observe the entirety of mortal-occupied creation. Across every world our Father chose to endow with life, the beasts and lesser beings roam. Only a fraction of a fraction have souls, warrant any attention from me at all, but so numerous are the worlds that it still takes time to examine them all. I cannot help but laugh at the workings of the mortal mind: Across a million languages and a hundred thousand planets, nearly all of their names for their own worlds translate, at least roughly, as "Earth."

And from the heights of the watchtower, I can see farther still. Farther out—and farther down. I can see into the Fire, and the demons and souls that writhe within. I swear I can even smell the brimstone, as nothing more than the faintest incense on the air.

Small. From here, it's so small. For a moment, I'm resentful, but only for a moment. I'm not down there anymore. I'm here, and I've time yet to prove that I'm *anything* but small.

I turn and, ignoring the continued glares and glowers of the others, return to my duties—and my Throne.

"I need to *what?*"

Raphael stands beside the Throne, his entire form radiant with light both physical and spiritual. His lip twitches, as he's apparently taken aback by my questioning. It's not that I failed to hear him—I'm just not certain I heard him *correctly*.

I've been distracted. I hesitate to admit it, even to myself, but it's true. In Hell, even when I'd grown largely accustomed to the constant agony, I was always *aware* of it. Every moment that went by was etched across my flesh, imprinted on my consciousness.

Here, though? Here, without the pain, I have occasionally gotten lost in my activities. I've even come to enjoy the occasional challenge inherent in the judgment. Why did this mortal do what it did in life? Why did it commit its sins? Where does the soul deserve to reside? It's…interesting.

I'm honestly not sure how long I've been here, now, not that time has much meaning in Heaven anyway.

But whatever the case, it took me a moment to pull my attention away from my task, to comprehend what my brother said to me. And now that I have, I find I have difficulty believing it.

"I said," Raphael begins again, "you need to come shape life."

And then, when it's become clear to him that I've no idea what he's talking about, "Follow me. Please." He *almost* manages to hide the resentment and exasperation on that last word.

He leads me once more to the parapets, far past the watchtower, to a corner I've yet to visit. At a spot that, so far as I can tell, is no different from any other, he stops and extends a hand. "Look."

So I do, and for an instant I'm not certain what I'm seeing. Just another world, of earth and oceans and sky. Yet nothing crawls upon it, nothing swims or flies. And even stranger, beyond that world, and its sun and its moon, lie…

Nothing. Darkness. Void.

"As the universe expands," Raphael tells me, "new worlds appear at the edges of Creation. Sometimes, those worlds are inhabitable. At which point, it is up to God—" and there can be no mistaking the sarcastic tinge, to both the title and the meaningful glance he gives me—"to shape that life."

"I am not Him, Raphael." I wonder how long he's been waiting to hear me say that.

"As I'm well aware. But He put you in His place, for the nonce. This duty is yours."

"I don't have that sort of power."

"You're looking at the expanding edge of Creation itself, Lucifer. The power is there. All you need do is shape it."

It takes a short while, as he instructs me in the methods of concentration and sculpting of possibilities, but in the end, he's right. The power's already there. It's almost…easy.

Again, I *could* design the race to suffer, to live and die in torment. And again, I'm fairly certain—despite the lack of explicit instruction to the contrary—that doing so would violate my agreement.

And I still don't want to go back.

I do not start with the end result, of course. No. Tiny creatures, primitive fish and crawling things. But I cast and build the energies around them, shaping the evolution of things to come. The height of the plants just so, the gravity and tectonics like this, the early predators like that. If I've done the job properly, the end result—some many thousands of millennia from now—will be a bipedal race somewhat akin to the monkeys. They will never be as intelligent as, for instance, humans—but neither will they be as unhappy. Their lives will be short, and likely without meaning, but pleasant.

It is not, I'm sure, what He would have done. But neither is it what, only a short while ago, *I* would likely have done, either.

It feels...

I shake my head, offer Raphael a shallow nod, and walk away. For some reason, I suddenly don't want to watch that world anymore.

For a moment, I can actually see through the priest's eyes, feel the flush of sweat and fear and unshakable faith on his skin.

As long as I've been here, holding down the fort on His behalf, I've never answered a prayer like this one. I rarely answer any; the overwhelming majority are from people asking for luck or fortune of some sort or another, and it was made quite clear to me that that's not my purpose here. For the most part, chance and nature run their course, for good or ill.

But then came this one. Rare, or so Raphael and Gabriel have told me, but not unheard of—and not, necessarily, to be ignored. Apparently, the forces of Heaven are permitted to act against the demons of Hell.

Strangely, I knew that already.

I watch the priest intone the ritual phrases, wave his hands and rosary and Bible through the proper rites. I even recognize the demon inhabiting the old man currently held against the mattress by the sobbing, terrified members of his family.

Tamiel. How long has it been since Tamiel bothered to possess a mortal? What, precisely, has been going on below in my absence?

Well, no matter. The priest's faith is strong, his use of the rites proper. Again my duties and obligations require me to take action where, left to my own devices, I very well might not. I see through the priest's eyes, and my power—or, at least, the power I currently represent—surges through him. The old man screams, the room quakes, and Tamiel plunges back into the depths of Hell.

I wonder if I am imagining a brief look of recognition and betrayal in his expression as he plummets from sight.

I open my own eyes, and I am back upon the Throne, with a line of souls before me and two of my brothers standing to either side. Raphael smiles at me; Gabriel nods his approval.

Their hatred and resentment are, if not gone, then certainly diminished. They are pleased with my decisive action, and with how I've been executing my duties to the waiting souls. The same holds true for nearly all my brothers, greater and lesser. Only Michael, of them all, yet clings to his anger, refuses to speak to me unless circumstances demand.

I don't know how long I've been here. And I realize, with no small surprise, that today—this exorcism—is the first time in a very long while that I've even *thought* of Hell.

"Hello, my son."

I cannot say I'm surprised, not in the slightest. Somehow I knew, as soon as I had my earlier revelation, that it would not be long before His return.

"Father. Is it time, then?" I try to keep the quaver from my voice; it's as difficult as keeping myself from squinting as I gaze into the light.

"It is." A portion of the floor disappears from off to my left. I feel the rush of heat even before I see the coiling, greasy smoke, or hear the pitiful chorus of screams. I cringe away, and hate myself for it.

"Perhaps."

I cling to that word with both hands. Staring, I no longer find it difficult at all not to squint. "Perhaps?"

"You can stay, Lucifer. Remain in Heaven, perhaps even work to regain a place at My right hand."

I see it coming, before He even utters the words.

"All you have to do is refute what you have done. All you have to do is apologize."

And that's really what this has all been about from the beginning, isn't it? He knew I'd never acquiesce, not when He first summoned me. But He's given me the "gift" of perspective. He's allowed me time to live outside the fire, to live free of pain. Even to see, for myself, a sliver of His perspective.

*All you have to do...*

I've been manipulated, and I bitterly resent it. Yet the bile burns in the back of my throat, threatening to choke me, before I can spit it out.

I don't want to go back.

*All you have to do...*

I feel a terror of the Pit like I haven't felt since the chains first closed. I have my freedom—freedom to act, freedom to live, freedom from pain. I know what awaits me below, and the notion of returning to it, of trying once again to grow accustomed to it, makes me tremble.

*All you have to do...*

I have, if not everything I could ever want here, then at least a vast preponderance of it. And I can keep it, all of it.

*All you have to do...*

If I give up being who I was. But after my time in His Throne, am I not, already, someone other than who I was?

*All you have to do...*

Either way, in a sense, it's over. Either way, I lose.

I take a deep breath, and I think I surprise neither of us when I give the only answer I can.

---

ARI MARMELL is a fantasy and horror writer, with novels and short stories published through Del Rey/Spectra, Pyr Books, Wizards of the Coast, and others. His most recent novels are *Thief's Covenant* and *False Covenant*, from Pyr Books, and *Darksiders: the Abomination Vault* from Del Rey. Although born in New York, Ari has lived the vast majority of his life in Texas-first Houston (where he earned a BA in Creative Writing at the University of Houston), and then Austin. He lives with his wife, George, two cats, and a variety of neuroses. You can find Ari online at mouseferatu.com.

# THE BLEACH

## *Karin Lowachee*

THE RUNWAY DISAPPEARED INTO the white desert. He rode his bicycle until the front wheel rubbed into the sand and stopped him. He looked over his shoulder but only the wavering heat of the pale horizon glared back. An endless tapering line of cracked and faded gray tarmac stretched out like some forgotten ancient road long neglected by the conquered. He was alone and he was safe. He looked up at the cotton heavy sky, and a pure haze made of some combination of sand and moisture weighed like gauze on his eyelids, and the round incandescent sun blared down at him with relentless insistence: *You can never go home again. You can never go home again.*

The white arrow on the runway pointed to the Bleach, as if to offer the inevitability of death to anyone who found themselves this far from civilization. Just in case the one hundred miles through desolate nothingness hadn't told you. He sat with one black sneaker pasted to the cracks and pocks of pavement, the other resting on the pedal, and he rubbed bruised palms on his black jeans and pushed at the tails of his shirt as they clung to his ribs. The white T-shirt underneath was covered in sand, sand in the straggles of blond beard on his chin, sand between his teeth and on his tongue, sand that made every blink feel like the world at which he looked was made of finely ground shavings of some god's dirty fingernails. He felt the stab of it even in the squinted wrinkles at the corners of his eyes.

Sand in the grooves of the gun tucked into the waist of his belt. And on the front of his T-shirt, blood.

*Congratulations, you've just killed the King.*

*So where,* he'd said, *is my money?*

He waited. The jagged gaps in the runway spread serpent-thin and struck across what was left of the yellow track lines. These dark rivulets lacking water, parched by the air. He needed water, he'd emptied his bottle and tossed it fifty miles back. He'd passed all the caches he'd buried over time and used up that water too. He'd come here to the end of civilization at full tilt, on his own steam, because anything mechanized would have been detected. Now he waited, and thirsted, and thought of the hailstorm of gnashing he'd left behind.

In the distance the sand dragons moaned.

The Barrurian helicopter kicked up tornados in its landing, forcing him to cover his face with the folds of his shirt. He climbed off the bike just as the heli's black struts touched down, and he picked up the bike and took it over to the passenger bay. A helmeted door gunner lifted the bike from him and he climbed on, and before his ass hit the seat they were in the air.

Across from him the fat man mopped at his pink forehead with a velvet piece of snakeskin, as if he'd been the one to hike those miles under the sun. "I'm surprised you're on time."

He said, "Where's my money?"

"Patience, patience."

He thought that patience was for fat fucks who couldn't pull the trigger themselves. He withdrew his gun and laid it against his leg, the barrel facing the Barrurian.

The snakeskin stopped its patting progress across the round folds of skin. "No need for that, my boy."

Boy? "I want those units now or you'll be next." A look at the door gunner. "Don't."

The gunner had a sidearm, but it was in a holster. The pilot had one too but by then it would be too late.

The fat man said, "Hold out your arm."

"No. Let me see it."

So the fat man reached into his suit's side pocket and revealed the data syringe. He waved it a little then held it out. The door gunner watched with eyes like the shells of beetles and when the sun caught them they flickered opaline. He had seen eyes like that on statues, but these eyes saw as clear as day in the night and if you were on the surface of the earth when this gunner put you in his sights, you were dead where you stood. He took the data syringe left-handed and didn't look away from either Barrurian. Instead he reached inside the front pocket of his shirt for the globe of blue putty, and he laid the putty on his thigh where it stuck to the warm material of his jeans. Then he stabbed the syringe into the putty and loaded the data. When the putty turned blood orange the fat Barrurian breathed a sigh.

He lobbed the empty syringe at the sweating man, then tucked his gun back into his waist and the putty back into his pocket.

"I told you it was good," the fat man said, fumbling the catch.

He didn't answer. He wasn't going to let political killers stick a needle in his arm, not even for twenty million.

"How does it feel to start a war?" the fat man said.

He didn't answer that either. He hadn't been hired for conversation.

Smoking and age had made his voice rough, like words were an endangered species or dune-dwelling creatures too solitary to be found. Kind words were virtually extinct. He was thirty-one and his eight-year-old son hugged him at the door. "Did you hear?" Jatey was crying. "The King is dead."

The heli had dropped him outside the Wall. He'd taken his bike and ridden into the town. The Barrurians had left and nothing stood between him and the thing he'd done but the Bleach, where no communication passed and the city-states didn't cross, not even to towns technically under their jurisdiction. Technically the Wall kept them out, even though technically previous kings had razed and owned the town, and owned it now. But who remembered those things? Only the dragons. He kissed his son and said, "I'm home. Go wipe your eyes. Where's your aunt?"

She came from the side door that led to the cement slab behind the house that she liked to call a garden. She was always trying to make things grow. She had a flower mien, a delicate head of red hair that bent toward him in greeting and he put his hand on the stem of her arm and kissed her cheek. "Hello," she said, as if it had only been two hours and not two weeks. "Go clean up for dinner," to Jatey, and by then the boy had dried his eyes and looked at them, and went off down the narrow hall toward the bathroom.

He left his sister and went to the kitchen sink and washed the sand from his hands. His sister said, "There's blood on your shirt." So he removed both his shirts and wadded them up and stuffed them in the garbage under the sink, and returned to the tap to splash water up his arms. "He's going to see the gun," she said, but he was listening to his son in the bathroom. He shut off the water and just listened, the boy splashing around in there, taking joy in water like he had since he was a baby. A fish born in the desert.

He removed the gun from his waist and walked by his sister, down the hall and past the bathroom to his bedroom that he shared with the boy because they just had two rooms for sleeping and when he was home he always wanted the boy near, like a talisman. He set the gun in his bedside drawer and turned around, and his sister stood in the doorway. She didn't want to ask out loud, but she asked with her eyes.

So he turned his back on her and took the blood orange putty from his pocket and put that in the drawer too. His son would never want for anything and his sister could take her silent judgment and go fuck herself.

He held a strange pleasure in watching his boy eat. Jatey shoveled the mashed potatoes and peas into his mouth like they were going to sprout legs and leap off the plate. He tried to ask his son about school, what he was learning, what he liked, because even if his jobs only took him away for a couple weeks at a time, he went often and came back usually at night. Sometimes he took Jatey into the dunes so they could look for sand dragons and they'd stay out overnight and listen to the mournful howls of the creatures calling to one another or calling to their gods like the feathermen claimed. He would sign off on the boy skipping school because being back home meant he was the father who could do such things, he wasn't his sister who made the boy memorize mathematics even after classes. But Jatey didn't want to talk about learning or sports or games—or even about sand dragons. He said he and Auntie Lida had watched the news break about the King and couldn't tear themselves away for hours. "Did you see, did you see how the King was killed?"

Lida stared across the table at him and he said, "You let him watch that?"

She said, "I thought he should. It affects us all. They've canceled school for three days."

"You were supposed to come in for Parent Day," Jatey said.

"I was going to go in." Lida touched the boy's arm.

"I wanted Daddy to, but now there's no school."

The boy was still at an age where he liked school. That was a time he wished the boy would never lose, even though he didn't know what he would possibly say to a room full of kids and he had forgotten all about it. But he watched his sister with her hand on his kid and he said, "When school starts up again, I'll go with you for Parent Day."

"You know you can't," Lida said.

"I'm his parent."

This made Jatey so happy he dismissed it from his eight-year-old mind as a done deal, and went on to the other thing that was in his thoughts. "Now the princes have no daddy or mommy. What's gonna happen to the princes?"

"They're rich," he said. "They'll be taken care of."

"But who's going to play with them?"

Jatey was a sensitive boy and forgot all about his food and instead concentrated on the upsetting idea that nobody would play with the Royal Princes, even if they had a shit ton of servants and relatives and nannies and advisors, not to mention the Council and the Royal Guard to look after them and give them anything they wanted. Tragic figures, they were even going to have the sympathy of an entire city-state. Maybe all of the city-states, except Barrur and the northern tribes that hated everyone and plagued the borders of the balding mountains.

"Don't worry about them," he told his son. "Eat your dinner and we can go play afterwards."

He watched through the window above the sink, how the boy rolled the ball on Lida's concrete garden with his feet like he was dodging away from unseen predators. Agile and showing that confidence with growing limbs that said he might be an athlete when he was older. He had been good at sports as a kid too, but he'd decided to use his hand-eye coordination and physical intelligence for other things. Now he washed their plates at the sink with methodical rhythm, circling each one with a rough sponge. The sun had dimmed and the air and light outside sat bruised and blue over the boy's pale skin.

"How could you do it?" Lida said, standing behind him where he never liked anyone to stand.

But he didn't move, just kept watching his boy and washing his dishes. Thorough. Clean. He wasn't going to bother to play dumb. He wasn't going to even answer.

"The King was a *good man*."

But he didn't have patience for this. "Keep it to yourself."

"One day he's going to find out."

His hands stopped and he looked over his shoulder at her. Her flower face seemed withered at the edges. The kitchen light aged her.

"He's going to find out you killed the King," she said.

"How? Are you going to tell him?"

"These things *always* get known." It sounded like a plea.

But he began to think of it as a threat. A reminder. It always sat at the back of his thoughts like some great regret of the past reaching toward an old man's fading memory. He turned back to the dishes and rinsed and stacked one on the counter top. Then he picked up the next dirty dish and began the rotation of sponge over its surface. More soap. Eventually she left him alone and he heard her disappear into her bedroom and shut the door. More than once he looked over at his comm unit to check if the light was live. He listened to hear a voice from behind her door. But there was no light and she was quiet.

After ball with his son he saw the boy through his clean-up ritual and into the yawning blankets of the bed they shared when he was home, and he slid to the middle of the layered and covered mattress where it was deepest and wrapped his arms around the boy like they did in the desert to ward off snakes and the cold. Both entities liked to feed on outflung limbs but they lay here like a mandala of security and he let his fingers trace the soft round of his son's skull and the scent of soap and boy filtered up as if he'd nudged a rose in bloom. This was the only peace he'd ever known and it coursed through him like blood and made his heart work almost healthy in the cage of his chest.

"Daddy," Jatey mumbled, "why doesn't Aunt Lida like you?"

"Why do you think she doesn't like me?"

"She's mad at you."

"Is she?"

"She says when you go away, you mightn't come back."

He pulled all the threads of his son's words together and saw clearly the overall stitching, what his sister had been weaving for months in the boy's head. "I always come back. And I won't be going away anymore."

"You won't?" Hesitant hope.

"I won't. Don't listen to your aunt, only listen to me."

"I don't have to do my homework when she says?"

"You do your homework 'cause *I* say."

"...Okay."

"Okay."

He listened for the boy to fall asleep. It didn't come, even if there was quiet. Eventually the boy said, "Is Auntie Lida scared of you?"

"Hmm," he said, with his eyes shut.

"Why's Auntie Lida scared of you?"

"Because I love you," he said. "More than her. Always remember that."

He walked his son to school, holding his hand. Lida hadn't come out of her room for breakfast and he disabled the comm unit before leaving the house. He took his gun with him too, hidden beneath his clothes. It was a sunny day but the sidewalk lay littered with blips of news, flickering under the sun every time they stepped on it. All of the news surrounded the murder of the King. Assassination. Mourning. Replayed footage of the man on the floor of his hotel suite, a fallen effigy. Blood in circles around his body. Grainy evidence out to the world that a heinous crime had been committed. The Chancellor vowing investigation and vengeance. Crying young princes. The King of Peace was dead. Hope was lost. Barrur was bulking their army at once. The world predicted war before the season passed.

"The only war worth engaging in is the war against lies. The war against ignorance. The war against intolerance. We must create the peace we want in the land through the peace we keep within ourselves. Be kind. Be open. Be as vast as the Bleach in your acceptance of others. Be vigilant against apathy."

The King's words followed him and his son, echoing up from the ground upon which they walked, as if rhetoric were made of stone. Yes the King was a man of peace. But he'd also built an army over the years in the event that his enemies decided to march toward the city. First they would breach the walls there, and then they would swarm across the Bleach and take every town in the King's domain brick by brick.

There was no better end to peace than a sense of vengeance, and the people of his town cried out for their share. It rumbled in the earth like dragons being born.

Thirty young faces stared at him from behind their screens. He saw his own faint image in thirty flat pieces of optimized glass, in reverse. The teacher stood to his right, near the windows, and his son sat in the front row directly before him, smiling. Other parents sat in a line against the left wall like convicts about to be mass sentenced. *This is Jatey's father. We are happy to have him here for Parent Day. Please be polite but feel free to ask him questions. We are here to learn.*

Some others had spoken. Teachers, engineers, courtiers, dancers, artists, technicians, house managers. Doctors. Soldiers.

He said, "I'm a mercenary." Because that was a kinder version of the truth.

The students shifted and sat up a little straighter. His son smiled wider. He felt the teacher take a step toward him as if to stop him, and all of the parents now stared like their children. Before anyone could say anything, a little girl stuck up her hand.

"Does that mean anyone can hire you? For money? And you'd do what they said?"

"One question only, Marda," the teacher warned, but sounded unsure.

"Not just anyone," he said. "But yes."

"Have you killed people?"

"Are you bad?"

"Where's your wife?"

"Are you rich?"

"Are you a murderer?"

Perhaps his sister was right. Perhaps this wasn't a good idea. The soldier in the room had tight eyes. Perhaps he should have lied outright, but it was a part of his registered identity that he was a mercenary. Because he had been long ago, when he hadn't lived in this land. The King had been the only King of Peace. In other places there was need for him and others like him.

"Is he a murderer?" He pointed to the soldier father of another student. "He's paid as well."

The children had no answer. The soldier looked offended. Then one child in the corner raised her hand and said, "But he fights for the King. Who do you fight for?"

They were here to educate. As adults and parents. He thought the better strategy in childrearing was to never lie to your kid, though you never told them everything at once. Now was a time for specific truth. He said to both his son and his son's classmates, "I fight for myself. That's a belief that can never be shaken."

Lida would tell him that was still a lie. But she had never understood that he never doubted himself. Other men were fallible, even the great King of Peace. Men like him, hired assassins—they were just efficient.

The state funeral ran long and broadcast on every channel. Lida forced the TV on and there would be no shutting it off without some kind of major argument. His son lay on the couch watching too. An hour into it and he told the boy to go to bed. "But why? I want to watch!" Go to bed. His tone was cruel and the boy ran off to his room in a pout. Lida looked at him and he left her with the pageantry on the TV and followed Jatey into the bedroom and shut the door. The boy kicked at him when he sat on the edge of the bed and tried to get a stubborn body to roll over.

"You didn't care when mommy died either!"

So much accusation made in ignorance. This was the forever battle between father and child.

"She didn't die," he said. "She left. But death is the endpoint. Your aunt lied to you about that and I'm sorry I never explained the truth."

The kicking grew worse. He grabbed hold and gathered up, and said nothing more. Death was something you understood the older you got, and for his son it would come eventually. Inevitably. The hatred would pass. The fairy tale had died. The King was dead. He held his son while the boy worked it out in breaths and rebellion, then fell quiet in his arms. The endpoint was this and sooner or later his son would realize that too. The endpoint was him, the father. The one who came from the desert and the one who would take him back.

The boy fell asleep in his arms and he tucked him under the blankets and kissed the soft blond hair. His gun lay where he'd left it after coming home from the school, set in the nightstand with the blush orange putty and the twenty million he now possessed. He picked up the gun and found a clip beneath his papers in the second drawer and loaded the gun with it and chambered a round. He left the bedroom and shut the door behind him quietly, then took the two steps to his sister's room and opened the door and slipped inside. The house was quiet and she lay in bed, her face to the moonlight as if that would make her grow.

The only mercy in this was that she remained asleep. He picked up one of the pillows and covered her head with it, then pressed the point of the gun into the soft down and pulled the trigger three times. It still made a sound but not enough to exit the walls of the house. Then he left her room and went back into his bedroom where the boy slept. Jatey had always been able to sleep through storms.

He gathered the putty and two more of his guns, ammunition, a couple blades, a change of clothes for both him and his son, some official papers and extra bottles of water from the kitchen. A couple hats. Everything else he'd buried long ago across the Bleach and those caches would serve him now, like he'd always known they would one day. When the bag was ready he went back to his son and shook him awake. "Come with me, baby." And his son followed him, holding his hand, as sleepy as the night but as unquestioning as the moon.

Finally as their steps across the midnight sand grew numerous in the hour, Jatey said, "Where are we going, Daddy?"

"We'll spend some nights out with the sand dragons, just like we always do. We're going north."

"Are we going to find Mommy?"

"No. Mommy's nowhere to be found."

The silence was born from thoughts. Then: "Is Auntie Lida lost too?"

"Auntie Lida is dead."

The truth began now, in parcels, in grains of sand. In footsteps. He looked ahead at the pale dunes and the inverted cranium of stars all blinking with their own thoughts and perhaps with some judgment. It didn't matter. Nothing else mattered when he felt the little hand caught in his palm squeeze back as if his son were afraid he, the father, would be the next one to be lost. The next one to die.

"Why is Auntie Lida dead?"

"Because I love you more." He looked down at the blond boy beside him, this miniature mirror to his own features, or some rewinding of his history. "Do you love me more?"

Tears coated the words. "Yes, Daddy." And the hand gripped him tighter.

They walked on across the Bleach.

"I don't have to go back to school?"

"Not soon."

"I'll miss school."

"I'll teach you now."

He leaned down and picked up the child in his arms, and held him as he walked, now only one set of footprints and soon even those would be swept away in the hot shuffle of the Bleach's whims and moods. When the sun rose they would rest. Eventually the boy fell silent again, asleep on his shoulder, and not even the sand dragons howled, as if they too lay buried in a dormancy only violence could reawaken.

---

KARIN LOWACHEE was born in South America, grew up in Canada, and worked in the Arctic. Her first novel *Warchild* won the 2001 Warner Aspect First Novel Contest. Both *Warchild* (2002) and her third novel *Cagebird* (2005) were finalists for the Philip K. Dick Award. *Cagebird* won the Prix Aurora Award in 2006 for Best Long-Form Work in English and the Spectrum Award also in 2006. Her second novel *Burndive* debuted at #7 on the Locus Bestseller List. Her books have been translated into French, Hebrew, and Japanese, and her short stories have appeared in anthologies edited by Julie Czerneda, Nalo Hopkinson, and John Joseph Adams. Her latest fantasy novel, *The Gaslight Dogs*, was published through Orbit Books USA.

# THE WOMAN WHO SHATTERED THE MOON

## *Jay Lake*

I AM THE MOST famous woman in the world.

That's something to be proud of, something no one else can say. It does not matter that the European bastards have locked me up for the past forty-one years, seven months and eleven days. It does not matter that they dynamited my stronghold and sealed off the steam vents that drove my turbines and powered my ambitions. It does not matter that Fleet Street and the American press and governments from the Kaiser's Germany to Imperial Japan have all forbidden my name from being mentioned in writing.

Despite all that, they cannot unmake me, because every night my greatest deed glimmers in the sky, a permanent reminder that I am the woman who shattered the moon.

Colonel Loewe comes to see me every Tuesday. He is proper, starched and creased in his lobster-red uniform with the white Sam Browne belt smelling faintly of oiled leather. His moustache is full and curved, something that must have come into fashion after I'd been imprisoned here in this hidden fortress, as it looks silly to me. In recent times, he has grown exactly nine white hairs hidden in the auburn of the moustache. The colonel's face is sometimes as red as his jacket. I am never certain if this is exertion or anger.

We meet in a tiny room with a knife-scarred wooden table between us. The floor consists of boards ten centimeters in width. There are thirty-six of them in a row most of the time. Some weeks there are thirty-seven of them. My jailors think I do not notice these little changes. It is much the same as the patterns in the dust and cobwebs, for nothing is clean in this place except what I clean for myself. I save my old toothbrushes to scrub out the mortared joins in the stone walls of my cell.

The walls of our meeting rooms are covered in stucco, so I do not know if they are stone beneath. I see patterns in the plastering, but they are never the same, so I suspect my own imagination may be at fault.

Either that or they have many more nearly identical rooms here than seems practical simply for the purpose of manipulating a single prisoner.

This week, Colonel Loewe has brought me a chipped stoneware mug filled with a steaming brown liquid which appears to be coffee. After eleven years and fourteen weeks as my interrogator, he knows my ways, so with a small smile, the colonel sips from the mug to prove to me that it is not something dangerous or unpalatable.

I inhale the rich, dark scent. There is of course the possibility that he previously took an antidote, but even in my darkest moments I recognize that if my jailors wished to kill me, they have had ample opportunities over the decades. Whatever my final end will amount to, I strongly doubt it will be poisoning at the hands of the colonel.

"Madame Mbacha." He always greets me politely. The coffee is a break in the routine.

I take the mug, the warmth of it loosening the painful tension that always afflicts my hands these years. The odor indicates a Kenyan bean. Another small politeness, to bring me an African variety.

"Good morning, Colonel." I follow our ritual even as I wonder what the coffee signifies. The routine is that he asks about my work, my machines, precisely how I shattered the moon from my East African mountain fastness. In all my years here, I have never revealed my secrets, though I am sure forensic teams extracted much from my laboratories before their terminal vandalism rendered my works into dust.

Why should I offer confirmation of their abuse? Why should I give them the secrets of gravity which I and I alone discovered, after being laughed away from the great universities of Europe and America for the inescapable twinned flaws of being African and a woman!?

What Colonel Loewe should say now is, "Let us review the facts of your case." That has been his second line for the entire time he has been my interrogator. Instead he surprises me by departing from his script.

"I have news," the colonel tells me.

I tamp down a rush of frustrated anger. In my years of incarceration I have become very good at containing my feelings. Long gone are the days when I could work out my troubles on some trembling servant or prisoner. Still, how dare he change our rules now?

"What news, Colonel?" My voice barely betrays my intensity of emotion. This cannot be good. Change is never good.

He clears his throat, seeming almost embarrassed for a moment. "Madame Mbacha, it is my happy duty to inform you that your parole has been granted by the plenary session of the League of Nations on humanitarian grounds. You will shortly be processed for release, and will be free to go where you will, within certain restrictions intended for your own safety."

I stare at the colonel for a long moment, then began to laugh. It is the only way I can stop the tears that threaten to well up.

Home. I can go home. The one thing I have never expected here in my imprisonment was to ever be allowed home again.

They bring me a newspaper with my supper. Such a thing has never before happened in my time in this prison. The change in routine intensifies my discomfort. At least the meal is consistent. I have been served the Tuesday menu. Sausage and cabbage, steamed so the meaty scent mingles with rankness of the vegetable. Also hard brown bread. The relief cook is on duty, I can tell by the way the food is prepared. Even that is part of the routine, though his shift does vary.

I glare at the folded newsprint as if it were a rat snuck into my cell. *The Times* of London, a respectable and credible outlet. The lead story concerns ongoing negotiations over changes to fishing rights in the North Sea. Apparently the cessation of lunar tides continues to exert significant effects on marine life, as does the changing rotational period of the Earth in the absence of lunar drag. Fish stocks have shifted catastrophically time and again in the decades since my master plan came to fruition.

At this I can only laugh. Long dormant emotions are beginning to stir within me. To be in the world, to walk under an open sky as I have not done since the last day of my so-called trial. Why, once more I can do anything.

I give vent to a rising bubble of glee. Even with my eyes closed, I could measure this cell to the centimeter. My voice echoing off the walls gives me an aural map just as accurate as my visual observations and memories.

The process of my release takes several more weeks. The newspaper left nightly with my meal mentions nothing of me or my fate, though I do learn much about the state of the world. Many of those things are incredible, even to me who mastered electricity, magnetism and gravity in the days of my youthful ascendancy. It took a combined Anglo-German army reinforced by numerous battalions of African *askari* to bring me down, in the end. Still, I had not anticipated the development of aeroplanes or thermionic valves or electronic switches. My world once consisted of iron and brass mechanical behemoths motivated by the pressure and heat of steam.

The colonel still comes on Tuesdays, but now I also have other callers. A milliner, to clothe me fit for today's street, at least its European variety. An alienist to discuss with me how people might be expected to behave. A geographer to inform me of the current state of empires, colonies and independent kingdoms in the West Africa of my birth and upbringing, and the East Africa of the years of my power.

"Kilima Njaro is preserved by the Treaty of Mombasa," the small, serious man with the Austrian accent informs me.

"Preserved?" I ask.

"Set aside by multinational acclamation as a natural area to maintain its beauty and bounty." His voice is prim, though he rattles off those words as if he does not quite believe them himself.

I smile at the geographer. Already I know this unnerves him. I am history's supreme villain, after all. My deeds rewrote the night sky, triggered floods and famines that altered the fates of entire nations of people. Self-satisfied white men such as this fussy little lavender-scented Herr Doctor Professor have trouble compassing the idea that a woman born of Africa could have accomplished such mighty perfidy. Even the prosecution at my trial at one point advanced the notion that I must have been a stalking horse for some unknown evil genius of European or American origins.

So my smile, coupled with the power of my personality that has faded so little with age, disturbs this man. Much to my delight. I ask in his native German, "And this Treaty of Mombasa was signed shortly after my capture, I presume?"

He sticks to the English that my jailors speak. "Ah, in fact, yes."

"So what they are preserving is the ruins of my stronghold. Lest some malcontent unearth the secrets of my strength and turn my lost machines against the Great Powers." I lean forward, allowing my smile to broaden further. "Or perhaps worse, prevent European scientists from successfully publishing my research as their own?"

Now the little geographer is completely flustered. I know I have struck home. So it goes.

The last time I see Colonel Loewe, he speaks more frankly than anyone ever has since I was first subdued and captured on the slopes of my mountain, fleeing my besieged stronghold. It is a Tuesday, of course. Some things do not change. I, who am about to see more change than I have in decades, choose to interpret this as courtesy on his part.

"Madame Mbacha." He once more offers me coffee.

"Colonel Loewe." I nod, grant him that same broad smile I have used to upset some of my other visitors.

His voice grows stern. "I must inform you that as a matter of personal opinion, I am not in favor of your parole."

*Interesting.* "Thank you for your honesty, Colonel. Why do you think thusly?"

"These people at the League of Nations do not know you as I know you." His fingertips drum briefly on the table. "They barely know of you, except as a rumored evil slumping into your dotage."

*Dotage!?* I will show them dotage. I hold my tongue, of course.

The colonel continues. "I am well aware that even I barely know you. Always you have guarded your tongue as jealously as any citadel's sally port." After a moment he adds with further reluctant candor, "Though for many reasons I wish matters were otherwise, I cannot help but admire your strength of character."

I am near to being enchanted by his words. Flattery is one unction that has been denied to me in the more than four decades since my capture. "Do go on," I tell him in a throaty whisper which even at my age can distract all but the most determined men.

"You and I both know full well you are slumped into nothing, especially not dotage. Age has not dimmed your fires, only brought you to a preternatural discretion. I have noted this in my reports over the years. In my judgment, you are still by far the most dangerous woman on Earth." Another drumbeat of the fingertips. "The most dangerous person of either gender, in truth."

"It is hoped," he continues, "that four decades of incarceration have mellowed you, and that what prison has failed to accomplish the inevitable withering of time will have managed. Your release is seen as a humanitarian gesture, proposed by some of the new regimes in the tropical lands that are slowly emerging from colonial patronage. You are a hero in the tropical villages of Africa, of Asia, and of South America, Madame Mbacha." He clears his throat, sending his moustache wobbling. "But we also both know you are still the greatest villain who ever lived."

I wait a long, polite moment to see if the colonel was finished speaking. Then I take pity on him, for he is flushed and perspiring, obviously uncomfortable with himself.

"They are not far from wrong," I tell him. "My years here have made of me an old woman. I do not have the funds or the equipment to embark on grand ambitions. Nor, frankly, the years." I take brief joy in imagining his precious London burning, choking in clouds of toxic chemical fog, assaulted by clanking monsters rising from the bed of the Thames. "Whatever is in my heart must remain there, hostage to age and penury, not to mention the watchers you and yours will surely be setting to dog my every step between the door of this prison and the grave I eventually find."

"Fair enough." His eyes flick down to his hands as if his fingers were an unexpected novelty. Then Colonel Loewe meets my gaze once more. "If you will, for the sake of all that has passed between us these dozen years, please indulge me with the answer to one final question." He raises a hand to forestall my answer. "This is my own curiosity. Not for any report I shall write, nothing to be used against you."

I wonder what could be so important to him now, though it would not be too difficult to guess.

"With all the unimaginable power you commanded, why did you lay waste to the moon? If you'd wanted to free the nations of the tropic world from colonial bondage, why not destroy London or Paris or Berlin, or sink the fleets of the world powers?" He sounds almost apologetic.

The question makes me laugh. A full-throated laugh, the delight I'd once taken in powering up a new machine, in uncovering a novel physical principle of material progress and destruction, in arranging a particularly baroque and painful fate for some interloping spy or traitorous servant. I'm certain it makes me sound mad to him, but what do I care now?

Finally I regain control of my voice. "Believe me, Colonel, once I'd perfected my gravitational gun, I considered those other targets and more. I could have altered the balance of the Great Powers in a single moment. But for every city destroyed, every ship sunk, every army brought to its knees, three more would have sprung up in their place. You Europeans are like the god Eshu, sly tricksters who make a lie of the world with the strength of your guns and gold. In a dozen years, you would have rebuilt and remade and convinced yourself my strike against you had never happened, or had been of little consequence. But who can deny the loss of the moon? So long as men and women live in the world and lift their eyes to the night sky, you will be reminded that at least for a while, there was a power greater and more fearful than even your own."

"In other words," he says quietly after a thoughtful silence, "you destroyed the moon because you could."

"Well, yes." I smile again. "And if my gravitational gun had not imploded, I might well have gone on to destroy London and Paris and Berlin. I chose my most lasting target first." I lean against the table, almost pushing it in to him. "I *will* be remembered."

When I walk out of the prison, the daylight is blinding. I have not seen the sun in over forty years. I stumble against the physical pressure of its brilliance. Guards flank and support me, corporals in the same uniform that Colonel Loewe wears.

I'd never known where my prison was. They had brought me here by night after my trial in a secret courtroom in Brussels, the capital of that mad despot King Leopold. Now *there* was a city I should have destroyed. I was brought not just by night but also blindfolded, as I'd been moved from armored omnibus to sealed railway carriage to a cabin on a boat or ship.

England, almost certainly, for where else would one take ship to from Belgium, at least for a short voyage? And English had always been the language of my imprisonment. Still, I am surprised to find myself on the verge of a busy city street amid scents of petroleum and cooking oil and hurried, unwashed people. Gleaming horseless carriages careen past with a clattering of engines and a blaring of claxons. Men and women wearing unfamiliar fashions throng the pavements alongside the roadway. Airships and aeroplanes dot the sky.

My breath grows short and hard as a headache stabs through my eyes to interrupt my thoughts with vicious distraction. Dizziness threatens, and despite my best efforts, I feel perspiration shivering on my face and about my person.

"'ere you are, missus," says one of the guards. He presses a cheap cardboard suitcase into my right hand. "They've put your walking money inside. I'd be careful of snatchers."

With that, I am alone and free for the first time in more than half my life. I take a deep breath, look up into the harsh, brilliant sky, and see a silvery band stretching from horizon to horizon. The Ring of the Moon, they call it. My signature upon this Earth.

Even amid the pain and panic of the moment, my smile returns a thousandfold. Then I set out to find my way home.

The borders around the Kilima Njaro Preserve are secured by soldiers from a number of European states. It seems that Africans cannot be trusted to protect our own. There is a wall, as well, topped in places with electrical wires and brass light pipes through which guards might spy on distant locations. Still, it is not hard to find men among the Kikuyu who know how to slip through the animal gates. They poach, and gather from the forests on the lower slopes of the mountains, and generally show the white men their asses.

These are not my people—I was born half a continent away—but they and I are of one mind when it comes to British, Frenchmen, Germans, Belgians, Russians and others. Joseph, my guide, has been engaged for a quantity of silver rupees I earned through various chicaneries and the sorts of petty crimes open to a woman of advancing years. Once I'd gained my needed funds, it had not been so challenging to slip away from Colonel Loewe's watchers in Mombasa, where I was but one among many thousands of old African women.

I have not told my guide who I truly am, and I am certain it has not occurred to him to guess. If nothing else, he was not even born when I shattered the moon. Tales of Madame Mbacha and her gravitational gun are surely just as legendary and improbable to a young man as are his parents' stories of the days of their own youth.

Still, whether he thinks me mad or simply lost in the world does not matter. Joseph smiles easily, his teeth gleaming in the dark. His ragged canvas shirt and duck trousers are sufficiently reddened with the ground-in dust of the savannah to keep him unobtrusive in these grasslands below my mountain. I myself am equipped with tropical weight camouflage which Joseph finds an endless source of amusement.

"You are an old woman," he declares, his Kikuyu accent inflecting his English in a way I had not known I'd missed during the years of my imprisonment. "Why do you want to look like a German bush ranger?"

"For the same reason German bush rangers dress like this. To not be seen."

He shrugs eloquently. "You do not come to fight. There is nothing to see here except what is here."

True, I carry no firearm. I never have. There were always others to do the shooting for me. Joseph has a rifle, an old bolt action Mauser that I suspect is more dangerous to him than to any lions or soldiers he might shoot at. "Sometimes seeing what is here is enough," I tell him.

He does not need to know.

We take our time, moving by night and sleeping by daylight against clay banks or hidden in low-lying hollows. The guardians of the Kilima Njaro preserve fly overhead periodically in small aircraft that drone like wasps. Twice we hear the chuffing clank of European steam walkers and even catch the scorched metal scent of their boilers, though we never actually see the machines. Neither do they see us. Joseph and I are small and hard to find, as if we were beetles on a banyan tree.

My only complaint, which of course I do not voice, is the heat. I, who once worked with great gouts of steam and the fires of a foundry to build my ambitions. I, who was birthed amid the parched plains of western Kamerun. Slowly I come to admit that the years spent entombed in cold British stone have sapped my bones of their youthful fire.

After four days we gain the slopes of the mountain. I am on my home ground now, and have begun to see traces of my old roadways, the supply lines that brought game meat, grain and other supplies from the surrounding countryside up to my stronghold. The heat seems more bearable up on the slopes, where the breezes can more easily reach us and trees spread shade from time to time.

"There is nothing here," Joseph says uneasily one evening as we break our camp. A collapsed, fire-scarred stump of one of my watchtowers stands close by. "I do not think we should go on. Haven't you seen enough?"

"I can find my way from here," I say politely. Back in my day, I would have had him whipped for cowardice and sent to take a turn stoking the fires of my industry. Now I must rely upon this man to stay alive. I press another sack of silver rupees into his hand. "Give me a water gourd and wait in this place for two days. If I do not return, make your way home and forget you ever saw me."

"There are ghosts here," he says uneasily. Then: "I will wait."

Perhaps he will, perhaps he will not. I tell myself this does not matter, that I am almost home.

I hike the last few kilometers alone. Even in the evening, the heat persists in bothering me, so to put my mind at ease I review the triumphs of my life. The moon, of course, first and foremost. But also how in my youth I bested the chief's son in my home village and left him crying for his manhood which I took away in a *muti* pouch. How I'd learned the physics and chemistry and mathematics of the Europeans while working as a cleaner in the universities at Heidelberg and Cambridge. How I'd carved out my own domain in the savannahs of Kenya and Tanganyika, laying the foundations for what would become my stronghold on Kilima Njaro.

Madame Goodwill Adeola Mbacha, scourge of the white race. When my resolve falters or my memories fade, all I need do is lift my eyes to the Ring of the Moon and I am reminded of all I have accomplished.

I come across the outer gates by starlight. They are shattered, their tumbled ruins covered with cloying flowers and acrid-scented shrubs. Vividly I recall the cannon fire that laid waste to my defenses. I walk past a row of nearly vanished graves, surely guards and servants of mine buried where they fell.

Ahead, where the walls of my stronghold should have risen, there is only a larger, night shadowed heap of rubble. No flowers there. I wonder if my enemies salted the ruins to keep them barren. Slowly, still sweating profusely, I make a deliberate circuit of the destroyed fortification, taking four thousand, one hundred and twenty-seven paces to do so.

It is all gone. My laboratories, the refineries. The little railroad that brought in wood and ore for my smelters has been ripped up completely and the bed trenched so it would erode.

Somehow, I'd thought there would be something more of home here. A doorway, a room, a place to start again.

My aching bones and shaking hands tell me that I am old. The heat tells me this is not a place to rekindle forge fires and drill anew for steam vents. The dusty, bitter air tells me I do not belong here.

For a while I sit on tumbled, fire-blackened stones and weep. I, who have not wept since earliest childhood, let the tears flow unchecked. Even the Ring of the Moon seems a mockery, my lost power glimmering in the sky day and night as the world rearranges itself around missing tides and deeper nocturnal darknesses.

In the morning I walk back down the mountain to where Joseph should still be waiting. I bid the graves farewell as I pass them. The slope is hard on my hips and knees. My mind should be awhirl with plans and possibilities, but I cannot summon the energy. It is too late in my life to start over.

I just want to go home. Is that giving up? The world lives with my mark. I've accomplished more than they can ever take away from me. Now I can return to Mombasa and allow Colonel Loewe's agents to find me. Having broken my parole, they will remove me once more to my cool, stone-walled room in the depths of London.

Home is where you live, after all. I have lived most of my life there, and there I will live the rest of my life.

"Colonel," I tell the uncaring thornwood trees and the bone dry wind, "I am coming home."

---

JAY LAKE lives in Portland, Oregon, where he works on numerous writing and editing projects. His 2012 books are *Kalimpura* from Tor Books, and *Love in the Time of Metal and Flesh* from Prime Books. His short fiction appears regularly in literary and genre markets worldwide. Jay is a past winner of the John W. Campbell Award for Best New Writer, and a multiple nominee for the Hugo and World Fantasy Awards. Jay can be reached through his blog at jlake.com.

# CHARITY

## *Julie E. Czerneda*

Throughout the labyrinth of pods and corridor tendrils that was the Ship, strings hummed into motion at the 3rd divide of the 4th cycle, pulling denizens to their assigned tasks, drawing others home from their labours. The procession was orderly and swift, for denizens built well and with forethought. Tails wrapped or claws did. Those with burdens took advantage of hooks. Like commuters anywhere, some gossiped as they traveled while others buried their broad snouts in readers or dozed.

The journey was a full 8th longer since the new pods had budded, ready to be coaxed into useful structures, but no one complained. More housing was a now-urgent need. The oldest pods were hollow, unlivable shells; the Ship would soon shed them. The denizen population, ever-growing, had been prepared, about to expand into the next cluster of freshly prepared and furnished pods, but that was no longer possible.

Others lived there now. Others who found the pods to their taste, if not the strings connecting them. He'd see some if he looked in what wasn't down, but was away and dark and narrow, for the others traveled the corridor's machineway, clinging to conveyors and assemblers and fabricators like bits of lint.

1055th Sanitation Engineer Tissop snapped his thumb over the decel string, releasing his tail's curl around the corridor string with an instant's delay that spun his body towards the waiting iris of his home. The flashy move gained him askance looks from those speeding past in either direction, but they were ordinary denizens and unimportant.

The iris membrane let him through, absorbing his momentum so Tissop entered his home with the calm dignity of someone now far from ordinary and exceedingly important.

To be greeted by floating green balls.

"Children! Catch dessert!" Raekl gave him an apologetic look as she herded their latest litter in chase. "A good cycle, husband?"

Tissop dodged the leading edge of the swarm only to collide with the mass that followed. His uniform, spotless through an entire shift, acquired blobs of sticky green goo.

"Sorry, father!" Rus, Ssu, and Spel bounced and tumbled through the

153

air in pursuit with the nonchalant grace of those raised in null-g, catching the errant food in open mouths; likely their plan all along. They were, he thought with proud exasperation, too clever for anyone's good. No leaving this set with a minder. They'd have the poor denizen tied up by his or her tail and locked in a cupboard in moments.

Gravity would help, but that required a home within a pod's gentle rotation, not blistered from a corridor. The Ship responded to such wounds with increased growth, so denizens took their turn living like this. That didn't mean they enjoyed it. Denizens belonged where they could use their pairs of strong legs and even stronger arms, where food could be lapped from proper bowls instead of sucked from bulbs, where bathing could be a properly luxurious soak instead of a process requiring a sack, scrub aerosols, and vacuum hose.

Soon, Tissop thought fervently. Soon.

"Your day?" Raekl reminded, gathering Ssu with her tail and eyeing the other two sternly.

Despite three litters and advancing age, she was handsome. Some silver on her magnificent snout and above those expressive eyes; a roundness to her shoulders and back from cycles spent at her consoles. Neither mattered. Raekl was exceptional in every way and much too good for the denizen he'd been.

Until now. At last, finally, he deserved her. "My day," Tissop proclaimed with satisfaction, "was—" He stopped short, nostrils flared at an unexpected, all too familiar scent. It couldn't be. It wasn't possible.

It was. Raekl dipped her snout in greeting as the other floated from the main room to join them in the antechamber. "There was a mix-up in the shifts," she explained. "I told Curtis you wouldn't mind."

He did mind. He minded each and every 5th cycle, when this two-armed, two-legged intruder in black arrived to share their table, but Raekl was only being kind. She worked with Curtis in the biolabs on the 5th cycle shift and the newcomer came for supper afterwards.

4th cycle, Curtis shouldn't be here. 4th cycle, Curtis belonged in a mid-cluster pod, with other refugees.

Oh, they had another name for themselves, albeit untranslatable, and polite denizens referred to them simply as newcomers, but the truth was what it was. They'd no home of their own—why, no one had explained. Rumour, that mainstay of news, claimed their vessels had been ludicrously ill-suited to deep space—yet, that's where they'd been, remnants of some disaster, adrift and desperate and alone, until the Ship passed by.

Or rather, here they were, for how could denizens ignore their plight?

Easily, Tissop grumbled to himself, glaring at Curtis. But those who guided the Ship hadn't asked the opinion of those forced to remain in substandard housing along the corridors while strangers took their promised homes. Yes, the Ship would grow new pods, especially, as was its way, having absorbed what it craved from the newcomers' vessels, but the process wasn't quick. By some accounts, the new pods wouldn't be ready until his latest litter needed homes for theirs. They'd be stuck in the corridors, exposed to null-g longer than any denizen should be.

Or so the rest believed, accepting their fate. Denizens were dutiful.

His skin tingled with pleasure, cilia rising along the insides of his arms, as Tissop contemplated the evening newsfeed. Oh, the uproar to come...the hasty explanations. How could such a thing happen?

Only he would know. Tissop the extraordinary. On the commute home, he'd fantasized telling his family what he'd done, imagined them sharing his triumph when all unfolded as he, Tissop, planned, but of course he mustn't. The result would be enough.

Of course, on the commute home, he'd been sure they'd be eating alone.

With Curtis somehow present—the matter of how being of considerable, if untenable, interest—the sour note in Tissop's stomach assured him anonymity was indeed best.

From Raekl's troubled scent, he'd been silent too long. "Why would I mind?" he declared with forced cheer. "Greetings, Curtis."

Curtis spread her lips, exposing flat, uninteresting teeth. She—for it claimed to be female despite lacking any feminine trait he could discern—hadn't learned this first, least lesson in courtesy, but then, the newcomers weren't ones for blending, Tissop thought with familiar irritation. "Greetings, friend Tissop. Clean any sewers?"

"Someone must." Tissop mimed her smile, ignoring Raekl's disapproval as he exposed the brilliant orange of his upper toothplate. It wasn't as if the newcomer could grasp the crudeness. "And you, Curtis? Cure any plagues?"

The creature laughed. The newsfeeds called it a fortunate congruence, that both races expressed humour in a similar fashion. Tissop had yet to be convinced Curtis' laughter had anything to do with amusement.

Shooing their wide-eyed children into the other room, Raekl slipped her tail into the crook of Curtis' arm as if to apologize for her husband's lack of manners. "I've made your favourite," she assured their guest. Tissop's stomach turned again. The offering that so pleased their foreign visitor gave him gas. "We can share our accomplishments at the table, husband," this with a hint of orange beneath her lip. "Once you change into clean clothes."

Cowed, Tissop ducked his snout in mute acquiescence.

Curtis smiled again.

Much as Tissop longed to access the newsfeed, given Raekl's mood, he dared not. He'd have settled for curling in his webbing chair with a bulb of fermented nectar to soothe his abused gut, but that small respite was denied. Their litter had learned a splendid new song in school today and nothing would serve after supper but the adults, including Curtis, stay hooked to the table to pay due attention to the performance.

Performance? Torture, as he'd feared. Rus was loud, Ssu tone-deaf, and little Spel, over-stimulated by their romp with dessert, sang faster and faster. With grim determination, Raekl kept her ears up and forward; every so often her eyes darted to check the state of his, in case he quailed.

Having noticed the high notes made Curtis wince, Tissop was more inclined to ask his litter for another song, but Raekl would have seen through it. She made sure he behaved as a proper denizen should and he was grateful, most of the time.

If only he dared tell her what he'd done for them all.

Just thinking of it, with Curtis in the same room, filled Tissop with a sneaky, inner warmth. Not sneaky enough, for Raekl's lovely nostrils flared with interest and she ran a thoughtful claw through the cloud of her mane in a way that suggested he offer to bath the litter and tie them in their sacks early.

"What shall we play?" Scent-blind and oblivious, Curtis pushed herself as deftly as any denizen from the table to the cupboard on the ceiling where Raekl stored the games. Not that corridor quarters had ceilings or floors, being without gravity, but the words were their own comfort. Denizens could be stubborn as well as clever.

Tissop sighed, the inadvertent exhalation sending him back towards the wall. He damped the motion with a stroke of his tail along the table edge and decided to make the best of it. The news would get out and these painful evenings would end. "Anything but glantstix," he offered generously. The newcomer's squishy digits gave her an unfair advantage.

"It's Raekl's turn to pick—" Curtis began.

Suddenly the lights dimmed, both table top and ambient, then pulsed a painful, warning orange.

The children sailed to their mother, clinging to her torso, while she, fearing the worst, soared to the emergency cupboard with a powerful thrust of both legs.

"It's not a breach!" Tissop blurted.

They all, children, wife, and guest, stared at him. Raekl took hold of the cupboard egress, but hesitated, her mane adrift. "How can—"

The orange faded and normal lighting resumed.

"See?" he said quickly. "A system test." But surely it wasn't. As Tissop waited for the announcement to follow, he found himself unable to look towards Curtis. He didn't fear her; the newcomers were a puny race by denizen standards and Curtis small for her kind. The children were more than a match, let alone Raekl or himself.

But he wasn't ready to see her face when she heard the news.

"Tissop?"

"Listen."

The lights brightened once more, then normal lighting was restored. The voice he'd expected filled the air. The denizen who spoke for the Ship was always calm and confident, managing to blend the soothing undertone of a minder with the precise snap of a leader.

Until now. This voice shook and stammered, words pouring out in an alarming flood. "Fellow—fellow d-denizens. A d-disaster of unprecedented severity has taken p-place. We remain safe, thanks to the Ship and thanks to you, but we're not out of d-danger. 6th cycle shifts are cancelled, without exception. String m-movement has ceased. Stay within your homes or workplaces until further notice."

Schooling his expression as best he could, Tissop waited impatiently for the rest, for the explanation and his triumph.

But the broadcast ended there.

"Mark my words," Curtis said carelessly, "it'll be the plumbing. Always is, on ships." She opened the games cupboard. "Might as well play. Glantstix, was it, Tissop? I'll spot you the first couplet."

Freeing herself from their trembling litter, Raekl gave Tissop a meaningful look. He tried to give back one of his own, but she lifted her lip and he lost. "You're welcome to spend the night, Curtis," he muttered without grace, though why his home should be violated, only the Ship knew.

"An excellent suggestion, husband. I'll find a fresh sack." Having settled matters, Raekl was in her element as host. She eyed their guest. "I believe one of the children's will do. You're so nicely compact, Curtis."

The com panel blinked a summons. Raekl made to answer, then stopped. "Tissop, it's your code. Marked urgent."

His? "I'll take it in our room," Tissop announced, trying to sound as though such summons happened every cycle instead of never. He pushed himself through the iris before Raekl could say another word.

His stained uniform floated accusingly in midair. Tissop used his tail to flick it aside as he passed, hands gripping the strings that made this and several actions feasible in null-g. At the panel, he took hold of the child-proof netting Ssu had dismantled twice, that they knew, and breathed on the intake to establish his identity. Steady, he told himself, his insides fluttering. He'd planned for this, planned for everything.

"All sanitation engineers suit and report to stations. 1st priority. Acknowledge."

A recording? His lips pulled back in frustration and the netting snapped in his claws.

"All sanitation engineers suit and report to stations. 1st priority.

Acknowledge."

1st priority meant a threat, occurring or imminent, to the populous. Or to the Ship, which amounted to the same thing, since denizens lived nowhere else. Disconcerted, Tissop curled his tail and hunched into a ball, floating in front of the com panel. What he'd done...there was no chance of harm to his own. He wasn't bent.

"—Acknowledge."

The recording would continue, louder with each repetition, until he did. Tissop keyed in his code with a claw, silencing the voice.

What could have gone wrong?

He pulled out his biosuit and began the tedious process of donning it, playing every possible scenario in his mind's eye, as he had each waking divide of every cycle since forming his plan. There was no flaw. No point at which his protocols could or would spread to threaten denizens or the Ship.

Revolving slowly between bedsack and laundry, Tissop slipped his hands into the glove bulb, waiting for the liquid to congeal over skin and claws to form a flexible, protective shield, and thought harder.

He'd been careful, yes, he had. The sanitation process was a simple one, really. Inform the Ship a cupboard was ready to be purged, and the Ship would do so. Nothing more than a change in scale to empty a pod the same way. The trick had been to deal with those inside the pod, for the Ship would not knowingly take life. Even if it would, he could hardly expect the newcomers to remain quiet while every wall collapsed and every ceiling cracked open to space.

He'd been clever, oh yes, and responsible. No one noticed wastes; very few knew or cared where they went—not until there was a problem, then no engineer slept. He'd found a plethora of little tweaks and almost mistakes waiting to be made, each innocent of itself, but their sum? Oh, their sum wasn't innocent at all.

At a time when he, Tissop, was home and asleep in his sack, the sum of little mistakes had bled toxins into a specific air supply. By the time the eager cries of his and Raekl's hungry litter had awakened him, nothing could have awakened those in the newcomer pod.

Sanitation took place as scheduled; the Ship, ever hungry for materials, gleaned what it craved from the debris before resealing the pod. That it destroyed evidence at the same time hardly mattered.

What did was a well-contained—tidy, he thought with content—catastrophe, affecting only newcomers. One pod, emptied by seeming accident. There'd be an investigation or several, but there was nothing to find. Everything he'd done was, of itself, harmless and untraceable.

Like himself, one of the anonymous thousands working in the Ship.

If that first accident proved insufficient, another newcomer pod would be cleansed, then another, in order but at random intervals. He didn't want to exterminate them. That would be vile.

He wanted them off the Ship, that was all.

They'd run, he was sure, as they'd run before. They'd beg the denizens to put them off somewhere, anywhere. A dozen systems lay in reach, any one of which suitable.

And he'd have his Ship back.

So why a 1$^{st}$ priority alert?

Tissop removed his now-gloved hands and pulled on both pairs of boots. He dealt with his tail last. He could have wrapped it around his waist, inside the 'suit, but that was crippling for the sake of convenience. It was worth the time to run the glove bulb from base to tail tip, pressing the appendage into the coating material. Careful, responsible, and thorough. Like any denizen.

Like his plan. Tissop resolved to join the ranks of his fellow sanitation engineers, be one among many, and learn what had happened.

The strings hummed along the corridor, empty of all but grim, suited figures, late heading home. 1055$^{th}$ Sanitation Engineer Tissop dutifully transferred to the decel string well before the iris of his door, letting it slow him to a stop before he entered.

"Raekl, I'm home." No floating globs of dessert greeted him, though it was suppertime. Tissop removed his headgear, careful not to let it float free. Check everything, they'd been told, and he'd done his best for a full cycle. His eyes burned; his mouth felt like pipe insulation. He wanted nothing more than sleep.

No, he wanted answers.

"I don't need supper," he called, to forestall any offerings. The suit came with rations; he hadn't had the stomach for them, not once he'd heard the report.

Yes, a pod had been accidentally sanitized by the Ship, one of the newcomers'. How fortunate none of them had been inside at the time.

Fortunate? Impossible. He'd scanned the pod for biosign before tripping the first of the mistake sequences. It didn't take an expert to read a display that counted hundreds.

For nothing. Not one newcomer was missing. Rumour was rampant, but unhelpful. The most popular involved some newcomer revel, doubtless exotic, gathering them all in another pod.

It made no sense— "Raekl?"

"Greetings, friend Tissop." Curtis slipped effortlessly into the antechamber. "The family's asleep. They stayed awake most of the night, waiting for news." The newcomer, for once, didn't smile. "Is there any?"

"Why are you still here?" Of course she was still here. No unauthorized movement was permitted, not yet, in the corridors. Tissop calmed himself with an effort. "My apologies, Curtis. A long shift."

"I'm sure. Come. If you aren't hungry, then drink with me."

A drink would be welcome. Being invited to do so in his own home was not, but Tissop couldn't find a reply that wasn't churlish. "I'll clean up."

For no reason, Tissop checked on the litter first. Rus, Ssu, and Spel were clustered near the ceiling, their little snouts, wrinkled in sleep, poked from their sacks. He felt a sudden impulse to wake them, to be sure they were fine, but restrained it. Raekl would have had trouble enough getting them calmed to rest, being confined to their quarters all cycle with a houseguest on top of it, and wouldn't thank him.

Drifting close, he inhaled their living breath. At least one, he noted wryly, had neglected to scrub his or her toothplates.

Leaving the children, he went to the room he shared with Raekl. It was dark and chill, the atmosphere reset to their sleep preference, but she'd tethered her sack near the iris to catch him coming home. Tissop managed to slip beneath without waking her. He stripped off the biosuit, tucking the pieces into his sleepsack, breathing deep. Raekl's scent differed from the children's, more complex, tainted with worry and exhaustion, yet above all comforting. He wished to stay; should stay.

Would, but for the alien in his home.

The light within the table was brighter than the ambient when Tissop reentered the main room, casting disturbing, unfamiliar shadows. Curtis sat at one end, having slipped her too-small feet into one of the table loops. An array of clear bulbs clung to the table surface; his entire supply, at a glance. "I didn't know which you'd prefer," the newcomer said blandly, as if Tissop's belongings were hers. The play of light and shadow emphasized the strange length of her jaw and hollowed the sockets of her deep-set eyes. She smiled, teeth bizarrely white. "I like preehn liquor, myself."

Preehn being Tissop's favourite and hard to come by, he scowled and swept up two bulbs of common ale as he came to the table, sending one tumbling at his unwelcome host. Curtis caught it and pressed it to her mouth.

There was a bladder of something more substantial among the bulbs. Leftovers, no doubt. Warmed by the homely gesture, Tissop decided he might be hungry after all and reached for it.

"Something different, that." Curtis chuckled. "We left supper to the little ones while we worked." She took another swallow, a convulsion traveling down her narrow throat. "Kept them busy, but Raekl said to warn you mumpsweets were the main ingredient."

Tissop redirected his reach to another bulb of ale. They'd worked together, in his home. His wife and this—this creature who should, by his calculation, be grieving, if not dead. He drank deeply, then ordered the ambient to normal levels, pleased to see Curtis squint.

The newcomer didn't appear overly discomfited, taking another bulb, this of preehn, and letting her hairless head tip back. "Quite a day. Do you have a deity, friend Tissop?"

He managed not to spew. Despite the air scrubbers, Raekl would notice the smallest tinge of ale. Until the Ship had taken in strangers, only those denizens engaged in trade communicated directly with other races. They'd come on the newsfeeds to instruct the rest, warning that cultural differences could be greater than the physical, urging denizens that offense could be given without intent. Spiritual beliefs were not, under any circumstances, to be discussed by those unqualified. He found he didn't care. "Do newcomers?" Tissop asked boldly.

"Some do, some don't. I'm inclined to believe after what happened today." For once, Curtis read his expression. "What—didn't you hear the report?"

He'd been told the same as the rest: a pod sanitized by accident, disappointingly without casualties. A report given to lower-ranked sanitation engineers might not, Tissop thought uneasily, be the one granted researchers like Curtis and his wife. "The problem was isolated," he said lamely. "An accident—"

"Then why the alert? Why—" with that rude smile "—am I still here?" Curtis held up her bulb of ale, appearing to study it. "What series of happy mistakes led to every inhabitant of that pod being assigned to other quarters on 3rd cycle? A god to thank would be convenient. Unless it was you, friend Tissop. Should we thank you?" Before Tissop could attempt to answer, the newcomer waved the bulb. "Or some faceless denizen, doing his or her duty less well or better than most. Ah! I have another notion—"

Curtis pulled herself closer to him and lowered her voice. "It was the Ship, protecting us." She spread her arms. "Thank you, Ship!"

No, it wasn't. The Ship was alive the way the sludge that ate denizen waste was alive. It didn't make decisions or take actions other than those dictated by the denizens within it. Ships without denizens lodged in asteroid belts, growing aimlessly, trapping hunks of rock to digest what they needed and ignoring the rest.

All of which Tissop kept behind clenched toothplates, abruptly afraid to match wits.

"Which does make me wonder," Curtis said next, seeming content to carry the conversation by herself. "None of us are missing. Why the alert, friend Tissop, unless—do you suppose?—some of you are?"

Fear fluttered in his gut, pushed a thick foul taste to the back of his mouth.

The biosigns. Something had been in the pod. Hundreds of "somethings." It couldn't be...He swallowed, hard. "Nothing's been reported."

"There wouldn't be, would there?"

Because there'd be fear, like his. Those who controlled the Ship couldn't allow the thousands crowded in its pods and corridors to feel this. Denizens had lived on a world once, improbable as it seemed. Minders taught that their kind adjusted so well to life within Ships because they'd evolved from ancestors who'd tunneled in groups and stayed together and had no need for sky. That didn't make them incapable of blind panic or riot.

What kind had newcomers been, Tissop wondered for the first time. What world, what life, could have favoured such frail bodies, such sensitive bulbous eyes, hands like an unborn child's...

"My apologies. You've worked hard and need your rest," Curtis said, words that would have been kind from Raekl or another denizen, but weren't, not uttered through such thin, writhing lips. "I'll tidy here, friend Tissop. Hopefully tomorrow will see good news and the end of all this."

First frightened, then dismissed like a weary child. In his own home.

Instead of anger, Tissop felt lost and powerless. Without a word, he stuck his empty bulb to the table, unhooked his back feet, and pushed himself through the air. He'd sleep.

Tomorrow?

He'd try again. He had to.

The strings hummed along the corridor. Machines and newcomers slid along on the conveyors below, as many as before or more. The handful of denizens on the strings avoided looking at one another or down. 1055th Sanitation Engineer Tissop stared so intently at his snout he almost missed the decel string before the iris of his door and was forced like a fool to lunge with tail and hands to catch it in time.

He clung to the wall, loath to enter.

Afraid, was the truth.

Oh, not of discovery. No one seemed to suspect him. But, no matter what he did, he couldn't trap a single newcomer. Another pod, the third, would be sanitized—accidentally—at the end of this cycle and he had no greater hope for it.

He'd tried. He'd brought an extra scanner, had dared pretend to be inspecting pod-corridor connection ports to use it from every direction, even stood watching as newcomers entered and left, smiling at him as if they knew.

There'd been a new report. The Ship had budded a bad cluster, that was all. It wasn't unheard of, though any flaws should have been caught during preparations. There'd be exhaustive tests run before the new pods were opened for habitation. Denizens were resourceful and resolute.

And missing.

If not officially admitted, the reason for the 1st priority could no longer be hidden. Denizens had failed to return to their homes. Had failed to arrive at work. Had vanished, so far as their neighbours knew, from the Ship. Three here. Two there. Heres and theres multiplied over and over until the numbers were appalling.

The restrictions on who could travel had been lifted; they had to be, denizens had to work, or crucial systems would begin to revert. The Ship must be tended.

Even if those who tended it were disappearing.

3rd divide, 7th cycle. The busiest time in a corridor. Shoulders hunched, Tissop made himself look along the homeward string. Made himself turn and look along the one heading out to the limit of the Ship.

He was alone. How could he be alone?

He made himself look down.

Newcomers looked up as they sped past in both directions. Offer our Shipmates space in your homes, the newsfeeds had urged last cycle. They've come forward to help in our time of need. Thank them.

What had he done?

Tissop thrust himself through the iris, desperate for the safety of home.

No dessert. The light—he blinked, wondering what was wrong, then knew. Curtis had dimmed the ambient to suit herself again.

"Raekl?" The word hung in midair, tenuous and fearful. Tissop took a deep breath then almost gagged at the smell. What was that? "Did you let the litter cook again?"

"Greetings, friend Tissop."

Curtis—but not. This newcomer was larger, with ridges above the eyes. Male.

"Who are you?" Tissop demanded. "Where's Raekl? My children?"

Curtis pulled herself into the antechamber, a hand on the shoulder of the male slowing her to a stop. She showed her teeth. "Don't worry. They've been assigned a new home. You've wanted to move into a pod, haven't you?"

A pod. "What pod? Where?" Not the one he'd—Tissop pushed himself toward the com panel to find it smothered by filaments, rebounded from that wall to the far one, grasping a string with his tail to stop. This had to stop. "You're doing it. Why? I don't understand!"

More newcomers joined them. Smaller than Curtis, larger. Thin and frail, but so many. His home was rife with them. All in black, living shadows with glistening eyes.

"What don't you understand, friend Tissop?" As Curtis spoke, they all smiled, teeth strange and white. "We're grateful, of course. You've saved us time and effort." She laid a hand on the wall. "The Ship is our home now."

It wasn't true. It couldn't be. "I killed you!" Tissop cried.

"You tried." Her smile widened. "One of you usually does. That's the beauty of it. Ships don't care what parasite infests them. We let you do the work for us, invite us in, then...take your place."

They'd done it before. To other Ships. To other denizens. And he'd helped, hadn't he? "Why didn't we know about you?" he whispered. "Why weren't we warned?"

Deep inside, he knew what she'd say before she uttered the terrible words. "Accidents happen, don't they, friend Tissop?"

Tissop curled his limbs against his aching gut. "Don't kill us all," he pleaded, thinking of his family, of what he'd done. "You don't have to."

"Oh, but we do," Curtis assured him. "Denizens are much too clever. Like you."

"Go now," the male said. "Die with the rest."

"Unless you'd like to stay for supper, friend Tissop." Curtis laughed. "It's the least we can do."

1055th Sanitation Engineer Tissop pushed himself out the iris of his home. He reached for the string that should have been there, that was always there, for denizens built well and with forethought, but the strings were of no interest to those who now called the Ship home, and had been cut. He found himself floating helplessly down the corridor, tumbling head over tail.

With every tumble, he stared down into the machineway, filled with newcomers about their business.

They looked up at him, and laughed.

---

When confronted with this anthology's theme, JULIE CZERNEDA's first thought was, no, I don't write villains. Her second thought was, well, who's a villain does depend on point of view. And her third and final thought was...oooh, what if? Thus "Charity" was born. It's a familiar pattern for this biologist turned award-winning science fiction and fantasy author, whose fourteenth novel from DAW Books, *A Turn of Light*, will be released March 2013. Visit www.czerneda.com for more of Julie's work, from novel excerpts to other short stories.

# MADDENING SCIENCE

## J.M. Frey

BULLETS FIRING INTO A crowd. Children screaming. Women crying. Men crying too, not that any of them would admit it. The scent of gun powder, rotting garbage, stale motor oil, vomit, and misery. Police sirens in the distance, coming closer, making me cringe against old memories. Making me skulk into the shadows, hunch down in my hoodie, a beaten puppy.

This guy isn't a supervillain. He isn't even a villain, really. Just an idiot. A child with a gun. And a grudge. Or maybe a god complex. Or a revenge scheme. Who the hell cares?

In the end, it amounts to the same.

The last place I want to be is in the centre of the police's attention, *again*, so I sink back into the fabric, shying from the broad helicopter searchlights that sweep in through the narrow windows of the parking garage.

If this had been before, I might have leapt into action with one of my trusty gizmos. Or, failing that, at least with a witty verbal assault that would have left the moron boy too brain-befuddled to resist when I punched him in the oesophagus.

But this isn't before.

I keep my eyes on the sky, instead of on the gun. If the Brilliant Bitch arrives, I want to *see*.

No one else is looking up. It has been a long, long time since one of... us...has donned sparkling spandex and crusaded out into the night to roust the criminal element from their lairs, or to enact a plot against the establishment, to bite a glove-covered thumb at "the man." A long time since one of us has done much more than pretend to *not* be one of us.

The age of the superhero petered out surprisingly quickly. The villains learnt our lessons; the heroes became obsolete.

A whizzing pop beside my left ear. I duck behind the back wheel of a sleek penis-replacement-on-wheels. The owner will be very upset when he sees the bullet gouges littering the bright red altar to his own virility.

I've never been shot before. I've been electrocuted, eye-lasered, punched by someone with the proportional strength of a spotted gecko and, memorably, tossed into the air by a breath-tornado created by a hero whose Italian lunch my schemes had clearly just interrupted.

Being shot seems fearfully mundane after all that.

Only the extraordinary die in extraordinary ways. And I am extraordinary no longer.

A normal, boring death scares me more than any other kind—especially if it's due to a random, pointless, unpredictable accident of time and place intersecting with a stupid poser with the combination to daddy's gun drawer and the key to mommy's liquor cabinet. I had been on the way to the bargain grocery store for soymilk. It doesn't look like I'm going to get any now.

I look skyward. Still no Crimson Cunt.

Someone screams. Someone else cries. I sit back against the wheel and refrain from whistling to pass the time. If I was on the other side of the parking garage, I could access the secret tunnel I built into the lower levels back when the concrete was poured thirty years ago. But the boy and his bullets are between us. I've nothing to do but wait.

The boy is using a 9mm Barretta, military issue, so probably from daddy's day job in security at the air force base. He has used up seven bullets. The standard Barretta caries a magazine of fifteen. Eight remain, unless one had already been prepared in the chamber, which I highly doubt as no military man would be unintelligent or undisciplined enough to carry about a loaded gun aimed at his own foot. The boy is firing them at an average rate of one every ninety-three seconds—punctuated by unintelligible screaming—and so by my estimation I will be pinned by his unfriendly fire for another seven hundred and forty-four seconds, or twelve point four minutes.

However, the constabulary generally arrive on the scene between six and twenty-three minutes after an emergency call. As this garage is five and a half blocks from the 2nd Precinct, I estimate the stupid boy has another eight point seven minutes left to live before a SWAT team puts cold lead between his ribs.

Better him than me.

Except, probability states that he will kill another three bystanders before that time. I scrunch down further, determined not to be a statistic today. This brings me directly into eye-line with a corpse.

There is blood all around her left shoulder. If she didn't die of shock upon impact, then surely she died of blood loss. Her green eyes are wide and wet.

I wonder who she used to be.

I wonder if she is leaving behind anyone who will weep and rail and attend the police inquest and accuse the system of being too slow, too corrupt, too over-burdened. I wonder if they will blame the boy's parents or his teachers. Will they only blame themselves? Or her?

And then, miraculously, she blinks.

Well, that certainly is a surprise. Perhaps the trauma is not as extensive as

I estimated. To be fair, I cannot see most of her. She has fallen awkwardly, the momentum of her tumble half-concealing her under the chassis of the ludicrously large Hummer beside my penis-car.

I am so fascinated by the staggering of her torso as she tries to suck in a breath, the staccato rhythm of her blinks, the bloody slick of teeth behind her lips, that it's all over before I am aware of it.

This must be what people mean by time flying.

I'm not certain I've ever felt that strange loss of seconds ever before. I am so very used to being able to track everything. It's disconcerting. I don't like it.

And yet the boy is downed, the police are here, paramedics crawling over the dead and dying like swarming ants. I wait for them to find my prize, to pull her free of the SUV's shadow and whisk her away to die under ghastly fluorescent lights, too pumped full of morphine to know she is slipping away.

I wait in the shadow of the wheel and hope that they miss me.

They do.

Only, in missing me, they miss her, as well. She is blinking, gritty and desperate, and now the police are leaving, and the paramedics are shunting their human meat into the sterile white cubes, and they have not found my fascinating, panting young lady.

Oh dear. This is a dilemma.

I am reformed. I am no longer a villain. But I am also no hero and I like my freedom far too much to risk it by bringing her to the attention of the officials. What to do? Save her and risk my freedom, or let her die, and walk free but burdened with the knowledge of yet another life that I might have been able to save, and didn't?

I dither too long. They are gone. Only the media are left, and I certainly don't want *them* to catch me in their unblinking grey lenses. The woman blinks, sad and slow. She knows that she is dead. It's coming. Her fingers twitch towards me—reaching.

A responsible, honest citizen would not let her die. So I slink out of my shadow and gather her up, the butterfly struggle of her pulse in her throat against my arm, and slip away through my secret tunnel.

I steal her away to save her life.

It occurs to me, when I lean back from the operating table, my hands splashed with gore, that I've kidnapped this woman. She has seen my face. Others will see the neat way I've made my nanobots stitch the flesh and bone of her shoulder back together. They will recognize the traces of the serum that I've infused her with in order to speed up her healing, because I once replaced the totality of my blood with the same to keep myself disease free, young looking, and essentially indestructible. The forensics agents will know this handiwork for mine.

And then they will know that at least one of my medical laboratories escaped their detection and their torches. They will fear that. No matter that I gave my word to that frowning judge that I had been reformed, no matter that the prison therapist holds papers signed to that effect, no matter that I've personally endeavoured to become and remain honest, forthright, and supportive; one look at my lair will remind them of what I used to be, what they fear I might still be, and that will be enough. That will be the end. I will go back to the human zoo.

I cannot have that. I've worked too hard to be forgotten to allow them to remember.

I take off the bloody gloves and apron and put them in my incinerator, where they join my clothing from earlier tonight. I take a shower and dress—jeans, a tee-shirt, another nondescript wash-greyed hoodie: the uniform of the youth I appear to number among. Then I sit in a dusty, plush chair beside the cot in the recovery room and I wait for her to wake. The only choice that seems left to me is the very one I had been trying to avoid from the start of this whole mess—the choice to go bad, again. I've saved her life, but in doing so, I've condemned us both.

*Fool.* Better to have let her died in that garage. Only, her eyes had been so green, and so *sad...*

I hate myself. I hate that the Power Pussy might have been right: that the only place for me is jail; that the world would be better off without me; that it's a shame I survived her last, powerful assault.

When she wakes, the first thing the young woman says is, "You're Proffes—"

I don't let her finish. "*Please* don't say that name. I don't like it."

Her sentence stutters to a halt, unsaid words tumbling from between her teeth to crash into her lap. She looks down at them, wringing them into the light cotton sheets, and nods.

"Olly," I say.

Her face wrinkles up. "Olly?"

"Oliver."

The confusion clears, clouds parting, and she flashes a quirky little gap between her two front teeth at me. "Really? Seriously? *Oliver?*"

I resist the urge to bare my own teeth at her. "Yes."

"Okay. Olly. I'm Rachel." Then she peers under the sheet. She cannot possibly see the tight, neat little rows of sutures through the scrubs (or perhaps she can, who knows what powers people are being born into nowadays?), but she nods as if she approves and says, "Thank you."

"I couldn't let you die."

"The Prof would have."

"I'm Olly."

She nods. "Okay."

"Are you thirsty?" I point to a bottle of water on the bedside table.

She makes a point of checking the cap before she drinks, but I cannot blame her. Of course, she also does not know that I've ways of poisoning water through plastic, but I won't tell her that. Besides, I haven't done so.

"So," she says. "Thank you."

I snort, I can't help it. It's a horribly ungentlemanly sound, but my disbelief is too profound.

"Don't laugh. I mean it," she says.

"I'm laughing *because* you mean it. Rachel." I ask, "How old are you?"

She blushes, a crimson flag flapping across a freckled nose, and I curse myself this weakness, this fascination with the human animal that has never managed to ebb, even after all that time in solitary confinement.

"Twenty-three," she says. She is lying—her eyes shift to the left slightly, she wets her lips, her breathing increases fractionally. I see it plain as a road sign on a highway. I also saw her ID when I cleaned out her backpack. She is twenty-seven.

"Twenty-three," I allow. "I was put into prison when you were eight years old. I did fifteen years of a life sentence and was released early on parole for good behaviour and a genuine desire to reform. The year prior to my sentencing I languished in a city cell, and the two before that I spent mostly tucked away completing my very last weapon. Therefore, the last memory you can possibly have of the 'Prof,' as you so glibly call him, was from when you were six." I sit forward. "Rachel, my dear, can you really say that at six years old you understood what it meant to have an honest to goodness supervillain terrorizing your home?"

She shakes her head, the blush draining away and leaving those same freckles to stand out against her glowing pale skin like ink splattered on vellum.

"*That* is why I laughed. It amuses me that I've lived so long that someone like you is saying *thank you* to me. Ah, and I see another question there. Yes?"

"You don't look old enough," she says softly.

I smile and flex a fist. "I age very, very slowly."

"Well, I know that. I just meant, is that part of the...you know, how you were born?"

"No," I say. "I did it to myself."

"Do you regret it?"

I flop back in my chair, blinking. No one has ever asked me that before. I've never asked myself. "I don't know," I admit. "Would you?"

She shrugs, and then winces, pressing one palm against her shoulder.

"Maybe," she admits. "I always thought that part of the stories was a bit sad. That the Prof has to live forever with what he's done."

"No, not forever," I demur. "Just a very long time. May I ask, what stories?"

"Um! Oh, you know, social science—recent history. I had to do a course on the Superhero Age, in school. I was thinking of specializing in Vigilantism."

"A law student, then."

"Yes."

"How urbane."

"Yes, it sort of is, isn't it?" She smiles faintly. "What is it about superheroes that attracts us mousy sorts?"

"I could say something uncharitable about ass-hugging spandex and cock cups, but I don't think that would apply to you."

"Cape Bunnies?" she asks, with a grin. "No, definitely not my style."

"Cape Bunn—actually, I absolutely have no desire to know." I stand. I feel weary in a way that has nothing to do with my age. "If you are feeling up to it, Rachel, may I interest you in some lunch?"

"Actually, I should go," she says. "I feel fantastic! I mean, this is incredible. What you did. I thought I was a goner."

"You nearly were," I say.

"And *thank you*, again. But my mom must be freaking out. I should go to a hospital or something. At least call her."

"Oh, Rachel," I say softly. "You've studied supervillains. You know what my answer to that has to be."

She is quiet for a moment, and then those beautiful green eyes go wide. "No," she says.

"I am sorry. I didn't mean to trade my freedom for yours. I thought I was doing good. For *once*."

"But...but," she stutters.

"I can't."

She blinks and then curses. "Stupid, I'm not talking about that! I mean, they can't really think that about you, can they? You saved my *life*. This... this isn't a bad thing!"

I laugh again. "Are you defending me? Are you sure that's wise?"

"Don't condescend to me!" she snaps. "That's not *fair*. You've done your time. You saved me. Isn't that enough for them?"

"Oh, Rachel. You certainly do have a pleasant view of the world."

"Don't call me naive!" The way she spits it makes me think that she says this quite often.

"I'm not," I say. "Only optimistic." I gesture through the door. "The kitchen is there. I will leave the door unlocked. I've a closet through there— take whatever you'd like. I'm afraid your clothing was too bloody."

"Fine," she snarls.

I nod once and make my way into the kitchen, closing the door behind me to leave her to rage and weep in privacy. I know from personal experience how embarrassing it is to realize that your freedom has been forcefully taken from you, in public.

I built this particular laboratory-cum-bolthole in the 1950s, back when the world feared nuclear strikes. I was a different man then, though no less technologically apt, and so it has been outfitted with all manner of tunnels and closets, storage chambers, libraries, and bedrooms. The fridge keeps food fresh indefinitely, so the loaf of bread, basket of tomatoes and head of lettuce I left here in1964 are still fit makings for sandwiches. I also open a can of soup for us to share.

She comes out of the recovery room nine thousand and sixty-six seconds—fifteen point eleven minutes—after; a whole three minutes longer than I had estimated she would take. There is stubbornness in her that I had not anticipated, but for which I should have been prepared. She did not die in that garage, and it takes great courage and tenacity to beat off the Grim Reaper.

"I'm sorry, Oliver," she says, and sits in the plastic chair. I suppose the look is called "retro" now, but this kitchen was once the height of taste.

"Why are you apologizing to *me?*" I set a bowl in front of her. She doesn't even shoot me a suspicious look; I suppose she's decided to take the farce of believing me a good person to its conclusion.

"It sucks that you're so sure people are going to hate you."

"Aren't they?"

She pouts miserably and sips her soup. It's better than the rage I had been expecting, or an escape attempt. I wasn't looking forward to having to chase her down and wrangle her into a straitjacket, or drug her into acquiescence. I would hate to have to dim that keen gaze of hers.

I sit down opposite her and point to her textbook, propped up on my toaster oven for me to read as I stirred the soup. It had been in the bloody backpack I stripped from her, and seemed sanitary enough to save. Her cell phone, I destroyed.

"This is advanced, Rachel," I say. "Are you enjoying it?"

She flicks her eyes to the book. "You've read it."

"Nearly finished. I read fast."

"You didn't flip to the end?"

"Should I?"

"No," she blurts. "No. Go at your own pace. I just...I mean, I do like it," she said. "Especially the stuff about supervillain reformation."

I sigh and set down my spoon. "Oh, Rachel."

"I'm serious, Oliver! Just let me make a phone call. I promise, no one will arrest you. I won't even tell them I met you."

"You won't have to."

She slams her fists into the tabletop, the perfect picture of childish frustration. "You can't keep me here forever."

"I can," I say. "It is physically possible. What you mean to say is, 'You don't *want* to keep me here forever.'"

She goes still. "Do you want to?"

I can. I know I can. I can be like one of those men who kidnaps a young lady and locks her in his basement for twenty years, forcing her to become dependent on him, forcing her to love him. But I don't want to. I've nothing but distaste for men who can't *earn* love, and feel the need to steal it. Cowards.

"No," I say.

"Then why are you hesitating? Let me go."

"Not until you're fully healed, at least," I bargain. I'm not used to bargaining. Giving demands, yes. But begging, never. "When no trace of what I've done remains. Is that acceptable? But in return, you must not try to escape. You could hurt yourself worse, and frankly I don't want to employ the kind of force that would be required to keep you. That is my deal."

"You promise?"

I sneer. "I don't break promises."

"I know," she says. "I read about that, too. Okay. It's a deal."

I spend the night working on schematics for a memory machine. I've never tampered with the mind of another before—I respect intellect far too much to go mucking about in someone's grey matter like a child in a tide pool—but I have no other choice. Rachel cannot remember our time together.

Rachel sleeps in one of the spare bedrooms. She enjoyed watching old movies all afternoon, and I confess I enjoyed sitting beside her on the sofa. We had frozen pizza for dinner, and her gaze had spent almost as much time on the screen as on my face.

In the morning, my blueprints are ready and my chemicals begin simmering on Bunsen burners. I find her at the kitchen table, drinking coffee and flipping through my scrapbook. It's filled with newspaper articles and photos, wanted posters and DVDs of news broadcasts. I've never thought to keep it in a safe or to put it away somewhere. Besides Miss Rachel, no one has ever been to this bolthole but me.

"You found the soymilk, I see," I say. She nods and doesn't look up from her intense perusal of a favourite article of mine, the only one where the reporter *got it*. "And my book."

"It's like a shrine," she says. "I thought you'd hate all these superheroes, but there's just as much in here about them as you."

"I've great respect for anyone who wants to better the world." I touch the side of the coffeepot—still warm. I pour myself a cup and sit across from her.

"See...that's what's freaking me out, a bit," she says. "You're such a..."

"What?"

"You seem like such a sweet guy."

I laugh again.

"What?"

"Don't mistake my youth for sweetness."

"I'm not, but...I don't know, you're not a supervillain."

"I'm not a superhero, either."

"You can be something in the middle. You can just be a nice guy."

"I've never been just a 'nice guy,' Rachel. Not even before."

"I think you're being one now." She leans across the table and kisses me. I don't close my eyes, or move my mouth. This is a surprise too, but an acceptable one.

When she sits back, I ask, "Is this why you were studying my face so intently last night while you pretended to watch movies?"

She blushes again, and it's fascinating. "Shut up," she mumbles.

I smile. "Are you a Cape Bunny after all, Miss Rachel?"

"A Labcoat Bunny, maybe," she says. "I've always gone for brain over brawn."

"Who are you lashing out against," I ask calmly, my tone probably just this side of too cool, "that you think kissing the man who has kidnapped you is a good idea?"

Rachel drops back down into her seat. "Way to ruin the moment, Romeo."

"That is not an answer."

"No one!"

"And, *that*, dear Rachel, is a lie."

She throws up her hands. "I don't know, okay! My mother! The school! The courts! The whole stupid system! A big stupid world that says the man who saved my life has to go to *jail* for it!"

"I am part of the revenge scheme, then," I say. "If you come out of your captivity loving your captor, then they cannot possibly think I am evil. You have it all planned out, my personal redemption. Or perhaps this is a way to earn a seat in that big-ticket law school?"

She stares at me, slack jawed, a storm brewing behind those beautiful green eyes. "You're a bit of a dick, you know that?"

"That is what the Crimson Cunt used to—"

"Don't call her that."

"Why not? The Super Slut won't hear me say it. Not under all this concrete."

"Shut up!"

"Why?" I sneer. "Protecting a heroine you've never met?"

"She deserves better, even from you!"

"Oh, have I ruined your image of me, Rachel? Am I not sweet and misunderstood anymore?"

"You still shouldn't—"

"What, hate her? She put me in jail!" I copy her and slam my fists on the tabletop. My mug topples, hot liquid splashing out between us. "I think I've a right to be bitter about that."

"But it was for the good! It made you better."

"No, it made me cowed. I've lost all my ambition, dear Rachel. And that is why I am just a normal citizen. I am too tired."

"But Divine—"

"*Don't* say her name, either!"

Rachel stands and pounds her fists on the table again, shaking my fallen mug, and I stand as well, too furious to want to be shorter than her.

"Asshole!" she snarls.

"And she was a ball-breaker on a power trip. She was no better for the city than I! The only difference was that she didn't have the gumption, the ambition, the *foresight* to do what had to be done! I was the only one who saw! *Me*. She towed the line. She kept the status quo. I was trying to change the world! She was just a stupid blonde bimbo with huge tits and a small brain—"

"Don't talk about my mother that way!"

Oh.

I drop back down into my seat, knees giving way without my say-so. "Well, this is a turn," I admit.

"Everyone knows!" she spits. "It's hard to miss. Same eyes, same cheekbones."

"I've never seen your mother's eyes and cheekbones."

"What, were you living under a rock when she unmasked?"

I smile, and it's thin and bitter. "I was in solitary confinement for five years. By the time I got out, it must have been old news. And I had no stomach to look up my old nemesis."

Rachel looks away, and her eyes are bright with tears that don't skitter down her cheeks. I wonder if they are for her mother, or for herself, or because I've said such terrible things and her opinion of me has diminished. They are certainly not because she pities me.

Nobody pities me. I got, as I am quite often reminded, exactly what I deserved.

"What does your mother do now?" I ask, after the silence has become unbearable. There is nothing to count or calculate in the silence, besides the precise, quiet click of the second hand ticking ever onward, ever onward, while I am left behind.

"Socialite," Rachel says. "Cars. Money. Married a real estate developer."

"Is he your father?"

She swings her gaze back to me, sharp. "Why would you ask that?"

"Why does the notion that he might not be offend you?"

Her lips pucker, and with that scowl, I can see it: the pissy frown, the stubborn thrust of her chin. There is the Fantastic Floozy, hating me through her daughter.

"It doesn't," she lies. She twists her hands in front of her again. "Fine, it does. I don't know, okay? I don't think she knows. She wants it to be him."

"So do you," I press. "Because that would make you normal."

She looks up brusquely.

"Please, Rachel," I say. "I am quite clever. Don't insult us both by forgetting. The way you do your hair, your clothes, the law school ambitions, it all screams 'I don't want to be like my mother.' Which, if your mother is a superheroine, probably means that you are also desperate to not be one of...us."

"I'm not," she whispers.

"I dare say that if you have no desire to, then you won't be," I agree. I lean forward to impart my great secret. She's the first I've told and I don't know why I'm sharing it. Only, perhaps, that it will make her less miserable. "Here is something they never tell anyone: if you don't use your powers, if you don't flex that extra little muscle in your grey, squishy brain, it will not develop. It will atrophy and die. Why do you think there are so few of us now? Nobody wants to be a hero."

"Really?" she whispers, awed, hatred draining from her face.

"Really," I say. "Especially after the sort of example your mother set."

Rachel rocks back again, the furious line between her eyebrows returning, and yes, I recognize that, too, have seen that above a red domino mask before.

"Why do you *say* things like that?" she asks, hands thrown skyward in exasperation. She winces.

"Don't rip your stitches, my dear," I admonish.

"Don't change the subject! You wouldn't talk about the Kamelion Kid that way, or Wild West, or...any of them! You'd have respect! What about The Tesla? You respect him. I've seen the pictures on your wall and you— why are you laughing?"

And I am laughing. I am guffawing like the bawdy, brawling youth I resemble. "Because I *am* The Tesla!"

She rocks back on her heels, eyes comically wide and then suspiciously narrow. "But you...Prof killed The Tesla."

"In a sense, he did."

Her eyes jump between me and the door to my lab—the only door locked to Rachel—and back to me. "You were a hero first."

"Yes."

"And it didn't work, did it?"

"...no."

"Because people...people don't want to change. Don't want to think."

"Yes. My plans would have been good for society. Would have forced changes for the better. But people just want a hero to keep things the way they already are."

She looks at her law textbook, which rests exactly where I had left it the night before, propped on the toaster oven.

"So you made it look like The Tesla was dead."

"Heroes can save the world. But villains can *change* it, Rachel."

She looks up. "I think I want to hate you, Olly, but I can't figure out if I should."

"It's okay if you hate me," I say. "I won't mind."

"Yes, I think you would," she says. She flattens her right palm over her left shoulder.

We sit like that for a long moment. I forget to count the seconds. Time flies when I am around Rachel, and I find that I am beginning to enjoy it.

Rachel sulks in her room for the afternoon, which bothers me not at all, as I've experiments to attend. When I come back out, she is sullenly reading her textbook on the sofa, and she has found the beer. One open bottle is beside her elbow and three empty ones are on the floor.

"It's not wise to drink when you're on antibiotics," I say, wiping my hands on my labcoat. They leave iridescent green smears on the fabric, but it's completely non-toxic or I would not be exposing her to it.

"I'm not *on* antibiotics," she mutters mulishly.

"Yes, you are," I counter. "There is a slow-release tablet under your skin near the wound."

She makes a face and pushes away her textbook. It slaps onto the carpet. "That's just gross."

"But efficient."

She looks up, gaze suddenly tight. "What else did you put in me?"

I walk over and take away her beer. And then, because it would be a waste of booze to dump it down the sink, and I have been on a limited income since I ceased robbing banks, and because I enjoy the perverseness of having my lips on the same bottlemouth as hers after having so recently admonished her for kissing me, I take a drink.

"Not that, if that's what you're implying, my dear Rachel," I say. "I'm more of a gentleman than that." She blinks hard, my innuendo sinking home.

"What? What, no! I didn't mean..." she splutters. "I just mean...where did you get the replacement blood? What kind of stitches? Am I bionic now?"

"No more than you were before," I say. "Nanobots are actively knitting the torn flesh back together, but they will die in a week and your liver will flush them from your system. The stitches and sutures are biodegradable and will dissolve by then. The rest of the antibiotic tablet will be gone in two or three days, and the very small infusion of my vitality serum only gave your immune system a boost and your regenerative drive a bit of extra gas. You are in all ways, my dear Rachel, utterly and completely in-extraordinary. Your greatest fear is unrealized." I finish off the beer with a swig, liking the way her green eyes follow the line of my throat as I swallow, and then go to the kitchen and retrieve two more.

I hand one to her and flop down onto the sofa beside her. She curls into a corner to give me enough room and then, after eyeing the mess on my coat, thrusts impertinent—and freezing!—toes under my thigh. "Dear me, Rachel, stepping up your campaign?"

"You started it," she says. "Re-started it. With the...bottle thingy."

I arch a teasing eyebrow. "Bottle thingy?"

She shakes her head. "I think I'm a little drunk."

"I think you are," I agree.

"Enabler," she says, and we clink beers. She drinks and this time I watch her. Her throat is, in every way, normal. Boring. I cannot stop looking at it. Her toes wiggle. "How can you read me so well?" she asks. "I mean, I didn't even have to say, 'I'm scared of turning into my mom,' but you knew."

I shrug. "I'm a great student of the human creature. We all say so much without saying a thing."

"Do you ever say more than you want to?"

I smile secretively, a flash of teeth that I know will infuriate her with its vagueness. "Rarely, any more. I've had a long time to learn to control my, as poker players would call them, 'tells.'"

"Hmph," she mutters and takes another drink. I swallow some of my beer to distract myself. She wriggles her toes again, and pushes them further. Soon they will brush right against my...but I assume that is the point.

"Careful, Rachel," I warn. "Are you certain this is what you want to do?"

"Yes."

"You are drunk and you want revenge on your mother."

"Maybe. Maybe I want to thank you for saving my life. Maybe I want to reward you for being a good guy."

"What if I don't want your thanks, or your reward?" I ask.

She smiles and her big toe tickles the undercurve of my testes. "Don't you?" she asks, and her expression is salacious. I provided her with no bra, I had none to give, and under my borrowed tee-shirt her nipples are pert.

"I do." I set aside both of our beers and reach for her. She comes into my arms, gladly, little mouth wet and insistent against mine as she wriggles her way onto my lap. Iridescent green smears up her thighs. "But maybe... oh!" I gasp into her mouth as clever little fingers work their way inside my waistband. I return the favour. Intelligence must be rewarded.

"Maybe?" she prompts, pressing down against my hand.

"Maybe I just want revenge on your mother, too."

She jerks back as if I've bitten her. "Oh my god, how can one man be such a *dick*?"

I press upwards so her pelvis comes in contact with the part of my anatomy in discussion. "I am honest, Rachel. There is a difference."

She sits back, arms crossing over the breasts I hadn't yet touched. "An honest supervillain," she scoffs.

I stand, dumping her onto the floor. "I think we're done here."

"Are we, Profess—"

"I've *asked you* not to call me *that*!"

She cowers back from my anger. Then it fuels her. "Fuck you, Olly," she says, standing.

"I thought that was the idea," I agree, "but apparently not."

"You're nothing like I thought you'd be!"

I laugh again. "And how could you have had *any* concept of how I'd be? Did the Dynamic Dyke tell stories? I bet she did. And you felt sorry for me. The poor Professor, beat up by mommy, hated—like you were. An outcast, like you were. Not good enough, like you were. Was I your imaginary friend, Rachel? Did you write my name in hearts on your binders? Did you *fantasize* about me?"

"Shut up!" she screams.

Her cheeks are red again, her eyes glistening, her mouth bruised, and I want to grab her, kiss her, feel her ass through the borrowed sweatpants. Instead I fold my hands behind my back, because I told the truth before—I am a gentleman. I say nothing.

"You're not supposed to be like this!"

"Be like what?" I ask, again. "Explain, Rachel."

She collapses. It's a slow folding inward, knees and stomach first, face in her hands, physicality followed by emotion as she sobs into the carpet. I stand above her and wait, because she deserves this cry. Crying helps people engage with their emotions, or so I'm told.

When her sobbing slows, precisely one thousand six hundred and seventy-three seconds later—twenty-seven point nine minutes—she unfolds and stands, wiping her nose. I offer her a handkerchief from the pocket of my labcoat, and she takes it and turns her back to me, cleaning up her face.

She picks up the textbook. She opens it to the back, to those useless blank pages that are the fault of how books are bound, and for the first time in a very, very long time, I am shocked.

The back of the book has been collaged with photographs. Of me.

Computer printouts of me when I was the Prof. Newspaper clippings of my trial. Me, walking down the street, hunched into the shadow of my sweater's hood. Me, buying soymilk. Me, through the window of the shitty apartment on which Oliver Munsen can barely afford to pay rent. Me, three days ago, cutting through that same parking garage.

Genuine joy floods my blood. A small shot of adrenaline seethes up into my brain and I can't help the smile, because I missed this, I really did. "Oh, Rachel. Are you my stalker? How novel! I've never had a stalker before."

She snaps the cover shut. "I'm not a stalker."

"Just an admirer?" I ask, struggling to keep the condensation out of my voice. "Or do you want me to teach you how to be a villain? Really get back at mommy?" Her expression sours. "Ah. But you already know that you can't be. You knew before I told you that you were born boring. So this is the next best thing." I reach out, grasp her elbows lightly, rub my callused thumbs across the tender flesh on the inside of them. She shivers. "Tell me, how were you going to do it, Rachel? Were you going to accidentally bump into me in that parking garage? Were you going to spill a beer on me in a bar? Buy me a coffee at my favourite cafe? Surely getting shot was not in the plan."

"It's not like that!" she says, but her eyes are closed, her lashes fluttering. Her chest bobs as she tries to catch her breath.

"Then what is it like?"

"I don't know! I just...I just *saw* you one day, okay? I recognized you, from mom's pictures on the wall, and I thought, you know, I should tell her. But I thought I would follow you first, you know, figure out where you live, or something."

"Except that I wasn't being dastardly and villainous."

"You sat in the bookstore and read a whole magazine. And then you *paid* for it."

I smirk. "How shocking."

"For me it was." She tips forward, breasts squishing, hot and soft, against my chest. "The kinds of stories I heard about you as a kid..."

"And you were fascinated."

"And I was fascinated."

"And so you followed me."

"I followed you."

"And then what, my dear Rachel?"

She wraps her arms around my neck and pulls me down for a kiss I don't resist.

"You seemed so lonely," she says, breath puffing into my mouth. "Are you lonely, Olly?"

"Oh, yes." I pick her up and carry her off to her bedroom.

The mattress is new, she is the first person to ever have slept on it, but it still squeaks. After, she drops off, satisfied, mumbling amusing endearments about how wonderful it is to make love to someone who is so studious, makes such a thorough examination of his subjects.

Tonight I decide to sleep. I don't do it very often, but I don't want to be awake anymore. I don't want to think. I close my eyes and force my dreams to stay away.

In the morning, I'm troubled. I think I've made a very bad choice, but I'm not sure how to rectify it. I am not even sure how to articulate it.

Rachel was right. I am lonely. I am desperately, painfully lonely. And I will be for the rest of my unnaturally long life. But Rachel is lonely, too. Desperate in her own way, desperate for the approval of a mother I can only assume was distant and busy in Rachel's youth, and then too famous and busy in her adolescence. Rachel wants to be nothing like her mother, wants to hurt her, punish her, and yet...wants to impress her so very badly that she is willing to take the ultimate step, to profess love for a man her mother once hated, to "fix him," to "make him better." To make him, *me*, good.

Only, Rachel doesn't understand. I don't want to *be* better, or good, or saved. I just want to live my boring, in-extraordinary life in peace and quiet, and then die. I don't want to be her experiment. And yet her fierce little kisses...her wide green eyes...

I look down at the schematics under my elbow and sigh. The scent of burning bacon wafts in through the vents from the kitchen, and the utter domesticity of it plucks at the back of my eyes, heating them. I'm still a fool, and I'm no less in over my head than I was two days ago.

I abandon the lab and rescue my good iron skillet from the madwoman who has pushed her way into my life. When she turns her face up for a kiss, I give it to her, and everything else she asks for, too.

And I can have this, because I am not a supervillain any more. But I am not a superhero either. If I was, I could turn her away, like I should.

After lunch, I hand her my cell phone. It has been boosted so that the signal can pass through concrete bunker walls, but cannot be tracked back to its location.

"What's that for?" she asks.

"Call your mother," I say. "Tell her you're okay. You're just staying with a friend. The shooting freaked you out."

She frowns. "What if I don't want to?"

"You were arguing that I should let you call."

"Yeah, before."

"Rachel," I admonish. "Do you really want *her* frantically looking for you?"

She pales. I imagine what it must have been like for her when she ran away from home for the first time. "No, guess not," she mumbles and dials a number. "Yeah, hi Mom. No, no, I'm cool. Yeah, decided to stay with a friend instead of coming home from campus this weekend. No, no, it's fine. I'm fine. There's no need for the guilt trip! I said I'm fine! God!...okay. Right. Sorry. Okay. I'll see you next..." she looks at me. "Next Saturday?" I nod. "Next Saturday. Right. Fine. I love you, too." She hangs up and places the phone between us. "There, happy?"

"Yes. I am curious Rachel, how do you intend on springing me on your mother? And how will you keep her from punching my face clear off?"

She picks at her cuticles. "I hadn't really thought that far ahead."

"I gathered." I stand from the table and go to do the dishes. I can't abide a mess.

She comes up behind me and wraps her arms around my waist and presses her cheek against my back, and asks, "What do you want to do this afternoon?"

"Whatever you want," I say. "I'm all yours." I turn in her arms to find her grinning. She believes me, whole-heartedly, and she should. I never lie, and it's the truth. For now.

When the week is over, I sit her down on my operating table and carefully poke around the bullet wound. In the x-ray, the bones appear healed without a scar. Her skin is dewy and unmarked. The stitches have dissolved and a scan with a handheld remote shows that the nanobots are all dead and ninety-three percent have been flushed from her system. I anticipate the other seven percent will be gone after her next trip to the toilet.

I scan a bit lower down, but there is nothing there to be concerned about, either. We have not been using prophylactics, but I've been sterile since I used the serum. It was a personal choice. I had no desire to outlive my grandchildren.

Rachel hops from the table, bare feet on the white tile, and grins. "It's Saturday!" she says.

"Yes, it is."

"Time to go!"

"Yes."

She takes my hand. "And you're coming with me, Olly. Then they'll see, they'll all *see*. You're different now. You're a good man."

I smile and close my fingers around hers and, for the first time in many decades, I lie. "Yes, I am, thank you." I use our twined fingers to pull her into the kitchen. "Celebratory drink before we go?"

She grins. "Gonna open that champagne I saw in the back of the fridge?"

I laugh. "Clever Rachel. I can't hide anything from you."

Only I can. I am. When I pop the cork she shrieks in delight. Every ticking second of her happiness stabs at me like a branding iron and dagger all in one.

I thought I would need a whole machine, a gun, a delivery device, but in the end my research and experiments offered up a far more simplistic solution: rohypnol. Except that it is created by me, of course, so it's programmable, intelligent in the way the cheap, pathetic drug available to desperate, stupid children in night clubs is not. My drug knows which memories to take away.

Clever, beautiful, dear Rachel trusts me. I pour our drinks and hand her the glass that is meant for her. I smile and chat with her as she sips, pretending to be oblivious as her eyelids slip downwards, giving her no clue that there is anything amiss.

I catch both her and the glass before they hit the floor. Tonight she will wake in her own bed. She will honestly remember spending the week with a friend she then had a fight with, and no longer speaks to. She will wonder what happened to her backpack, her cell phone, her law textbook. She will not remember the Prof, or The Tesla. Her mother will be annoyed that she will have to tell her the stories over again, stories that Rachel should have internalized during her childhood.

And I will shut down this hidey-hole and go back to my apartment and cash my welfare cheque and watch television. And it will be good. It will be as it should be.

The stupid boy with the gun might have been the bad guy in our little melodrama, but I am the villain.

I am the coward.

---

J.M. FREY is the author of *Triptych* (Dragon Moon Press), "The Once and Now-ish King" in *When the Hero Comes Home* (Dragon Moon Press, August 2011), *The Dark Side of the Glass* (Double Dragon Publishing, June 2012), and "Whose Doctor?" in *Doctor Who in Time and Space* (McFarland Press, Fall 2012). She holds a BA in Dramatic Literature, where she studied playwriting and traditional Japanese theatre forms, and a Masters of Communications and Culture, where she focused on fanthropology. She is active in the Toronto geek community, appearing on TV, radio, podcasts, and live panels to discuss all things fandom through the lens of Academia. *Triptych* received a Publishers Weekly starred review and was one of PW's top ten SF/Fantasy books of 2011. It was a Lambda Literary Award finalist and won Best SF/F in the San Francisco Book Festival.

# BIRTHRIGHT

## Clint Talbert

KHRANDOR HAD HOPED FOR a bright morning, for blades of sunlight to stab the nightmares that plagued him. Instead, clouds snagged on mountain peaks and their frayed tendrils roamed like wraiths through the valley, filling every rocky shadow with an imagined terror. It would only get worse as they neared Idren. Idren—one place he'd never thought to return. But here he was on this accursed road, and every landmark reminded him of the night he fled propelled by fear, with bandaged hands and snow biting his feet. He fidgeted with the reins. Once he settled his father's accounts and took control of the gold mines, he could be away. Another memory flashed, like a spark in a moonless night: Kassandra. Was she still as beautiful as she had been at fourteen? Had she grown into the woman he imagined each night before falling into his hellish sleep? Were her hands still strong, was her hair still the color of setting sun, were her lips still welcoming as soft pillows? He remembered fumbling moments in her father's shop, the heavy smell of shoe leather covering them like a blanket.

What if his father wasn't dead? What if this was a rebel trick? He glanced at the fifty loyalists and mercenaries he'd hand-picked. They were good men. He had survived ambushes with far less. And if his father was still alive...Khrandor could see the old house, the bastard standing on the steps. Khrandor imagined riding up those steps, swinging his axe through the bastard's chest. Chills of victory rippled through his body, leaving goose bumps in their wake. Maybe he would draw out the man's death, using the tactics he'd learned as an interrogator. Maybe breaking the bastard would end the trauma of the nightmares that endlessly pursued him through the black, restless nights.

As if he'd called their names, images of last night's evil came to mind. He'd dreamt of the last time he saw his father. He could smell the corn whiskey on his father's breath, feel the big paws on his shoulders as his father pushed him into the fireplace. He remembered the stinging pain as he pulled the log from the fire and hit his father with it. His breath came in short gasps, the scars beneath his gloves ached. He coughed and spat. *Stop thinking about it. The bastard's dead.*

They crested the southern rise of Idren's valley. Khrandor halted his horse.

He had stopped here on that fateful night when he was fourteen. That boy had looked back, not out of remorse, but out of terror that his father would be galloping up the road in the moonlight, his riding crop salivating for Khrandor's flesh. Kassandra had bandaged his hands. He remembered that she packed snow into the bandages to stop the burning. He'd begged her to come with him. Back then, she wouldn't leave her father. *Will she now?*

Idren looked much as it had thirteen years ago. The river still fell in roaring cataracts down the far side of the valley and passed swiftly beneath the two bridges. There were more homes with slate roofs, fewer with thatch. Khrandor's eyes went to one large house at the north end of the valley, the prison of his youth. What demons awaited there? Who might be behind one of these naked aspens? Was his father even now fitting shaft to bowstring? Khrandor pulled his axe free.

"Sire, what is it?" Colonel Girath said, eyes sweeping the valley.

Khrandor spat. He tried to swallow his fear, lest his voice tremble. "Trust no one here. Remember, Gorick drafted many of them to fight us. We do not know if the summons is another rebel trick."

"T'would be a vile one, lying about your father—"

Khrandor snorted. "That's what makes me think it real. In Idren, everyone knows there was no love between that bastard and myself." He turned to the men. "Circle up. Arms ready." Ten men rode ahead; arrows notched.

As he followed them downhill, his eyes fixed on the ancient, gnarled pine on the edge of town. Kassandra would meet him beneath those low boughs, her body warm, her lips wet. Would she still cling to this icy backwater? Surely not, he was no longer a boy with no prospects fleeing a vengeful father. He was prince of the united lands. How could she resist being his queen? As he passed the tree, the memory changed. He had been waiting for her there when Brennan appeared. Khrandor shuddered. Brennan had come armed with a heavy staff, whereas he had nothing. Khrandor tried to clear his mind, but the memory clung with iron claws. He could feel his ribs cracking beneath the blows of the staff. He remembered the awful stink when he lost control of his bowels. Brennan had nailed his soiled trousers to the meeting tree in the center of town. Khrandor recalled the horror on Kassandra's face when she arrived hours later, finding him broken and bloody and naked. He'd been certain he would die. She bound his wounds, washed away the blood with her tears, but her actions merely delivered him to his father's hungry riding crop. The iron and leather hilt of Khrandor's battle axe bit into his palms as he tightened his grip.

"Sire," Girath's gauntleted hand touched his horse's neck.

Khrandor blinked, freed of the memory. He chuckled at the ragtag line of men arrayed across the road armed with rusted swords and pick axes.

"You'll find no shelter here!" An old man brandished a pitted blade.

*Master Resivak? Surely not.* Khrandor remembered Resivak tending his wounds after a beating when he was five or six, not long after his mother had died. Resivak had been ancient even then. Father had threatened the old man, and Resivak had ignored Khrandor since. The old man's blade shook with palsy.

Khrandor dismounted, raising a hand to stay his men. "Master Resivak? Is that you?"

The old man's eyes widened; the blade clattered onto the road. Khrandor saw his men instinctively charge forward, weapons raised. He held his hand high. These were good men.

"Khr—Khran—Sir—Lord Investigator—I mean General—Khrandor?"

"Yes." Khrandor grinned at the collection of titles from his service in Gorick's army. He flashed his best interrogator's grin: disarming, sly, cunning. "You sent word that my..." Khrandor swallowed, struggling not to say *bastard*, "father had died. I am here to settle his accounts and take ownership of the mines."

"What are you doing here?"

The voice came from a young man with thinning brown hair. Hurovan. "Hello little brother," Khrandor said. "Were you planning to usurp my claim to the mines?"

"We need them!"

Khrandor gestured with his battle axe, roaring. "I need those mines. Until I crush Prince Rajan there will be no peace." He stepped closer, lowering his voice. "I need the gold mines. And as the eldest, it is my right to claim them." He pointed the curved blade toward his brother. "Do you object?"

Hurovan's eyes glanced from the axe to the mounted men. He sighed. "Welcome home, Khrandor."

Khrandor smiled. *So the summons is real, the bastard is dead. This will be simple.* He mounted and rode through the line of villagers. They walked fast to keep up with the horses. Resivak babbled about the hardships they had suffered while other men nodded their heads. In a few moments, they had crossed Idren to that accursed stone house on the north side of the village. The pitched roof looked like his father's angry, arched brows. Khrandor had felt less fear leading a phalanx into a hail of arrows. His mouth went dry. The oak door stood open, like a demon's gesture, welcoming him into its shadows and horrors. He checked his sword, it slid easily in the sheath. Dead or alive, his father would not hurt him again.

"Sire, is something wrong?"

Khrandor looked from Girath to the house. He did not trust his voice, so he shook his head. Resivak and Hurovan stared at him, as though they expected something. "What?"

"We were just talking about the hardships we've suffered. And I do hope that you will keep some of the profit from the gold mines here, so that we can provide for our people. After all, Idren is your hometown, Lord Khrandor." Had Resivak just demoted him from Lord Investigator to some miserable noble?

Khrandor laughed. "You will still be paid for your work in the mines, if that is what you are worried about."

"I can oversee them for you, brother. I've been helping father with it for..." His voice trailed off as his eyes met Khrandor's. "For...some time."

*Hurovan. Little coddled Hurovan. Father didn't slap you, did he? He didn't burn you, did he? No, you were always the bright one. Always the baby. You never worked in the mines. You never dug until your hands bled. You never felt the lashes on your back. You have no idea how to run those mines or how to ensure I get paid. In fact, you probably administered them for Gorick, didn't you, little brother? Do you think I'm a fool?* Khrandor swallowed the urge to backhand the privileged imbecile. "I have my own men for that."

Khrandor took the steps to the veranda two at a time, hand on his hilt. The men followed. His father lay on a table in the middle of the receiving room. It smelled faintly of rot. The bastard appeared asleep, and Khrandor immediately wanted to silence his footsteps lest he wake him. His palms sweated. *Plunge the dagger through the bastard's heart before he wakes!* No, he couldn't appear superstitious before his men. He had to show them he was in control. The damned villagers followed him inside. Khrandor looked at the bastard's bushy eyebrows, the receding hairline of salt and pepper hair braided in a short queue, the thick mustache. Hatred simmered under his skin, pooling into pearls of sweat on his brow. Heat prickled up his shoulders, along his neck. The wool cloak burned against his skin, the chain mail crushed his lungs. Any moment now, the bastard would sit up. He would swing his legs off that platform, crop in hand. Khrandor's knees shook. His breath came in gasps. The bastard would smile that demon smile and raise the crop...and...and...

Sweat ran down the scars on his back. The melted skin on his hands ached. The nightmare's blackness encroached on his vision, threatening to swallow him. *Calm down. Calm down! The bastard is not moving. Calm down.* Khrandor took a shallow breath. From a safe distance, he spat on the corpse's face. The bastard didn't move. Khrandor exhaled. The room expanded, giving him space to breathe. Blackness receded from his vision. *Thank the gods, the bastard is dead.*

Murmurs rippled through the crowd behind him like sunlight flickering across a river.

"Burn him," Khrandor croaked.

More murmurs.

Hurovan spoke over them, voice confident. "Brother, his wish was to be buried in the mines."

Khrandor whirled, smashing his fist into his palm. "I will not have that bastard's ghost haunting my mines!" *Calm down. Don't be hysterical in front of the men.* "He will be burned."

"But Lord Khrandor, we only burn criminals," Resivak said.

"This man sinned against me." Khrandor leveled a gaze at Resivak—he should know. "And I am the prince of the united lands. I administer justice in this kingdom, and I declare him a criminal." Khrandor stabbed a finger toward the corpse, keeping one eye on it at all times. "He. Will. Burn!"

"No!" Hurovan rushed toward him. "I will not—"

One of the mercenaries cracked his gauntleted fist against the back of Hurovan's neck, sending him to his knees.

Khrandor forced his interrogator's smile again. "It doesn't matter what you want, little brother. I will let you keep this damned house. Cross me again, and I'll burn it down too. Resivak, have Umaya draw up the documents for the mines."

"Umaya is four years dead, milord."

"Who is your judge?"

"I am, sir."

"Would you do me the honor, Master Resivak?"

"What is the ratio of profit sharing?"

"I told you. The men that work the mines will be paid. As they are currently paid."

"But, Lord Khrandor, it has been several hard winters. And the 'men' that work those mines are mostly children. The men were drafted into Prince Gorick's army when you—" Resivak swallowed. He stepped backwards.

Resivak may have been old, he may not have known the difference in noble titles, but he was smart enough not to remind Khrandor that Idren had been drafted to slay him when he rose against Prince Gorick. "I saw many familiar faces in that battle. And I am sorry they were drafted into that fool's army. I gave Prince Gorick a chance to surrender."

"You gave him a chance to surrender his daughters to you. What sane man would agree to those terms?"

The outburst came from a tanned face, with curly blond hair, and a scar down the cheek. Khrandor's spine tingled. "Why, Brennan, well met. Were you there?" The interrogator's thrill opened like a flower in Khrandor's gut, replacing the abject fear caused by the corpse. "Yes, those were my terms. I could not risk Gorick turning against me as I continued the advance east; I'd have been trapped between armies. You obviously don't understand tactics of war."

"I understand well enough."

"Your understanding must have aided Gorick immeasurably." Khrandor smiled at Brennan, relishing the way it made the man recoil. "Master Resivak, is that profit sharing not to your liking?"

"But, sir, lord, I thought that since Idren is your hometown—"

"If I give you special treatment, every damn place I've lain my head these last thirteen years will want special treatment. I will review the accounts and see if the wage can be increased, but for now, things stay as they are."

"Khrandor," said his brother, still pinned on his knees by the mercenary. "I said, now."

"Yes, milord," said Resivak.

"Are you going to let him bully you into that? You know that if they keep those wages we'll never make it through winter!"

"Brennan, do you not have the courage to question me directly?"

Khrandor crossed the marble entryway, boots clicking on stone.

Brennan flattened his mouth into one line and studied his worn shoes.

Khrandor continued. "Perhaps you'd like to offer me some of your wise council? Perhaps you'd like to tell me which tree to hide in so that you can spear me down like I did with Gorick? Was that the war counsel you gave him?"

Brennan remained silent, but his fists clenched.

Brennan was easy to control; he'd be even easier to break. Khrandor stood a little too close, talked a little too softly in a voice that would echo down the man's spine. "It's funny how the tables turn, isn't it? Once you beat me. You nailed my pants to the meeting tree in the square. And now, look at where you are. You stood on the wrong side of Gorick's battlefield, didn't you? Tell me, did it give you pleasure to leave me half dead beneath the pine? Did it?"

"It was a long time ago—"

"I still have the scars." Khrandor circled him. "Do you know that my right knee has ached in cold weather ever since?"

"No...I didn't—"

"I will take what I want, Brennan. And not you, not Prince Gorick, not Prince Rajan will stop me. Do you understand?"

Brennan nodded, slowly. His fingers twisted on the hilt of the notched blade that he still carried.

*Swing it at me.* Hurovan called his name. Khrandor held a hand up, and heard the jingle of mail as the men restrained his brother. Khrandor continued circling Brennan, lowering his voice so only his victim could hear. "Do you know where Kassandra is?"

"Leave her out of this."

"So you do know where she is."

"I said, leave her out of this."

"Why? She's a grown woman now, why are you protecting her? Did you marry her?" Khrandor swallowed his revulsion, not letting it disrupt his interrogator's smile. He was close now, he just had to nudge Brennan over the edge. Khrandor dropped his voice to a rotten, insinuating whisper. "I will take whatever I want. Kassandra. The mines. All of it. I will take what-so-ever I want."

Brennan spun, raising his blade. Khrandor stepped inside the swing, batting Brennan's arm away and landed a punch in the man's neck. Brennan's blade clattered to the ground as his hands grasped at his throat. He doubled over, wheezing. Steel sang from sheaths behind him. Khrandor grinned. These were good men, but he'd wanted Brennan's blood for many years. He laced his fingers behind Brennan's head and kneed him in the face three times. A wonderful lightness filled Khrandor's heart. No interrogation had ever been so sweet. Khrandor held Brennan up with his left and pummeled him with his right. Bones crunched, blood splattered. For the first time since setting out for Idren, Khrandor laughed. He should have come back years ago to crack his gauntleted knuckles against Brennan's bones. He let Brennan's body fall to the floor, kicking the crumpled mess once for every nightmare where he'd relived the beating under the tree. Blood pooled on the marble. Exhilaration sang through Khrandor's muscles. His smile beamed.

He turned that grin onto the villagers. They flinched. Joy loped through his body like a wolf. He wanted to dance. "Get this bloody mess out of my brother's house." Mercenaries threw the broken body down the stairs of the front veranda. "Now, before we were so rudely interrupted, I think we were talking about drawing up the documents for the mines. You'll have those for me tomorrow, Master Resivak?"

"Yes, milord. I'll have them for you tomorrow morning." Resivak said to the floor.

"Wonderful. And tonight, we burn that bastard." The villagers fled the house. Hurovan was locked in his room. Khrandor took the account ledgers, the keys to the mines, and stationed some of his most trusted men there. That evening, over half the village turned out for the burning. Khrandor stayed long enough to ensure they went through with it. Once the pyre burned well, he stalked back inside. He would keep no vigil.

"Khrandor."

He knew that voice. It had called him out of nightmares for years. When things were blackest, he'd awake, thinking she would be there next to him, red hair pooled on the pillow, but she was never there. "Kassandra."

"Why did you beat my husband?"

His eyes followed the shape of her body in the flickering shadows from the pyre outside. Her beauty at fourteen had blossomed into a woman more ravishing than he'd imagined. Her face had lost none of its shape; her fiery hair was still long. He guffawed. "Husband? Brennan? Time has been good to you, but it has not made you wise."

The corners of her mouth flicked up, then back into her frown. "Why did you do it?"

"Why did he beat me all those years ago? Remember when he beat me under our tree? Remember when he tried to burn me at midsummer's eve? Remember when he pushed me into the stream in winter, and I fell beneath the ice? The real question is why do you stand up for him now, and why in the name of the gods did you marry him?"

"Because you left me." She sighed. "And because his family offered an amazing bride price to me and my father. It let Papa spend his last years in peace." Tears pooled in her eyes.

"I begged you to come with me! I begged you!"

She looked down, wiping her eyes. She swallowed. "I didn't think you were actually leaving. And...I was scared. I've never been out of this valley. I didn't know what Papa would do without me. I'm sorry."

Khrandor crossed the room, put his finger under her chin and lifted her gaze to meet his own. "Come with me now. Leave all this behind. I have a beautiful castle, in the south, where it's warm. You can have anything you want. You will be queen of the world."

"No." She pulled away.

"No? Would you rather stay in this icy hell waiting for winter's bane to find you? You'd rather stay with that lout of a husband you have? Had I known that, I would have killed him and settled your choice for you."

"Khrandor! That's why I won't go with you. I refuse to live in a world where you relish murder!"

"Is that what I do?"

"Yes."

He laughed. "Kassandra, someone has to be the leader. I rose to the occasion because the Princes were fools. Tell me, was Gorick any better?"

"Under Gorick, at least we had enough to eat. You should know. You served him. You were his general."

"Gorick was weak! This world only rewards the strong, and I will never be weak again. Come with me. You can have anything you want, anything in the world."

"No. The boy I knew believed there was more to life than being the most ruthless person in the world. The boy I knew loved to create things, to build things. All you do is destroy. When was the last time you held a hammer? A paint brush?"

"Don't you realize what I am creating? I am re-creating the world. If you want to die in an icy backwater, then hammers and paint brushes are wonderful distractions from reality. But if you want to change the world, if you want to make something of yourself, then you need a sword. The strong rule the weak. I've seen it again and again. Hell, the man who taught it to me is that bastard on the pyre. The strong rule, and I intend to rule. I intend to make the world I want. And I want you in it. You will come with me."

"Congratulations, Khrandor. You've become your father."

"Bitch!" He backhanded her. She caught herself on the long dining table. An icicle drove through his heart. She would pay for that. He pushed her down onto the table, pulled her skirts up.

"Khrandor! Stop! Stop!"

"You will come with me!" He was nothing like his father. He smiled at the way her hands curled into claws, the way her fingernails raked the wood. She tried to push herself up, but he forced her down. Blood throbbed through his loins. "Will you come with me?"

"Khrandor, don't do this, please."

He pulled his trousers down. "Say you'll come with me, and I'll stop."

"Khrandor, please."

"Come with me."

"No! You are no better than—"

She screamed. Even in his imagination, he'd never believed taking Kassandra would feel this good. Her screams died into growls, then whimpers. The table creaked across the floor. "You will come with me, Kassandra. You. Will." His hands tightened on her hips as a thunderous joy reverberated through his body, his back arched, his breath caught. Kassandra was unlike any other woman; she could banish the nightmares, banish them forever.

When Khrandor released her, she sank to the floor.

At length, she spoke. "Is this the world you want to create, Khrandor? How many lives will you wreck to create it?" She wiped the blood from the corner of her mouth with her sleeve. "I say to you it will not last. One day this patchwork of princedoms will fall apart. You will be alone again. Only this time, no one will come to save you because you've hurt everyone who cared."

She would be a challenge to break. The interrogator's grin crept across his face. "You will come with me, Kassandra. I'll not leave here empty handed."

"You have your mines."

"I want you."

She spat blood toward him. As he dodged, she was on her feet, trying to run past. He caught her and dragged her upstairs. She struggled as he tied her to his bed. Every time she winced as he pulled the ropes tighter, his heart hammered in his loins.

"Let me go, please. On all that is holy, let me go."

"There is nothing holy, my dear." Khrandor dropped his clothes on the floor. "Say you'll come with me, and this will all stop."

"I—" Her eyes caught the dagger in his hand. She tried to shy away from the point.

Khrandor's heart danced. He'd tortured plenty of women, but it had never been so luscious as this. "You will come with me, my dear." He sliced through her dress, marveling at her exposed body. So beautifully vulnerable. So beautifully afraid. So ripe to be broken. He traced the curve of her breast with the point of his knife, careful not to cut her. Not yet.

"Khrandor, please. Let me go. Please."

"Only when you agree to come with me." He lowered his body onto hers, relishing the feel of her trying to squirm away from him and not finding any escape. "Sweet Kassandra."

He smothered her screams with his mouth as he forced his way between her legs.

It was nearly dawn when Khrandor went downstairs to find Colonel Girath. He and the men slept in the entryway. "Sir?" The colonel said.

"We leave now. Saddle the horses."

"The documents?"

"We have no need. Commander Regen is controlling the mines and has the keys. I have the prize I came for. Best we leave before these people cause us trouble."

They rode through the dozing town. Gray light pooled behind low clouds that wreathed the mountains, threatening snow. Khrandor's heart leapt as they rode south, imagining his return to the sunlit, white castle walls, the banners flying high. He glanced at Kassandra. She'd resisted and cursed him until deep in the night when he resorted to pain. Now, she obeyed his every demand. Even in his old riding clothes, she was beautiful. Dark circles bruised her eyes. The welts he'd left on her back would sting against the heavy wool, but would heal without scarring. She sat the horse awkwardly, every step of its gait pressing into a different part of her soreness. He smiled. She said nothing, shoulders hunched forward, mouth pressed into a firm line. She stared at her hands tied to the pommel of the saddle. With the gold mines to fund the army and Kassandra to chase away the nightmares, he'd be invincible. He envisioned Prince Rajan fleeing before him.

Pain shot through his left shoulder, shattering his reverie. Kassandra's face was next to his, tears in her eyes, mouth frowning in savage determination. The hilt of a dagger protruded from beneath his shoulder blade. It burned as she pulled the knife free.

"Sir!" The men were slow. They circled the horses; their steel sang.

"I will not go with you!" she screamed. The swords kept her from advancing on him again. He noticed her hands had come untied, and she held the old dagger he'd always kept under his mattress. Her horse pranced sideways, uncertain, neighing at the swords arrayed against it. "You're a sick man, Khrandor, no better than your father!" She looked around, as though she expected something to happen. Worry crossed her features. Khrandor's vision swam. He tried to put pressure on the wound, but he couldn't reach it. Blood trickled down his back.

"Kassandra. I love you."

"You have no idea what that means." She glanced to either side of the road.

One of the mercenaries grabbed her from behind. She twisted out of his reach. "No!" She plunged the knife deep into her stomach.

"Kassandra!"

Khrandor spurred to her, jostling his men out of the way. He caught her as she fell, but they both tumbled to the ground. Shouts erupted on either side of the road. A wild arrow sailed overhead. Khrandor tried to stop the blood that soaked rapidly through her clothes. "Attack!" shouted Khrandor, waving one arm. "It's an ambush, you fools!"

As the horses wheeled and steel sang against steel, Khrandor held Kassandra, wiping sweat-matted hair from her face. All he had ever wanted was to see her brown eyes smiling at him in the morning, to hear her laugh in the evening, to fall against her lips as the moon rose, and to discover safety from the inevitable nightmares in the circle of her arms. Thirteen years. Thousands of leagues. Rivers of blood. And yet, she would choose death over him. A constriction burned at the back of his throat. His eyes stung. He was certain this was his own death, finding him at last, just as she foretold. He found it hard to breathe around the blockade in his throat. But instead of dying, he convulsed, and wept, rocking back and forth.

"Sweet Kassandra...please..." He rocked back and forth as his tears fell on her pale brow. She was right: he had become his father. Merciless, sadistic. "Kassie, I won't hurt you again. Kassie, I'm...I'm sorry."

Her eyes flicked to him, recognizing the old name. She touched his face. "Too late for that, Khran. I'd hoped...you'd be different. Was going to warn you..." She convulsed.

"No, no, please, by the gods, Kassie, Kassie!" He shook; all his fear, all his terror, all his hatred streamed down his face. "No, please. Kassie, I'm so sorry, I'm so..."

He touched a soft, loving kiss against her perfect lips as her heart shuddered and stopped.

---

CLINT TALBERT started writing at a very young age—when he'd read all the King Arthur stories in his backwoods Texas library—because he figured the world needed more Camelot. He lives on the ocean in California with a very cute Boxer puppy. This is his first fiction sale (of many, hopefully). His debut novel, *Last Stand of Darwony*, is forthcoming from Barking Rain Press. Follow along with his progress at www.cmtalbert.com.

# BROKEN CLOUDS

## *Rachel Swirsky*

ALEX WALKED HOME THROUGH light rain that was almost soundless as it silvered the sidewalk. The whole world seemed colorless: overcast sky, grey drizzle, endless cement.

The empty, grasping ache in her abdomen gnawed at her, not just because of the pain but because of the frisson of loss that accompanied it. She was like a glass with the water poured out, a vacant vessel.

Would it ever stop? Did anyone ever recover from having the magic torn out of their flesh?

Her house came into view as she turned the corner, its dilapidated single story dwarfed by the apartment buildings on either side. It always seemed to be cowering, as if the neighboring giants might decide at any moment to crush it into oblivion. Its faded wood siding was the same grayed-out blue as the rainy sky. Battered shutters held tight against wind and water.

Rain had swollen the doorframe. Alex grunted as she put her weight into tugging it open. Hinges screeched. Slanting rain pooled inside the threshold.

Alex squished into the entranceway and pulled the door closed behind her. She abandoned her boots and threw her messenger bag beside them; its sodden contents were worthless now.

Her socks left a trail of wet footprints as she made her way into the kitchen. Alex's older sister, Jenny, sat at the table, cutting coupons out of the newspaper, the way no one did anymore except for Jenny. She wore a loose t-shirt and jeans, cozy and cheerful despite the weather. Jenny was that kind of person. She woke up happily at dawn and hummed through her daily routine.

Jenny smiled as she looked up. Green irises swirled with hints of yellow, summer grass dappled with dandelions.

The empty place inside Alex ached.

Jenny held up a coupon. "Good deal on gardening supplies. Two bags of soil for the price of one."

She chuckled as she returned the coupon to the pile. Alex and Jenny didn't have a garden. A lot of coupons were like that. They offered deals on stuff you didn't need, hoping you'd suddenly be inspired to buy a blender when you really just wanted the 20% off on microwave dinners they were offering two rows down. Jenny clipped them all, though, just in case.

Alex tried to chuckle back, but the sound came out false. Jenny slid her a skeptical look. Alex tried to keep her face blank so that even Jenny, who knew her better than anyone, wouldn't know that something was wrong.

Jenny stood. "Want some tea?"

"Sure."

Jenny pulled their kettle out of the cabinet above the sink. The sound of water pouring into battered metal twinned the sound of rain on the shutters. It was the sound of something that had been high up falling to the ground. It was the sound of water breaking.

Jenny didn't remember dying.

Alex had checked as thoroughly as she could without asking Jenny outright. Her sister was completely unaware anything had happened. She didn't even remember not remembering something.

It was probably for the best. It meant Jenny didn't ask questions Alex didn't want to answer.

The day Jenny died had been rainy, too. To celebrate Alex's high school graduation, the sisters had decided to bike out to the suburbs and visit the park where they'd played as kids, back before the car crash that killed their parents and left eighteen-year-old Jenny with custody of her ten-year-old sister.

Visiting the park was supposed to resolve things, to tie happy memories of the past to the success of the present, wrapping up Alex's childhood like a bow. Instead, it just hammered home how much everything had changed in eight years, how the old streets looked weary, the houses dingy behind chipped paint, the lawns parched and brown.

They remembered the landmarks—the bright blue roof on the two-story between Ford and Applegate, the elementary school, the enormous oak that cast its shadow over three front lawns. Somehow, though, they couldn't find the park itself; they rode back and forth, tried every turn they could think of, asked people passing by. The park was always really close now, just a block away, if you turn back, keep going, go left, head right.

Wet and tired, Jenny and Alex decided to bus back home, and set to walking their bikes to the nearest stop. There was one major street to cross in order to get there: a busy, forty-five mile-per-hour avenue that led to strip malls in either direction. They stopped at the corner, waited for the little blinking man, and started across the asphalt.

The crosswalk was empty until it wasn't.

Some hard-core drunk, already blasted by three p.m., came speeding down at sixty-five. He tried to brake. His tires spun. Rubber shrieked; metal struck. Jenny shoved Alex to the ground.

Alex barely had the chance to look up before she saw her sister falling under a bright, metal wall. The driver was a dark silhouette behind the windshield, hands shaking on the wheel. Tires chewed the bike into scrap then bit into Jenny. A wet crunch. The smell of blood bloomed, mixing with the rain.

Taillights streaked past as the coward fled. Bruised and dizzy, Alex pulled herself toward her sister's body.

Afterward, there had been an ambulance and a declaration of time of death and doctors who wanted to know how Alex was related to the victim. "She's my sister," Alex said. "She's been taking care of me since I was ten."

They asked more questions, but she didn't answer. Jenny was dead and she was alone.

Jenny stood by the stove, watching the kettle heat. "Winter's coming. We need better weather stripping."

Rain tapped on the shutters. Cool wind blew through poorly insulated walls.

"Maybe I can find a coupon for it," Jenny continued.

She smiled, inviting her sister to laugh. Alex couldn't even manage her hollow chuckle.

"What's wrong?" Jenny asked.

Alex couldn't look her sister in the eye while she lied. She counted cracks in the linoleum. "The days are getting shorter. I miss summer, that's all."

"Stroke of luck. I've got twenty percent off on a full-spectrum lamp," Jenny said. "No, seriously. I found it today."

Alex still couldn't laugh, but this time, the screaming kettle provided a distraction.

After Jenny's death, Alex walked around in a daze. She had nothing to do, felt no connection with her former classmates. There was a little money left, enough to see her through six months or so. She could have gotten a job before then, but she couldn't bear the idea of working minimum wage while she grieved, weeping silently at the cash register between customer orders.

She took long walks, rode her bicycle, read books, spent hours staring at nothing. She visited the library once a week to refresh her pile of mysteries. One Tuesday, somewhere between Grafton and Hillerman, she got lost in the stacks.

She'd been browsing a perfectly ordinary shelf, filled with rumpled paperbacks, but suddenly, everything was different. Tall, narrow mahogany bookcases formed an endless, twisting maze, their shelves populated by dust and spiders and books far too old to belong in a local library branch. She scanned for a way out, but saw nothing except corridors of books.

She jumped as a crooked man stepped around a corner. He was lean and dark like an evening shadow. He wore an old-fashioned suit with tails, elegantly cut but shabby. Tattered lapels sported desiccated flowers that had withered where they were pinned. Long, pointed fingers poked out of holes in his pockets.

"Wh—What do you want?" Alex stammered.

The man grinned jaggedly. "It's good to see you." Beckoning with a gnarled finger, he turned and darted through the stacks.

Alex hesitated before following, but then she realized—with Jenny gone, what did she care if he led her someplace dangerous?

She raced to keep up with his grasshopper-long legs. She whipped around corners only to see ragged coattails disappearing.

At last, she turned to find him standing beside an iron gate that led into a section of the library that looked even older than the mahogany shelves. Light from mounted torches picked out patterns in the gate's scrollwork. They read: DARK MAGIC.

The crooked man tapped the gate with his forefinger. It swung open.

"You can go in," he said. "If you want."

She started forward. He moved to block her path.

"Lots of people have the talent for dark magic," he said. "Only a few reach the point where they truly don't care whether they live or die. This is a place for the hopeless."

"I want to go in," Alex said.

With a cavernous grin, the crooked man stepped aside. When she looked over her shoulder, he'd disappeared.

Inside the mysterious archive, books populated the shelves sparsely, as if quarantined from each other. Dried blood streaked old vellum covers. Everything smelled of bones and mold.

All around, the shadows watched. Strange figures took shape in the corners, wagging their tongues and making obscene gestures, baring their genitals and grinning when Alex shied away.

Fingers pointed in a dozen, conflicting directions. Alex followed them at random. Despite dead ends and false starts, the shadows seemed to be herding her toward something.

She knew immediately when she saw it: a carrel upon which a single book lay open, a black silk ribbon marking the page to which it was turned.

The heading was written in old-fashioned, slanting script. It made her heart beat faster.

*Resurrection.*

Alex's mouth dried. She ran her finger down the page, memorizing the directions for enchanting a dagger that would steal its victims' souls. The magic spelled out an easy equation: twelve stolen lives for one resurrection.

She could bring Jenny back.

The shadows writhed and laughed.

Jenny brought their mugs of tea into the living room. She set Alex's on the coffee table and pulled the chain that turned on the overhead lamp. Under the direct light, Jenny's skin shimmered with the rainbow colors of the eleven souls Alex had collected to save her.

Eleven out of twelve.

The magic book had been clear on the number:

> *One for body*
> *One for breath*
> *Two for memory*
> *Three to pay death*
> *Four to mend the broken soul*
> *And a last, like wax, to seal the whole.*

Without the last soul, the spell would have nothing to hold it together. It would disintegrate into dust on the wind and Jenny would die again.

Jenny, unknowing, settled in their broken-down but still plush armchair, and sipped her tea. "This stuff may be more expensive, but it's totally worth it." She raised her cup. "Are you going to have some?"

Alex ached for her lost magic. She couldn't help remembering the crosswalk: the screeching tires; the apple-red metal, washed clean by rain; the driver's frightened eyes.

Alex stepped back. She couldn't watch Jenny die again. She shouldn't have come back to the house. She should have gone somewhere else. Back to the library to find the crooked man. To the train station to buy a ticket for someplace far away. Anywhere but here.

"I've got, um, some errands," Alex said. "I need to get some stuff. You know, from the drug store."

"Now?" Jenny asked.

"It'll only take ten minutes."

"It's raining."

"Ten minutes," Alex repeated plaintively.

Jenny glanced down at Alex's mug. "Drink your tea first?"

Steam rose from the mug into the cold air. It smelled like peppermint, humid and sweet.

Alex hesitated. The spell required that the twelfth soul be paid by nightfall. It wouldn't fall apart until then.

There were still a few hours left. Alex could give Jenny some of that time and still be gone before her sister died.

She picked up her mug. It was warm in her hand. She blew and her breath rippled across the placid, dark surface.

After she found the book in the library, Alex set to work.

That night, when the fireflies emerged, she cast a seeking charm that caused a trail of them to glow red instead of gold. She followed the path of blood-colored lights to the door of the driver who'd killed her sister.

He was middle-aged, clothes well-chosen but rumpled, eyes red though it was only evening. He opened the door with a suave smile, expecting someone else. He frowned for a moment when he saw Alex, but recovered with slick charm. "Can I help you?"

When Alex stabbed the man in the throat, his eyes brightened with surprise. He seemed unable to imagine why anyone would have a reason to hate his smooth, handsome self.

Alex stumbled down his front step. She hadn't brought anything to clean herself up with. She hadn't even brought gloves to hide her fingerprints. Her hands were slick with his blood, matching the fireflies above her.

Alex had always been timid. She'd lost so much so young. She knew that life was full of precious, fragile things that you had to hold carefully because they could break at any moment.

Now there was nothing left to break.

The smell of the man's blood was bright like a penny. It was the smell of vigor and freedom. It was the smell of possibility.

She followed the firefly-trail down dark, deserted streets. From time to time, headlights swung toward her, and she should have cowered, fearing discovery. Instead, she walked boldly on, and each time the cars pulled away, never coming too near.

Then, as Alex passed under a streetlamp spotlight, she heard someone gasp. "Goddess! Are you all right? Is that blood?"

A blonde woman stood on her apartment's front step. She looked older than Alex, probably college-aged, but somehow she didn't look like the type who'd gone to college. She wore a peasant-style blouse tucked into an ankle-length skirt. Wide, blue eyes stared with alarm.

Alex could have turned and ran, but she was someone new now. She was predator, not prey.

She held up her bloody hands. "It isn't mine."

Instead of screaming, the woman approached. "I can smell the magic in the air." She glanced up at the blinking red trail of lights. "The magic came to me when I was about your age."

Startled, Alex staggered back. The woman continued undaunted.

"I remember what it was like, starting out. No one to guide you…

no idea what's happening...I'd fight some demon in the dreamlands and stumble back, all covered in its ichor, and wish I wasn't on my own." She gestured Alex toward the door. "My name is Lyric. Come inside. You need to clean yourself up."

Alex wasn't sure at first why she followed Lyric. She only knew that once the offer was made she was desperately curious to find out how Lyric lived.

Her apartment was cheerfully cluttered with sheet music and various instruments. Enchanted items gleamed here and there: crystal globes and charmed angels' feathers and vials of golden powder. They were artifacts of a magic that looked nothing like what Alex had encountered in the library, a different kind of magic altogether.

Slowly, as Alex washed her hands and listened to Lyric burble, she realized what it all meant. If there was a dark magic then there must be a light magic, too.

A magic for people with hope.

What do you do on your last day with your sister? Sky-dive? Ride in a hot air balloon? Drink and dance? Weep and gnash?

What do you do on your last day with your sister when she doesn't know she's already dead?

Alex stood in the kitchen and watched Jenny mix spices and roll out dough. She listened to her plan for winter. She watched the shadows that the rain made on the shutters and wondered what would happen when the sky stopped falling.

Lyric was an Iowa-transplant. She'd left home at eighteen, moved to the city, and taken a new name. She was a singer-songwriter who earned extra income playing in a piano bar. Hence: Lyric.

She knew all about magic. Her kind of magic, at least.

"There's a secret world overlain on this one," she said. "It's like we're on one side of the mirror. The other side is right in front of you. You just have to press your nose against the glass and look."

Lyric introduced Alex to her community of magical friends. There was Sabella, a strange woman who always wore a plain, black mask that lacked eyeholes. She could use anything to scry the future, even piles of trash. Alex's favorite was Dirk, a four-foot-tall man who wore a long trench coat to conceal the dusting of golden fur that revealed his cat-magic heritage. Fingerless gloves left his claws sharp and bare.

Alex knew it was stupid to spend her time with a community of good witches. She kept her secrets to herself, but she was still risking discovery.

When she met them, Alex hadn't had anyone else in her life. Her house echoed with the lack of her sister. Even once the accumulated souls restored Jenny's body, at first she was only a shell, void of personality and volition.

It was good to have sun-dappled afternoons in Lyric's apartment, listening to Sabella's grim forecasts and Dirk's exaggerated exploits.

"There will always be a place for you here," Lyric told her more than once. "A place to rest when the world and magic and everything are too much."

Alex knew that snub-nosed, open-hearted Lyric was making promises she couldn't keep. Despite everything, it was comforting to hear.

"I've been thinking," Jenny said as they sat down to dinner.

The scent of rosemary rose from roast chicken, mingling with the aromas of cinnamon-baked apples and diced red potatoes.

"I'm not sure it's good for us to stay here, in this house," Jenny said. "It made sense when you were younger, but now that you're out of school, we're going to have two incomes. We can move somewhere that isn't full of old memories about Mom and Dad. Somewhere that doesn't make us sad. This place won't get much on the market, but it'd be enough to get us a new start somewhere else. I could get a better job. You could take night classes."

Alex looked down at her plate. "I couldn't get into college."

"Junior college. You can get your AA then transfer."

"I don't really want to go back to school," Alex said. "That's more your thing."

Alex felt old guilt stir in her stomach. Jenny had been about to leave for college when their parents died and she'd had to drop out to take care of her sister. Alex knew it wasn't her fault, but from time to time, guilt whispered in her ear that, in a way, it was.

"I'm sorry," Alex said.

Jenny knew what she meant. She shrugged. "It was a long time ago." She reached across the table to take Alex's hand. "I wouldn't trade my years with you. You know that, right? The me who left home, who went off to college, I'm not that person anymore. I like who I am."

"You could go back to school," Alex said. "I'll work to pay for your classes. You can be her again. The you that you were supposed to be."

Alex knew it was stupid to say. Jenny was going to die. She was already dead. But Alex felt better for the fraction of a moment when she could believe it was true.

Jenny chuckled softly. "I'm too old to go back to school."

"Of course you're not!"

"Oh, God. Writing papers. Raising my hand. I don't think I could survive."

Jenny was trying to laugh it off, but Alex could hear the desire in her voice. "You'd be great!" Alex said.

Jenny pulled her hand away from Alex's. She stood to clear the table. "We'll talk about it." She paused thoughtfully as she piled dishes by the sink. "Yeah. I think it'll be good for us to move away from here."

The sink bubbled with dish soap as Jenny plunged her hands into the water. Dishes clanked. Dinner smells faded as leftovers cooled, waiting to be cling-wrapped and tucked into the fridge.

Alex's resolve hardened. Jenny had already given up her life once. Alex wouldn't let her do it again.

She'd find another way.

Alex's second kill was a neighbor who kept convincing the police to ignore the domestic abuse calls, even though they could see her husband slumping behind her in the doorway, cowed and bruised.

Third: a policeman who'd raped a number of prostitutes after threatening to arrest them. Fourth and fifth: a sister and brother who ran a pyramid scheme that stole millions from the elderly. Alex killed the sister first. During the long seven days before the spell called for the brother's soul, he lived in fear of the vengeful hand that had slain his sister. He wept when Alex found him. He promised her money. When that didn't work, he vowed contrition. Still, she cut away his soul.

The sixth death, the seventh, the eighth, all fell easily beneath her blade.

Those were the easy weeks, the weeks when she felt no guilt, when the smell of blood wasn't only the smell of magic and triumph but also of self-righteousness. She was a vengeful sorceress, cleansing the world of those who needed to die.

Her first victims had come so easily that, when the time approached for her to take the next, she never doubted that an appropriate lamb would present itself for the sacrifice.

None came.

She spent her nights prowling. The alleys were full of shadows and strangers, none dark enough to invite her knife.

In the final hour, she steeled her resolve. If she couldn't find someone who deserved to die then she'd kill whoever she found.

The victim walked straight up to her. A drunk boy, a little older than Alex, scrawny and bright-eyed. He leaned heavily on Alex as he asked her to walk him home. A college student. Philosophy.

Afterward, when she unpacked his bag, she found poems written in the margins of his text books. Silly limericks for his sister and purple sonnets for his boyfriend.

The expression on his face as he'd died had been one of confusion. He wasn't shocked, wasn't alarmed, was simply puzzled. His eyes seemed to ask: Are you really doing this? Why?

His name was Aaron.

When she got home, Alex locked herself in her room. Crying and shaking, she read his poems over and over again, trying to make some sense out of what she'd done. The pages wrinkled and his handwriting began to fade, but she found no answers. He was dead and she had killed him. There was no justification to be found. Those were the only things that mattered.

Still, when the time came for her next kill, she ventured into the night.

After Alex excused herself from the table, she returned to the front hall to recover her messenger bag. She pulled open the flap and dug inside for her bespelled dagger.

Her victims' blood had disappeared into the strange, translucent blade. She held the knife up to the light and watched soul-colors shift beneath the surface as they sometimes did beneath her sister's skin.

When she'd possessed her magic, Alex had sensed the blade as a kind of cold, dark magnetism, pulling the heat and life from the room. With her magic gone, the blade was only ordinarily eerie. Watching it with only her mortal senses felt odd, as if she was trying to make out something without opening her eyes.

Alex palmed the hilt. She crossed the house to her room. Noises came from the kitchen, her sister washing dishes and humming off-key along with the radio. Outside air crept beneath her window, filling her room with the scent of wet soil.

Alex sat on her bed. She looked at the dagger in her hands. She no longer had the magic to lure an unwilling soul, but perhaps the spell would accept a sacrifice.

And if it didn't—so what? The magic had found Alex because she had no hope.

The sacrifice would work or it wouldn't. It was all she had left to give.

Victim eleven was an old woman living alone on the first floor of a run-down brownstone. She was a piano teacher, her rooms filled with dusty magic books and battered pianos. The magic whispered that her tissues were breaking down, that she only had a few years left. What was that against Jenny's whole life?

When she was finished, Alex surveyed the remnants of the life she'd taken. Framed photographs of former students lined the wall. One caught Alex's attention: a smiling blonde girl with an upturned nose.

Lyric.

What followed was one of those moments that only makes sense in the context of magic, when the push and pull of dark forces against light creates what would otherwise be a staggering improbability. Lyric, coming on a whim to visit her old mentor, treaded lightly on the porch stairs, her hand twisting the doorknob, her face appearing in the crack of the opening door.

Alex darted aside, hiding in the shadow cast by a heavy, velvet curtain.

Lyric ran toward the corpse. "Mrs. Mueller? Oh, no! Mrs. Mueller!" She knelt in the pooling blood. "What happened to you?"

Alex crept toward the door, trying to escape while Lyric examined the body, but the noise of her shoes on the hardwood summoned Lyric's attention. Piercing blue eyes went straight to her face.

"Stop! Who are you? What did you do to Mrs. Mueller?" Lyric rose, all furious outrage, and then recognition dawned. "Alex?"

There was no more point in hiding. Alex stepped forward, holding her dagger between them. The spell was very specific about when she had to make her kills—it would ruin everything if she took another soul now. But Lyric didn't know that.

"I don't want to hurt you," Alex said. It was true.

Lyric's expression had turned from surprise to horror. "The blood on your hands when we met... it was human?"

Alex tried to laugh. It was so ridiculous. Only Lyric could have been so convinced it was blood from a magical beast that she hadn't even considered otherwise. But Alex had no mirth in her; the sound came out a dry husk.

"Magic can be volatile..." Lyric ventured. "Sometimes it creeps inside you...overwhelms you...makes you do things you wouldn't..."

Alex backed toward the open door, waving the dagger in front of her. "I'm going now. Don't follow me."

Lyric started toward her anyway. Alex tried to harden her gaze, to make it flat and murderous so that Lyric would be forced to see her as she was.

"I'll kill you if I have to," Alex said.

She could see what a struggle it was for Lyric to believe the worst of anyone, even with the evidence right in front of her, but fear won a moment's hesitation.

Alex ran.

Alex looked down at the dagger in her hands. She thought of all the bodies she'd bled. Would the spell accept her sacrifice without magic to guide her soul into the blade? Perhaps. Dark magic was like the shadows in the library: mocking, mercurial, cruel. It would like the chance to drink her life.

She pressed the blade against her throat, but hesitated before it bit too deeply. A drop of blood ran down her neck. Its scent mixed with the rain, just as her sister's had that day in the crosswalk.

The last sensations of her life: blood and rain, her sister's humming drifting from the kitchen, the empty ache of her missing magic.

The blade trembled as her hand shook.

For her twelfth victim, Alex found a drug runner. The year before, he'd been peripherally involved in a drive-by shooting, riding as a passenger behind the guy who shot the gun. He didn't deserve the death penalty, but better him than another college student or music teacher.

She sent him a message proposing an exchange. They settled on a location: a deserted alley positioned between two massive brick buildings that stared, windowlessly, down at the dumpsters and cracked asphalt.

The dealer leaned against brick. He was a skinny white kid with a cocky sneer. He kept glancing furtively in both directions, but concentrated on the north, where the alley led to the back of a bar.

Alex approached from the south. The fog-charm she'd cast silenced her footsteps. She kept her hand inside the messenger bag, fingers closed around the dagger's hilt.

Suddenly, the kid looked her way. She couldn't stop the sharp intake of breath that seemed to echo from wall to wall. How had he known she was there?

No, his gaze wasn't settling on her; it swung further up, to the top of a neighboring building.

A golden figure leapt down from the rooftop, trenchcoat streaming behind him. It was Dirk, twisting in the air so that he landed gracefully on his feet, directly between Alex and her prey.

"What the hell?" the kid spluttered. He took in Dirk's tawny fur, the glint of light on his naked claws. "What the fuck are you?"

Dirk ignored him. "We know you're here, Alex. Give it up."

Alex tried to think clearly despite her pounding heart. She was still wearing her fog-charm. Maybe she could escape without Dirk hearing her.

Before she could try, Lyric came blazing into the north end of the alley. The masked prophetess, Sabella, followed a step behind. Her finger rose, pointing straight at Alex's heart.

"The girl is there," Sabella intoned. "She's come to this place to kill, just as I saw in the patterns."

Dirk turned, tail whipping, and hissed at Alex.

Alex stepped back. "Leave me alone."

Lyric shook her head. "I'm sorry, Alex." Her blue eyes were infuriatingly more sad than angry.

"Sorry?" Alex repeated. "I'm a serial killer. I killed your music teacher. Be furious. Be frightened. Be righteous. Don't be sorry."

She pulled the knife from her bag. It rippled with the rainbow light of the souls she'd taken. Dirk hissed. Sabella held up her hand as if trying to shield herself from its aura.

"One more life," Alex said. "My sister raised me. I owe her everything. One more life will bring her back."

Slowly, Lyric shook her head. "No more lives."

Alex snarled. "If you kill me, then you're just as bad as I am! You're murdering my sister!" She twisted the knife in the air. "You know I won't let you do that!"

Lyric turned back toward Sabella. The prophetess nodded. "We have to," Sabella said.

Lyric sighed. Gathering herself, she strode toward Alex, blonde hair burning behind her like a golden flame, eyes cold and blue like the winter sky. Sabella flanked her. As they passed, Dirk fell into formation, teeth bared and eyes slitted.

The shred of light beneath Alex's windowsill was a deepening navy. There was no more time to waste.

Alex drew the blade across her throat.

Nothing happened.

There was no fireworks burst of pain, no red slashing her vision. She didn't grow faint from blood loss. She didn't die.

She moved the dagger so that its point thrust under her chin. The sharp metal stung as she swallowed. She gritted her teeth and stabbed.

Nothing.

She threw the dagger down. It fell onto the rug, spinning like a bottle until its tip pointed toward the window.

Alex touched her throat. No blood, no slash. Only skin. Her fingernail scratched the dried blood from the scratch she'd made earlier. The dagger had been sharp then, when she'd tried to slash but hesitated. It was as if it had only become harmless after she'd made her decision to die.

That was probably exactly what had happened. The cruel, mercurial dark magic had decided it would rather see Alex suffer her sister's death than savor Alex's blood.

She looked down at the dagger. Rainbow colors rippled across it, disconcertingly bright against the drab backdrop of her room.

She'd had hope for a while. Hope that her sister would live.

She should have known better. Dark magic was for the hopeless.

Dirk and Sabella pinned Alex to the ground. She watched the alley behind them, the way the grey of the cracked asphalt blended into the dirty bricks. The whole place was broken-down and dirty and abandoned; it belonged in the Dumpsters with the trash. Even the drug dealer had run off.

Lyric bent over her and then Alex could see nothing but lashes fluttering open over an eternity of guileless blue.

Lyric plunged her hand into Alex's stomach. Her fingers penetrated flesh and organs. Alex clenched in pain. She tried to draw away, but she was pinned too tightly to move.

Lyric's fingers stretched and searched until, finally, they closed around something. Alex could feel what they held, but she couldn't give it a name. It was something ineffable but essential, something she'd never be complete without.

Lyric's hand withdrew. Her fingers opened. The thing in her palm was black and wriggling. It writhed and spat as it tried to escape. Lyric pursed her lips and blew. Like an extinguished candle flame, it disappeared.

Her soul's magic. Gone in an instant.

At Lyric's nod, Dirk and Sabella released Alex. Lyric looked down, mouth half-open as if there was something she wanted to say. In the end, she stayed silent. The three light mages departed, leaving Alex mutilated and alone.

After a while, when it began to rain, Alex retrieved her messenger bag and began the silent walk home.

Alex made it into the kitchen just in time to see the dish that Jenny was holding tumble through her hand and hit the floor.

Jenny cursed and bent to retrieve it, but her hand passed through the shards.

"Damn it," Jenny grumbled, her confusion audible beneath the frustration.

Alex stopped a few steps away. She'd automatically extended her hand, ready to wave Jenny away and go for the broom, but it was pointless to pretend that this was like any other mess. She couldn't clean this up. Broken things were broken forever.

Jenny frowned as her fingers failed to close on a triangular wedge. She tried again. On the third pass, as her fingers became transparent, she made a choking noise and jumped back, as if it was the glass that had caused her to become intangible.

She looked up, searching for an explanation. Her eyes lit on Alex. They were no longer bright green, but some muted, shadow shade.

The pale, rippling rainbow colors of the stolen souls passed through Jenny's translucent form, shining like the iridescence on a soap bubble, and bled into the air.

Alex's tongue felt numb in her mouth. "I'm sorry," she said. "I tried to save you, but I couldn't. I'm so sorry."

She was hoping she'd see something in Jenny's eyes before she died, some moment of understanding or forgiveness, something other than the confusion and fear that clouded her expression in the last moments before her body lost all definition, becoming only a silvery translucence, like a vaguely woman-shaped drop of rain.

All at once, Jenny's essence lost coherence. The glistening outline shattered. She broke against the ground.

It was too late. It had always been too late. Too late for them to move to another city. Too late for Jenny to start college. Too late for Alex to love someone who wouldn't leave her.

She crumpled onto the floor, shoulders shuddering, wishing she could make herself so small that nothing could see her, so small that she couldn't even see herself. Her skin tingled with the strange feeling that comes with being watched. She wondered what she would see if she still had her magic. The crooked man, leaning against the wall? The shadows, leering and laughing?

How much had they done? Had they lured her to the spell only because it amused them to watch her fail? Had they been involved before that? Had one of shadows wrapped itself around the driver's foot on the gas pedal, goading him to go faster and faster?

Lyric had said there was a magical world overlaying this one like a mirror. All one had to do was press one's nose against the glass. But what if what looked back wasn't elves and angels and dream-mages, but something dark and howling?

Alex wept. There was nothing else left.

---

RACHEL SWIRSKY holds an MFA in fiction from the Iowa Writers Workshop. Her work has appeared in Tor.com, Subterrnean Magazine, and a number of other venues, and been nominated for the Hugo Award and the World Fantasy Award. In 2011, she won the Nebula Award for best novella. Her first collection, a slim volume of poetry and fiction, *Through the Drowsy Dark*, came out from Aqueduct Press in 2010.

# THE MISCIBLE IMP

## Tony Pi

TREG'S NEW BOTTLE WAS tall, narrow, and square, and he hated it. It was cramped inside, and the thick flint glass distorted his view of the outside world. But Myrina had been adamant: he must ride inside this bottle or not come at all. "I hain't carrying a prissy vial that'll break from a sneeze, and if it's round it'll roll underfoot when I set you down," she said. "You don't want to spill, do you?"

The magic that gave Treg life came with a curse that trapped his essence inside bottles and jars. Within the confines of a glass prison, he could possess and animate any liquid it held, but he could never hold thought or shape beyond the vessel's mouth. Therefore he needed Myrina to retrieve Old Man Reeve's notebook from its hiding place; without notes, he'd never learn how his former master made him. If he had the formula, he might discover how to halt the strange decline of his genius. To live simpleminded was a doom worse than death to Treg, and Myrina was living proof.

*Let her have her small victory*, Treg thought. Without his counsel, she'd still be scum in the gutters.

Myrina slipped out of the shrubbery and held his bottle up so that he could see Alchemy Hall. "Which window, Yer Impship?"

Treg pressed a liquid eye against the glass. He hadn't seen his first home since he and Apprentice Leech fled the university two years ago, and the sight of it made him uneasy. Was it remorse over what they did to Old Man Reeve, or just his potion-body reacting to moonlight? Nerves aside, the ivy-covered building was still the most majestic at the University of Norwesternesse. Yet under the gibbous moon it acquired a menacing cast.

"Third storey, fourth window from the right. See that gargoyle above it? It inspired my shape. Old Man Reeve left his elixir of intellect on this ledge, thinking it had failed, but did I ever surprise him." He grinned. "And if the new alchemist's a perfumer, as you say, she might even leave that window open to air out her lab."

Myrina crinkled her nose. "You sure Professor Lavender hain't ferreted out the notebook already?"

"Quite certain," Treg said, indignant. "It takes three key concoctions poured in the right sequence to open the secret panel. No one's clever enough to figure that out, or lucky enough to stumble upon it." Reeve wouldn't have told anyone the combination, either. Last he heard, the alchemist was a drooling guest at the local sanatorium and couldn't even remember what a chamber pot was for. Water-of-lethe in the professor's midnight cordial had robbed the man of his mind, a parting gift from Treg and Leech to repay their harsh master.

"A bloody alchemy lock? You should've told me," Myrina skulked across the green to the wall and hid amidst the shadow and ivy. "Have we got everything we need?"

"I understand you're nervous, Myrina, but I will walk you through the steps. You just focus on what you do best and get us there. We're a team, remember? Your skill, my brilliance? We can be rich, but only if we work together."

"Like how you made Leech rich?" she whispered. "Oh, wait, he's in a coma."

"Not my fault that he messed things up," Treg said. "How was I to know the fool would use bear's piss where I specifically told him to use a bull's? When it comes to alchemy, be careful what you mix."

"I'll try to remember. What did I ever see in that fool, anyways?" Myrina kicked off her shoes, tucked Treg back inside her satchel and began to climb.

He envied Myrina her freedom. Humans might be blood bottled in skin, but because of their flesh they could do things he couldn't. Sure, he had the spells he learned from a bottled djinn drifter to allow him to escape into another bottle in case of danger, but that magic relied on him being able to see his destination. Being in the satchel blinded him to the world.

They shouldn't even have been back here. The three of them had a simple scheme to strike it rich: sell strength potions to prizefighters and bet on the outcome. But Leech's bright idea to improve the draught worked all too well. The boxer who drank the potion sneezed so hard, he broke almost all his ribs before the match. When the poor man's brothers paid Leech a visit, Myrina had the foresight to grab Treg and clamber out the bedroom window. If she hadn't, Treg might have been thrown off the roof with Leech.

"We're in," Myrina whispered. She took him out and set him down on the ledge.

"I'm impressed—I didn't even hear the window creak." Treg began drinking in the moonlight with his substance. It tickled. "Myr, I'm ready for the catalyst."

Myrina uncorked his bottle and produced a small phial. Treg opened his mouth and caught the catalyst she poured into his bottle. The liquid burned pepper-hot as it mixed into his potion-self, setting his substance aglow. He delighted in the dose of vigor it gave him.

When his illumination lit their corner of the laboratory, Treg was surprised by what he saw.

Old Man Reeve had always kept the lab orderly, his glassware immaculate, and his alchemical supplies arranged by name and function. For all their gripes about their master's obsessive cleanliness, both Treg and Leech kept the same standards when they set up their own workshop. But the perfect order that once ruled the lab had been storm-tossed. Where once there was one cavernous hall where no student could hide from the watchful eye of the professor, mismatched storage shelves now rose like stalagmites, creating small pockets of workspace. Hastily labeled oils, elixirs and philtres shared the shelves with bottled vapors, perfumes and effluvia. Stacked tomes perched on top of a chair, while a moldy sandwich lay forgotten on a table crowded with alembics and crucibles. Treg could hear drips and bubblings elsewhere in the lab, likely experiments left to simmer overnight.

Worse, the air reeked of strange scents, sour and musky and cloying. He didn't know much about perfume alchemy; that fledgling art wasn't part of his vast alchemical knowledge. He was just glad when Myrina re-corked his bottle.

"What next, Yer Impship?"

"You can't see it, but at the other end of the lab there are two grotesques carved into the mantelpiece over the fireplace," Treg revealed. "First pour a dram of kraken ink into the right one's mouth, and a half-dram of ant venom into the left." He'd give her the final key later.

Myrina gave him a look of exasperation. "Where do I even start? What do they look like?"

If the lab had been left in the same configuration as Old Man Reeve's, Treg could tell her exactly where to find them, but now that notion was moot. "We'll have to try shelf by shelf. Read out the labels, assuming you can decipher that wretched handwriting."

"How about I just hold you up to the shelves?" Myrina snapped.

"If I must," Treg said, wondering what he had said to irritate her. "These look more like finished potions, not raw materials. Let's start at the far end of the hall. Maybe we'll get lucky."

Myrina carried him deeper into the lab. The bubbling and dripping sounds grew louder, and when Treg saw the source of the noise at last, it was too late to warn Myrina. A great automaton with eyestalk lenses and brass spider-like legs reached out with a pneumatic arm to catch the thief's neck in its pincers.

Though Myrina was quicker, tumbling out of the way, her grip on Treg's bottle slipped. Luckily for Treg, the impact on the stone tiles didn't break the flint glass, and neither did he roll...but as the monstrosity moved to catch Myrina, its metal foot was poised to crush Treg's bottle.

In panic, Treg painted the decanting spell on the side of the glass and targeted the first bottle he saw, trading places with the contents. Unfortunately the smaller bottle couldn't hold all of Treg's potion and popped its stopper, spilling glowing liquid on the shelf and the floor. Treg tasted the remnants of the previous contents as they mingled with his potion: gummy and pasty. Glue? He did feel his imp shape sticking to the walls of the new bottle.

To Treg's surprise, the Contraption (as he had just dubbed it) didn't crush his former prison underfoot, but only stomped on the ground beside it. However, it noticed Treg, who was still shining inside his new bottle. It plucked him off the shelf with a claw.

"Myrina! Help me!" he cried.

But the burglar was having problems of her own. As quick as she was, she couldn't outrun a cloud of gas. The Contraption blasted Myrina with a greenish vapor. She choked, stumbled, and fell.

The claw raised Treg's bottle before an eyestalk lens, giving Treg a chance to glimpse inside the Contraption's bulbous torso. He could see bubbling flasks and piping caged within, the source of the alchemical reactions he heard earlier. Was this drip-drop spider programmed like a golem, or was it truly thinking?

No matter. It reminded Treg that he was mind and will, and the potion-body an afterthought. He drew a variation of the decanting eye, a spirit-leap spell that allowed him to tear his mind from the glow potion and piped only his force of will into the new bottle. He claimed the liquid within and shaped it into his next body.

Strangely, his new body floated up against the top of the flint glass flask, and a wave of sadness overtook him.

Treg realized that he had taken possession of pegasus tears, which only fell skyward.

He fought the urge to weep. Whenever he took a new potion-body, he gained the power of the substance, but sometimes the magic changed his mood as well. These pegasus tears sent him into a deep sadness that made him want to drown his sorrows in a bottle of whiskey.

The Contraption was examining Myrina with a long eyestalk lens, while its other eyes scanned its surroundings. Poor Myrina! If she was discovered here in the morning, it was prison for her. Though he knew his newfound affection for the thief was probably a side-effect of the pegasus tears, it pained him too much to leave the woman to her fate. But what could he possibly do to help her? He was just a useless imp stuck in a bottle.

Yet...if he could find smelling salts or spirit of hartshorn, he might be able to rouse her. Surely he could find some in an effluvium lab like this. But he couldn't keep hopping bottles without knowing what was in them. He couldn't always read the labels. What if he ended up in water-of-lethe? Thought and memory were all he had. Forgetting everything would equal death.

At least he could now read some of the labels on the neighboring bottles. Vessels of all shapes and sizes contained one's pick of liquids, powders or fumes. He saw jackalope droppings. Unicorn breath. Ambergris. Tincture of mandragora. And was that kraken ink? More jars with handwriting that he'd have to decipher.

The problem wasn't finding the spirit of hartshorn. It had to be kept close at hand in a lab where one wrong whiff would steal consciousness. In fact, a bottle of the liquid lay on the same shelf...but pushed to the back, behind the kraken ink and a phial of sneezing powder. How was he going to get the spirit of hartshorn to Myrina? Even if he did wake her, how could they bypass the Blasted Contraption?

Treg studied the drip-drop automaton. He knew nothing about pneumatics or clockworks, but the Contraption was designed to protect the lab, and it couldn't do its job unless it knew not to break bottles or upset tables. Proof: it had stepped aside to avoid crushing Treg's bottle. But was it truly reasoning, or simply following the dictates of its mistress? Treg wondered if Professor Lavender had discovered the notebook and mixed another imp like him to control the Contraption, but he gave up that hope as a foolish dream.

Those bubbling potions running through the Contraption's head must be its set of rules. Treg could mess with that, but he didn't know how those alchemical reactions worked. However, if it was moving, it must have an alembic engine for its heart. That, Treg understood.

The alembic engine required three fluids reacting in balance: ruby, emerald, and bronze. Wait, those weren't right. Why was his memory failing at such an inconvenient time, on such a rudimentary reaction? He bashed his head against the glass. Ruby was...phlogiston. Emerald was oil of philosophers. What was the bronze?

He cursed his fading intellect, and hoped he would recall it later. He drew a spirit-leap sign and left his bottle, possessing the kraken ink instead. Although the spell took him into the new bottle, he wasn't able to coalesce a body out of the liquid. He could see nothing, and it scared him.

Could it be that the djinn's spells diminished him every time he cast them? Maybe it had been a mistake to assume djinn magic would work safely for him. He should never have left his original elixir!

But the fear of being stuck as formless ink forever pushed Treg to keep trying. It seemed an eternity before he could shape a hand, and the rest of his potion-body followed.

The Contraption stood over Myrina now, running drip-drop drip-drop like clockwork.

Talosian ichor! That was the bronze liquid he had forgotten. If he could replace the ichor with tonic orichalcum, the orichalcum should stop the alembic engine dead. But if things went wrong...the Confounded Contraption might blow up, taking Treg and Myrina with it. Treg shuddered just thinking about it.

Unfortunately, he needed Myrina to find the tonic orichalcum in this mess, which meant waking her and keeping the Contraption from knocking her out again. Even getting the spirit of hartshorn to Myrina would be a challenge. If he could break a bottle of it next to Myrina, the fumes should be enough to rouse her. He supposed he could spirit-leap into the hartshorn, trade places with the kraken ink, then roll this brittle bottle off the shelf. But could he get out of the falling container in time? He was afraid he wasn't fast enough. Unless....

Treg regarded the bottle of pegasus tears again. The buoyant tears were contained in a vessel of heavy flint glass to prevent the whole thing from floating into the air. His current prison was made of more delicate glass. With the right sequence of spells, it might work.

First, he spirit-leapt into the pegasus tears. While Treg was struck by another bout of sadness, his fears thankfully subsided. He could pull this off.

Treg targeted the ink bottle again, but this time he used the decanting eye and swapped the pegasus tears with the kraken ink. His tear-made body pushed against the top of the thin glass, levitating the entire container. The glass clinked against the roof of the shelf.

The Contraption heard the noise and turned an eyestalk his way.

Rolling the ink bottle from the inside, Treg forced his container to the edge of the shelf's roof, then cast his decanting eye and exchanged places with the spirit of hartshorn. With the hartshorn unable to keep the jar afloat, it fell and bounced off the shelf. Treg's current bottle was too heavy for his tear-made body to levitate high enough for him to see, but he did hear the sound of glass smashing to bits.

"Myrina, if you can hear me, play dead," he shouted. "I bet the Contraption's too dumb to tell that you're faking sleep."

The sound of his voice drew the Contraption's attention. A pair of claws snatched him from the shelf.

Treg had been counting on it. When the automaton brought his bottle close enough that he could see its glassy innards, he leapt spirit-wise into the reservoir of talosian ichor. He forced his imp shape onto the viscous ichor, withholding any droplets of his new substance from leaving his new glass cage.

The drip-drop rhythm stopped. The Contraption sputtered, and Treg felt heat rising from the pipes connecting the reservoir to the alembical heart. The phlogiston was reacting to the oil of philosophers without the talosian ichor acting in counterbalance, and that wasn't good.

Could he perhaps stay in the Contraption, regulating the drip of ichor into the alembical reaction? It was a tempting thought. He might even be able to control the automaton and actually touch things and move!

But there didn't seem to be enough substance to keep the alembical heart beating. Professor Lavender must replenish the reservoirs daily. It wouldn't do to have his ichor-body consumed by the process!

"I can't hold this Contraption for long, Myrina," Treg said, his words slurring from the thick nature of the ichor. "I need tonic orichalcum to stop it for good. For the love of glob, find some and hold the bottle up!"

Myrina stood, rubbing her eyes. "What's it look like?"

The Contraption was shaking now. "Just read the damn labels," Treg shouted.

"What's. It. *Look*. Like."

"Oh." Treg realized what Myrina was too proud to admit. "You can't read?"

"Lots o' folks can't, but it don't mean they hain't smart." She grabbed a golden potion off a shelf. "This it?"

Treg squinted at the label. "No." The heat from the pipes was growing insufferable, and the Damned Contraption was rocking wildly on its legs. "Show me another. Quickly, before it blows!"

It was the wrong thing to say. Myrina backed away from the Contraption. "Sorry, Yer Impship. You're on your own." She turned and sprinted for the window.

"Come back, you cask of ungrateful blood!" he cried, but she was gone.

Without Myrina, Treg had no choice but to try finding the tonic orichalcum himself, but he couldn't see anything clearly beyond the hull of the Infernal Contraption, much less see the hue of a potion or read the labels. Maybe Myrina had the right idea. He could come back for the notebook another day. It was time to get out of here.

He saw the narrow and square bottle he arrived in, which now held glue. He traced a spirit-leap sign and—

The Contraption blew up.

The force of the explosion sent tables, flasks and books flying, just as Treg's spirit flowed through the spirit-leap sign. Instead of pouring into his intended bottle, however, the blast threw a different flask in his path, forcing him to infuse the unknown liquid with his mind—

The outside world went dark, and Treg lost the strength to keep his shape and thought.

When he awakened, Treg imposed his imp shape on the liquid he now inhabited, wondering where he had ended up. Scant sunlight peeked through the chaos of twisted bronze, sundered wood, and broken glass around him. He wasn't sure what the potion was, except that it was sweet and smooth. Treg had a sudden longing to see someone, anyone, though he couldn't say exactly why.

"Myrina, are you there?" he cried. "Anyone?"

A hand pushed through the debris, clasped around the neck of his bottle and lifted him up. A red-haired woman in her thirties smiled at him from the other side of the glass. Professor Lavender.

From the moment Treg saw Lavender, he knew she was the one who had been missing from his life. She was the taskmistress he longed for, the brilliant mind he admired.

He was stuck inside a love philtre, he realized...but looking at his truelove, he was just fine with that.

"What a strange thing to find," Lavender said. "What might you be? And do you know what happened to my workshop?"

"Why, there's a tale in that, Fair Lady Lavender, and a gift of a notebook at the end of its telling," Treg cried with heartfelt words. "But I, Tregnum your loving servant, must first sing praise to your beauty."

As Treg sang of love and devotion, he wondered if Mistress Lavender would rebuild the Contraption for him. But she wouldn't need bubbling potions to control the blasted thing. Not when his brilliant mind would do wonders in their place...

---

TONY PI always wanted to be an alchemist, but organic chemistry in university proved to be his downfall. That's why he's a linguist and writer now. A writer based in Toronto, Canada, Tony was a finalist for the John W. Campbell Award for Best New Writer, and his work has appeared in many places such as *Clarkesworld, Intergalactic Medicine Show, Fantasy Magazine, Beneath Ceaseless Skies*, and *When the Hero Comes Home.*

# MANMADE

## *Leah Petersen*

THE CASTLE CALLED TO him. Lord Andrew Rorin rode on through the creeping grey mist of dusk, determined to spend the night within the castle walls. In a sack tied to his saddle, the head of a king bumped a pleasant tattoo against the horse's flank. Rorin smiled and urged the horse faster toward home.

The siren song of the keep danced together with visions of meats roasting over the fire, fat sizzling and popping on the coals below, of spiced mulled wine to warm his bones, and a wench or two to warm everything else.

The gates came into view and Rorin's pulse quickened. He was eager to show off his latest trophy. He loved the expressions on their pretty little faces as they looked at, while trying not to see, the grisly proof of his latest conquests. That this was the head of a man only sweetened the victory.

For Lord Rorin's intolerance for other men was legendary. He allowed no man in his presence save the heads of those he had killed, carefully bound with spells so that their last expression of fear or pain or the sweetness of surprise was forever preserved.

The lights in the windows were a cheery glow and the bustle of activity in the courtyard was proof that the castle had rallied its inhabitants to welcome their lord home. Rorin galloped through the gates and reined his horse to a stop in front of the great doors where, turned out to serve their lord and master...were a dozen men. Tall, hairy things like a grove of blight oaks planted in his yard.

Rorin flew off his horse, trembling with rage.

He stumbled to a stop in front of a thick, furry one. The words rushed to his lips, power gathering in his cupped hand.

Something massive darted in his peripheral vision, slamming into his side. Rorin fell. A moment before he hit the cobblestones he was snatched up by the very blur that had knocked him down.

"Don't, my lord."

The deep, resonant voice sent red fury racing through Rorin's veins. He rounded on the speaker. The man was tall and beefy, with hands that looked capable of snapping small trees in half.

"What is the meaning of this? Get out of my sight! Where are my servants? Charlotte!"

"Here, my lord," the same man answered.

Rorin stared at him.

"They call me Charles, now," he amended after a long pause.

It was so absurd Rorin sputtered, a spray of astonishment and rage.

Charlotte, his current favorite, was thin at waist and wrist, plump where it mattered—breast, hips, lips. Her hair was the color of new wheat, eyes the strange, enigmatic dusky color of moss in the dry season. She was the loveliest of the ladies he had acquired in the forty years since he'd claimed the keep.

This thing, this *man*, couldn't have been more different. Although the hair that brushed his powerful shoulders and shadowed a strong jaw was the color of new wheat. And under thick, knitted brows his eyes were the enigmatic, dusky color of dry moss.

"Don't you ever, ever touch me," Rorin hissed, clenching his teeth against the involuntary shiver the man's touch had excited.

He wouldn't have time to craft a spell with the man's eyes on him. "Don't even speak to me you lying, disgusting, monstrous—"

Snatching his belt knife, he thrust it two-handed at the man's neck. The man's hands flashed up and snatched at his wrists, a painful, crushing grip. Rorin gasped in a breath but before he could do anything with it, a beefy fist slammed into his temple. As darkness descended he heard a faraway, "Forgive me, my lord."

The silence was startling. After nearly a month of the constant, muted cacophony of travel, the soundless hum of the keep brought Rorin awake with a jerk.

He was alone and in his own bed. He didn't remember climbing the stairs, or entering his room, or undressing, though he was in only his underclothes now. He didn't remember anything after the courtyard and the men—

He shot upright. Fury, confusion, and fear rushed through him in equal measure.

He spluttered a rather hysterical chuckle. A dream. Of course. That was the only explanation. Rorin was the most feared magician in the fifteen lands. No handful of servants would dare vex him this way. No power could thwart him within these walls. The castle thrummed as if in agreement.

He drew breath to roar reproaches at whoever dared to attend their lord in so shoddy a manner, but he caught himself on the inhalation and closed his mouth in lingering doubt.

He tossed the blankets aside in disgust.

"Charlotte!"

The door opened at once, as if someone had been waiting outside for his summons.

A head popped around the doorframe, a mud-haired, mud-eyed young man just acquiring his first muddy-colored whiskers.

The edges of Rorin's vision blurred red. The swell of anger strained under his skin. "Where is Charlotte!"

"I'll get him, my lord," the lad answered in a disturbing combination of rumble and squeak.

Rorin paced in front of the fire, hands reflexively clenching and unclenching as he ground his teeth.

"You sent for me, my lord?"

The deep bass voice had a familiar lilt and cadence, and for a disconnected moment it was soothing, welcome, like music. Rorin clenched his jaw on a wash of despair and longing.

"What is the meaning of this?" he bellowed. "Who—" he indicated the man with a dismissive sweep of his hand. "What are you?"

The wheat-haired man dropped into an aborted curtsey which morphed into an awkward bow. He blushed.

"A fortnight ago, my lord, we went to bed as always and woke like this."

"Impossible."

"And yet..." The man looked down at his hairy hands, turning them over and back again before looking up at Rorin. He shrugged.

The rise and fall of broad shoulders held Rorin's gaze and for a couple of breaths he just stared. Rorin jerked, turning his head away.

"Insolence! I will not be contradicted in my own home. This is impossible. It's nonsense. No magician but one of the blood can effect any kind of magic here. I killed all of them long ago. The castle acknowledges *me* as its master. You lie!"

"I swear it is the truth, my lord."

"What have you done with the women who were here?"

"We *are* the women who were here. I give you my word." The man turned to someone behind him, out of sight in the hall. "Get Mitchell."

Rorin ignored it. "Your falsehoods mean nothing. Who sent you?"

"I'm here by your sufferance, as always," the man replied, a saucy half-smile quirking at his lips, his shoulder tilted forward; the unconscious flirtation so second nature, so familiar in any of his servants, so pleasing in the women.

Rorin's hands spasmed into fists. He flew at him. The man drew himself up and suddenly he was like a wall. Rorin stopped short, his breath catching in his throat, trembling with unspent fury and a muddle of feelings he couldn't afford to think about. The side of his head throbbed with remembered pain and something indefinable but disorienting.

A soft shuffle sounded in the doorway and a gaunt, withered old man appeared.

Taking a deliberate step away from Rorin with a long exhale, the man gestured to the elder. "Mitchell, come here."

The shriveled, wrinkled figure was both less and more disconcerting than the robust specimens. Rorin shrank away from the man's tottering bow.

"This is Martha, my lord," The man nodded to the oldster. "Show him."

The old man extended one trembling arm, pulling back his sleeve to the elbow. There, shiny and bald among the wrinkles and patches of hair, was Rorin's mark. "Put there by your brother," he rasped. "Going on forty years ago."

Rorin squinted at the mark, sure he could find evidence of duplicity. But the brand was long healed, only a blemish being slowly reclaimed by the sagging skin around it.

He slapped the old man's arm away.

"This is outrageous! I won't stand for it." He turned to the younger man. "Bring in new servants, then. Women. Send these away. And you too, once you've done."

"It won't do any good, my lord."

"And how do you know?"

"Because it's already been tried. That is, Janie and Hera were out hunting the night it happened and they were not changed. But when they returned three days later, the moment they entered the castle walls they became like all the rest of us."

"I don't believe it. Bring me some young women at once."

"And where should we get them, my lord?"

"There are villages, aren't there? You're capable of the two day journey, I hope? There are dozens of you brutes here now. Can't you manage to plunder and ravish? Only, don't think I will tolerate any of you taking liberties with them. They're for me."

The man's eyes narrowed.

"What?" Rorin demanded. "Are you jealous?"

When he realized he'd made that statement to a man, he shivered so dramatically that he lost his footing.

"Just do as I say!" he roared. They departed without another word and Rorin slammed the door behind them.

Rorin slumped against the stone wall, sliding down until he plunked into a disconsolate heap on the floor. He thumped his head back and groaned.

Turning his cheek to the cool stone, he lifted a hand and laid his palm against the wall. The familiar pulse of the castle's life was an unspeakable relief. Rorin knew this keep in his very soul and it knew Rorin; its touch was more tender than any mother with her babe, more welcoming than cruel, changeable people. The life of the castle recognized and enfolded him; a warm vibration, like the murmur of lips against skin, just there under an insubstantial curtain of stone.

Rorin let the sweetness of reunion wash through him and sweep away all the anger, fear, and violation. His home, his castle had been compromised and Rorin didn't know how.

It was Rorin's first and only friend. It knew Rorin, had chosen him when Rorin was still a boy, even before he killed his own father and older brother and freed the castle to be his. Rorin needed no father or brother or mother or so-called friend, so long as he could turn to the castle.

And it had always been there for Rorin. Everyone else who had witnessed Rorin's childhood humiliations had laughed, beaten him with fists and words. His father had whipped him, even as Rorin pleaded, "It's not true!" or "I don't!"

It was enough that his brother suspected, and called him the names. They said it was a weakness in Rorin, a failing. And sometimes Rorin believed them. If he couldn't make it go away, stop the feelings, then he was weak. Broken and wrong.

No. It wasn't Rorin who was weak in the end. It was his father's head on the wall in the study, and his brother's, not Rorin's. Sometimes Rorin wished he could bring his father and brother back so he could show them how wrong they'd been. How he wasn't what they thought. How he'd banished all men from his very existence decades ago. He would prove it to them.

And then kill them again.

He closed his eyes and drifted past the barrier of the wall, into the heart and mind of the keep. The web of spells cast by generations of his ancestors to create, preserve, and protect the living structure wrapped around him like a blanket. He knew this weaving like he knew his own body.

How could anyone impose their will in competition with his own? Who could even try? Why had the castle allowed it?

Betrayed him.

The flash of his anger ignited an answering pulse of something like guilt. No, shame. Rorin seized it, followed it. *You didn't betray me, did you? What did they do to you?*

He wandered through the web of enchantments, examining it as if for the first time; a child with his hand extended, touching everything because everything was new and wonderful. There it was, like a loose thread in a tapestry. He picked at it and it unraveled as if it wanted to be found.

"Hello there, my nephew." The rich, warm tones of a woman's voice washed through his mind.

No, this wasn't possible.

"I think you know you have found only the message I left for you and not the enchantment that so torments you at present. Don't trouble yourself, even if you do find it—and perhaps you will—you cannot remove it. My blood ties run deeper than yours."

Rorin glowered. She was dead, he had killed her himself. Though hers was the infuriating gap in his collection, her head the only trophy he'd never collected. He'd never found her body, but no one could have survived that fall. Surely she wasn't alive?

"You were always a wicked boy, Andrew. Your murders over the years have been appalling, but they were all your rivals and I don't begrudge you your ambition, however much it offends me. But you went too far this time. King Daviel was no threat to you. He had done nothing to you that you did not cause yourself. Your petty revenge may destroy everything I've worked for over the past two hundred years. I will sit by in silence no longer. Consider yourself duly punished." Her voice took on a self-satisfied tone. "I know this is an enchantment you will find particularly trying."

She knew. They'd told her. Rorin had been so sure his father would never speak of it. It was a shame on the family name. He wouldn't have told anyone. No. She couldn't know. No one knew. He'd killed everyone who had even suggested, hinted.

"I urge you not to incur my wrath further," she said. "However distasteful you find this situation, it's nothing to what I'll do if you force my hand."

Rorin growled low in his throat.

"You have been warned, nephew. Find some other occupation. Your days of senseless and butcherous meddling are at an end."

Rorin jerked out of the castle heart so quickly his head spun. He dropped his head back against the wall and roared.

Lord Andrew Rorin was not so easily defeated. He would not be forced to endure this mockery, this torture.

And so the master of Rorin Keep kept to his chambers. At night he snuck out to retrieve books and scrolls—all the books of magic collected and histories recorded by dozens of the castle's former masters—desperate to find a solution to this problem.

The next morning's knock on the door startled him, sending a stack of tomes crashing to the floor.

"Go away!"

"But your breakfast, my lord." The man's voice was placid, untroubled.

"Leave it in the hall!"

"And your bath?"

Rorin groaned. He did so hate cold water, but the thought of men in his chamber while he was naked and vulnerable...A violent shiver sent another book toppling.

"Go away!"

Five days later a rather bedraggled and still unwashed Rorin stood on the wall, struggling to look lordly and dispassionate as a dozen of his *men* approached, leading four young women. In spite of his orders to the contrary, the man who had been Charlotte stood a few paces away. Rorin was very aware of him, like a spreading flush on the back of his neck, but a jittery feeling in his stomach made him reluctant to dismiss him.

Three of the women were tolerably handsome, if trembly and teary. A grin spread across Rorin's face at the thought of all the fun he could have with that—a weepy virgin was one of his favorite toys. But all his attention was for the tall, raven-haired beauty behind. Her face was set, her mouth a determined line. Rorin chuckled to himself. This one might make the whole ordeal worth it after all.

The guards and their captives passed through the gate. Rorin turned to watch them emerge into the courtyard, unchanged. Grinning in triumph, he rushed down the open stairs.

But before he reached them, a chorus of screeches erupted from the women. They gaped and goggled at each other in horror as faces and limbs thickened, horrified cries dropping an octave. They huddled, arms clasped over ripped bodices, covering breasts they no longer had. The first three burst into noisy sobs.

The beauty who trailed them, now big and dark with arms like a blacksmith, cast a quick look around and with a mighty blow to the guard's jaw, toppled his captor and sprinted back through the gate.

Rorin stared for only a moment before shock turned into an explosion of rage.

"Shoot him!" he yelled to the archers on the wall.

"Stop! Don't shoot."

Lord Rorin spun to face the man in dumbfounded astonishment. "How dare you?" He grabbed a nearby bucket, hurling it at him. "How dare you!"

Gathering power crackled in Rorin's other palm. He picked up a shovel and pitched it as well, keeping the man at a distance long enough to complete the spell.

A discarded horseshoe was in his hand when the man rushed him, grabbing him by the arms. Spinning Rorin around, he jerked the lord's arm up behind his back and the power in it drained away with a stabbing pain. The man yanked him backward into his body, locking his other arm in a crushing vise over Rorin's chest. The heat of him was like a brand everywhere they met, and Rorin's mouth went dry, heart thudding in a thrill of terror.

"Let me go," Rorin's voice had an undignified waver.

"Stop throwing things." Rorin felt the reverberations of the man's deep tones in his whole body.

"You have no right to command me."

"And you have no right to kill that man, or me."

Rorin's pulse jumped against his skin. Apprehension, confusion, and excitement hummed along every nerve. The man released him slowly, his hands hovering, his body tense and waiting.

Dusting himself off to hide his sudden trembling, Rorin turned. "Get them out of my sight," he spat. "I'll be in my room."

Rorin stumbled through the castle's heart, gripping the web of spells and enchantments in desperation. The flavor of his aunt's weavings was not new; it had been a part of the whole for as long as he'd known this tapestry. It was stronger now, fresher, but it was still bound old and deep, impossible to separate or remove. He felt so helpless—he who had spent decades doing whatever was necessary to be strong, to inspire fear, to feel safe.

When he finally pulled away and came back to himself he found Charlotte—Charles—in his room, directing a few servants who were filling a tub set in front of the fireplace. When they'd topped it up with steaming water, Charles ushered them out and closed the door behind them.

"Your bath, my lord."

"I didn't order a bath." Rorin's protest was weak.

Charles made no answer.

"Well leave, at least," Rorin snapped.

A smile ghosted at Charles' mouth. "Am I so frightening, my lord?"

"I'm not afraid of you."

"I should hope not. Come, let me help you. You haven't changed your clothes since you returned."

"I would if I could, but I haven't any clean travel things and all my other clothes are impossible to get into without help," he huffed.

"I know. Go ahead and get in, I won't look at you. I'll lay out your things while you wash."

Rorin didn't like it, but he didn't like the way he smelled either. He waited until the other man had turned away before he scrambled out of his clothes and into the tub, sinking with a sigh into the water and closing his eyes.

He settled deep into the heat and the familiar sounds of someone attending him. He was so tired, so thoroughly exhausted, that he let his consciousness drift, seeking peace in the lingering touch of the castle's mind. At first, he was barely aware of the sensation of hands in his hair, the strong smell of soap, and the crackly sound of lather.

"Tip your head back."

The voice brought him bolt upright, water sloshing to the floor.

"Don't touch me!"

The hands disappeared.

"As you wish, my lord."

Huddling low in the water, Rorin sluiced water and soap from his hair with trembling hands, giving a cursory swipe to the rest of his body, and snatched at the towel laid out in front of the fire. He whipped it around his nakedness before he was standing, the bottom half wicking up soapy water.

"You're dismissed," he cast over his shoulder. "I can do it myself."

"You cannot."

Rorin whirled around. "Get out!"

Charles hesitated, holding Rorin's eye for only a moment. He bowed.

"Yes, my lord."

For a long time Lord Rorin stood shivering in front of the fire, clutching the towel around him like a blanket in a snowstorm. After all these decades, after a lifetime of fighting, after all he'd done to destroy this, was he to be undone by something so simple as a bath?

He put on the clothes he could manage, the breeches and the shirt, though he couldn't manage all of its ties, and sank into the chair at his desk, still littered with the books of magic, his intended saviors. He laid his forehead on a cool leather cover and squeezed his eyes shut.

When Charles entered his room the next morning, Rorin said nothing. He did not acknowledge him when he set the breakfast tray on the table, or as he tidied up the room. When Charles began to absentmindedly hum that little tune Charlotte would sing, Rorin almost yelled at him to stop, but then he didn't.

When the voice came from just behind him, he jumped.

"Have you found anything, my lord?"

Rorin spun around in his chair to find Charles peering at the text from over his shoulder.

"Step away!"

Charles took two steps backward but didn't leave.

Rorin turned back to his book, closing his eyes for a moment to block out the smell of him, the desperate craving bubbling up within.

"If I'd found anything, you'd know it."

Charles went back to work, but after a moment he said, "I hated it at first. Who would want to be a man if he could be a woman?" He wasn't looking at Rorin, but there was a hint of teasing in his voice. "I'm getting used to it, though. There are even some advantages."

Rorin scoffed. "Of course there are. Being a man is infinitely preferable. I would never be one of those delicate things; weak and weepy, taken advantage of by any passing brute, despised."

"Despised?"

"I mean— Never mind, I didn't mean despised. Just, I'd never let myself be less than others simply because they were bigger and stronger, stupid and cruel. I'd kill myself first."

"Or other people, if you thought it would help."

Rorin's head shot up. "What does that mean?"

Charles shrugged. "Just a thought."

"Your thoughts are not needed or welcome in my room."

"Yes, my lord."

He had spent many nights bent over his books, and it was very late. Rorin linked his arms over his head and stretched sore muscles, dropping his neck forward.

He jumped when warm hands settled on his shoulders, massaging with strong, familiar strokes.

"Stop," he said.

The hands stilled but were not removed.

"You used to like for me do this," Charles said, his voice quiet and very near.

"That was before." Rorin's voice came out rough and hoarse.

"Am I really so different now?"

Of course he was, but that wasn't really the problem. Rorin silently cursed his weakness. Though whether it was the weakness of wanting, or of being afraid to want, he was no longer sure.

"You're completely different," Rorin rasped.

"And when you close your eyes?" The voice was closer now; he could feel the heat of breath on his ear.

Rorin shivered. "You feel different."

"Different isn't always bad."

The brush of fingers ghosted over the sensitive skin on the back of his neck and Rorin gasped, leaning into the caress without meaning to.

"Don't touch me like that." It was barely a whisper.

The fingers withdrew and were replaced by the brush of firm lips. "Like this, then?"

Rorin opened his mouth but the words didn't come, only a soft moan.

A quiet chuckle tickled his neck.

Charles took his hand and pulled him up. Rorin kept his eyes closed. Strong arms pressed him into a broad chest and he dropped his head on a shoulder higher than his own. He knew he should hate this feeling, but he couldn't remember why.

An intoxicating vision of giving up this struggle, of just not fighting any more, made him giddy and lightheaded.

Charles took his hand again and pulled him in the direction of the bed.

Rorin didn't move.

The hand slid away but the voice was soft, husky, melty.

"Shall I go?"

Rorin trembled, his mind racing, his body aching with confusion and need.

"I'm sorry," Charles said. "I'll go."

Rorin's eyes flew open. "No."

Charles turned back but stood still, waiting.

"No?"

Rorin closed his eyes, bowing his head, clenching his fists. "Stay. Please?"

He opened his eyes and looked up at Charles.

Charles' smile was warm, soft.

"Yes, my lord."

---

LEAH PETERSEN lives in North Carolina. She does the day-job, wife, and mother thing, much like everyone else. She prides herself on being able to hold a book with her feet so she can knit while reading. She's still working on knitting while writing. Her first novel, *Fighting Gravity*, is available now from Dragon Moon Press.

# THE LORD OF THE SOUTHERN SKY

## J. P. Moore

LORD SET, BROTHER OF King Osiris, watched ghostly arms of dust weave among the sandstone columns, through shafts of white sunlight. The dark of the underworld seeped up between black marble tiles and blanketed the temple floor. So, the world of light was far above. The realm of mortals was dark and low, and men were like insects at the feet of the gods.

This was Ombos of the Upper Nile. Arid, hot, and dead. This was Set's home.

Panahasi, short with a broad bald head and big ears, crouched like a monkey in the shadows. The priest spoke.

"You do not look like Lord Set. It has been years, but I remember Set well. You are not Set."

"But I am," he hissed.

Panahasi approached, his staff clacking against the marble so sharp and loud that Set thought the stone tiles might shatter. The far, high dust whorls shuddered with each strike. The old priest squinted at Set. As he did, his forehead furrowed and his ears tipped forward. He looked even more like one of the monkeys, one of the chimps from the jungle.

"Your ears are like a giraffe's," Panahasi said. "And your snout is an aardvark's snout."

"You do not see beneath my robes."

"What is there?"

"I am a jackal," Set said. "An animal."

Panahasi's face burst in surprise.

"A demon!" the priest shouted.

"No," Set whispered.

"Prove it. Tell me something that only Set would know."

Set thought for a moment—a moment too long, he feared. Panahasi would strike him with that holy staff and send him to the floor, to the cold tiles. Set looked at the floor and thought he saw his reflection, the image of his monstrous transformation, in the infinite black depth of that marble. Indeed, he was a strange beast. He was many animals. He had once been a striking man.

"My brother Osiris once lost a race for me."

"Doubtful," Panahasi said, looking into the sky. "He was a fast boy. No one would believe that he could lose."

"He was fast," Set agreed. "But you should remember this. He was winning. There were ten of us on the racecourse. I tripped and Osiris turned to help me. I pulled him to the ground and ran ahead. Another boy had already won, but I pulled my brother down as he helped me, just to beat him. You said, 'Set, why did you do that? You are an animal.'"

Panahasi hummed and nodded.

"You felt the back of my head," Set continued. "You said that I had a bump at the base of my skull. And you said that was a sure sign that I was descended from beasts that our grandfathers' grandfathers had killed and eaten when the jungles receded and the Nile wound up from the sea."

The priest looked at him, boring a sharp gaze from tight black pupils right into Set's forehead.

"I remember. I also remember that your brother nevertheless mastered a beast that day. Tell me what it was."

"A ram stood on the ridge over the racecourse. It kicked and stomped like it was going to charge us. Osiris climbed the ridge and wrestled the ram to the ground. He broke the ram's neck with his own hands."

"Yes," the priest said. "You are Set. I see it now. What has happened to you?"

"I do not know."

"Your brother is dead, you know. King Osiris is dead."

"I killed him, Panahasi. I have come to see my mother. I have something for her."

Osiris had presided over a tyranny of benevolence. Set considered this as he walked the bank of the Nile, his feet sinking into the black mud and leaving dog tracks with the gait of a man. Osiris and Isis had created opportunity and abundance, as if the very power of their breath, some tingling magic that rose from the delta of their chests, fell to the land like magic seed, like powerful dust from the sun itself.

Set knew that it had been his duty to kill his brother.

To win, to lose—this was the order of things. Gods ruled it. The wilderness preserved it day in and day out, for the lion and the beetle and everything in between. No king or queen could deny it. No edict could forbid it.

"We are sport for the gods," Set said to himself. "Most of us are meant to suffer."

The royal couple had even approached their station with a nauseating humility. They wore simple clothes and eschewed the entourages and riches of their fathers and grandfathers. Osiris dismantled the great memorials, using the stone for aqueducts to carry fresh, sweet water from sparkling pools in the hills to the slums of the cities, where the Nile was a muddy and diseased thing. He did much of this work with his own hands, standing beside the workers and slaves. He ordered the witches to cease their explorations into potions and curses, and instead charged them to learn the magic of the seed and flood. The priests turned from royal astrology to intense study of the clockwork of the harvest that Osiris insisted the gods had scribed into the stars. Isis was mother to all. Peasant mothers spoke of Isis offering her breast to their children. Though it was a figure of speech, the dirty crones had such a look in their eyes that Set believed they had seen the poor, toothless children of the desert suckling in the arms of the queen. That milk cured all disease and sated all hunger.

Set reached the broken column, a monument to some ancient tyrant. A short walk from this, and Set was on the edge of the racecourse. This was a simple thing, a rough track worn into the dirt. Nothing would grow here. Some said it had been the sight of devilish massacre. The legend was that soldiers had killed thousands of escaping slaves. The children of Ombos still raced here. They had raced three decades earlier, when Set and Osiris were children.

Osiris had once been the king of this course, and nothing more.

Three young boys now ran the course, kicking clouds of dust into the air behind them. One boy lagged far behind the other two. And the leader, a tall and thin boy with sandy hair and foreign eyes that were slightly too far apart, like the eyes of Osiris, stopped and turned to help the fat, far boy at the end of the line. Set licked his lips and groaned. It was disgusting. Here, this boy—he could win, but he refused.

It had been nothing to kill Osiris. And then nothing to dismember him. What would it take, he wondered, to kill this kind boy? The legend, the ghosts of shrieking slaves, vibrated through the sand and sent red clouds to the sky. It would be nothing. A twist of the boy's neck, and that would be all.

Set opened his robe and threw back his cowl. He walked onto the course and made straight for the boys. The fat boy was still on the ground, clutching his ankle. Where, Set wondered, was the strategy in this? The trickery? The fat boy was no hunter, no beast. He did not take advantage of his comrade's compassion.

Set was growling. His voice rolled in his throat and broke now and then into yelps. The three boys turned to see him and froze. Their eyes widened in horror. The kind boy lifted his fallen companion and tried to escape, pulling the fat boy through clumsy steps. The third boy was already far gone. Set was now close to the lagging pair. He could smell their musk and hear their quickened hearts. He could sense their tracks around the course, around and around. As he felt and saw all of this, as he heard their footfalls in the track and, now, in the softer ground at the foot of the ridge as they retreated, his hunger spiked. Drool fell in glistening strands from the corners of his long mouth.

So close, now—Set could smell their panic.

The fat boy dipped, took a rock and threw it. The stone hit Set square in the forehead. Set's vision shuddered and he stumbled for a moment. He lost the boys in explosions of color and light. Shapes spiraled in sickening swirls. Set rubbed his eyes with the backs of his paws. He tried to stand still, but the ground seemed to move and swell beneath him. He was then on his knees, rocking and swaying like a cultist worshipping the desert moonlight.

The kind boy pushed his fat friend forward, then stopped and turned.

"You are a fool," Set said. "You would stop to help me?"

But the kind boy did not hear, or perhaps did hear, and turned to run, to guide his friend to safety.

So, Set thought. He had failed to save the world from another Osiris.

"Your mother's tomb," Panahasi said. The priest was leaning against a column, gesturing toward a cave. Inside, a sealed stone door displayed fine, colorful paintings of Set's mother and father, Nut and Geb. Beneath both likenesses, ages of priests and family had left sacrifices for the couple's nourishment in the afterlife. Wilted flowers and rotten food baked in the heat. Blue flies buzzed about this carrion.

"I have news," the priest said. "Do you wish to hear it?"

Set said nothing, but grunted as he passed through the first pair of columns at the head of the colonnade that led to the cave. Panahasi turned and walked behind Set.

"You no longer hide yourself," Panahasi said. "You are quite a mystery. Quite a demon."

"Children ran from me," Set said.

"I do not doubt it."

"But I had tried to kill them."

"They escaped?" Panahasi asked. "That is good for them."

Set snarled. Osiris was dead, but it was little consolation for this latest defeat on the racecourse.

"What is that bundle you carry?" the priest asked.

"A gift for my mother."

The two walked in the gravel for several steps, their feet crunching. The sharpness of that sound spiked in Set's head, in the knot at the front where the stone had hit.

"Do you want to hear my news?" Panahasi asked. He spoke loudly, as if to the sky and hills rather than to Set.

"No."

"Isis is with child."

Set stopped. He looked at the bundle in his left hand, and then at the priest.

"It is not possible," Set said.

"You see," Panahasi said. "I have now heard all about it. I have heard how you poisoned your brother and set him adrift on the Nile in a coffin made to his exact size. I have heard how you transformed into an animal. Tell me, though. How did Osiris come to be maimed?"

"I did that," Set said. "I wandered the banks of the river. I ran between the feet of soldiers who were sent to kill me. They were looking for a man, but I was no longer a man. I slept by their fires and ate their food. One morning, after the floods had receded, I found my brother's casket lodged in a tree by the riverbank. The lid had fallen away and Osiris was there, smiling at me. His eyes were open. I am certain now that he was dead, but..."

"But what?"

"He was smiling. He was watching. I tore him to pieces."

"Fourteen pieces," Panahasi said. "And you scattered them to all of the corners of the kingdom."

"Yes."

Panahasi leaned close and whispered.

"Do you want to know what happened next?"

Set closed his eyes.

"Isis found them," Panahasi said. "All but one. And she wrapped them in linens and made him whole again. And the missing piece—the courtiers attached a gold phallus to Osiris. And there was magic as Isis danced, and the gods descended, and a great storm of lightning shook the desert, and Osiris was alive again!"

Set opened his eyes. The sunlight beat off of the sand and nearly blinded him. He blinked and turned to Panahasi. Blotches of light pulsed in his vision and obscured the priest's face.

"It is not possible," Set repeated.

"As impossible as a man turning into an animal?"

Set closed his eyes again. "Is Osiris still alive?"

"No," Panahasi said. "He lived just hours, but long enough to give a child to his wife. It will be a son. They will name him Horus."

Set stepped forward, into the darkness of the cave, and knelt before the image of his mother. Nut stood, facing the west, in the blue dress that she wore when Osiris married. She held Geb's hand. And the writing, which Set could not read, not because it was faded or marred but because he could no longer read, must have proclaimed the glory of their lives, of their gift to the Nile with the birth of Osiris. The writing must have promised a treasured corner of the afterlife to them, but how could it be? The gods had willed an order, a way.

Osiris had broken the natural world. He had elevated peasants and destroyed monuments. But, then again, the gods had allowed it to happen.

"Tell her what you have done," Panahasi called. "And tell her the news. She will be a grandmother!"

Set knelt, bringing the bundle to the table at his mother's feet. A sack of rough brown cloth, not larger than a fist—dried blood was just a darker brown in its fabric. The flesh within, by now, was a hunk of leather.

"Mother," Set whispered. "I have killed your son, my brother. I bring him home to you so that he might nourish you in the afterlife."

Panahasi knelt before a fire just outside of the colonnade. He blew into the embers and smiled as the fir caught and consumed the scraps of brush and twigs. He raised his palms to the weak flame as if its warmth were significant. Set kicked the fire, watching the sparks spread across the sand and die into darkness. Panahasi frowned.

"Where do you go now, Lord Set?"

"To the desert. To the jungle. Perhaps I will drown myself in the river."

Panahasi exhaled loudly through his nose and gazed at the stars. It was night. Set felt the attention of tombs, of ghosts. Many caves dotted the ridge. Each was a portal to the afterlife. Through each, the dead watched him. Places like these, at times like these, were powerful. Things passed between worlds in such places, and both worlds became different.

"See?" Panahasi said, pointing. "There is Ma'at in the stars. The feather of Ma'at. The balance. And there—there you can see the last light of Ra fading. The last of the sunset still lingering on the horizon. And above that. Do you see those three stars?"

Set nodded.

"That," Panahasi continued, "is the belt of your brother. Do you see him? Do you see him raising his arm? He fights the ram. Do you see?"

"My brother is now a god."

"You have created a new world, Lord Set. You have created a new world, and you say that you will kill yourself in the river. Look up! Do you see the river? Do you see the ribbon of stars?"

Panahasi swept his arms across the whole sky, as if plowing it all away. Set swallowed hard, imagining those stars gathering into a glowing mass at the edge of the priest's arm as he pushed them from view. And there was a tight, dim group of them left. They burned far and cold, blue specks in the infinite black.

"Do you see?" Panahasi said. "That is Set, Lord of the Southern Sky."

"I am a god," Set whispered.

"Balance, Lord Set. There is the animal, and there is the man. And there will always be the animal and the man. This is the world that you have created."

Panahasi lowered his gaze and smiled. The corners of his mouth rose so high that his nose, his ears, his eyes climbed upon his small face.

"Why do you smile?" Set asked. "Do you think that you will be my priest? You will control my gifts? I will not be controlled."

"Nor they," Panahasi said.

Down the slope, some distance to the south, campfires dotted the plain all to the way to the banks of the Nile and beyond. The river was a black snake through this camp, which seemed to grow as Set watched. More and more fires flared, and the encampment soon stretched as far as he could see. The fires were like the stars, a mirror of the night sky. Set moved forward, nearly falling down the gravelly slope. He strode across the plain, reaching the edge of the encampment in just several minutes. Panahasi was far behind, but running to catch up with Set. Set was bounding, his robes falling away and billowing. He was on all fours, heaving, the cool night air of the desert rushing through his fur and pinning his ears to his head. He raced through the crowd. They were peasants and slaves, soldiers, foreigners. Osiris had provided for them, but Set knew that he offered something that made more sense to them.

He arrived at the center of their camp. A bonfire reached to the stars. Men chanted, beat weapons against their chests, and bowed to his constellation. They promised blood and sacrifice, smoke and embers.

Set climbed the rippling heat of their bonfire. The flames singed his fur. His ears burnt away. He ascended to the stars but a frame of his physical self, but with the power of a god. It took him days to find his place in the black of the sky. All the while, they chanted and worshipped. As he watched them from his perch in the sky, he knew.

They would follow him.

They would carry his world to the son of Osiris.

---

J. P. MOORE writes in southern New Jersey—a long way from the settings of his novels and stories. He has fond memories of a childhood in the Jersey Pine Barrens, where endless tracks of mossy wilderness informed the spirit behind his fiction. *Toothless*, his first novel, won the ForeWord Book of the Year 2010 Gold Medal in Horror. Praised by critics and fans alike for its original spin on the zombie apocalypse, Publishers Weekly hails *Toothless* as "moving, intriguing, and highly entertaining."

# BACK IN THE DAY

*Ryan T. McFadden*

VERNON ARCHER SLUMPED IN his leather chair, listening as lawyers debated the usual topics: sorcery, slavery, drugs, magic, lycanthropy.

He just wanted to take a nap.

Twenty-five years ago, he was just another grunt fighting in the trenches for a slice of the pie. Now, he fought in the boardrooms for the whole pie. *Fortune* magazine listed Vernon Archer as the 179th highest paid CEO in the world. If he'd declared illegal holdings and transactions, he'd have rocketed into the top thirty.

The boardroom door hissed open and the room fell still—the door had been magically and mechanically locked; it shouldn't have opened before their business was complete.

A small man stood in the doorway, spectacles perched on the end of his nose. LaFage, the Friendly. Vernon was suddenly very awake.

"Meeting's adjourned," Vernon said. When no one moved, "Now." There was a flurry of papers stuffed in folders, briefcases shut, and electronic equipment beeping.

When they were alone, Archer said, "I thought you were dead, LaFage."

LaFage placed a wooden four-inch box on the table.

"You owe me a favor, Vernon. I trust you haven't forgotten?"

The favor given to him at the beginning. Before boardrooms, before suits. Back when Vernon was a nobody. He hadn't forgotten the favor because how could he? It was the keystone of building his empire.

"What do you need?" Vernon asked, gaze tracing the perfect finger joints on the box. He wondered if there was a way to open it, like a puzzle box.

"You need to deliver this to a client."

Vernon took the box, judged the weight. "What's inside?"

"Confidential."

"I don't want to break the contents."

"You won't."

"Where am I delivering it?"

"To Sam Hurst."

The name scratched at Vernon's memory. Perhaps an acquaintance from his past.

"I'm sure you understand," LaFage continued, "this requires your services, and your services alone."

"And where do I find Sam?"

"He's somewhere in the city." LaFage stood, straightening his ruffled shirt. "This must be delivered tonight."

"Tonight? I'm an old man, LaFage. I don't have the energy to find this Sam fellow. Let me make a call. I can have my best men deliver this within the hour."

LaFage swept his hand at the board room, to the glistening glass windows, to the cherry conference table, to the leather executive chairs. "It appears that you have used my favor to its fullest potential."

Vernon sighed. He knew better than to underestimate his visitor. The favor LaFage had granted twenty-five years ago was potent—the reason that Vernon was captain of the underworld. And yet, he knew his power paled next to LaFage who was driven by obscure motives like a demi-god out of a Greek tragedy.

Even more importantly, however, was that Vernon had been waiting for LaFage all these years, wondering when he'd come to collect. Vernon was a man who repaid his debts, and this was the last one. He was tired of the business. Tired of working. Tired of wearing suits. But every morning, the favor hung over him.

LaFage bowed graciously then shuffled from the boardroom.

Vernon stood, his back sore. He had to go back to the streets. Just like the old days.

*Showtime.*

He straightened, flexed his fingers, shook them to get the blood flowing. He parted his suit jacket, revealing the hip holsters carrying his twin SIG-Sauer P220 semi-automatic pistols with shortened barrels and slides. Newer models had hit the market, but these were the guns he'd used to get to the top. He wasn't going to abandon them now.

Vernon took a couple of deep, even breaths.

With a quick motion, he reached for the pistol grips. The first 9mm twisted, then slipped off his finger and spun to the floor. Compensating, Vernon gripped the other too tightly. With a pop-pop-pop, he fired three bullets into one of the wall-to-floor windows. The glass exploded in a cloud of shards.

"Crap."

He glanced around sheepishly before retrieving the pistol. Didn't matter. All he needed to do was deliver one little box.

One small favor.

He probably wouldn't need his 220s.

In the wardrobe at the back of his office, Vernon changed out of his William Fioravanti suit into street clothes; street clothes he'd worn twenty years and three inches ago. A Kenneth Cole double-layer sweater, $175; denim 5-pocket jeans $225; and ox-blood, cracked leather loafers, $235. He shrugged on a double-stitched leather jacket $875 to complete the outfit.

Then he typed his personal code into the secret drawer of his bathroom vanity. With a click, it popped open. Vernon reached in, grabbed the container, unscrewed the lid, and slathered the cream onto his face.

The cream was $625 an ounce in New York's finest skin salons. Proven to remove wrinkles and signs of aging. Except no matter what skin creams or conditioners he used, the brown age spots on his hands and cheeks refused to retreat.

He judged himself in the mirror, turned sideways, sucked in his gut, let it back out, and sighed. He shut off the light. Vernon was always surprised at the old man staring back.

Vernon took the elevator to his limo in the parking garage. His driver, the Kid, opened the door for him.

"Where to tonight?" Kid asked.

"The Highwayman."

"Where?"

Vernon sighed. Passed on the directions. How could a modern-day criminal not even know the location of the Highwayman?

As they drove across town, Vernon pulled the box from his jacket and studied it. Why did the name Sam Hurst sound familiar? No matter how hard he tried, he couldn't recall anything beyond a vague familiarity. He returned the box to his pocket.

The car crawled to a stop along a greasy sidewalk. The black glass partition slid down.

"You sure this is it?" the Kid asked.

"This is fine."

Vernon Archer shifted from the limo, straightened his jacket, and took a deep breath. Perhaps he had grown a little soft over the years, his reflexes a little slower, but his mind was as sharp as ever.

"I won't be long." Vernon saw a flicker of confusion cross Kid's face. "This isn't about a woman. This is business."

"I'll follow."

"Kid, I used to do this stuff for a living."

Kid's disbelief was apparent. Vernon was having a hard time believing it too.

The Highwayman Tavern was the place for information. If anything was going down, it could always be traced back to the Highwayman. And if someone needed to be found, no matter how deep they were, this was the place to start.

Vernon Archer pushed on the front door of the Highwayman.

Except here, wasn't the Highwayman anymore.

A small bell tinkled above the door. The air smelled sweet, like sugar and honey.

A young woman was smiling at him, eyes blank as if possessed.

"Things have…changed," Vernon said.

"Have they?" she said. "We had some renovations, but that was a year ago. We'll get you settled in."

She sat him at a booth, a '50s diner table with rounded metal edging, except this table doubled as an aquarium. Vernon gave a tap on the Plexiglas. The goldfish inside weren't moving.

A family of four sat beside him, twin girls working on a deluxe sundae. In the booth across from him, a couple was on a date, taking turns feeding each other ice cream.

The woman with the dead gaze was smiling at him again.

"Our specials today are Three Cheers for Sundae and Field of Creams." He wondered if she was a zombie, but her coloring looked a little too alive. Perhaps she was spawn.

"I need to talk to someone," he said.

"At Tastes, there's always a party."

And she stood there.

Finally, Vernon turned his attention to the menu, picked the first one he saw. "I'll have the Field of Creams."

"My favorite!"

Then she was gone.

He felt a twinge of something. Regret? Nostalgia? The ultimate den of villainy had been transformed into a family dessert bar. No matter, he didn't have time for this. Vernon knew another place, a little further away, a little more dangerous.

The Cage.

He flipped open his cell phone, hit Kid's number.

"This is a dead end, Kid. I need you to pick me up." He paused as the Field of Creams was placed in front of him. A plate awash in vanillas, white creams, strawberries, and angel cakes.

"Give me five minutes."

The Cage was tucked away between dumpsters at the end of an alley cordoned by barbed wire. Vernon squeezed through a cut in the fencing, the ice cream and cake churning in his gut. Maybe he shouldn't have eaten the whole thing. Too late for regrets.

The building could've been a box factory, or a slaughterhouse, or a warehouse.

Except for the Minotaur who stood beside the open door, arms crossed.

Beyond him, laser lights and drum beats poured into the alley.

The Minotaur snorted and barred the way.

"Where's Norm?" Vernon asked.

The minotaur rolled its head, then replied, "Huuuooohar."

"Right. Well, the name's Vernon Archer. I should be on your list."

"Huuuahaaroo."

"Look, buddy, I'm always on the list. I'm on every list."

Vernon tried pushing past but a massive hand clutched his chest. Vernon swayed backwards and used the Minotaur's momentum against him. Eight hundred pounds of bovine slammed into the concrete. Vernon tapped his pistol against the Minotaur's temple.

"Is there going to be trouble?"

The Minotaur narrowed his eyes, did the math, then shook his head. Vernon straightened, holstered his pistol, and extended his hand. Except when the Minotaur took the offer, his immense weight caused Vernon's back to pop.

The Minotaur dusted himself off, then thumbed Vernon inside.

"Thanks, chum." Vernon stood there, afraid his back would give out completely. So he breathed deeply, tried to bury the discomfort, and wobbled into the cacophony of the Cage.

*No ice cream here.*

The crack of a cue ball cut through the din of conversation washing over cheap tin roofing and exposed asbestos insulation. A permanent haze clung to light bulbs dangling from the ceiling.

He smelt fermenting piss, beer, and vomit. It was good to be back.

Six trolls played Russian Roulette with a .44 Magnum. One troll was already on the ground, his brains splashed across the floor.

Vernon made his way to the bar.

Despite indigestion and a strained back, he felt good, leaning against the bar, foot up on the railing. He avoided staring at the shattered backbar mirror. It threw a thousand reflections, and in every one, Vernon still looked old. But standing there made him feel younger—like back in the day.

"Vernon Archer? *The* Vernon Archer?"

Of all the voices he didn't want to hear, this one might've topped his list. He sighed, prepared himself, and turned around slowly. Yet the face from his memory didn't match the face staring at him. Dmitri Sokolov was older, rounder, his cheeks and forehead covered in spider veins. Back in the beginning, they had been partners. Back before Vernon decided to invoke his own shotgun clause and oust Dmitri.

Three goblins, dressed like Old West gun slingers, escorted Dmitri. They may've dressed the part, but they slobbered and drooled. Hired muscle, real knuckle-draggers but nasty in a fight.

"I see you're keeping good company, Dmitri."

"These are my boys." Dmitri snorted. "They're dependable. Trustworthy. *Loyal.*"

"Cheap, you mean?"

"They wouldn't leave me holding the bag against an eight-pack of Hooked Emperites."

"Are we reminiscing, Dmitri? Or is there something else you want to say?" He parted his jacket to reveal the SIG-Sauer on his hip.

"You know how long I've wanted to meet you alone? No Kid, no special units? Just you and me."

"And three goblins."

Dmitri shrugged. "Now you're worried that this might not be a fair fight?"

"This is a fight?"

"Wasn't that always your philosophy? Have the fight finished before they even knew it had started?"

"I'm looking for someone."

"You think I'd help you, Vernon?" The goblins were flanking him. "The thing that hurts most, is that I would've stepped aside. Taken a buy-out. You didn't have to backstab me like that."

Vernon drew first but Dmitri's knife was already at his throat. Except now it wasn't a knife. It had morphed into a black mamba. *Christ, he's fast, or I'm just slow.*

"We were friends, you son of a bitch," Dmitri spat.

Vernon wanted to tell him that he had no friends, which was why he now ruled half the Eastern Seaboard while Dmitri was slumming it at the Cage. The snake tongue tickling his throat convinced him to be quiet. Sweat beaded along Vernon's neck and his heart beat quicker than it had in years. And yet, the speed of the world slowed, as if his mind was trying to savor the last moments of life.

"His name is Sam Hurst." Vernon gasped. "I need to find him tonight."

Dmitri blinked. "Sam?"

"You've heard of him?"

With enviable speed, Dmitri re-sheathed the snake-turned-dagger into the folds of his jacket.

"Who told you about Sam?" Dmitri asked cautiously.

"I need to deliver something. Tonight."

"To Sam?"

"That's right. You know where he is?"

"I'm probably the only one who does."

"Where?"

"At the Bone Factory."

"The cemetery?"

"That's right. Dead, gone, buried, six feet under."

"How do you know he's there?" Vernon asked.

"Because I'm the man who put him there. Under your orders. Funny how fate has a way of coming back around."

Vernon considered. LaFage had never said that Sam was alive.

"Thanks for the information, Dmitri. I owe you."

"Anytime, *friend*."

Vernon pushed his way past the drooling goblins.

"Hey, Vernon," Dmitri shouted over the din.

Vernon paused, but didn't turn around.

"Back in the day, I wouldn't have been able to beat you. You're nothing but an old man now."

Vernon left to Dmitri's laughter.

"Take me to the Bone Factory."

Kid stared through the rearview mirror. "Boss?"

"You heard me. The Bone Factory."

The night wasn't even half over and already Vernon wanted nothing more than to be soaking in his oversized bathtub, listening to *Enrico Caruso* over his Ohm Model F's loudspeakers.

Instead, his back hurt like a son of a bitch, and his stomach twisted and churned. He crunched down a lactose pill even though he knew it was too late. *One small favor.*

Kid let him out a block away. Heavy layers of fog muted the sounds of traffic, and vines smothered the buzzing street lights.

The Bone Factory stood at the end of the street like a skeletal cat ready to pounce. Extending beyond the building was the graveyard proper, ringed with a fungi encrusted stone wall. Razor wire was strung along the top; Vernon got the impression that the wire was positioned to keep people in, not keep intruders out.

Vernon rapped three times with the knocker. He heard a slow shuffle and the left door ground open.

An undertaker stood in the entrance, a lantern in one hand, a heavy tome tucked under his. Black ink stained his fingers.

"Yes?" The undertaker spoke with a sibilant lisp.

"I'm here to see someone."

The undertaker was dressed in a black coat, satin pin-striped trousers, and patent leather shoes. His eyes were black marbles sunken in a face seemingly molded of wax, and his lips a deep shade of red.

"Of course, of course. Please, come in," he lisped.

Vernon stepped past the undertaker into the skeletal Necropolis. Though there wasn't a hint of wind, the torches guttered in their sconces.

"No electricity?"

"Hmmm? Electricity? No, no. It upsets our guests, unfortunately."

"I see," Vernon lied.

"My name is Doctor Vanblud. I am the Undertaker of this institution. We don't receive many visitors at this time of night."

"You receive visitors during the day?"

"No."

Doctor Vanblud led him down the corridor of statues. He opened an oaken door and shuffled into an office stacked floor to ceiling with papers, binders, and leather-bound books. The doctor sat behind an old, beaten mahogany desk. He clicked on the green desk lamp and ushered Vernon to sit opposite him.

Vanblud opened the tome, gave his finger a lick, and flipped the pages.

"Ah, here we go." He turned the book around and pushed it to Vernon. "All visitors must sign here." Doctor Vanblud offered a quill.

Vernon signed, dated, then printed his name in the ledger. He noticed the last entry was twenty years ago. The name was Dmitri Sokolov, checking in someone under the moniker Sam Hurst.

"I'm looking for someone. A *guest* of yours."

"Do you know what plot he's in?"

"I was hoping you could help me. It's urgent."

Doctor Vanblud took back the ledger, inspected the name, and raised his eyebrows. "Vernon Archer?"

"Yes." He smiled. His name was sometimes more valuable than any bribe or form of intimidation.

"Interesting."

"I'm looking for someone. His name is Sam Hurst. I see he was actually the last person listed in the ledger."

"This is quite unusual, Mr. Archer."

"I know, it is. He may be dead, but I still have this package for him. I have to deliver it. Tonight. Now if you could let me know the plot—"

"I don't mean him. I mean you. It's just that…" Dr Vanblud paused. "Well, most of our guests don't come quite so…alive."

"I can be gone in a few minutes. I need to find this man."

He sensed the door opening behind him.

"We already have a plot set aside for you." Doctor Vanblud's face cracked into an emotionless smile. "Are those your burial clothes? Usually our guests prefer something a little more…formal."

Vernon heard a shuffle behind him.

"Does the name Vernon Archer mean anything to you? I'm a man of some renown, Doctor," Vernon continued.

"Renown is usually a nice way of saying butcher. You've had a plot reserved for quite some time. Now, our morticians are the best in the business but you may find yourself in some discomfort during the evisceration process."

"You're not listening. Is this about to get violent?"

"Oh dear me. I pray not. This is a house of the dead. Not a place for rabble-rousing and other disturbances."

"Call off your henchmen and we can discuss this like businessmen."

"I'm not in business."

"If this is a question of money—"

"It's a question of integrity."

Vernon kicked back his chair, reached for his weapons, turned, and aimed.

Behind him were two perfect duplicates of Doctor Vanblud. So perfect that he wasn't sure if they were the real ones and the man behind the desk was a fake.

Each of the doctors was smiling. Both carried butcher's knives, chipped and covered in past grime. Outside, he saw another Vanblud manning an empty gurney.

"You don't know who I am, really, do you?"

"You are the occupant of plot A15."

"I'm Vernon Archer."

Vernon started firing. He dropped two of the doctors. *Damn, missed one.* Which meant: a knife was coming for him. Vernon deflected it with his pistol and he realized the time for playing fancy was over. He shot the knife-wielding doctor four times, sending him sprawling onto his own gurney.

That left the one doctor still at the desk. All Vernon needed was one.

Vernon whirled, saw the doctor twisting for cover, but Vanblud was too slow. Vernon shot him in the lower back and dropped him.

Vernon holstered his 220s. The doctor dragged himself along the floor.

"Now, Doctor. You and I were having a conversation. You were going to tell me where I could find Sam Hurst."

"There are privacy concerns…"

Vernon stepped on the doctor's back. The doctor screamed, his mouth wide, forked tongue dancing.

"I wasn't always a businessman. Once, I did things a little less savory. A location. It's all I need. Then we can be finished with this. Understood?"

The doctor's pale complexion had turned sallow. Vernon dragged him to the ledger.

"Show me where he is."

"C54," he gasped.

"Show me."

The doctor flipped through the ledger, pointed to plot C54. Vernon followed the line over to the occupant name: Sam Hurst.

"Thank you. If Sam's not in C54, I'll be back for you. Understand?"

The doctor gave a sickly nod and Vernon released him to crumple beside the desk. Vernon left the necropolis through the rear double doors.

Outside, the graveyard was organized in nice, neat rows with identical tomb markers. Nothing fancy, just a granite slab with an etched plot number. Vernon walked quickly through the yard. Plot C54 appeared no different than any of the others. Heavy crab grasses covered the ground, unmolested for quite some time.

He retrieved a shovel from a freshly dug site and returned to C54 to begin digging. His sore back became nearly crippling. He tried to keep his enthusiasm high by concentrating on the results, not the details. Finally, after all these years, the debt to LaFage would be done.

When the shovel struck wood, Vernon fell to his knees and brushed aside the last of the moist dirt. He dug out the locks, retrieved the shovel, and smashed the first lock open.

*Thump-thump.*

The body in the coffin was anything but dead. Vernon smashed the other locks, pulled his gun, and opened the lid.

The occupant of plot C54 blinked and sat up.

Despite being in a box for untold number of years, the man was quite rotund, with dark eyes set in a pock-marked face. He wore a white leisure suit with a black, perfectly pressed shirt.

"Vernon?"

"Doyle?" Vernon wondered if perhaps his body was reacting poorly to the Fields of Creams. Doyle Archer, his brother, had been dead for twenty years. Or should've been dead.

"Damn, you look old," Doyle said.

"I am old."

"I knew you'd come for me. How long I've been in here? A couple of months?"

"Something like that." Vernon sat back against the earthen wall, suddenly feeling every year of his age. He smiled as if understanding the joke. He imagined Dmitri, somewhere, laughing his ass off. Laughing because there was no Sam Hurst.

"Oh boss, Dmitri, he's gone crazy. Bastard stuck me in this box."

"Did he now?"

"He got the jump on me. Put a bag over my head, worked me over, stuck me in this hole. You can't trust that guy."

"Doyle...it wasn't Dmitri. It was me."

Doyle blinked, frowning. He never was very bright. Even after all these years, locked in a coffin, somehow kept alive, he had never touched upon the truth. Never even considered the possible betrayal. Which was why Vernon ruled the underworld, and Doyle had been trapped in a box.

"You're the only one who knows about the favor."

"The favor?"

"That's right."

Doyle processed the information, but instead of rage, he appeared saddened by the realization.

"You did this to me? All you had to do was ask and I would've disappeared."

"No one disappears, Doyle. Look—I found you and it only took one night."

Vernon pulled back the blue slide on the Sauer to see the bullet in the chamber.

Doyle's gaze fixed on the gun. "So this is how it ends?"

"This is how it ends, Doyle."

"But we're brothers."

Vernon Archer shot him in the chest. The entry wound was small—no larger than the size of a quarter. But it was precise. Through the heart. Doyle tried to take a breath, and died.

Vernon couldn't draw his eyes from his brother.

Vernon had fooled himself. Fooled himself into thinking that he was a businessman, a captain of industry. He destroyed people with money, with commerce. And if those methods weren't successful, he pressed a button and that person would disappear. He didn't have to fire guns or strangle enemies with his bare hands. He didn't have to murder his brother.

Vernon smelt the bitterness from the gunpowder. But he didn't feel remorse. What scared him was that he felt nothing.

Vernon stood, reached into his jacket and pulled out the box. He was going to toss it into Doyle's coffin but thought otherwise and returned it to his inner pocket.

Doyle didn't need it now.

Vernon flipped open his cell phone and called Kid.

"I found what I needed. Come get me."

Back at his office Vernon Archer changed into fresh clothing. He sipped from a highball. In front of him sat his personal ledger and the box.

Vernon stroked LaFage's entry out of the book. He closed it, melting back into his chair. The books, after all these years, were balanced. But he knew that some ledgers, like his own, could never be balanced.

With the butt of his pistol, Vernon smashed the box until the joints broke. He knew what was inside even before sifting through the wood splinters.

Nothing.

RYAN McFADDEN is an Aurora-winning fantasy/SF author from London, Ontario. He has been nominated for two Auroras in 2012 for his work on the 10th Circle Project—a ten-volume shared world project (the10thcircle.com). Recent writing credits include *Blood and Water* (Bundoran Press, 2012) and an untitled anthology from Edge SF&F (due in early 2013). His website is ryanmcfadden.com.

# ROBIN REDBREAST

## *Todd McCaffrey*

"Parolee Beaumont reporting in," I said as soon as my call was answered. "No, I haven't been drinking," I said in response to the first question. "No, I haven't left the state," I said to the second question. The voice on the other end sounded familiar.

"Goodi TwoShoes, is that you?" I knew he hated it when I called him that. Tough. He could change his last name—but he's a stubborn Indian.

"And what if it is?" Detective Inspector Paul TwoShoes asked gruffly. I sorta expected him to argue over "Goodi"—officially there was no such thing as the Global Order Of Detective Inspectors. Of course, the name fit like a...shoe.

"What, did they drop you from the force?" I asked. "Is this all the work you can get now that all the big, bad evil-doers are behind bars?"

"There's at least one evil-doer not behind bars," TwoShoes said. Yeah, me. Mean ol' Robin 'Redbreast' herself. All one hundred and five pounds, five foot three inches of dangerous post-adolescent.

"Is that so?" I said, sounding surprised. "Well I've no doubt you'll be able to catch him just as easily as you caught my dad."

"I'm certain of it," TwoShoes said. "As long as *she* doesn't figure out some way to beat the ankle tractor."

*She*—meaning me.

"Don't worry, I've seen the error of my ways."

"Where are you now?"

"I'm at home, as your electronic gadget will tell you," I said.

"The lights are out," TwoShoes said.

Oh! So he was watching my place. Interesting. Not really a surprise but interesting.

"I'm in bed," I said. I lowered my voice and added a bit of a purr, "Wanna come up?"

"I don't rob cradles," TwoShoes said.

"Oh, yeah, you do!" I shouted over the phone. "I was in mine when you robbed me of TEN YEARS of my life!" I shouldn't have lost my temper, I know it but—damn —how could he say such a thing?

"Sorry." And—dammit!—you know, but he really did sound sorry.

"That's nice, Goodi," I said. "It's a bit late. You coulda said that when they went for sentencing. When they sent me up for all my childhood." My eyes were watering now as too many nights came back to me. "Do you know what they did to me for the first three months I was there? Do you know they put me in solitary? 'For my own good'?"

"No," and Goodi had the sense to sound repentant, "I didn't know until I checked up on you."

"And when was that?" I demanded.

"Three months after you were incarcerated," Goodi said quietly.

*Oh!*

"So I'm supposed to thank you?"

"No," TwoShoes said. "They'd already moved you when I found out about it." A pause. "All I did was make sure that the prison governor was removed for cause." Goodi Twoshoes would never say 'fired'; he really had earned his nickname.

"Unh." I was getting tired; tears do that to me. Stupid tears. I rubbed them off my face angrily. I'd sworn, ten years ago, never to cry again and here I was—only a day out of the joint—bawling like a...like a kid who was sent to jail when she was only twelve.

For a crime everyone knew I didn't commit. Not that it mattered. The jury didn't give a shit, nor did the judge, nor did dear ol' Goodi TwoShoes when it came to it. Someone *had* to pay, the crime was too enormous —"a crime against humanity so heinous that it revolts all common sense to even consider it"...and my dad was dead.

So li'l ol' Robin, "the notorious Robin Redbreast" as the newsies decided to call me— 'cuz they couldn't call me "Red Robin" or they'd get sued— little twelve-year-old pint-sized me got to take the fall.

They even attempted to try me as an adult.

I was like all of five foot at the time, flat-chested, freckle-faced, ninety-five pounds dripping wet, with flaming red hair and "beautiful, baleful blue eyes."

At the time, I really didn't care. Hell, let them kill me was what I thought back then. There wasn't anything left to live for. My dad was dead, thousands had died because of—"a heinous act of premeditated murder"—no, really, a mistake. A mistake for which I cried every night of those three months in solitary until I finally realized that that was all it had been: a mistake. My mistake, so maybe I deserved some of the punishment.

But not all of it. No, not for a mistake.

"Make sure you report in tomorrow," Goodi TwoShoes said now. "And don't think of leaving town."

"Sure, no problem," I said. "Is that all?" I knew better than to hang up on him. The shit would probably have revoked my parole just for that alone. Goodi TwoShoes.

"That's all," he said and hung up.

I was in my room, just like I said. Of course, I was in the room that no one had ever found, not even my dad.

Maybe if they'd've found my room, they wouldn't have sent me to jail. Maybe not. I've had ten years to learn how people will close their eyes to the truth. How would the public have handled my room, all kitted out in pinks and Barbies? It wouldn't have fit with their nice post-Emo terrorist girl image of me. The kid with mascara tears, the pierced nose, the punk haircut, the intense expression—how is anyone supposed to look when they learn that their father's dead, that he's convicted in the eyes of the public of being a mass-murderer/terrorist and that they're considered his happy accomplice? Would I have looked better if I'd've smiled? With all those blackened teeth in my face?

Did anyone REMEMBER that it was Halloween? How was I supposed to look, trick-or-treating with my dad?

I spent a year being mad at my dad. Maybe I would have spent longer but strange things happened in the joint, things I never would have expected. I suppose the strangest thing of all is that I lived—that and they let me out.

It's true that my dad wanted to be the most notorious evil genius in history. And he tried, he really did.

He almost succeeded in creating a mini-blackhole gun. I had to work *really* hard to handle that one and, even so, we ended up with the Anomalizer.

When that didn't work, he tried to make "Evil Genius Pills" and that's where the trouble began.

My dad was really, really, really smart. And he never set out to be evil. He made mistakes. But because he was really, really, really smart his mistakes were worse than most.

My mom died in childbirth. The car had broken down because dad had stolen some parts for his infinite poker player—the machine that was supposed to make it so he could never lose at poker. Because the car stopped along the highway, dad had to deliver me himself. Biology wasn't his specialty—even after, he was never really good at it. He wouldn't say—but I read the police reports—Mom died from a ruptured artery. It's rare but not uncommon. Her death was ruled "death by misadventure."

So I grew up with Dad. And he tried. He never really *saw* me though. Because whenever he *really* looked, he saw my mother and he couldn't bear it. So, instead, he saw a girl-clone of himself. My mother was arty, airy, light-hearted, heavy-humored, and totally the sort of person my dad needed to keep him grounded. Only she was dead and I was supposed to be my dad's clone. So for him—by day—I was the emo-Goth super-scientist nerd lab Egor.

At night, in my special room, I could be me and draw pictures of butterflies, play with Barbies and pretend I was a normal girl. I even managed to get pink dresses and I'd put them on when I was playing.

My mother's memory preyed on him. I guess I was maybe four or five when I finally realized what my dad was trying to do—back then—and that was bring my mother back to life. He studied biology and he worked on resurrection, revitalization, and several things.

He came up with some good ideas but, somehow, ChemCo always seemed to patent them before he remembered to file. So he was never given the credit he deserved. He'd threaten to sue; they'd rattle their lawyers; and finally there'd be a small settlement—enough to distract him and off he'd go in a new direction, sure that this time he'd find the answer and bring mom back to life.

For the first two years or more, I was his willing accomplice in this. He'd tell me all about my mother when he was working and I got this brilliant image of her, I could see how much he loved her and how great our lives would be with her back—maybe I'd have her in my special room and we'd play tea or house. Maybe—and I only thought this in the deepest, secretest parts of my mind—maybe she'd let me wear *dresses* to school! And then maybe (and now I couldn't even really bring myself to think this even in the deepest, secretest parts of my mind because it was just too miraculous and impossible), maybe I'd get friends and I wouldn't have to take karate classes and break all the bullies' bones at recess—and then I'd never get sent to the principal again.

But that stopped the night he tried to dig up Mom's body. I was asleep, I guess he couldn't bring himself to take me, so I only found out about it when the police banged on the door and barged in, throwing all our stuff around and scaring me so badly that I almost wet myself.

Dad was sent to jail and I was sent to a foster home while he was there. They wouldn't let me wear dresses, they were convinced that I *liked* being goth and, after a while, out of loyalty to Dad, I stopped trying.

Things were very different when he got out. He looked warier, meaner. I suppose I looked the same, too—because I discovered that the cops had found my special place and they'd taken all my pretty toys and clothes, "for evidence." I guess none of them believed that I could actually want the stuff.

I was about eight, then, and I cried myself to sleep—when I could sleep—for the next year. I started wetting the bed again, too, but I couldn't tell Dad, so I learned how to clean the sheets myself and finally figured out how to stop the bedwetting, too.

Everything was different. School was worse, way worse. Finally, one day, some mean kid shouted, "Why don't you go home and stay there?" I really wanted to but I knew I couldn't.

But when I got home, I started to find out why I couldn't. By the end of the week, the school received an official notification that I had transferred to the NightBridge school. They called the school to be certain and a very lady-like voice answered and assured them that, indeed, Robin Beaumont had been accepted and was currently enrolled there. It was the first time I used a voice-changer and I really liked it.

After that, every day Dad would send me off to school and I'd go back around the house and upstairs to my special room. I studied very hard and my grades were excellent—I made sure that dad got regular report cards. And I really *was* studying. I studied Math, Science, Thermodynamics, Philosophy, Sociology, Criminal Law—everything. I learned French (they say I sound like a Belgian), German (they say I sound French), Japanese (they say I sound Chinese) and a smattering of Chinese (they say—you probably guessed—Japanese). I learned computer programming. And I don't meant that baby web-programming stuff that the kids on the net brag about. I mean *real* programming. Because the first thing I needed to do was break into my dad's computers to find out what he was doing.

You see, I'd decided that I never wanted to go to a foster home again. And the best way to do that was to make sure that Dad never went to jail again.

And for four years, I did just that.

Breaking into his computers was the easy part. As soon as I managed that, I had to get a spy eye into his lab and follow his calculations. So, while I was downloading his data, building a microtech robot that looked like a mosquito but could fly soundlessly when I wanted, I was also learning Calculus, Tensor Math, Manifolds, Number Theory, Quantum Mechanics, and sub-atomic element theory.

Because I discovered that dad had been trying to build a time machine. Only, after getting out of jail, he was now trying to build a mini-blackhole gun. And, from what I could tell, he was just about to complete it.

Yeah, I know, what's a ten year-old doing learning about black holes and stuff? Well, from the time I could speak, I could say, "Black holes warp space-time." I mean, who couldn't? Dad taught me a lot growing up and if we didn't do regular girlie things we did build model rockets—the kind with real liquid propellants, not the kind you can buy in a store—we learning rappelling, skydiving, hang-gliding and all sorts of stuff. When I was six, I got a microscope and, at seven, I got a telescope. I did mention that my dad was really, really, really smart, didn't I? I forgot to mention that my mom was really, really, really, *really* smarter. And I'm smarter than both of them put together. Really, I'm not joking — they made me take the damned IQ test five times in the joint, they couldn't believe the numbers. In fact, I flubbed the fifth test on purpose and that's the number they used. So, as far as the rest of the world is concerned, I've got an IQ of 129—not the 229 that I scored on the first four tests.

Anyway, Dad was good. And that mini-blackhole gun? Just about ready. It would've worked too, except I was smarter. Just as he was about to finish with the mini-blackhole gun, I perfected the anti-blackhole shield. So when

Dad first tried his gun on the door of the First Intermediate Bank—because he was flat broke after that year in jail—I knew it wasn't going to work because I'd added my anti-blackhole circuitry to his gun while he'd been sleeping. So Dad thought it didn't work. Hell, *I* thought it didn't work. I'm smart but I'd been rushing things too much and hadn't bothered with the math beyond the first solution.

Of course, I knew it wouldn't work so while Dad was banging on it (not a great idea with a quantum fusion reactor), I said to him, "You know, Dad, there's usually more money is selling the tools of the trade than there is in doing the grunt work yourself."

"What?" Dad looked up from pounding on the gun. Fortunately, he decided to stop at that moment—which was a good thing. "What do you mean?"

"I was thinking, rather than do the robbing yourself, why not sell the tools?"

"Sell the tools?"

"Yeah, you could advertise."

"Where?"

"Soldier of Fortune, Evildoers Anonymous, on-line," I said, adding with a shrug, "the usual places."

"I don't know..."

"Well, I could help," I said. "After all, I'm kinda good at that sort of stuff." I had managed, after he got of jail, to convince him that I could help him by finding suppliers. That gave me a leg up in figuring out what he was trying to do — hence, the anti-blackhole shield.

"But your common evil-doer is so dumb!" Dad complained.

"Well, that's it, then!" I told him. "Just make an evil genius pill or something."

"An Evil Genius Pill?" Dad said, trying out the sound of it. He gave me an approving look. "You know, that might just work!"

"Hey, and if it does, will you come trick-or-treating with me for Halloween?"

"Trick-or-treating?" Dad sounded dubious.

"All the kids do it," I said. I could see that he wasn't impressed. "And if people don't give treats, then I can do some really good tricks."

"Oh," Dad said, sounding suddenly enlightened. "And what tricks do you have in mind?"

"What tricks do you suggest?"

Dad thought for a moment and then listed four or five really nasty tricks ranging from letting air out of tires to infecting toothbrushes with teeth-removing bacteria.

"Wow, Dad, you're really good at this!" I told him. Maybe I could distract him enough, and maybe slow him down enough that I wouldn't have to worry about him going back to jail.

"But first, I'll need to make those Evil Genius Pills," he said. I could tell he really relished the idea, even without his rubbing his hands together and laughing maniacally. But that was Dad—when he did something, he did it all out. Which is why I should have been more careful.

You see, even I didn't think that Dad could come up with something in the four weeks before Halloween. So I slacked off, checking out Halloween costumes that I could wear and that Dad would approve. I finally settled, after having regretfully shelved the Pistol-packing Pink Barbie outfit, on emoGoth girl. Complete with blackened teeth and a tear-drop out of one eye. When I mentioned it to Dad, he merely said, "We've still got to get the Evil Genius Pills perfected."

"Come on, Dad, with your brains, it's got to be easy!" I told him. "Just do the whole little girls thing and corrupt it."

"What?"

"Well you know, they say that little girls are made of sugar and spice and everything nice," I told him, being very careful to scowl and roll my eyes—something I wasn't quite faking because while I might like to wear pink, I honestly couldn't subscribe to the whole girls-as-wimps thing. "So just take that and *corrupt* it—make it evil."

"Huh," Dad said. He frowned and shook his head. "I don't think it'll be that easy."

"Well, it's worth a shot," I told him.

Dad got that far-off dreamy look he got when he was thinking deeply and following his intuition. "Hmm, maybe some plutonium and some anti-protons coupled with a degenerate DNA interferon bacterial transport..." he looked back at me again. "I'll be in the lab."

As soon as he was out of sight, I raced up to my room and fired up my computer. I wanted to know what he was doing. And, as I said, I'd promised to look at the whole marketing angle. I made a mistake, then, and got totally lost in an article in Soldier of Fortune— "Girls, the next superweapon?"

When I finished, it was way late and I was too tired. I should have checked in on Dad but I didn't.

The next morning, he was late for breakfast. Heck, he was late for lunch. So I made a pair of sandwiches—roast beef with horseradish and chili peppers, just the sort he likes—and ran up to the lab with it. I knocked but no one answered.

Worried, I keyed in the combination to the lock. The normal combination, the one Dad had given me. But the door didn't open. So I left the tray by the door and ran back to my room. Inside, I fired up my computer and did a quick security scan, then I turned on the spybot in Dad's lab. He wasn't there. I turned on my tracking device and discovered that he was in the downstairs john. I turned everything off—with a super-genius Dad you can never be too careful—and raced back down.

"Dad?" I asked, knocking gently on the door. "Are you in there?"

"I know what went wrong," Dad's voice came rasping through the door. It sounded echo-y and I couldn't figure out what was up until I heard him retch into the toilet again. "Oh, no!" he sounded weak. "That's the twenty-third time."

"Should I call a doctor?" I asked. Dad had never barfed more than twelve times in a row with his previous experiments and then he'd had to get his stomach pumped. This sounded serious.

"No, no, at least it's not green anymore," he called back weakly.

"Should I make toast or tea?" I asked, just wishing for something to do, some way to help.

I heard the toilet flush and my Dad open the door. I stood back, ready for anything. I wasn't ready for pink. And I wasn't ready for the hair.

"What's wrong?"

"Your hair!" I said, pointing at it. I didn't dare mention the pink—Dad has a thing about pink. He turned and looked into the bathroom mirror. He jumped and slapped his hands to his face, crying desperately, "I'm pink!"

"I'm sure it'll wear off," I told him quickly. His face, hands, every part of his body was the color pink that I dreamed about. Guiltily, I wondered if somehow I'd managed to infect his project, to somehow project my hopes into his actions—after all, neither of us could ever tell for a certainty that Dad's old Psychic Projector hadn't worked. "You should drink some water, get some rest."

"Not now, not now!" He said, moving past me and climbing back up to the lab. "I've got it, I know I've got it."

"What?"

"The Evil Genius Pills, I know what to do now!" Dad exclaimed.

"How?"

"I took some and now I know," he told me. He gave me a grateful look that at was spoiled by the deep, pulsing pink that had filled the whites of his eyes. "Sugar, spice, everything nice—and plutonium! That's just the start, Robin, just the start! Today the pills, tomorrow the world!"

He dashed inside before I could say anything and then, just as quickly was back with a piece of paper in his hand. "I need you to get these for me. Have them sent immediately. Use the Hermes guys."

"What, are we ordering flowers?" I asked, glancing down warily at the list.

"No, no, the overnight guys!" he said, waving a hand dismissively. "You know the ones I mean. When it absolutely has to be here tomorrow—make sure it comes tomorrow. There'll be a full moon."

"Okay," I said as my insides turned to jelly. Full moon? Overnight? This was sounding serious.

"And place those ads!" Dad said, turning and rushing back inside, locking the door behind him.

Okay, now I was freaked. Dad had used the Evil Genius Pills? Or the first version, at least? And he'd turned his hair white and his skin pink! What if they actually worked? What then? What if, suddenly, there weren't just dozens but hundreds—thousands or even tens of thousands of evil geniuses on the planet?

I looked at the list and tried to make sense of it. It included aspirin, alcohol, sugar, spices—including mace—and a whole bunch of other things including—I could hardly believe it—Gummee Slops! Apparently, Dad took whole fruit Gummee Slops—so that's where they went!—and rolled them around the plutonium-DNA-retroviral core to make the whole mess swallowable. Or, thinking back to the bathroom, at least initially swallowable.

I ran up to my room. How could I stop this? How could I make these pills not work but do so in a way that Dad wouldn't suspect and he'd still make money?

I scanned the list. There was one thing on the list that fairly jumped out at me—vinegar. Apparently the pills were supposed to be packed in vinegar to preserve them. Hm...what if they weren't packed in vinegar? What if they were packed in something like brine or olive oil? Hmmm...it'd have to look the same.

I got online and searched. It took me all night to get the list just right and then I placed the order.

And I placed the ads. And I made the little video. I thought it was pretty cute, really. Okay, I admit it: I really got into making the video. I mean, I thought that maybe someone would see it and say, "Who's that girl? She's got a great voice!" And then, well, you know, I was all of twelve and I liked dreaming. Is that so terrible?

But maybe, if I hadn't been dreaming, none of this would have happened.

The stuff came in and Dad allowed me to take charge of bottling so he never knew about my "secret ingredient." He smiled when he saw my ad but I could tell that he wasn't really that impressed—maybe I should have added those explosions and fake headlines I'd thought of.

Anyway, orders started pouring in. Slowly at first, and then more and more until we were making Evil Genius Pills day and night. And we were finally getting money in the bank.

"So, I can go, can't I?" I said to him the day before Halloween.

"What, Robin?" Dad said, looking up from the latest sales figures. "What did you say?"

"I said, can we go trick-or-treating?" I repeated. "Halloween's tomorrow, and I've already got my costume." I'd bought it without telling him when we made our first hundred thousand dollars. Evil Genius Pills don't come cheap and we were selling thousands of them.

"Well, sure, if there isn't anything on the news," Dad said.

"It's early, Dad," I assured him, secretly relieved that there'd been no news stories about Evil Genius Pills. I was sure, because of that, that they didn't work. I still can't believe that I was so wrong. "So can we? It'll be fun."

"Yeah, okay," Dad said distractedly. But I knew I could hold him to his word. So I ran over and gave him a hug.

"Great," I said, "we can start out at seven when it gets dark."

"Okay, honey."

"And you don't have to worry about a costume, Dad," I told him. "With your white hair, all you have to do is wear your lab coat and pretend that you're an evil genius." The pink skin, by then, had faded back to just a healthy glow (as it were).

"But I *am* an evil genius!"

"See? So, no problem!" I ran up to my room and then into my secret room where I looked at the dark emoGoth costume and wondered, just for a moment, what it would be like if I had a father who would have been cool with a Pistol-packing Pink Barbie outfit. But, still... it was better than nothing.

And then it was Halloween. We rushed out about a thousand orders that day and I'd re-ordered a whole bunch of supplies, the overnight guys were non-stop at our door and some of them were complaining—and some of the neighbors had started to look at me funny when I answered the door.

I ignored them or waved as nicely as I could and then either handed off the packages or carted them inside. I couldn't wait for the night. If we weren't so swamped maybe I would have had time to look at the news or the internet or something.

But I didn't know about the manhunt until it was too late.

"Come on, Dad!" I called as seven o'clock came and went. "We're late!"

"Just one more batch!" Dad called down from the lab.

"You promised!" I wailed, getting ready to throw a certain-to-succeed tantrum.

"Okay!" Dad called back. He was down a moment later, in his white lab coat. "How do I look? Am I scary enough?"

"Yup, you are," I assured him, grabbing a bag and pulling him out the door behind me. I was pretty sure I heard it latch. Pretty sure.

We went down our street first, then around to the next block. Dad was really getting into the whole evil genius thing—even as the Evil Genius Pills were getting into everyone else.

We tricked and treated for about an hour and... honestly, it was the greatest night of my life! Finally, I was tired and told Dad that we could head home.

We saw the lights when we rounded the corner to our block.

"Is that our house?" Dad shouted, breaking into a run. "It's on fire, Robin!"

Dad raced way ahead of me. I was tired, my feet hurt, I had a full bag of candy... none of it really mattered, though. If I'd known, I would have dropped the bag, I would have torn after him, maybe stopped him but—

Four shots rang out and I saw Dad stagger, clutch his chest and stumble.

I dropped my bag then, you can bet, and I ran, and ran, and ran and I was screaming and I ran right into the first policeman—Goodi TwoShoes himself—and I started clawing at him, I raked my fingers on his face and I tricked to kick him and beat him and—rough hands pulled me off and held me, no matter what karate moves I tried and I screamed and screamed and still kicked until I had no more energy and then—

"Robin Beaumont, you are under arrest, everything you say can and will be held against you..." Goodi TwoShoes read me my rights.

You see, I didn't know it and Dad never found out. But that was the Night of the Zombies. The night that everyone who ate too many of our Evil Genius Pills turned into stark raving mad, flesh-eating zombies. And, all over the world, they killed tens of thousands of people before they were finally destroyed.

It was Goodi TwoShoes who figured it out, who traced the outbreaks to us, who set up the arrest, who thought that Dad was another raving zombie—the white hair gave them all away—and shot him four times in the chest while a fireman hosed him down with gasoline.

They never lit the match. My assault had done that much.

And so that's how I lost my father and ten years of my life.

The cops found everything, took it all. Except my room. I guess if I hadn't been working so hard on it, maybe my Dad would still be alive. If I'd told him about the anti-blackhole shield or what happens when you combine it with an equally strong mini-blackhole generator, maybe he'd still be alive. But I didn't. I was afraid. And...to be totally honest, I thought that this one time I could have something that was all my own.

The Anomalizer. What happens when a blackhole generator and a blackhole shield operate at the same time? An anomaly. A void in the space-time continuum. Whatever is inside is no longer here or there—it just is.

Which is why no one found my room.

And which is why Goodi TwoShoes will never worry about my next report. Because in five minutes, I'm going to attach my special micro-Anomalizer to that prick's car and he's going to go nowhere...forever.

And after that? We'll see.

My name is Robin Redbreast. You killed my father. You stole my childhood. Prepare to...

TODD JOHNSON MCCAFFREY wrote his first science-fiction story when he was twelve and has been writing on and off ever since. Including the New York Times Bestselling *Dragon's Fire*, he has written eight books in the Pern universe both solo and in collaboration with his mother, Anne McCaffrey; appeared in many anthologies, most recently with his short story, "Coward," in *When the Hero Comes Home* (2011), and with "The Dragons of Prague" in *Dr. Who - Short Trips: Destination Prague* (2008), and the mini-anthology *Six*. Visit his website at http://www.toddmccaffrey.org

# CYCLE OF REVENGE

### Erik Buchanan

"Melviiiiiin! Melvin!!!"

*I hate that stupid name.*

Melichor Blackheart shook his head and tried to focus his eyes.

"Melvin Bright! You get your skinny ass down those stairs and get your chores done now!"

A woman's voice.

Ms. Janet Wilkin's voice.

*It worked! It worked!!!!*

"Melvin, I will take my strap to you if you aren't in this kitchen in one minute!"

Melichor's grin stretched his face. He hadn't felt this exhilarated since he'd fed Wolfe-Bergerdorff's larvae into the water supply at Newton Station. Those things multiplied a thousand times in an hour once they were inside a host. He'd watched a thousand colonists die that day, eaten from the inside out.

And damned if the larvae didn't turn into the prettiest butterflies.

"You hear, boy? I'll whip you bloody!"

*Not this time*, Melichor thought.

Melichor had stepped into the time machine in desperation. His pistol had been out of charge. He'd killed a dozen of the black-clad, armoured, machine-enhanced police—the last two with a knife. His gang had accounted for dozens. And now?

Now Melichor could wreak havoc on the entire universe, thirty years before they even realized he was a threat. That would show those bastards. He'd kill the generals while they were still privates; cut their wives and children to ribbons in front of them.

*And the whole time, they'll never know why.*

It was delightful, really.

"Melvin!"

*And I'll start with that scrawny bitch downstairs.*

He couldn't wait to see the look on her face. He rolled to his feet and headed for the door.

The door was too big.

Melichor was a strong, tall man. Then he'd had biomechanical implants to make him well over two metres tall. He should have had to duck to get through the low door of his attic room. Instead, he was barely above the handle.

*Oh, no.*

He yanked open the door and ran to the bathroom.

*Oh...*

In the mirror, he saw a seven-year-old. A too-skinny, brown-eyed, tousle-haired moppet, with skin brown from the sun, wearing only a pair of shorts in the boiling heat of the Klaridian summer.

*...Fuck.*

His fist slammed down onto the counter, making hardly any noise at all.

*It wasn't supposed to work like this!*

"MELVIN!"

A hard hand grabbed his ear and twisted, hauling him up onto his toes.

Ms. Wilkin shoved him out of the bathroom and dragged him by his ear down the stairs to the kitchen. Still pinching his ear, she began whipping him with her strap. Melichor screamed as the hard leather licked his skin with fire.

*It's not fair! I'm a fucking warlord!*

*I had my own planet!*

The strap licked out again and again, and Melichor wailed and cried and finally collapsed on the floor. The woman kicked him until he got up, then sent him stumbling out of the kitchen with two heavy buckets of pig slops.

"And don't you spill it boy, or you'll get it again, you hear me?"

*Fucking old bitch.*

He'd been the richest warlord on the edge worlds. He'd had his own spaceships. He'd had his own slave race. He'd had kings and politicians and business leaders grovelling on their bellies before him. He'd had their daughters on their knees. And their sons, if they were pretty enough.

*And now I'm this pathetic, whining thing.*

The time machine had been a whim, really. He'd taken it because he liked the thought of owning something no one else had. The old man who'd tried to sell it to him had given him no guarantees that it would work.

"We know it is possible for independent particles to jump through time," the old man had said, "but there's no evidence it will work for people. And then there's the question of whether a person can inhabit two places at the same point in time."

"But you're pretty sure it works, are you?" said Melichor, looking at the contraption the man had taken three days to set up in Melichor's rec room. It had two wide, thick pillars, with a glassed-in section in the middle. On one column was a simple panel with numbers and a small screen. The other was blank.

"Fairly sure," said the old man. "And knowing you appreciate the unusual, I thought I would sell it to you, to fund my research."

"Hm." Melichor looked at the machine, decided he wanted it. "You thought wrong."

He grabbed the old man's arm in one biomechanical hand. Melichor heard the bone snap and the man scream as he shoved the old fucker into the machine. Melichor's top lieutenants cheered as he typed in -100,000 years, then hit the big green button.

The machine lit up so bright it blinded them all. When they could see again, the old man was gone.

He'd intended to try something a little more practical, like sending himself a note six days before, or putting one of his men through to the previous year to kill a rival he hadn't known about then.

Then the police had come, and everything had ended in fireballs and blood. *Assholes.*

Now, his hands ached from carrying the buckets. His small, thin back and legs smarted and stung from the strap. And seven-year-old Melvin could do nothing but what he was told. So he heaved the buckets of slop down the path to the pig barn.

*I am NOT Melvin, god-dammit. I am Melichor.*

A farm. Of all the places to be raised. A stupid, ugly, stinking farm.

*Well, now I know that one person can't physically exist twice in the same time.*

Solar collectors on the roofs of the buildings, charged by the two suns above, powered everything mechanical. Muscles powered everything else. Because no matter how technologically advanced people became they still needed food, and the most expensive food was hand-grown, organic, pure earth food, raised by labour and the sweat of a farmer's brow. It was a hard damn life, but it paid so well that most folks could retire in less than twenty years, if they worked hard.

And when the folks who raised such expensive food said they needed labour, well, what better place to put a young boy with no real prospects?

*I still can't believe they sold me to this place.*

When he was twenty-five and out of prison, he hunted down his parents. He cut their bellies open, tied their guts around the central support pillar of their house, and then lit the place on fire.

God, it had been fun, watching them run screaming, intestines like giant umbilical cords dragging behind them.

He'd wanted to kill the Wilkins, but they had both died while he was in prison. He settled for burning the farm to the ground with its new owners inside.

*But that was last time, wasn't it? It's all different now.*

He stepped carefully with the slops. He needed to heal, first. And to find a knife.

*After all, accidents happen all the time on organic farms.*

But the accidents never happened.

Three years passed. At ten years old, Melvin—*Melichor. I'm still Melichor*—was starting to gain some of his height, but was still gangly. He could carry the slop buckets without spilling and fork the hay into the pig pen. He could take care of the chickens and the eggs and spend whole days in the fields letting the sun burn the pain from the bloody marks on his back.

But he hadn't been able to kill the Wilkins.

Every time he tried something, every time he thought of a way to kill Ms. Wilkin or her bastard husband, every time he tried running away, something would go wrong, or they would notice something, or his child's body just couldn't do what he needed it to.

Then it was the strap from her or the fist from him or both, and nights sleeping on the cold floor of the cellar.

Melichor tried to remember what had happened the first time he'd been a child, so he could figure out how to change it. It had been so long ago that it was a haze. He remembered some of the beatings, but couldn't remember what they'd been for. He couldn't remember if he'd plotted revenge before, or just took it like the snivelly little bitch boy he had been.

"Mel! Mel, wait up!"

He remembered the pest, though.

Angel, they called her. Angelica Yin, really—all golden skin and golden hair and perfect round face. Two years younger than him and worse, a girl. Brought her in the year he turned nine. A pretty little thing with a quick mind and small nimble hands.

Melichor got her into trouble in her first three days, and watched with glee as Ms. Wilkin's strap licked up and down her legs. It was so much fun, he did it again, and got to watch the old man turn her over his knee and apply the flat of his hand to her bare backside.

"Com'on, Mel! Wait!"

Melichor just kept on walking. The Wilkins were gone for the day, driving a truck-load of animals to the spaceport for sale. Melichor had finished his chores early and was free. He was going to go for a swim, then sharpen his knife and kill something.

But Angel would want to talk, and find out how he was doing, and braid flowers for him and play silly games. He didn't want any of it.

*I don't play tag. I'm a warlord, for fuck's sake.*

"Mel! WAIT!"

Melichor remembered how he'd sent one politician's family into the sun in a small ship that kept out the radiation but not the heat. He'd put cameras in and made the politician watch as everyone he loved died on fire, screaming.

*Pity I can't do that to the pest.*

*Yet.*

"Are you all right, Mel? He beat you pretty bad last night."

"I'm fine."

"You got two black eyes, Mel."

"Yeah, well..." The old bastard had discovered him about to cut one of the cats.

"I wish you'd be better, Mel. You'd get in a lot less trouble," said Angel. "The Wilkins ain't bad folks. You just got to do what you're told."

"I do!" snapped Melichor.

"No one told you to go try and kill the cat," said Angel.

"I wasn't going to kill the damn cat!" yelled Melichor. *I was going to cut off one front leg and one back leg and toss it in the field to see how well it could outrun the Carnivori. And it was going to be fun.*

"Mel! Don't swear!"

"Fuck off, pest."

Angel pouted but still tagged along behind him. "Where you going?"

"The pond. Come with me so I can use you for fish bait."

"Ain't no fish in the pond," said Angel.

"Then I'll use your body for pig food!" said Melichor, grabbing her arm.

"Stop it! Stop it, stop it, stop IT!"

She lashed out with her foot on the last word, catching Mel in mid-step and making him trip and lose his grip. She danced out of his reach. "You touch me, I'll tell Ms. Wilkin. She'll whip you until you can't walk."

"I won't hurt you and you know it," sulked Mel. He tried to make nice. "I was just joking, anyway. I'm going swimming. You going to come?"

Angel looked suspicious. "You really want me to come?"

*Only so I can watch if you drown.* "Sure I do."

"All right." Angel skipped on ahead, smiling.

Life was just plain unfair. How could she still smile?

*That little bitch needs to make another "mistake."*

He watched her skipping ahead, singing.

*I'm gonna kill those Wilkins. Then I'm going to make their little angel my little slave.*

And for the next five years, that thought was the only thing that kept Mel sane.

He worked hard, did his chores, and kept trying to kill the old bastards.

When he was twelve, he taught himself mechanics so he could rig the harvesting machines to break down. He managed to take the threshing machine apart and put it back together, and was going to change its setting so that it would cut the old man's hands off. Then the old bastard stepped out of the shadows and announced that, since Melvin was getting so good with machines, he could damn well earn his keep by keeping them all fixed, and the neighbours', too.

From that day forward his chores doubled, and he'd be beaten if any machine had the slightest flaw or any chore was left undone.

Meanwhile, Angel scored high on the online school test, and was allowed to take classes over the net. Every time her grades slipped, Ms. Wilkin was there with the strap.

At thirteen, Mel learned everything he could about the animals, hoping to find a way to make them sick or die without being caught. There was not a damn thing. The best he could do was make sure the fence was down so the cows could go into the neighbour's field and graze on the twistweed (a native plant, delicious and mighty toxic to cows).

Unfortunately, it wasn't fatal.

Mel spent a week cleaning up and dodging the end result of irritable bovine bowels. And the old man took a set of horse leathers to him every night for letting them out in the first place. Then Mel was made to inspect and replace every single inch of the four miles of fence around the property.

Eleven-year-old Angel caught a baby Carnivori. She got bit half a hundred times over the course of the year, some needing stitches, but managed to turn the vicious thing into a pet that could kill any farm pest. She won a gold ribbon and a cash prize for rat catching at the fair.

The Wilkins rented her out to neighbours for clearing barns, and made Mel go with her.

In desperation, Mel turned to electronics. He taught himself computers and programming and hacked into the Wilkins' system. He had been hoping to make their money go away or make it look like their taxes were behind or that they had been ripping off the neighbours. But he discovered they had up-to-date software and anti-viral protection and that anything he did would set off alarms.

Instead he spent his time on the computer studying—supposedly for a correspondence course in husbandry. It lasted until Ms. Wilkin caught him studying firearms. She twisted his ear nearly off as she whipped him while explaining the important virtues of non-violence and peaceful co-existence. He called her a hypocrite and was beaten until he was nearly unconscious.

Angel snuck down to the cellar to hold his hand and tell him everything was all right. She tried to convince him to be better; to study hard and work harder so he'd stop getting beaten.

Mel made something look like her fault the next day, just so he could watch the old man take his hand to her.

Mel hated Angel. Even more than he hated the Wilkins.

Angel kept her grades good enough that the Wilkins let her join one of the local farm clubs (and heaven help her if she was late coming home). The club went to fairs and competitions and even put on a play. The Wilkins made Mel go and watch. Mel added a half-dozen laxatives to the punch bowl for revenge, figuring a shitty performance deserved a shitty reception.

He managed to get away with that one, but the old man found something else to beat him for.

Mel turned fifteen. He was nearly as strong as Mr. Wilkin—maybe stronger, since the old bastard had made him do almost all the work. He was tall enough to stare Ms. Wilkin in the eye when she screamed at him.

And, finally, he had a plan that was going to work.

Mel took it slow, bits at a time. He took to finishing his chores early so he could spend fifteen minutes a day on his plan. It took six months to get everything he needed. Some things, he stole from the Wilkins—nails, ball bearings, screws and wire. The gunpowder and batteries and electronics he'd stolen from elsewhere, sneaking out at night and getting back before morning. The explosives he'd made himself. He kept the device hidden under the floorboards of the shed, where no one would find it.

*And it's going to work, just like it did on Tyrene.*

He'd been twenty-one in the Tyrene prison. The leader of a prison gang didn't want to share his drug profits with Mel.

After the explosion, Mel dragged the bleeding, armless man in front of the surviving gang members and stomped on his head until it split, just so everyone knew who was in charge.

*In two days, I'll blow them all to hell.*

"I know what you're doing, Mel," said the pest, from the doorway of his room that night. The Wilkins were out visiting the neighbours. Mel was sitting on the floor, reading a comic he'd stolen.

The pest was starting to turn into a real girl. Her hips were wider and the breasts he'd told her would never be more than pimples were filling in.

"No, you don't," said Mel, pretending to still be reading.

"You're building a bomb."

*Little bitch is smarter than she looks.*

He put down the comic book. "I don't know what you're talking about."

"Oh, come on, Mel, I'm not stupid! I know nails and fertilizer and ball bearings are missing and I saw what you hid in the bottom of the shed!"

Mel stood up. "There's nothing at the bottom of the shed."

"There's a bomb, you jackass, and you're so stupid you probably built it wrong anyway!"

"I'm smarter than you!" snapped Mel, coming closer so he could look down at her. "I was always smarter than you!"

"Then why am I getting out of here and you're still stuck, Mel? Why?"

"Getting out?" The idea froze Mel in place.

"I got a scholarship to the boarding school at Transfer Station 6. I'm leaving at the end of the week!"

Rage, long simmering, long held back, exploded out in a word. "LIAR!"

"I'm not a liar!" she screamed at him. "I worked my ass off to get that scholarship and in four days, I'm out of here!"

"I'm out of here in four days, too, if you keep your mouth shut!"

"You can't kill the Wilkins!"

"Why the fuck not?"

"Because everyone will know you did it, fuckhead!"

"Oooo!" Mel made a big, phoney surprised face. "She swears! She's almost a real girl!"

"You bastard!" She shoved him, hard enough to move him back. "You sick, torturous, moronic bastard! Who do you think they're going to blame?"

"Maybe they'll blame the precious little Angel!"

"They won't, because I'll tell them if you don't take it apart!"

"Fuck you, you little suck up!"

"I'm not a suck up! I'm just not a screw up!"

"I *bet* you're not a suck up! I bet you sucked the old man off so you could go!"

Angel's hand flew up hard against the side of Mel's face, rocking him back. "You asshole!"

He grabbed her hard and spun, throwing her onto his bed. She tried to get up and he shoved her back, then sat on her legs so she couldn't move. He grabbed her shirt in both hands and pinned her body down with his.

"You will not fuck this up for me, you hear me?" he growled into her ear. "You may be pretty and perfect and little miss righteous, but I am Melichor Blackheart and I will not be fucked over again!"

"What?" Angel's face twisted in confusion. "What are you talking—"

"I'm a fucking warlord!" he screamed, shaking her with his every word. "I've waited eight goddamn years to get these bastards! And once I'm done with them, I'm going to fuck the entire universe! You hear me?"

Memories that had been fading in his head surged back to life. Men and women dying at his hand. His gang of a hundred loyal murderers, ready to do his bidding. Girls and women lying underneath him just like this.

He grinned. "And I am going start with you!"

The pest screamed and tried to fight. He ripped her shirt open and pinned her arms above her head. She wore a pretty pink and white bra and he was going to rip it off her and strangle her with it.

"I'm back!" he said, his hand closing around the front of her bra. "Melichor Blackheart is back!"

His hand yanked hard on the sheets beneath him.

"Melviiiiiiin! Melvin!!!"

He was alone.

His arms were small and thin and the room looked too big.

"No." Panic shivered through his body. "No. No, no, no, no, no no no no no no NO!"

"Melvin Bright! You get your skinny ass down those stairs and get your chores done now!"

*It can't be possible.*

He jumped up and ran to the bathroom mirror.

"Melvin! NOW!!!"

He saw a seven-year-old. A too-skinny, brown-eyed, tousle-haired moppet, with skin brown from the sun, wearing only a pair of shorts in the boiling heat of the Klaridian summer.

*Oh, god, no.*

A hand closed over his ear.

*Not again!*

"Again and again and again," said the old man. "Until the cryo chamber wears out."

"That," said Colonel Flint. "Is the most awful thing I've ever heard."

"I just sent him home," said the old man. He rubbed his hand over the cryo-chamber where Melichor Blackheart lay suspended in time. "I was in the other cryo-chamber. I had it programmed to wake me when he stepped into it."

"You used a phoney time machine to lock him into a permanent loop of the period in his life he felt the most helpless, and then put him in stasis so he could stay in that loop virtually forever," said the colonel. "Command takes a dim view of such things."

The old man shrugged. "Do you remember Newton Station?"

"I heard of it."

"My family was there," said the old man. "I was away at a conference on psychology, physiology and technology. My ship docked two days after Melichor put the larvae in the water."

"I understand your motive," said the colonel. "But I can't allow you to do this. He needs to stand trial."

"There is no way to take him out without killing him," said the old man. "Which would also be fine with me, I assure you."

The colonel sighed and reached for his tablet. General Angelica Yin was of the "catch and rehabilitate" school. She was not going to be happy at all.

---

ERIK BUCHANAN grew up on the Canadian prairies where he spent his spare time acting, writing, studying martial arts, and reading everything he could get his hands on. He moved to Toronto, Canada, and combined his love for history, mythology, weaponry, and theatre into a 13-year career as an actor and fight director. Erik left the business after the birth of his daughter and now makes his living as a writer and communications professional. His novels *Small Magics* (2007) and *Cold Magics* (2010) are both published by Dragon Moon Press.

# THE PRESUIL'S CALL

*Gregory A. Wilson*

*For Senavene*

JA'KETH ARALOCK, FOURTH WARDEN of the Hammers, servant of the Successor King and Supreme Ruler of the Do'vend Empire Ar'sheth, was tired.

It was more than tiredness, really; it was bone-weariness, practically full-on exhaustion. Not from exertion, though he'd had plenty of that over the past few days. Tracking a bellinot was no easy affair, even when the thing was careless. But this was no ordinary bellinot; it had been trained well by its masters, and in truth it had not been far from the border, scuttling rapidly on its eight segmented legs with barely a whisper of noise, when Ja'keth finally caught up to him. The fight had been swift and deadly, with little doubt about the ultimate outcome. In fact the bellinot seemed somewhat listless during the fight, disinterested, as if it had already accepted its fate and had decided to commit suicide by allowing Ja'keth an easy way inside its defenses, and one powerful slash with his axe had ended its life forever.

Still, this was minor compared to the kind of tracking he'd done before, even with all the work beforehand in discovering who or what had trained the bellinot in the first place. And as for what he had done to the trainer…

"Sha'nac's Blood, leave it alone," he growled to himself, running a hand over his furry snout in mild annoyance while the other hand tightened slightly around the strap of the pack slung over his shoulder. The thoughts he had when he was this fatigued were reason enough not to let himself get this way. But he knew a few hours of sleep wouldn't be enough to feel fully rested. His heart was tired, and for that there was only one place which promised respite: Belor's Reach, and home.

The Regent General Es'peth Bartuul, graying muzzle locked in a frown, had said little when Ja'keth had made his request; Es'peth always kept his true feelings to himself, even when they were (as was often the case) less than generous.

"One week."

"One week? That's—thank you, Regent, I am grateful—"

"Show your gratitude by doing your work all the better when you return," the Regent General said as he turned and strode away. "Which will be on the eighth day by noonsun," he added over his shoulder, not looking back, "or your notice of removal from the Hammers will come on the edge of another Warden's axe."

That very day Ja'keth had set out for home, traveling for a day by wagon over the border and into Steumgard. Few creatures lived on the road between the Imperial City of Edreath and Steumgard, other than guardsmen and an occasional fox or rabbit that darted away as the wagon approached, and for this Ja'keth was grateful. He even chose to sleep in the wagon rather than pay for an inn, or commandeer a room from the owner as Imperial law permitted him to do. He'd had more than his fill of the usual fearful silence which quickly pervaded the places he entered, and the hateful glances or whispered curses from the more foolish creatures within earshot now inspired more weariness than anger. The next morning he continued his journey on foot, traversing the remaining miles to the lower hills before turning off the main road and up onto the gentle grassy slopes.

There was no path for some time, and indeed none was needed; it was early fall, and harsh weather was still several months away. Ja'keth passed no one as he trudged up the grassy sward, the sun warming the soft breeze which ruffled his fur, but for once he not only needed but welcomed the solitude. There wouldn't be much of it when he got to Belor's Reach—he hadn't been back for four years, and then only for a few days. Certainly Far'sha would be happy to see him, and Mor'leath...*even Ca'rrack, Blood poison the old fool*, he thought with a slight grin. And Har'eth, of course. Har'eth would be the happiest of all.

It would be a strange feeling to be welcome anywhere. Respect was easy; his cloak and Warden's brooch ensured that. But to be admired—or loved— that would be an odd sensation indeed. He needed it. The promise of rest was drawing him home, but the possibility of peace...a few days or even hours with no missions, no discipline, no iron axe at his back while a fugitive ran from his relentless pursuit...was even more intoxicating. Far'sha would probably scold him and demand he cut some firewood behind the inn as penance for his lengthy absence, but even that felt like grace and comfort.

Hours passed as Ja'keth steadily climbed, watching as the angle of the rolling hills became more pronounced and the grass slowly gave way to scrub brush and rocks. He had encountered little wildlife beyond insects and the occasional bird overhead, and as he left the grass line behind and the temperature grew colder even those creatures became more rare. As a child he had rarely come even this far below Belor's Reach; he was a full grown adult before ever setting foot on the road leading to Edreath. Now he had been to almost every corner of the Empire, met members of races from every part of the known world, and the places of his younger days had become the foreign territories. But there were ghosts and shadows here, resonances he remembered echoing deep within him. He was nearly home.

The sun had long since passed its zenith when he finally reached the path leading from Belor's Reach to the watchtowers, twisting and turning as it wound from the lower foothills of the Kalatas Mountains into the upper hills of Steumgard. Here the grass was almost completely replaced by rocky outcroppings and occasional brush, and as Ja'keth turned onto the final stretch of the path leading to the village he stopped and breathed deeply. The air had a cooler, crisper flavor, but summer had not entirely given up its hold. He was no more than a half hour away now, and he had half a mind to ask Far'sha for a bowl of her best stew as soon as he arrived, no matter how upset she was.

Then he heard the sound.

It was a strange, high, warbling noise, rising like a feather on the breeze before fading into a vanishing whistle. Distress? Pain? Or a warning call— but certainly not an Imperial one, or any that he knew. It came again, slightly tremulous and louder before dying away. Ja'keth hesitated and turned, his eyes narrowed slightly as he looked to the western sky where the sun was turning a slow orange in its descent. It would set in an hour, and the remaining light would be gone a half hour after that. Again the noise sounded, this time somehow sweeter and lighter, before fading as quickly as before. It couldn't be far away, but his time was short. And what did it matter what some strange noise—

Again he heard it, this time shrill and piercing, almost desperately intense, and he winced for a moment before the sound dissipated again into silence.

"Blood," he growled quietly. "You just can't leave it alone, can you? Can't let a loose end..." He sighed, then shook his head again and, turning from the path, set off at a good pace up the hill to his right in the direction of the noise. If he hurried, he could find out what in Sha'nac was making that sound and be back on his way home with plenty of time to spare.

It continued as he went, alternating from loud and piercing to cool and soothing with each new call, and after twenty minutes he began to wonder how badly he had misjudged the distance. It seemed no closer now than when he had started, though the echoes made by the rocks surrounding him made it difficult to tell for certain. He had just about decided to give up and turn around—the sun was sinking fast, and Las'ken take him if he was going to wander the hills at night in search of a meaningless noise—when he made his way above the crest of a hill and stopped short at the sight in front of him.

He had come to a small clearing of sorts, with stones and rocks of various sizes littering the ground. A few pillars of rock stretched twenty or more feet above his head, extending from the side of the cliff wall which fell abruptly away perhaps fifty feet in front of him, the orange light of the setting sun casting strange, impossibly long shadows across the rough surface of the clearing. And there, lying on the ground at the base of one of the pillars, seated amongst a shower of rocks as if it had been placed there, was a small basket.

Suddenly the trilling sound rose from inside the basket, so loud this time he nearly covered his ears before it faded again. He set down his pack and walked slowly over to the source of the noise, hesitating for a moment before looking down. Some kind of wool or hair lined the inside of the basket, and lying atop the wool—

He saw a tiny creature, wide beak opening and closing, covered in bluish-gray down, squirming and struggling while its miniature wings worked feebly. Ja'keth's mouth dropped open.

A presuil.

Immediately the Warden's head snapped up and turned, hackles raised, his eyes scanning the area out of habit before his rational mind took over and reminded him of the facts. A prank? A dangerous one if so—and violating at least four Imperial laws and edicts he could think of off the top of his head. But even if some young kalock from Belor's Reach was stupid enough to bring a presuil here, how could he have done it? Villagers seldom strayed more than a mile or two outside of their own lands, and that only if they were traveling to sell goods in Edreath. Even those travelers wouldn't be able to procure a presuil, not without going through the black market, which was risky enough. Traders found guilty of buying and selling outside sanctioned markets would have their tongues cut out if they were lucky. And anyone found with a presuil within the boundaries of the Do'vend Empire would be executed in short order.

Not a prank, then. A trap? For whom? Besides Es'peth Bartuul and a few residents of Belor's Reach, who even knew he was here? And what kind of trap? Ja'keth sniffed the air and smelled nothing more unusual than the presuil, and there were no rocks large enough to conceal someone watching in any case. He walked to the edge of the clearing and looked down. The wall was sheer here; from this edge the drop would be a hundred feet at least to the treeline below, and there were no creatures visible as far as he could see in any direction.

The keening call floated again from behind him, loud and insistent, and he turned away from the edge of the clearing and walked back to the basket. The presuil seemed impossibly small to be making a noise this powerful, and he watched in a mixture of fascination and mild distaste as it trilled itself into silence again. He'd never seen a presuil this young before; in fact, he wondered if any kalock, even a Warden, had seen a baby presuil, given the dangers involved in being found with one. Suddenly a flash of color next to the basket caught his eye, and kneeling down he carefully moved the basket away from the rock pile.

A hand, covered in feathers, lay underneath.

Frowning, Ja'keth moved more rocks out of the way, taking care not to set the pile moving again, until the arm attached to the hand was exposed. Another minute of clearing revealed the torso, and soon thereafter the head. It was an adult presuil, clearly female from the angle of the eyes, her head broken and covered in congealed blood. The coldness of her body told the Warden she had been dead for some hours, and the size of the wound on her head was enough to tell him what she died of. Rockslides, especially small ones, were a constant problem in this area of the Kalatas foothills. Those who grew up in the area knew the signs to look for: newly disturbed stone, rattling and shaking nearby, long open paths closed or long closed paths suddenly open. But unprepared strangers to the region could easily find themselves on unstable ground or buried under loose stone and rocks in a matter of moments. On rare occasions, the result was death.

Ja'keth rubbed the back of his neck and sighed. It was probably just as well. A presuil found inside the border of the Empire would be killed on the spot...and depending on the guard doing the finding, the death might have been much more painful than this. But why a presuil would bring her hatchling into Steumgard in the first place, and why here in particular...

The loud call of the infant presuil jarred Ja'keth out of his reverie, and with a soft growl he looked back down at the squirming creature in the basket. It was miraculous that it hadn't died already, in truth. It certainly looked healthy enough, despite how many hours it must have been without food or shelter. He blinked as the late sun's light passed the level of an overhanging rock and shot into his eyes. *Better get it over with if I want to get home*, he thought, and with another sigh he unfastened the hand axe at his belt. "Time to follow your mother," he said gruffly as he lifted the axe high above the basket.

Then, for the first time, the presuil opened its eyes, black as ebony, and looked right at the Warden for a moment before crying out again. But this time the call was soft and quiet, very short, and Ja'keth's eyes widened. His axe nearly slipped from his hands, and he stared mutely at the presuil as he sat back on his haunches.

*I'm too tired. Been on the road too long. It can't have said—*

Again it called quietly in its strange, high voice, the same short sound, its eyes fixed steadily on his while its wings worked and body shifted. It wasn't possible, but it sounded as if it had spoken in kalock; a simple word, an old one...

*Sarva*, it said. Mama.

And suddenly a scene flashed through Ja'keth's mind, one he had not thought of in many years: him running as a young cub across the fields on the other end of Belor's Reach towards his home, fields small enough for him to know every blade of grass on their surface and large enough to be his kingdom. The late sun shooting across the landscape past the house, silhouetting it and the kalock standing on the back steps calling him, *Ja'keth, come home, Ja'keth, it's time for dinner, Ja'keth, come home.* And the young Ja'keth laughing and calling back, *I'm coming, sarva, sarva, I'm almost there.*

It was gone as quickly as it had come. Ja'keth the Warden remained on his knees beside the infant presuil and its dead mother. He waited for a few moments before almost unconsciously reattaching the axe to his belt. The presuil was quiet now, its eyes still focused on him. "Las'ken take you," Ja'keth growled finally after a few long moments, but there was no menace in his voice. He stared at the presuil before letting his gaze slip to the mother. Her legs were still covered by rocks, but most of the rest of her was now uncovered, and Ja'keth saw a hard wooden case strapped to her belt. Carefully unfastening the clip which held it to the belt and opening it he saw a mass of cloth and wool, within which sat four small glass bottles filled with some kind of whitish liquid, each one capped with a rubber tip.

Suddenly he heard voices growing louder from behind him—kalocks. They had probably heard the presuil's call just as he had. But if they found it here…

Ja'keth hesitated. And then, for reasons he could not explain, he scooped up the small basket and case and strode to his pack, pulled out the spare cloak and hood from inside and replaced them with the wooden case and basket. He had time to close the pack again and lay the cloak and hood on top of it before three kalocks carrying scythes came into view, stopping as they saw him. Two were young, squat with brown fur; but the third was almost his age and height, covered in mottled black and brown, and after a second he broke into a grin and stepped forward.

"Never knew you liked spending time at the edges of cliffs, Ja'keth," the black-brown kalock said in a gravelly voice. "Or does the Empire train you to search rock piles?"

Ja'keth smiled. "Only when nearby villagers can't keep their lands clean of them, Har'eth."

Har'eth barked a laugh. "We're not educated enough out here to learn cleanliness," he replied as he strode to Ja'keth and embraced him. "Blood, it's good to see you," he said, stepping back and looking him up and down with an appraising eye. "The army hasn't made you fat and lazy yet." Suddenly he blinked and turned, gesturing to the two brown-furred kalocks behind him to come forward. "Ba'leth and Cha'keath Farakech, my nephews. They were away from Belor's Reach the last time you were here, and before that they hadn't even been born. And this," he said to the two kalocks as he nodded in Ja'keth's direction, "is Ja'keth Aralock."

"This is the Warden?" Ba'leth yelped before wincing and lowering his head.

"Yes," Har'eth acknowledged with a frown. "But as I told you before, Ba'leth, he's here to rest, not talk about his time with the Hammers." He grinned as the young kalock nodded sullenly. "Ba'leth's been interested in joining the Imperial army since a solider came to Belor's Reach three years ago—he's spent more time daydreaming about battles and war and glory than doing his chores."

Ja'keth nodded. "I felt the same way before I joined. But I wouldn't rush to leave the village, Ba'leth. We all grow up soon enough."

Har'eth laughed again. "You're turning philosopher on me, Ja'keth. That can't be right for a warrior. If I—"

"What do you have in your pack?" Cha'keath suddenly said.

Ja'keth felt his throat constrict, but before he could think of a reasonable answer Har'eth jumped in. "What kind of impolite nonsense is this?"

"I saw the cloak on top of his pack move," the young kalock replied. Har'eth smiled wryly and opened his mouth as if to scold his nephew again, but suddenly his grin fell away as he caught sight of something. He walked past Ja'keth, who turned to see him stop and stare down at the dead presuil in the rock pile. He looked back at Ja'keth, his lip curled in an expression of disgust.

"Did you do this?" he asked Ja'keth, who walked slowly up to the pile.

"No," the Warden replied, pointing at the presuil's bloody head. "The rocks killed her long before I got here, probably hours ago."

"Killed *it*, you mean," Har'eth said in a low growl, turning his gaze downwards again as a wide-eyed Ba'leth and Cha'keath came alongside, the mysteriously moving pack apparently forgotten. "Pity you didn't. It deserved to die slowly, not with a simple blow to the skull."

Ja'keth looked at his friend's face, contorted with anger. *It's never gone away, has it? Not even after all this time.*

Har'eth stared down silently for a few more seconds, then spat forcefully and turned away. "We were on the way back from the eastern fields when we heard this strange calling. Normally we ignore noises around here, but I knew you were due to arrive and wanted to make sure nothing unusual had happened." He looked at Ja'keth, a question in his eyes.

Ja'keth nodded. "I heard the same thing. When I got here, this is...all I found."

"Blood," Har'eth swore. "What's the Empire coming to when it allows this filth to come here unchallenged?"

"When I get in the army I won't let it happen, uncle," Ba'leth said, gripping his scythe with a growl. "I'll stop 'em before they get anywhere close to Belor's Reach."

Har'eth cuffed his nephew lightly on the back of his head as a faint smile returned to his face. "First you need to stop the frost from getting into the cabbages," he said, not unkindly, but Ja'keth could tell his thoughts were elsewhere. Then he blinked and shook his head. "Don't have time to deal with this now...the sun's almost set. We'll have to send someone up here to clean this place properly when we can." He glanced at Ja'keth. "Unless the Empire's going to want to look into this."

Ja'keth shook his head. "The Hammers have bigger things to attend to than a dead presuil that took a wrong turn," he said with an attempt at a smile.

Har'eth nodded thoughtfully, searching Ja'keth's face for a moment. "All right, then. Grab your gear and let's be on our way. Far'sha will have both of our heads if I don't get you into the village before nightfall." Ja'keth slung the pack over his shoulder and laid the cloak and hood over his arm as the four kalocks left the clearing, but not before Ja'keth took a final look behind him at the pile of rocks in the dimming light, feeling the basket in his pack shift slowly.

Night had indeed fallen by the time the kalocks reached Belor's Reach, but despite his friend's prediction, Far'sha was so happy to see Ja'keth that he was more worried about suffocation than decapitation as she hugged him fiercely. He ate as quickly as he could manage without being insulting— Far'sha's temper was nearly as legendary as her *crozil* stew—and, having escaped with a plea of fatigue and a promise to be up bright and early to help fix the inn's leaky roof, retired to the room upstairs where he had stowed his pack. Whether from fear or its own exhaustion, the infant presuil had been silent since they left the clearing, and Ja'keth was worried it might not have survived the trip. But there it was, twittering softly at him as he pulled the basket from the pack and set it on the table near his bed.

He watched the iridescent wings shift as the beak opened and closed, wondering what was keeping it so calm...or him, for that matter. One of the presuil's cries would send the inn and half of Belor's Reach into an uproar, and if he were found with it in his room, Sha'nac only knew what he'd say to explain it. Yet for the first time in years, his senses were quiet, dully peaceful. "Tired," he growled gruffly to himself as he watched the presuil kick its tiny legs about. "Too tired to think, too tired to care."

Reaching into the pack he drew out the case and opened it, removing one of the bottles and holding it to the light of the lantern on the table. The presuil's twittering grew louder, and looking down he saw it straining its neck upwards. He hesitated, then inverted and lowered the bottle. When it was just a few inches away, the presuil grabbed the tip in its beak and began to suck greedily. And there Ja'keth sat, Fourth Warden of the Hammers, bloodsworn to defend the life and dominion of the Successor King of the Do'vend Empire, feeding an infant presuil.

Days seemed to blur into each other, each with the same pattern: he'd wake up, groggily feed the presuil, then return the basket to his pack and place it beside his bed before heading downstairs where Far'sha and another resident of Belor's Reach would be waiting to greet him—always with a smile and request for aid, anything from tracking down a wayward goat to helping harvest a wheat field to fixing a failing fence gate. He didn't mind, though oddly he now felt more at peace taking care of the presuil in his room than he did with the villagers. It slept most of the time and only ate twice a day, no more than a third of a bottle each time—which was good, since Ja'keth had no idea what he was going to feed it when the milky liquid was gone. On one occasion he clumsily steered the mealtime conversation towards the subject of feeding practices for children, confusing to no end Far'sha and old Ca'rrack, who had come to visit.

"You've been spending a lot of time in your room," Har'eth observed one cloudy afternoon as they were threshing the wheat in one of the fields at the far western end of the village's borders. "I would have thought you'd want to take all the time you could with us."

"You don't think I have?" Ja'keth replied, grunting slightly as he swept his scythe across the swaying grain. For the first time in the week since he had arrived in Belor's Reach the sky was clouded over, and a growing wind and the dampness of the air promised rain. "I've spent every spare second tending to a sinkhole in a field or a creaky floorboard. And if I have to track down Mor'leath's goat one more time, I'll send the Blood-cursed thing to Las'ken myself." He laughed, but Har'eth did not smile.

"That's not what I mean, Ja'keth. You've been almost silent since you got here. I thought you wanted to come home to get away from the problems of the Empire. Instead it feels like you've brought them with you."

Ja'keth dropped the blade of his scythe to the ground and leaned on the handle, looking at Har'eth. The faintest bit of gray had snuck into the black and brown around his muzzle, and the skin around his eyes betrayed a slight wrinkle. *Blood, he's getting older,* Ja'keth thought. *But then, so am I.* But he simply shook his head and smiled. "Sorry. Life in the Hammers is…difficult to get away from, sometimes."

"You mean the people around you won't let you get away from it?" Har'eth replied. "The ones who curse you, spit at you? Who think of you as one of Ar'sheth's trained dogs that he throws raw meat for his enjoyment?"

Ja'keth's head snapped up, eyes narrowed in anger as his hands tightened around the scythe, but Har'eth did not step away. "I've heard the stories about the Hammers, Ja'keth. Most people in Belor's Reach don't know what you do, but I do…at least some of it." He shook his head and sighed. "I can't pretend to know what it's like, of course. You always saw more than I did, thought more than you told me, even when we were cubs." He looked away, into the horizon where the clouds were darkening. "And if what you do helps—helps stop what happened to…" He trailed off and blinked, then turned back to Ja'keth with a fierce expression. "Then it's worth it, no matter what anyone thinks of you. It's worth it to me." He held Ja'keth's gaze for a moment, then turned away and walked off, holding his scythe loosely in one hand as the Warden watched him go.

That night was a bad one for Ja'keth, the worst he'd had in several weeks. He tossed and turned in restless sleep. Flames licked the edges of the city where he wandered with his axe, seeking survivors while the cries of the dead and dying fell thickly on the air until he thought his lungs were too full of it to breathe. Loud explosions sounded nearby, and the wind whipped the stinging smoke into his eyes. Suddenly, very close by, he heard a loud, twittering cry, and coming around the corner of the house in front of him he saw three birdlike creatures, two adults and a child, huddled together. One of the adults stood up shakily.

"Please," it said. "Please, you've already won. Leave them alone. Take me instead."

Ja'keth's vision was tinged with red, the roar of the sulfurous wind in his ears. "No," he said, and his voice was a deep snarl, hoarse and guttural, "no, not instead." And with a spin, he brought his axe down diagonally across the presuil's chest as the others screamed. Then the house next to him exploded, throwing him clear—

—and he found himself awake, panting on the floor by the side of his bed. The window of his room was banging wildly, sheets of rain sweeping through the opening. The door to his room was ajar, and his pack lay open on the ground.

The basket was gone.

Before he could process what had happened, he heard Far'sha crying for him downstairs, and springing to his feet he seized his hand axe and cloak from the table and ran downstairs to find her, wrapped in a blanket, pointing at the door of the inn. It had been broken from its hinges, and kneeling next to it was Ba'leth Farakech, Har'eth's nephew. The Warden strode over to him and lifted him by the scruff of his neck to a standing position. "What's going on?" he barked at Ba'leth, who struggled in his grip. "What have you done?"

"It's my uncle," Ba'leth howled back. "He broke into the inn—said he needed to see something. I followed him in, and then I heard a banging sound upstairs. Then he ran past me and shoved me into the door."

"What was he carrying?" Ja'keth growled angrily, teeth bared. "Where was he going? Tell me now, or I'll do a lot more than push you into a door."

"I—ow!" Ba'leth wailed. "I don't know where he was going...he wouldn't tell me. He was carrying something, but I couldn't—"

"What was it?" Ja'keth snarled.

"I—ow! A basket—it looked like some kind of basket!"

By the time Far'sha reached Ba'leth's whimpering body slumped by the door, Ja'keth was already halfway out of Belor's Reach at a full run. Har'eth could be anywhere, but as Ja'keth sprinted up the path, leaping over fallen trees and seeking purchase in the loose rocks at his feet while the driving rain blinded him, he knew there was only one place he would choose to go now.

*Yes, only one place.*

It had taken Ja'keth and the other kalocks a little less than half an hour to make their way from the clearing by the edge of the cliff to Belor's Reach five days ago, but that was at a regular walking pace. Ja'keth was running now, and Wardens were famed for their stamina and speed when tracking a target, tireless and surefooted. Still, he was running on muddy, unstable ground in wind so fierce he could see small stones scattering across his path, and he was pursuing someone even more familiar with the terrain and its contours than he was, with the same ability to see in the dark. So it still took him about twenty minutes to reach his destination, and when he first crested the hill and slowed to a stop his heart sank; he saw no sign of Har'eth, and for a moment he thought he had been wrong. Then the lightning flashed behind him, and a bright burst of light from the opposite edge of the clearing blinded him. Blinking to clear his vision as the clap of thunder rolled across the sky, he saw its source.

Light, reflecting off a blade.

On his knees, only a short distance away from the edge of the cliff, was Har'eth, his fur matted, lifting a long dagger into the air. And below him on the cold stone ground, its basket gone, lay the baby presuil, squirming and flapping its wings uselessly.

"Har'eth!" Ja'keth barked. "Har'eth, stop!" The blade froze for a moment, then began its upward track again. "In the name of the Successor King, I order you to stop!" Ja'keth shouted again as the wind whipped around him. The blade stopped again, and this time Har'eth looked in his direction as another bolt of lightning in the sky illuminated his eyes, wild with hatred.

"The Successor King," Har'eth cried mockingly as the thunder rolled. "That's something, Ja'keth, even for you: call on the name of your Emperor when you've been committing treason by sheltering his enemies."

"I'm sorry, Har'eth," Ja'keth replied, taking a step closer. "I found it here with its mother, and I...well, I don't know why I took it with me. It seemed like the right thing to do—"

"The right thing?" Har'eth screamed in a rage. "It was the right thing to feed and shelter this filthy vermin in Far'sha's inn—to bring this excrement to the village where you were raised? To give comfort to a presuil?"

*Please, it said. Please, you've already won.*

"It's a child, Har'eth, not a warrior," Ja'keth shouted. "A helpless infant."

"An infant that will grow into an adult which will kill us if it can, like every one of these Blood-cursed pieces of filth. Which killed—" Har'eth stopped, his speech choked with a sob.

*Leave them alone.*

"We fight for order, not vengeance," Ja'keth yelled back. "None of this will bring Shar'eth or Cy'ril back, Har'eth."

"You fight for what you will," Har'eth screamed. "You sell your honor for whatever you want. I swore an oath on their graves, and this fulfills it!"

*Take me instead.*

Suddenly the presuil called out, the noise piercing, almost agonizing, and crying out in pain Har'eth lifted his dagger again. Then time seemed to slow as Ja'keth drew out his axe and in one smooth motion hurled it towards Har'eth. The dagger was beginning its downward plunge when the axe hit it square, knocking it clear from Har'eth's hand and sending it plunging over the cliff's edge with a clatter. Har'eth howled in anger and charged at Ja'keth, who dropped low as Har'eth reached him and undercut his legs, sending him flying over his body in a heap. Ja'keth backed up slowly as Har'eth got to his feet, panting heavily as the rain drove down on him.

"Presuil-loving filth," he growled. "Blood-cursed cur!" He ran towards Ja'keth again, who without thinking spun away at the last second as his Warden training had taught him. Har'eth threw his arms out but missed, and with no chance to stop himself went flying over the edge with a rapidly fading howl.

Ja'keth scrambled to the edge and looked down into the dark. "Har'eth!" he shouted, but his voice was caught up by the wind which roared in mockery as he sank back. *I—I had no time to—I reacted the way a Warden should—*

Except he was not fighting an enemy of the Empire. This was his friend Har'eth, and he had killed him.

Suddenly there was another flash of lightning followed by a crash of thunder. But as the thunder died away, Ja'keth heard an odd whirring noise over the sound of the tempest, growing louder by the second—a noise both foreign and strangely familiar. He looked back over the edge. Rising from the void below was a feathered creature, wings flapping strongly against the wind. And in its arms it carried...

*Har'eth?*

The adult presuil was indeed carrying Har'eth, and Ja'keth watched as it flew over his head and landed softly in the clearing behind him before laying the black-brown kalock's motionless body on the ground and turning to face him, its massive wings folding smoothly into place behind its back. It cocked its head at him. "Klock caught before the trees," it said at last in heavily accented kalock. "Not dead." It looked past Ja'keth, who continued to stare at it in wonder, and caught sight of something next to him. It walked to his side and bent down. Slowly, gently, it lifted the baby presuil, wet and quietly twittering, and gazed into its face, tilting its angular head and trilling back softly. After a moment it looked up at Ja'keth. "This mine...my—cher—chould? Last one."

Ja'keth swallowed. "Last child?"

The presuil moved its head in what Ja'keth assumed was an approximation of a nod. "Most family killed by klocks months ago, except for mate and our—childs," it said, still struggling with the word. It stopped, twittering for a moment as if remembering. Lightning flashed in the sky again, but farther off now, and the downpour was lessening. "Escaped, mate and child and me. Flew north, but mate was hurt, couldn't fly far. Stopped here to rest while I looked for food and way home. Got back and found…mate dead, child gone." It paused. "Thought I'd stay and die here too."

"But you didn't," Ja'keth said.

"No. Flew everywhere looking for child, found nothing. Suns rose and set. Finally storm came."

"But why would you catch Har—the kalock?" Ja'keth said. "He wanted to kill your child."

The presuil twittered quietly. "You klock. Didn't kill child." It moved its wings in an odd way, almost a shrug. "Life is life…" It stopped, struggling again. "Life…comes from life. Must come from life. Nothing else. Even klock's life."

Ja'keth nodded slowly. "And now?"

"Now we go home." It turned and walked to the edge of the cliff. After a few steps it stopped and turned, its head cocked. "Why—why klock save child? Klock hate us, yes? Like other klock?"

Ja'keth opened his mouth, then closed it. Before he could try again, the baby presuil lifted its head over its father's hand and twittered softly. Ja'keth hesitated a moment longer, then shrugged.

"Life is life," he said.

The presuil held the Warden's gaze steadily for a long moment, then turned without a word and, spreading its wings wide, sprang from the ground and flew off, illuminated one last time by a fading flash of lightning before vanishing into the gathering darkness.

The next morning Far'sha, having finally fallen asleep from exhaustion, woke to find a note on the counter in the downstairs room of the inn.

*Far'sha,*

*On my way back to Edreath—left money upstairs to pay for damage to room. Har'eth is at his home, safe. When he comes to find you, please tell him I tried to help…him and someone else. I've never been a wordmaster, but…*

*Anyway. Life is life. Tell him that.*

*Sha'nac protect you,*

*Ja'keth*

---

GREGORY A. WILSON is currently an Associate Professor of English at St. John's University in New York, where he teaches creative writing and fantasy fiction along with various other courses in literature. He has published on many academic subjects, and his first novel, a work of epic fantasy entitled *The Third Sign*, was published in 2009. He regularly serves as a panelist at conferences across the country and is a member of Codex, the Writers' Symposium, and other author groups. He is also the co-host (with fellow speculative fiction author Brad Beaulieu) of *Speculate! The Podcast for Writers, Readers and Fans*, located at www.speculatesf.com. He lives with his wife Clea, daughter Senavene, and dog Lilo in Riverdale; his virtual home is www.gregoryawilson.com.

# THE MAN WITH LOOKING-GLASS EYES

## Rosemary Jones

THE PRINCESS BROKE THE ornate spear across her knee and tossed the pieces out the open window.

"That was the start of a potion," said the glass swan balancing on the fireplace mantle.

"No, no," said the brass monkey on the bookcase, "I think it was a direction, a beginning for the path to someplace important."

"Don't you remember?" she asked. Her reflection in the darkened glass of the half-open casement made her look ghostly, quite appropriate since she was busy haunting the wizard's house of memories.

"How can we remember anything?" the swan and the monkey spoke in unison. "We're only fragments ourselves."

"More appropriately, we are devices," said the tortoise at her feet. "Loci. Ars Memorativa."

"Some of you seem more aware than others," she said.

"Naturally," said the tortoise. "We were given voices, to speak at the necessary time, to direct, as it were, the course of the journey. But, even so, we can only indicate the route."

This was the seventh or the seventeenth room that she had systematically torn apart. Her own memory was necessarily poor in this place, a matter of protection. Somewhere, elsewhere, the princess slept, or so she thought. If she concentrated, she could feel the silken sheets beneath her, hear the subdued murmur of her attendants as they fought to stay awake and keep vigil beside her dreaming body.

The tortoise bumped against her as it began its clumsy, bumbling route across the room toward a previously unnoticed door. The princess followed it. The beast seemed quite willing to guide her through the house. She wondered if its absent master knew that his random creations made such poor guards for his mansion.

She opened the door and found a chamber full of gems. Diamonds and pearls cascaded from open boxes, forming glittering drifts across the parquet floor. Emeralds studded silver ropes that looped from the ceiling.

Rubies surrounded a giant mirror that reflected the shimmering treasures.

"What could he have buried here?" she queried the tortoise without hope of a sensible answer. When she had appeared in the long hallway leading to dozens of rooms, the tortoise roused itself from a nap beneath a potted palm to offer its services as a "locator of lost items and important moments." Since then, she found its conversation lacked coherence and it rarely held to a straight line in its wanderings.

When pressed, the tortoise claimed that it most certainly did know the shortest route between two points, but such a course might not serve as well as a circular tour through certain rooms.

In this room of wealth, the beast unearthed a small wooden box buried under the diamonds piled upon the floor. The princess snatched it up. The lid popped easily open to reveal a rusted key.

"So, now, what is this for?" she wondered.

"To open a lock," the tortoise sounded supremely uninterested as it nosed among the diamonds and pearls.

"Not a lock that is open often," the princess said, lifting the key out and turning it over in her hand. It looked ordinary, something that might fit a padlock or trunk.

"Some locks should not be opened more than once in a lifetime," said her reflection from across the room.

The princess scowled at the girl in the ruby-rimmed mirror. She looked foolish with her hair cascading down her back and the most ridiculous little crown perched precariously atop the riotous red curls. She resisted the urge to pat the top of her own head to see if the glittering crown was there. Certainly, looking down, she could see that she was dressed in the same impractical blue ballgown and golden slippers.

"I should be dressed in something sensible, like armor from head to toe," she said to her reflection. "There might be dragons."

"You don't remember armor," said the girl in the mirror, twirling around and holding her skirts wide. "Not the way you remember this dress, the one you wore to your very first ball. You stared at it for hours in the mirror."

"I do remember armor perfectly well," the princess said. And she did. It reflected the flickering torches held by her servants as she knelt in the mud and lifted the helm off the head of the dead man, her beloved father, the first of the royal family to fall victim to the wizard's deadly spells.

"Stop that!" shouted her reflection. "Put that memory away. Do you think he won't notice? He remembers that battle, too. The day his magic killed a king."

The tortoise nuzzled her little gold slipper. "He keeps that memory close, the memory of his first victory. You will find it in a bedroom just across the hall. You can destroy it if you want."

"No!" Her reflection stamped the same foot and the princess noted that no tortoise appeared beside her in the mirror. "The clocks are ticking rapidly toward dawn. You must go on. Taking away that victory will not destroy him."

"Oh, if it is destruction that you seek," the tortoise said, "I suggest the back stairs. They lead to the grotto under the house."

The princess met the man with looking-glass eyes upon the winding stair. He was climbing up as she was going down, and she saw his crooked shadow against the wall before she heard the footfall of his steps.

He stopped upon the stair and stared up at her.

"How did you come here?" he said.

She looked down into a face impossibly young and handsome. Inky curls tumbled across a wide smooth brow. Dressed in beribboned velvets and gilded leather, she might have taken him for an elvish prince or a knight of a dreaming realm if she had not spotted the slender wand of ebony that hung from his hip.

Because the truth can be twisted into deception and defense, she answered his question as simply as she dared. "I fell asleep," the princess said. In her left hand, she curled her fingers tight around the rusted key that she had found earlier. She shook down her sleeve to conceal it further.

The wizard climbed up the last three stairs to stand beside her. The narrow step broadened to hold them both. A long window appeared upon the wall to allow moonlight to brighten the landing where they stood.

"I heard footsteps in my house," he said. "Rooms that I closed long ago seem to be open."

As the princess gazed up into his puzzled face, she saw only her own reflection in the silvered perfection of his mirrored eyes. Even here, in the house built by his mind, he cast that spell of protection to keep her away from his soul.

"I fell asleep," she repeated, "and found myself here."

He reached out a hand. His fingers passed through the fluttering gauze of her sleeve. She stayed as still as the doe who hears the hunter's hounds panting through the brush.

"You are nothing more than a dream," he said. "Or perhaps a shadow of someone I met long ago. I know your face, I am sure of it, but you are none of my company tonight. How do I know you?"

"What do you see?" she said, unwilling to tell lies that could so easily twist into snares.

"I see a girl with shadowed eyes, a girl of fifteen or sixteen summers who carries some winter sorrow in her heart."

She nodded. "That is what I see reflected in your eyes." And still she spoke no more than the truth.

The wizard sighed and fingered the death-dealing wand that looked so innocent upon his hip. "I will remember your name. I am sure of that, for all my memories are here," he said. "But I must retrieve the pieces of a spell tonight for a battle tomorrow. Will you walk with me in the garden?"

The princess dared not refuse. The long window became a door leading out to the moonlit paths that passed under the shadowed trees and curled around the fountain spraying a cold silver mist into the air.

"I crossed the Northern Sea twice," the wizard said, "to discover a spell to shatter the heart of my enemy. In the swirling waves and flying spray, I found it." He reached his hand under the jet of water falling from the urn of a stone maiden. As the water trickled across his skin, it glowed with a brilliant cold light.

"As water wears away stone, this wears away the years, ravaging both strength and vigor, turning the young old and the old to dust," he said.

"And does your enemy deserve that?" the princess asked.

"That and so much more. For, every battle waged has stolen the young by the thousands and led them to their graves. Now one hundred stand in circle around my tent, the last of the thrice-bannered army that marched across the mountains. In these dark hours, my incantations must bind and snare, or all will be lost with the dawn. Victory balances on a blade's edge tonight."

His voice dropped lower and lower as he walked the perimeter of the fountain, gathering up his spell from the frothing water.

"Where are we?" she asked to distract him. Under the shadow of brush, the princess spotted the tortoise. The creature was carrying a clock in its mouth and she knew that time was ticking away for her. Once the wizard returned to the waking day with his spell, nothing could be done to save her kingdom.

She had fought so long, come so far, and now, in a garden growing in the mind of the world's greatest wizard, she could see a grave opening beneath her feet.

"Be careful," cried the wizard, turning away from the water to motion her back from the long hole that appeared in the center of his lawn. "That tomb is not meant for you. Look away, look away, before it consumes you."

The princess danced back from the edge. "Tell me where we are?" she begged as prettily as she knew how. It had been many years since she had asked anything of anyone but herself, and the words sounded falsely sweet to her ears. But the wizard bent to her and crooked his arm in invitation. She placed one insubstantial hand upon it. As formal as any court dance, they paced side by side across the smooth grass.

"This is my place, built out of recollections and magic," he said. "In the house I stored all my memories, cataloged each encounter, memorialized every friend and foe, placed my past behind locks and bars, so no one could steal it from me. No matter how far I travel, I need only close my eyes and come home to all that I hold dear."

"Yet you keep your most powerful spell outside the house?"

He smiled and the moonlight glittered in his looking-glass eyes. "Are we outside or in?"

She glanced around. The trees stretched up, carved pillars that supported a painted sky. Behind them was the bottom of the winding staircase. In front of them was a plain wooden door.

"What is it?" she asked.

"A protection," the wizard said. "Behind it dwells my only defeat."

She tilted her head and wheedled as nicely as she could: "Tell me the story."

Clenched in her left hand, the rusted key bit into her soft flesh. A drop of blood fell from her palm to spot her golden shoe.

"Once a great and terrible king invaded my country, trying to bind with iron and fire all the magic there," the wizard said. "We fought in the forests, and the mountains, and by the banks of the rushing streams. At last, in the mud and muck of a field that once sprouted with sweet corn and fair flowers, he fell and his army fled."

"Then you won?" she said.

"Then we lost," he replied with a rueful shake of his head. "For he had a child who seemed as innocent and fair as he was terrible and cruel. So we let her go home, not knowing her heart was as blackened and burnt with witchcraft as his. And that the armies who would swear loyalty to her would be far greater and more demonic than any that bowed head to her father."

Even as he spoke, she stepped forward to unlock the door with rusted key that she held in her bloodied hand.

A great wind came howling out of the door, a wind that smelled of winter and war, of witchcraft and thwarted spells, of all the enchantments that she had so long thrown against the wizard with looking-glass eyes.

The storm ripped through the grotto, uprooting spells and tossing memories into the maelstrom. The tortoise swirled away in the wave of water washing out of the fountain. The mirrors that protected the wizard's eyes shattered. With a cry, he collapsed to his knees. Bloody tears rained down his face to splash at her feet.

"I know you," the wizard gasped as he gazed up at her sweetly smiling face.

"And I remember you," she said. She bent to kiss him, gently as a sigh, and pluck out his eyes with her long fingernails. "I remember how you prattled of mercy and justice as they burned my father's body upon the battlefield."

She raised her hands and let loose the winds of her rage. She sent the storm spiraling through the house, smashing open every door, breaking every lock, destroying the wizard's mind and power one memory at a time. Then she woke.

In her chamber, the queen rose from her bed. The twelve maidens surrounding her dais slumped from exhaustion, only the cords that bound them to the chairs keeping them upright. Streaks of silver ran through their hair and deep lines marred their once youthful faces. She passed them by without regret or praise, calling for her attendants.

Her witches came running with robes, jewels, and unguents. Even as she stalked to the throne robe, they arrayed her in splendor. When the queen swept into her chamber, all bowed their heads to her terrible beauty and power.

As she settled onto her silver throne, the queen glanced into the hand mirror swiftly raised by one of her ladies. Her reflection had none of the sweet aspect of the princess that she had been so long ago. The once riotous red curls were now bound and braided beneath her iron crown.

With a pleased smile, the queen waved away her attendants and motioned to her generals to come closer.

"What word?" she said.

"We overran their camp at dawn, as you ordered," said the largest demon in smoking armor.

"The wizard?"

"A mindless husk mewing on the cold ground."

"The one hundred champions?"

"Eighty-two were killed and all the rest were captured."

The queen nodded. "Very good. Send the eighteen who lived home."

"Home, your Majesty?"

She nodded. "In chains. Execute the villains before their friends and family so their people know well my mercy and justice. Then set up new princes and dukes to rule as we have discussed."

"Very good, your Majesty."

They bowed and withdrew.

The queen sat on her throne, considering the wisdom of building her own memory house to store her magic and protect her soul from her enemies. In one room, she thought, she would place a man with looking-glass eyes. Then she would close and lock that door and never think of him again.

---

ROSEMARY JONES writes adventures set in shared worlds like the Forgotten Realms and Cobalt City as well as short stories for numerous publishers. Mostly she writes about ordinary people struggling to be heroes in extraordinary settings, but she appreciates the opportunity to be a little wicked in this anthology. When she's not writing, she's collecting books or reading. Which only goes to show you can take the girl out of the printed page, but you can't take the printed page out of the girl—or something like that! To learn more about her current projects, visit her website at www.rosemaryjones.com.

# STARKEEP

## *Gabrielle Harbowy*

FLAMES DANCED AT THE periphery of Riss's vision and consumed the air in her chest. She scattered the black water in the scrying bowl, summoning ripples across the surface until she could only feel the aching in her neck and hunched shoulders, not the crackling heat that had engulfed Lord Blackburn and half his men. The vision of their soundless screams pounded in the silence between her heartbeats.

"Well?" Arabella Blackburn's long-fingered hand tangled into the back of Riss's hair and twisted, pulling at the knot and pushing knuckles at her skull, so that no direction she could squirm would bring respite. Riss curled her damp fingers around the rough, unglazed edges of the stone bowl, turning away from the glassy surface as the water rose to meet her. Flames or no, she didn't relish a dunking.

"Fire," she said too quickly, too loudly, just to make the pushing stop. She silently cursed herself for revealing even that much. Now she would have to see it through. "They found the den, and the dragons. And there was fire. Death." Riss swallowed, tasting ash. A powerful headache was starting to build behind her eyes. Maybe a dunk would be refreshing, after all.

Lady Blackburn abruptly tugged Riss upright. Dampened ends of her hair landed cold and heavy across her flushed cheeks. The room spun, giving motion to the heavenly bodies woven into the hanging tapestries. The oily droplets and the fields of celestial blue quenched the last flames from the edges of her sight. When she spoke again, her voice was stronger, less parched. "They expected to capture one, on its own. They cannot defeat a whole flock. The survivors are retreating home."

"And my husband?" The hand tightened and twisted. The guard at the door shifted, fingers curling around the hilt of his sword.

"I did not see his face among the dead, my lady." It was the truth. But only because the side of him she could see had been burned away.

Lady Blackburn released her grasp. Riss bent over the claw-footed pedestal again, exhaling a slow ripple across the stale water. Only the midnight-blue glaze at the bottom of the bowl greeted her. No visions. When she pulled back her focus to the surface, she saw her own troubled reflection. Behind her, Lady Blackburn, with thin-pressed lips and eyes sharp as a crow's. The lady straightened and disappeared from the image, but Riss didn't dare relax the tension in her arms just yet. She knew she might still end up face first in the water, or worse. Silence hung, thick and cold as the droplets clinging to her cheeks. Finally, angry footsteps retreated, followed by the clank of the guard's armor, and the heavy door on the east wall slammed shut.

Riss took a trembling breath and straightened, feeling air sting the raw skin where she'd clutched rough stone. She flexed her hands gingerly and looked down at her fingers. They were short and dirty, where Lady Blackburn's were long and graceful. The tiny, delicate gestures of Arabella's fingers had brought so much cruelty down on Riss, and on people Riss had known all her life. Cruelty she had learned from her lord. Riss tried to mimic that imperious flick of the fingertips, and frowned—she only managed to look like she was flinging porridge at a wall. And missing.

It had been called the map room in Riss's youth. The plan had been to completely ring the round stone room in tapestries that mapped the known sky, but Starkeep had been taken before the work was complete. Four of the heavy tapestries hung: one at each cardinal direction, offering slices of the heavens in pale blues, silver and gold on fields of midnight. Lanterns between filled the room with harsh, wavering light.

The narrow door hidden behind the southern hanging was simple wood, painted convincingly with the shadows and stipples of the surrounding stone. Even if it were exposed, one would have to touch it to realize that its surface was smooth; Riss had been exploring these passages for most of her eighteen years, and it still fooled her eye. Yet, in all the evenings Riss had been watching her, Lady Blackburn had never even glanced meaningfully toward the tapestry. She didn't know the door existed, Riss was sure of it. The same with the hollow bench with the spyholes in the great hall, the trapdoor in the observatory, the kitchen cabinet and the bedroom wardrobe with the false backs—all leading to a web of tunnels and passages. Never so much as a glance. Riss wasn't sure whether she should be relieved or disappointed. Did they not have hidden passages at all in the Westlands? Who conquered an enemy keep and then didn't explore it to find its secrets? Sloppy work, truly.

Perhaps when this was all over, she'd take the lady on a tour and charge a sterling for each secret door and tunnel the woman had missed. Mistress of Starkeep indeed, when a dozen mousers and Riss could slip quickly between places Lady Blackburn hadn't even dreamt were connected.

Riss shut the hidden door behind her and felt for the lantern on its hook. A turn of the wheel produced just enough of a glow to see by, and she hurried down a stone passage narrow enough to scrape both her elbows. Behind the kitchens was a rounded intersection where three paths met. The fifth stone below the sconce was a false front, and from behind it Riss drew a cinched velvet bag.

"Wine for the mistress." Riss froze. She recognized the chambermaid's voice through the false backing of the pantry; the rustle of cloth and the hollow clanks of metal and glass.

"Any news of the lord?" The cook's assistant. She had already been old when Riss was a child.

"She'd not say, but she's angry as a storm. A bit of that loaf, too, if you don't mind. Something to soak up the wine a bit so it doesn't overflow into her temper."

"Take some cheese in, too. Here..."

More kitchen sounds, and a sigh from the young chambermaid. "So calm around here, innit, with Lord Blackburn gone. That gash he gave you is almost healed."

At the mention of his name, the flames from the scrying bowl flickered at the edges of Riss's vision and a wave of dry heat baked her cheeks. She'd been so focused on what to say to Lady Blackburn that it hadn't sunk in for herself, but now the realization struck her so suddenly that she had to lean her forehead to the cool stone. The fire. Lord Blackburn was dead. It was done.

"You hope his men come home soon," the cook teased. "What's the name of that one you fancy? The tall one, with the exotic Eastland eyes..."

With the velvet bag secured in a fold of her skirt, Riss rushed on. The kitchens were excellent for gossip, but her own appointment with an Eastlander was more urgent.

She followed the narrow hallway, extinguishing the lantern and emerging through the hinged panel into her own bedroom—which had once been the library, before Lord Blackburn had ordered the burning of the books. Bare shelves lined the walls, their edges splintered. She paused a moment to catch her breath and tug her sleeves down over her raw elbows. Though it was pointless, she straightened her hair in the looking glass she had propped in an empty shelf and made sure there were no smudges on her face. She left via the proper door and took the main stairs up the tower and into the southern dome, forcing the slowness of a casual wander to her steps as she passed a pair of guards.

Starkeep wasn't quite a castle or a keep, for all its imposing mountaintop grandeur and supposedly defensible stone. It wasn't just an observatory either, despite having two tall sky-watching domes. Starkeep wasn't even where stars were kept—and learning *that* had been perhaps the greatest disappointment of eight-year-old Riss's life.

Then the invasion from the Westlands had come, claiming the keep in some centuries-old border dispute. Ellis Blackburn, still a boy-prince then, had been given Starkeep by his father to let him practice ruling and to keep him out of the way. He was as displeased to be shuffled off to Riss's remote home as she was to have him in it, and he expressed that displeasure by taking it out on those around him.

Thus, Riss had learned what disappointment *truly* was. In the ten years since, Lord Blackburn had not let her forget.

The astromancers who had raised Riss, who had used their grand sky-domes to map the heavens and study the way of the stars, had all displeased their spoiled young master sooner or later, and had either fled for the sanctuary of the Eastland foothills or had been dispatched to the heavens, themselves.

It was only Riss who could not leave. It was tradition for Eastland royalty to receive their instruction at Starkeep, and she was meant to be its steward when she was of age—a parallel which Blackburn's father must have knowingly mocked. Instead, her freedom had been traded for security—the king must also have known that the Eastlands would not seek to take back the keep while their only heir's life was poised under the Blackburn thumb. But within the confines of the walls, she could roam freely.

Using the contact crystal was like trying to angle a bit of mirrorglass so that someone across the room could see the reflection of their own left eye in it, without the benefit of being able to ask them which way they needed you to tilt it. It took considerable time and even more patience, and Riss was running dangerously low on both.

Finally, the glow of filtered starlight passed through the condenser lens at just the right angle and caught in the shallow cup of carved quartz, making it resonate subtly in her fingertips. Carefully, without spilling it, she turned the lens aside, brought the vessel to her lips and blew across it. Fine quartz powder misted up into a shimmering cloud and resolved into the ghost of a shape. Scrying was neater (if wetter), but the benefits of the contact crystal's magic were many. One of them was sound.

"Where are you?" Riss and the figure asked each other at the same time. The words always carried the buzz of bees at first, before the dust was thick enough to transmit the vibration properly. There was an awkward silence as each waited for the other to answer.

"The observatory," Riss said into the pause.

"My father's observatory," her apparition of a visitor answered sharply.

The view from the sky-domes was so spectacular that Lord Blackburn had made the northern one his bedchamber. They had been built in such a way, with complex mixings of dusts and light, that they were shielded from outside view completely; an astromancer who wanted complete dark for sky-gazing in one tower would not be hampered by the light needed by an astromancer writing up his notes in the other. And since Lady Blackburn had a dome all to herself, she had no interest in visiting its twin. It was a place where Riss could be almost assured of privacy.

"*The* observatory," Riss said again. "Don't go down that bitter road now, Mother. We haven't time." Each of her breaths across the cup wafted more of the fine powder, gradually reinforcing the ephemeral shape into something vaguely familiar-looking, filling out the face and hairline, depicting what she knew to be dark in ghostly pale. "I saw the fire."

It strengthened the voice, as well. "I, too. What does she know?" the shape asked.

"Only that they've failed and are retreating. I couldn't keep that much from her. They'll be slower to return than if he'd succeeded and flown home on dragonback," Riss answered. The spectral head tilted slightly, and Riss could feel the weight of her mother's pointed gaze. She scuffed a foot. "And...maybe I wanted her to have a taste of concern." She didn't add that she'd been intimidated into it, or pressured, or that the base of her scalp still ached, or that she could have been run through. It had been ten years since they'd seen each other in the flesh, and her mother worried enough about her as it was.

"You've done well. You know what knowledge you must keep from her. I'll ride out with the troops at first light. You'll see me in two days." The queen's ghostly form raised a hand and passed one fingertip over the steep slope of Riss's upturned nose.

Riss made as if to rub her nose clean—not such an act, with the powder the spectre's movements left behind on her burnished brown skin. "I'll watch your progress as I can, but she's in a mood now. I don't know how much of a chance I'll have."

There was another awkward silence, this one born of two people trying *not* to speak the same words. Without knowing what tomorrow would bring, it always felt so final to cut off contact, never being quite sure if you'd ever have a chance again.

"Get some sleep, Larissa," Riss's mother said. "It must be done." Perhaps a feeble way to say *I understand* and *I miss* and *I wish*, but one that worked and was simpler than all those things.

"It must be done," Riss answered. It had become something of a mantra.

Her mother slipped away first, the cloud of dispersed dust falling without her energy and mass to support it. Riss caught it mostly in the cup, but knew she'd have some careful and reverent sweeping to do before she got any of that promised sleep. Even then, with so much weighing on her mind, sleep would not come soon.

Two guards flanked the entrance at the top of the winding stairs. This was new, and it made Riss's stomach flop over. She straightened her shoulders and waited for one of the guardsmen to knock and open the door, then stood uncertainly just inside the doorway of Lady Blackburn's sky-dome. Riss was surprised that the lady had waited so long to summon her. She hoped it wasn't a bad sign.

Lord and lady sometimes took their meals at the small wrought iron table in the chamber, and that was where Arabella Blackburn was seated now, gazing out at the night with a dragon-clawed silver goblet held tightly in her hand.

"My lady?" Riss ventured quietly.

Silence held for long moments. Lady Blackburn took a long swallow and refilled her goblet from the pitcher Riss had heard them preparing in the kitchens. More graceful movements of those delicate, deadly hands.

"I remember the first time I saw you," Lady Blackburn said quietly. "It was in the great hall, at my betrothal feast. Do you remember? He hung that great purple dragon head, and had a cloak made for me of its scales. He sat you at the end of the main table. At the far end, with empty place-settings all around you. He wanted you to feel exiled, but to me you looked like a treasured little porcelain trinket on a shelf, set apart to be admired. An exotic princess, captured under glass. How old were you?"

Riss's throat worked on the second try. This was the most that either Blackburn had ever said to her at once, to her memory. "Fifteen, my lady." She remembered that feast. She had been so excited to dine in the grand hall again, as she had in her youth. She remembered the way her stomach sank when she was shown to her place. She remembered sitting quietly with an empty cup and plate, with four days' hunger gnawing her middle apart while the Westlanders feasted and danced and the scents of meat surrounded her, and the severed dragon head watched her with its cold black eyes, its parted jaws laughing at her discomfort, as its lord did.

"And you'd been how old when Lord Blackburn took the keep?"

Riss wasn't sure where this was going. "Eight, my lady."

The mistress of the keep lost herself in thought again, drinking her wine. Pouring. Drinking. The bread and cheese were still untouched on the platter. Her lips were stained red, like Lord Blackburn had been in the vision. Riss tasted blood. Not Lord Blackburn's, she realized, but from the inside of her own cheek.

"He was twelve when the king gave him this place. And you were a part of it, where I had not been." She set the goblet down. "Speak freely."

Riss looked down at her awkward hands with their short, chipped nails. "I...I am at a loss for words, my lady. I would not presume to know my lord better than you. For all that we have both been here, we do not share a childhood in common."

She had explored the secret passages with Arin, lovely Arin, who had been the obvious object of Riss's free time and thus the boy-lord's first kill. The lady still watched her silently, so she continued. "I apologize that it seemed so, to you. There was fighting, lady. Horrible fighting, and then he came, and I was moved to the shadows. And I, in great thanks for his generosity and my freedom within the keep, make pains to honor my lord and remain unseen, save when he summons me. Then I serve fully, in loyalty to him, and you, and the rule of the Westlands over Starkeep by ancient right."

Had that been respectful enough? Had she spread it on too thick? *He took my home from me*, she wanted to say. *He murdered my teachers, my only friends, just to see whose loss would make me cry most. He took away everything good and noble about this place, and locked me in its hollow shell; mourning behind its empty eyes, like the dragon's, that no longer explore the sky.* But she knew that such insolence had its price, and that she only need hold out a little longer.

Lady Blackburn turned inward, filled the goblet with more wine. It flowed black in the harsh light. "A whole flock, you said. How many killed?"

"Of us, lady?" Carefully *us*, not *you*. "Half, it seemed. I saw the wounded tending to the dead. I did not see my lord, but if he was giving orders, he would have been out among the most capable."

Lady Blackburn seemed to accept that, nodding slowly to herself. Riss felt the moist squish of sweat between her shoulder blades and hoped it would not also drip down her front and betray her.

If Lady Blackburn knew her lord husband were dead, she would send word to his father and flanks of reinforcements would arrive from the Westlands. But it was vital that Starkeep be unprepared when Blackburn's body arrived—on the shoulders of the Eastlanders who had slowly replaced half his personal guard, and at the head of her mother's column of Eastland soldiers, reinforcements who would meet them at the mountain waypoint. Arabella could not know.

Further, if she knew that those Eastlanders had replaced half his personal guard—the surviving half, not coincidentally—she might suspect the veracity of the information that had led him to take his full personal guard to go and trap a lone dragon in the first place.

But for now, it seemed, she suspected nothing. "He insisted on keeping you, you know. He said a castle was no place for a child like you. He wanted to spare you the indignities of being in line for the crown, you see, because it is what he knows. What he has always been. He opened his home to you, even though he risked your anger—it would have been yours by now, you know, if we'd not come along."

Riss could not find the appropriate, nonviolent words to express that yes, indeed, there was never a moment when she did not think about that particular bit of knowledge. How generous of the young lord with the hard eyes to spare her from the horrible burdens of family, and freedom, and royalty, and stewardship of a great academy, and the secrets of the stars. She remained quiet and dipped her head to keep from glaring. Let the lady think it a move of submission; let her think her attempt at manipulation subtle. If, with that much wine, she was still thinking at all.

"I can scry in the morning," Riss offered, "try to catch a glance of him." She knew he would be shrouded and indistinguishable in the supply cart, but Arabella did not need to know what Riss knew. "I may be able to give you names of those who still stand."

"Names matter not," Lady Blackburn muttered, flicking her fingers dismissively. Those fingers that always looked like they were meant to launch fairies into a great aerial dance with the little gesture, not splatter cold porridge.

Riss held in a sigh, letting it leak slowly enough to be silent. Not much longer.

Lady Blackburn had trailed off again, frowning into the empty pitcher and empty goblet. "What is their position, Riss?"

Riss blinked. She couldn't just scry out of nothing, with no—

"Larissa."

She looked up, into cool gray eyes lined with the red of uncertainty. "What was the state of them, when you last saw?" she clarified. After a moment, quiet as a mumble, she added, "Please." Or perhaps it was some chirrup of a little night-mouse, and not her at all.

Riss took a breath. Flames warmed her fingertips. "It was slaughter. The den was settling down to mate. It's the time when it's most dangerous to disturb. My lord loosed a dragonsbane arrow at the only one they could see, and it went through his wing and into the rib of his beloved, whom he was sheltering." She told the story without passion. She had not been there. "It injured the male where it passed through, and its poison killed the female. The male roared, I assume, from the way he lifted his head and tilted his wings forward as if to guide the sound. And then more poured out from that same mountain and ones nearby we'd not even checked for Dragonsign. The front ranks were crisped. Nothing left but bone flakes and ash. The rest of the dead have...that is, there are...remains."

Riss's eyes focused on the present once more. "I cannot see the future. I know only that he is with them, in some condition, hidden away because it is in their best interest to hide him; perhaps merely because he is the leader." A calm, controlled lie. *He is dead, my lady. He rots. And you will rot with him soon.*

Lady Blackburn turned in her seat and cradled Riss's cheek with her palm. It was the first time in an age that someone who was not her nursemaid had done so, and Nurse had been dead these three years. It brought stinging tears unbidden to fill Riss's eyes. She dared herself not to blink.

This tenderness wasn't the prelude to a thrashing, which made it even more confusing still; the lady actually seemed to mean it, grateful for the information even though she still worried about the bits Riss left unsaid.

Riss lowered her eyes with something that would look like humility. This wasn't something the lady should thank her for. "Two days, my lady. Tomorrow we'll set out the linens, prepare the ritual baths. I'll help you clear the tombs. I'll help you organize the families so that when the bodies arrive you can focus only on your lord's health, and all the rest of that busy-hands work will be done."

"You speak of him in the present," the lady said hollowly, without the epiphany of afterthought, turning her gaze beyond the distant mountaintops once more.

Riss's stomach flopped over again; at least it was back in its true position now, if the flops had been of even intensity.

In the present. Not as one flustered and caught off-guard might speak of someone whose death they've seen, if they're caught nervous in a lie. Of course that had been her game. Why had Riss not seen it?

Riss's cheeks flushed hot; the lady could assume her blush was some sort of misguided humility. "Of course, my lady. Does he not still rule over these halls?" She made her eyes a bit too wide, too innocent, but that could also be read as surprise.

"He rules over fewer now. So many men lost. He will be in a right fury by the time he returns." A sigh, a real unguarded sigh, left Lady Blackburn's throat. "Thank the gods for leaving you with us, Riss. We need you in a crisis."

Arabella stood, curling into the curve of Riss's arm like a child. Two princesses, relying on each other to not learn what they relied upon each other for. Wrapping an arm around the slender, paler Westlander, Larissa N'Eastlanden steered her toward the black iron bed with its curling, thorned vines. It was more manipulation. Riss knew it. And yet...

"Do you remember..." Arabella murmured weakly. "He used to slide all the way down the staircase rails. He got in trouble for it, because he'd fall off at that sharp turn, but he tried and tried, because he'd seen you do it and hang on."

Already hollowed-out, Riss had nothing left with which to react to that. She was a sponge, long out of water and dried in the sun, all her hollow chambers having stiffened into uncomfortable, empty shapes. She shook her head.

"He'll be home soon. Lie down, my lady. I'll begin drawing lists for the servants. Everything will be ready for you tomorrow."

There was no resistance, so Riss kissed Arabella's forehead—why had she done that?—and left.

At dawn on the second day, trumpets sounded from beyond the gates. Riss, already dressed and expectant, nudged away the mouser that lounged across her feet and rushed to her window. There was the small company of personal guard, bearing their injuries boldly, with the solemn wrapped bodies in stained white cloths. Behind, Riss's mother, having gained considerable age about her face and, apparently, a fondness for the color blue. The army glittered behind her in their armor, the reflection of stars on water. Her glory was captured in all of them.

Riss took the twisting hidden passages and was among the crowd at the keep's entrance before Lady Blackburn arrived at the wall.

"Present!" Riss's mother shouted from mid-ranks in the outer courtyard, in that contralto military voice that instinct obeyed before mind could catch up to what it had heard.

The unit at the front stepped forward and three men presented a white-wrapped body, then knelt and raised it high. Lady Blackburn stood in silence for a moment, turned, and started slowly down toward the gate. She stumbled when she was even with Riss, and without thinking Riss moved to steady her elbow. They walked together, like brides to the altar, down to the courtyard that now served duty as a gravesite.

The guards unwrapped the face as Lady Blackburn approached. Riss winced. Just as in her vision, one side was cruelly melted away. The other did not fare much better; just enough for a lover to recognize, if no one else.

"Lord Blackburn is dead. Long live Lord Blackburn," one of the men said, voice hoarse from smoke and fire. He took a swig from a canteen but grimaced; the water burned.

"Long live Lord Blackburn," the lady herself answered, and as she surrendered herself into the custody of the Eastland soldiers in their gleaming armor, others took up the chant. Riss threaded her way between the ranks, and found herself enfolded in arms without any powder to get in the way. Except one dab square on her nose, joined by her mother's impish grin.

"Long live Lord Blackburn," Riss said with a half-sardonic smile.

Riss's mother shook her head. Pride looked enigmatic on her, like she was hiding something. And she was. "Long live Larissa, Steward of Starkeep."

Riss's eyes filled again and she turned away. "What will you do with him?"

Riss's mother smiled, not kindly. "His head will grace the spike of honor, of course, so that all may see it."

Riss bowed her head. "Lady Adrienne, Royal Majesty, allow him burial on the grounds. He is royalty too. And he grew up in Starkeep every bit as much as I."

Her mother lifted Riss's chin and peered curiously into her eyes for a long moment. She nodded, stepping back, and offered Riss her hands. The Talent was strong in the family, and she may well have read important things there. "It must be done," they said together. And then, finally then, hugged properly. It was the end of the Blackburn reign and a closing of the distance of ten years, and all the rest could wait.

# A LOT OF SLY WORK AHEAD

## Ed Greenwood

THEY BURIED THE KING in the Ghost Tower this morning. Feet high and head down, with a slim silver blade through his heart to keep him from walking. Of course.

The true and loyal are so damned *persistent*. Not like we slyboots.

As they set the graven stone over the withered royal heels, I was loath to turn away. I knew who would be waiting for me, wintry eyes above sneering smiles. The Wyrmcloaks.

Stornan, tall and grand with his dagger-like beard and new high-cowled robe, every arrogant inch the mighty wizard. Beside him, Aeregul, storm-haired handsome and knowing it, hands toying with the dashing blade he wore and gaze fixed smugly on me because—for once—there were no ladies to make smoldering eyes at. At Aeregul's shoulder, Hamreth; fat, surly and sour. And beside him, the fourth and last Wyrmcloak: Lrentorn, as balefully ugly as he'd come from the womb, his lopsided hatchet face alight with malice.

Four wizards who would prefer to rule the new king themselves.

Four wizards who soon would. I could overmatch any one of them, perhaps my choice of two, but...they stood across my path, with lesser mages behind them, and many dark-armored warriors of the realm, too.

"High Vizier Glardrim, a word with you." Stornan's words were a cold and drawn blade.

I shrugged. "Treason? Is that your one word, lords?"

"Aha, you know your own guilt," said Aeregul, gloating openly. "You also know the penalty, I believe."

"The things you believe, Aeregul," I replied, striding straight at him, "are among the problems besetting Duskember."

He flinched back, and with a snarl drew his sword. "Stand and surrender, old man!"

"*Such* discourtesy," I replied sadly, speaking to the folk behind the four Wyrmcloaks, as I felt the chill of cold iron sliding through me—as I stepped through it. "Here in the Chamber of the Fallen Kings. Let us meet this evening in the Room of the Riven Throne. *After* the memorial feast."

"When you've had time to prepare for us?" Stornan snapped. "Not garruling likely!"

Aeregul was busy collapsing and retching, tears of helpless pain on his cheeks, and the men beyond him were hastily giving way before me.

No wonder. They'd just seen me step right through a man as if I was a ghost—and that man was all too obviously feeling all the yawning agony of his body stretched by magic colder than any grave.

I turned, gave Stornan a tight smile, and replied gently, "I am *always* prepared for the likes of you, Stornan of Haelmantle."

I kept on turning, so as to favor Hamreth and Lrentorn with my smile. As they writhed and staggered in the aftermath of having the fell magics they'd just cast at me thrust right back into them.

Oh, yes, magic hurts.

As I knew all too well—and would be reminded of anew, all too soon. When the memorial feast was done.

"Marl Glardrim, know this: you are High Vizier of Duskember no longer!" Stornan's voice rang with warm satisfaction.

He seemed to be expecting some sort of reply, so I nodded.

The thirty-three other men in the room waited tensely for my outburst, wands of warding raised and ready. They expected me to lash out with spells, not knowing how few I had left.

The women of Duskgard expected even more; there was not one of them in all this wing of the castle. That much, the tatters of my failing magic still told me.

"You were born in the village of Thaler's Bridge," Lrentorn spoke up, "and to there you shall return. In lasting disgrace."

"For your tyranny, you deserve death many times over," Aeregul put in. "For what you did to our great king, all of those passings should be slow and agonized." His voice went bitter. "Yet we dare not, because of what you have done."

I nodded again, not bothering to add a smile.

Their words held no surprise for anyone in the room. Everyone in Duskember knew Marl Glardrim for a murderous villain.

Everyone in the chamber around me knew I'd risen ruthlessly to become the realm's most tyrannical High Vizier, manipulating a weak-minded, frail old king and his equally weak-minded young crown prince. I'd started wars and finished them, wars that had raised Duskember from a backwater kingdom into the mightiest empire this vast world of Aglirta had ever seen. As King Baerence Wyrmgar sat mumbling on his throne, I'd played kingdom against kingdom. Malaunt, Narsym, Pelevvar, and Thondur... slowly Duskember had swallowed them all, the blood of thousands shed in the doing. As, closer to home, I played archmage off against archmage.

I got very good at it all. And very tired of it all.

This ruling from behind thrones was a demon steed. Once mounted, you were trapped in the saddle; the only end for this wild ride was death.

Baerence had been a good man, once. I had sickened of ruling him. Crown Prince Aladar Wyrmgar was a spineless weakling, whom I detested as much as he hated me, and I was revolted at the thought of ruling him.

So I merely nodded.

"We have discovered," Hamreth growled, his voice heavy with distaste, "that we dare not execute you. Yet. Because of all the magics."

I felt like smiling then, but kept it off my face and merely regarded him patiently.

They needed this time to gloat and toy and justify, these four spineless malices, before they carried out whatever unpleasantnesses they had planned for me.

They dared not kill me, indeed. I had made myself indispensible. Without lifting a finger, by merely willing one thing or saying another, I could hurl this palace and the three greatest castles in Duskember down into ruin right now, on the heads of all inside.

Cutting out my tongue or manacling me spread-rigid wouldn't stop me. I had enjoyed thirty years of crafting new magics and altering old enchantments, to make myself the focus or keystone of them all. And I had used those years well.

If I died suddenly, before these Wyrmcloaks put in a decade or so of hard and exacting spellcasting, Duskember would fall with me, leaving them ruling a realm of rubble, whirling magical storms, and chaos.

"Too many magics," I admitted softly, keeping my eyes on Hamreth's face. "Done with the purest of intentions."

"To raise yourself to be a tyrant," he spat scornfully.

"Just as you four are now attempting," I said calmly. "With the purest of intentions, of course."

I ignored their sputtering responses. For it *had* begun with the purest of intentions. When I'd first set foot in Duskgard, it had been a softly sinister place of warring vipers, courtiers who led good Baerence astray daily for sport and their own waxing gain. I'd bound magic after magic to me for the good of the realm. I dared trust the future of Duskember with no one else, you see.

No one who's not a fool dares trust anyone, these days. As all the world knows, one can always trust a dragon—but nothing and no one else. And it seemed there were precious few dragons around these days.

They'd been rare since the rise of archmages who exalted themselves above mere wizards, by crafting dragonscale cloaks that could hold dozens of spells in their shimmering scales and so make a spellhurler mighty. Rather than remaining mere neighbors who had to putter all day to ready one magic, and so stay easy prey for any thug with a cudgel.

Aye, dragons loath to part with their scales—that is, every last living wyrm—had become rare indeed.

Men stepped forward at Stornan's signal, and my throat was suddenly ringed with glittering swordpoints. Freshly polished. Ah, such an honor.

"Stand still," Stornan ordered.

I shrugged and spread empty hands.

When one blade darted at my fingers, I slapped it away, shaking its wielder with a child's spell that sent sparks racing up his steel to snap out of his nose and mouth. Through streaming tears, he backed hastily away, trying not to sob aloud.

The other swordpoints slid in closer.

Hameth and Lrentorn were casting now. Unfamiliar magics, slow and complex.

"The spells now being laid upon you," Stornan announced, lifting his long-bearded chin in satisfaction, "will you keep you awake and aware throughout what follows. Experiencing every moment."

He smiled then, and it was not a pleasant sight. "It may be that you will not sleep again for years."

And then the man with the forgehammer came in.

I was glad I'd bought that little time before the feast to prepare. Among other things, what little I'd managed blunted the worst of the pain. Discomfort the Wyrmcloaks wanted to go on for years.

The years it would take them to trace, identify, and alter every last spell in Duskgard that held up sagging roofs, spires, and domes, that buttressed aging walls, that painted and stuccoed so many grand ceilings and tiled so many floors. Not to mention the three castles.

I hoped they'd remember the three castles.

The man with the hammer had broken every joint of my limbs—and then my jaw—with careful, brutal precision. For which I was grateful.

Then they'd strapped my flopping, bleedingly useless limbs to my body with far more pack-straps than were necessary, binding me into a bundle, and packed me off to my home village in an open horse-cart that same night.

With me in the groaning, rattling conveyance was a geased-to-serve-me servant, a quiet, drab young girl named Flaer, who regarded me with cool gray eyes. Presumably she was really "Flaera," but my jaw was in no condition to ask her anything, and learn of her kin and home village. So in frosty silence she fed me gruel, watered me, and sluiced away my wastes with the same deftness, doing what the Wyrmcloaks wanted: keeping me alive in agony.

With the cart rode knights bearing a proclamation from the new king. One of them took some delight in reading it to me. "The villain Glardrim is to be kept alive and in the best of health, but confined in the village and not allowed to speak to any visitors save My envoys. You need not treat him with respect. He caused the deaths of uncounted thousands, and ruined more lives besides, and has earned his lasting punishment. On no account trust him, in matters small or large."

Well, that was astute enough. More than I'd thought Aladar capable of, if one of the Wyrmcloaks hadn't written every word for him. And possibly signed it for him, too.

Eventually the long torment of the cart ride had ended. Here I was, back in Thaler's Bridge. Lying alone in the dark, with Flaer snoring faintly in the next room.

My shattered joints merely ached now, as I lay still, but inside me I could feel the slow, shifting nausea of one more spell anchored in me being dissolved into an anchor elsewhere. The Wyrmcloaks were already hard at work hastening the moment of my irrelevance.

Also inside me was a weapon they knew nothing of, hidden from their pryings among all the spell-nodes—the hundreds of pebbles I'd had sewn into my body over the years rather than trusting in a dragonscale cloak someone could steal or slash away in battle. One of them let me read the uppermost thoughts of anyone touching me, another made me...but enough; my thoughts ramble.

Three small glass vials of lorarra. Enspelled dragonblood. The instruments of my revenge.

Enspelled to me, so the moment a mere drop out of my vials sank into the flesh of a living person, they will fall under the influence of my mind. Vials that had been riding inside me for years, put there by that fell sorceress Lady Summertide, who'd once been a war-prisoner of Duskember.

Fiery-tempered and lash-tongued, eyes like two burning flames of fury... Ieira Ahmruth, a dusky-skinned, willow-thin outlander from the hot jungles of Surruth over the mountains, nicknamed "Lady Summertide" because she came from that warm country. I'd spared her life and arranged her escape in return for my three vials. That had been long and long ago; what had become of her?

Ah, but the past is the past, and here I was in the present, crippled— and strapped into a bundle so my limbs would henceforth be bent and deformed, when they did heal. A prisoner of my own shattered body.

I had a few feeble spells, and one other little trick. The nails of the smallest fingers on each of my hands were cut as sharp as bright-honed daggers. Usually I coated those nails nightly with the sleep-inducing venom of the river adder, but my bottle of that was behind me in Duskgard, well hidden. The smallest nail of my right hand bore another sort of coating: arraul, a deadly slay-at-a-touch poison I was immune to, thanks to years of sickening treatments. Best held in reserve until I was no longer strapped to a board, and had healed enough to move about.

In the meantime, if I could expel just one vial of lorarra, dip my left nail in it, and scratch villager after villager, as they handled me...

Had Flaer been reading my thoughts? I hadn't sensed her mind in mine for an instant, but upon awakening she'd silently drawn a knife from low under her shift. Then she'd calmly dipped it in a bowl of wine, sliced open my side in exactly the spot where the uppermost vial rode between ribs, eased out that tiny glass cylinder with a minimum of pressing and tugging, used more wine to sluice clean the cut and her fingers, and bound the wound with swift skill. Then, stonefaced, she'd immersed the smallest finger of my left hand in the vial, ere making knife and vial both vanish beneath her shift.

It had been ease itself to scratch her, but when I tried to command her, she ignored me, and I felt no mind-thread. Either she was as guarded against lorarra as I was, or the geas on her was stronger than its lure.

I couldn't be sure, because I couldn't feel her mind at all, let alone read it. No matter how I stared and concentrated, I couldn't win past the gentle, inscrutable smile she was giving me now.

She turned her back on me to pull her kirtle on over her shift, then reached for her worn linen-and-leather overdress. I stared at its patchwork of scraps settling into place over her.

How had she known about the lorarra? And why arm me so?

I smiled. Another one scratched, this one not even noticing.

Soon Marl Glardrim will reign in Thaler's Bridge.

Soon I'll have all your daughters. Soon...

Not that I'll be in any shape to *do* anything to any of them.

My healing was slow. After an entire season of enduring the daily taunts and spittle of Thalen-folk, I still ached, my body forever curled into a twisted ball despite the straps being long gone. I could crawl and drag myself along like a legless beggar, but not stand or be deemed less than hideous in anyone's eyes.

Just as the Wyrmcloaks intended, of course.

Yet I'd scratched a goodly number of villagers, not quite three out of every four Thalen-folk, and my influence over the village was strong and growing stronger. I could summon many to me, and order them about as if I was their emperor. These nights I dined on the best of their food and wine, not the rotting scraps they'd brought me when that damned cart had dumped me in their midst.

"Little toad of an emperor," some of them called me now, when they were far from the rooms they'd given me. Thinking of that title always awakened my best wintry smile.

The one that made Flaer turn away.

She turned away often, these days. She seemed not to approve of my grooming and pruning of Thaler's Bridge. I used my power over those I'd scratched with ruthless care, making those I commanded eliminate fellow villagers I knew to be spies for the Wyrmcloaks, but always staging such passings as "accidents." Accidents that were now spreading to the ranks of the more dangerously energetic of the villagers who hated me deeply.

Soon I could set about ruling Thaler's Bridge in earnest, reordering the village to make it prosperous and strong without much outward show. I'd have my own spies, to report to me daily of any strangers, and every little village incident. It would be tiresome tedium for the most part, but I wanted them to *know* they were being ruled, with daily reminders—for what good is villainy unappreciated?

Then would come the time to recruit capable villagers to be my agents, to go and slay Wyrmcloaks in suitably painful ways.

Ah, starting over. A lot of sly work ahead, but then…that's life.

The nights were noticeably cooler; winter was coming. It was finally time. As my second summer in Thaler's Bridge since the breaking of my body headed swiftly towards the cold to come, my rule was at last nigh complete.

Which meant I no longer needed Flaer, my oh-so-attentive servant. My attentive Wyrmcloaks spy.

She was emptying my chamberpot right now, her face as calm and unreadable as ever as she went past. Not knowing her doom.

They would be here soon. Ten-and-six daughters of the village, assembling at my silent mind-bidding this bright morning, coming here with their knives and cleavers to slice and pickle harvested thuldoons and peppers for winter storage in my cellar.

It would be messy, but—

Cheerful chatter outside, laughter, and the bang of our warped front door. The first were here.

Six of them, brisk and noisy and bustling all about, peering into the crocks I'd had Flaer wash and put ready, turning to the sacks of thuldoons as the seventh and eighth came in to join them, and Flaer slipped back into the room. Into their midst.

Here hail the ninth, then four more all in a bunch, chuckling over some shared jest. Enough to do the deed.

Surround her now, not obviously, but get you over here and you there and you *there*, so as to have her from all sides.

Ah, I'll miss you, Flaer, but—

*But nothing. Back away from me, all of you. Blades DOWN.*

The retreat to the walls is a scrambling rush, faces as pale and wide-eyed in surprise as I know mine must be.

My mind is caught in a dark grip, risen out of nowhere to tighten hard.

I am more astonished than afraid as her face turns to me. Two fires burn deep in her eyes, the rest of her face the usual serene mask.

*Marl Glardrim ably controls many. Is he truly so blind that he cannot see that someone can as easily control HIM?*

Well, so I must be. Have been. And—

Flaer's face never changed, and she barely lifted a finger, but the spell that lashed into me then flung me into worse shrieking agony than I'd ever known before.

This was it at last, my slaying stroke...

Out of red writhing I slid, slowly but then faster, plunging helplessly down, down into...the waiting cold darkness.

I came awake.

Well, *that* was a surprise.

I'd never expected to awaken, ever again.

My agony was gone, and the young women of the village, too. I was still in the same room, facing Flaer's serene face, the two of us in almost the same positions.

Almost. Fresh astonishment: I was floating.

In midair, a few feet off the ground, with a cane in my hand.

"Push at the floor with that," Flaer told me calmly, "and so propel yourself along."

"To where?"

"Down the room, and back. Practice."

I obeyed, straining as I did to feel her mind lurking in my own, but finding nothing. Yet I'd not felt her before, when she must have been there...

The knack of pushing with the stick to move myself along was a simple one, and I was at the far wall already. It seemed I could "walk" without functioning legs.

Back, she'd said. I turned around and returned to where I'd been, staring at her unreadable face as I came.

"Why have you spared me?"

That brought a steely smile.

"Do you know me not, Marl?"

I stared hard at her. There was something about her eyes...I'd gazed into them before Flaer, but...

"Who *are* you, lady?"

"You spared a sorceress, once."

"Ieira *Ahmruth*?"

She nodded. "Henceforth, your new master. Who will work with you to hurl down the Wyrmcloaks, and return to Duskgard."

I gaped at her.

For a long time.

Too long, it seemed. She sighed. "No gratitude? Or are you too much the dazed dullard to appreciate my mercy, my forbearance in these years since the cart ride that came so close to killing you?"

"Gratitude?" I dared to say, as bitterness flooded up to nigh choke me. "So from being a crawling cripple, I am now a floating cripple?"

I slammed the cane against the table, making all the crocks rattle. "I ask again, why have you spared me? Is this your notion of prolonged punishment?"

Flaer—Ieira Ahmruth—shrugged.

"By all the gods, I hated you," she whispered. "Yet for all your ruthlessness, your driving need to control everything and smash everyone and everything you couldn't control, you were the best ruler Duskember—nay, all Aglirta—ever had. You ended the petty wars of the princes, the endless butchery that bled kingdoms dry and left us all scratching for frozen turnips in deep winter, amid the yawning skulls of the fallen. Glardrim, you are a sly serpent and a right vicious prowling beast—but you are *useful*. To me, if no one else. And our aims ride together: to destroy the Wyrmcloaks."

She came closer. "You have been the greatest tyrant the world has ever known. Trusting no one, always alone."

She smiled again, friendly this time, almost entreating. "You can again be the greatest tyrant the world has ever known, trusting no one—but no longer alone. I've spent my life alone, and am heartily sick of it. We need not trust each other, but I ask you: is it not better, as the years pass and find us older, not to be alone?"

I was gaping at her again, but thinking hard.

And she waited in silence, thank the gods, giving me time to ponder.

It was some time before I dared use the cane to approach her, to reach out my hand to her.

"I find myself persuaded," I told her, and meant it. "Use me."

Slowly, Ieira Ahmruth took my hand.

It occurred to me then that I could use my arraul to slay her. Somewhat to my surprise, I found I really didn't want to.

It had been a hard winter, but we'd kept ourselves from freezing by much sly and distant night-work against the Wyrmcloaks, harming those who served them and the King.

Carefully, always carefully, never doing anything that would bring down fierce suspicion on a crippled husk of a man out in the countryside. We mind-smote men halfway across Duskember when they were precariously balanced on bridges or leaning out high windows or riding in perilous weather, and let long falls do our slaying for us.

Patience was something I and the lady who now ruled me had both mastered very well.

As the days passed, and the unseen Wyrmcloaks far away at the glittering heart of the realm reached out into me again and again, as they'd been doing since they'd shattered me. Reaching to shift spell after spell from anchors in me to their control.

Those nauseating movements in my innards came more slowly these days, for the swift and easy magics were long done and only the harder, more complicated ones were left. Here came another, a roiling no less painful for its slow unfolding, a—

From out of the depths of my mind into that firming grip on the spell lashed a mind-blade swift and terrible, sliding deep even as it rose into fire that cooked a distant wind so suddenly that—

Hamreth barely had time to try to shout.

His mind went abruptly silent while the echo of his straining mind-shout was still rolling through our linked minds.

Unless one of Hamreth's fellow Wyrmcloaks had been sitting with him, they'd not have time enough to trace who'd slain him, and would find only a mind-melted corpse, drooling his own brains out into his lap. His own reaching out had left him unguarded before the waiting Ieira Ahmruth.

Who now blazed ruby-red in my trembling mind, aglow with satisfaction, the heat of her deadly bolt still washing through me. I was spasming helplessly, the cane cracking off a distant wall, my maimed limbs vainly and frantically flailing the air—

My right hand struck something, slashing into flesh, rolling me over in midair to—

Stare at Ieira Ahmruth, aghast.

Her fingers had darted to a slice on her arm. The work of my poisoned fingernail.

"Milady Summertide," I blurted, still struggling to speak as new spasms seized me, "I never meant to—"

"I know," she replied briskly. "I've watched you, this winter, thinking of meaning to, several times, then refraining. Be not upset, for I am unharmed. Arraul works not on dragons."

"On...dragons?"

She gave me the thinnest of smiles. "Where did you think I got dragonsblood, dolt?"

Just for a moment, her eyes held golden slits, her delicate nose flared horribly to snort out smoke, and she opened her mouth to show me an ocean of glittering fangs.

Still writhing and spasming, I tried to cower back, but already she was herself again, her smile warm and wry.

"Yet worry not, Marl Glardrim. For as all the world knows, you can always trust a dragon."

I stared at her, my mouth as open as any fool's—then started to laugh, great bellows that roared out of me. I couldn't stop.

I was rolling over and over in midair from my own mirth by the time she joined in.

Ah, starting over. With a partner this time.

Which changed nothing. There remained a *lot* of sly work ahead.

But then...that's life.

# THE HEIR APPARENT

## Mercedes Lackey and Larry Dixon

"ONE DAY, ALL THIS will be yours," Dominic Verdigris III proclaimed solemnly, and gestured broadly with his right arm.

The short, burly man beside him removed an unlit cigar from his mouth, and snorted. "If you're waiting for a Monty Python quote, you're gonna be waiting a long time, Dom."

Verd sighed. "Oh Rancor, you have no sense of humor." He dropped his arm, and surveyed the weedy lot before him. It was approximately five acres in a shabby part of Memphis Tennessee, fenced in by eight foot chain-link with razor wire on the top, and a bent-up sign proclaiming "City Property — Keep Out" on its heavy welded-pipe gates. Inside that property was a three-story, square brick building, whose front façade proclaimed that it was "Rogers School." Or rather, "Roger s School," since the first "s" hung crooked.

"So," the man that Verd had addressed as "Rancor" continued. "Obviously this dump isn't what it looks like. And you're the one that's always going on about how much time equals money. We're wasting time, which is money, ergo—"

"All right, all right." Verd frowned. "You have no sense of drama either. Come on."

He led the way around to the side of the building, where there was a much smaller gate, and pressed his thumb into the pipe just above the lock. The pipe clicked, the lock opened, and the gate swung freely. "After you," said Verd.

Rancor examined the pipe before passing through. "Okay. Galvanic sensors. Now that impressed me."

"Prepare to be amazed." Verd adjusted the cuff on his linen suit, where his pajama top had bunched up for a moment, and mimed straightening a tie.

A hidden trigger switch at a boarded up side door won them into the interior of the building.

It looked inside like what it was outside; a long abandoned school building, probably constructed in the 1930s with WPA money, too big and drafty to heat and cool economically, and not on property desirable enough that the city could sell it. Light seeped in through the cracks around the plywood over the windows. Many of the windows were broken. The corridor they stood in was floored in split, worn-out linoleum. The walls were chipped white paint, with graffiti all over them where kids had broken in and added their personal touches. The stucco ceiling sagged and light fixtures hung precariously from wires.

But…something was slightly off….

Rancor moved close in to the nearest wall, and got a good look. There was something wrong with the graffiti…

He turned to look at Verd, accusingly. "No kid did this. This is from an airbrush, not a spray-paint can."

Verd aimed a finger at him. "Well spotted. Not one person in a thousand would have noticed that."

Rancor began examining everything else in the hallway as minutely, and as Verd knew he would, he clearly came to the conclusion that the air of decay was entirely artificial. Only the smell was right, that "school smell" of aged desks and books and old sneakers and too many cafeteria lunches.

He waved a hand at the hallway. "This is all fake."

"Of course it is!" Verd gloated. "Even the black mold is painted on. Now, come along."

He led the way up the stairs to the cafeteria, and watched as Rancor noted all the carefully placed signals that would reinforce to anyone else "nothing to see here, move along." Rancor nudged open a door as they passed, surveyed the bolted-down desks, the blackboards, cracking and falling off the walls.

Perhaps the only thing that gave the game away was that, under all the creaking of thin, warped floorboards and the precarious look of dangling fixtures, everything was as structurally sound as a bunker. If you ignored the sound of walking, and concentrated on the feel, you'd realize that. It had been calculated not to scare away any fence-jumpers or county inspectors, but rather, to bore them, and give a vague sense of unease.

The cafeteria looked to have been stripped of anything useful, including the old walk-in cooler. There was just a hole in the wall where it once had been, and shocks of broken tile edging and chopped-through conduit. Verd led the way inside. Rancor followed him…carefully.

As soon as they were both in the space, Verd pushed the remote he had in his pocket, and the floor began descending.

Knocked out, splintering boards yielded to metal walls; a new "floor" slid in above them, and the LED lights embedded in it lit up the shaft. Rancor nodded.

"Okay. More impressed," he said.

The metal walls continued for two stories below the level of the school basement. Then the elevator came to a slow and graceful stop. One of the walls slid aside to reveal a corridor that would not have been out of place in any one of Verd's corporate labs. Lights in the ceiling came on at the touch of another button on the remote, sequencing away from them and then splitting down the adjoining corridors.

Verd sighed, and patted the wall. "My first lair," he said, nostalgically. "Home sweet home. You never forget your first, you know. I wanted the United States and then the world, so I set up shop here. Central to everywhere. Drowsy locals. Good infrastructure for moving everything from lab equipment to superbombs by highway, river or rail. Convenience counts when you're doing high-end crime." Verd traced fingertips on the stainless steel trim. "I've had a lot of bases of operation, but there's just something about returning to your first lair that always feels like coming home. I did some good business here. Good times. Come on, I'll show you around."

"How'd you get your hands on this place?" Rancor asked. "And how the hell do you keep the city from noticing the power drain?"

"Racketeer with a wrecking firm sold it to me, and got me rotating, no-questions illegal labor for the construction work. I installed my own power plant. My design, of course. I don't use every isotope I get just for weapons, you know." Verd chuckled. "Anyway, the racketeer didn't know it was me, of course. It was one of my shell-personas. He hardly even had a chance to enjoy the payoff too, before his fatal stroke." Verd shook his head sadly. "I kept telling him, lay off all that butter."

Rancor snorted. He knew more than enough about Verd's ventures into biological research to know that butter had very little to do with that fatal stroke...unless, of course, butter was the delivery system for some untraceable nanobot that had caused the stroke in the first place. Verd gave the stubby man a raised-eyebrow sideglance in response to that snort. Rancor was the first person Verd had found who could figure out nearly everything Verd was doing, even if he couldn't deduce the means, or have invented them in the first place. But given a tool, he was an absolute genius at coming up with uses for it.

Verd opened the first door on the corridor, and as he did so, motion-activated lights came up inside. His hand caressed the doorframe as they entered. The room had been rigged out as a high-tech garage.

"Remember the Murdercycle?" Verdigris grinned. Of course Rancor would remember it. It had been one of his early favorite assassination tools. "This is where she was conceived, born, improved and repaired." He had loved the Murdercycle. The only reason he had stopped using her was that ECHO had caught on to what he was doing with her, and not even the color-changing paint and shape-morphing bodywork was going to keep her and her rider from being tracked and caught.

"Now that was a sweet ride." Rancor nodded, smiling slightly. He walked around the room, picking up a tool here, a spare part there, examining everything, while Verd leaned back against the doorway. "We could still use something like that, if we kept it to night rides and switched the venue to high speed, superhighway intercept with a capture vehicle down the road. Hit the target at 120-plus miles per hour."

*Huh. Clever.* "I'll put that idea on the list," he promised. "We'd need a meta with enhanced reflexes to pull the job though, at those speeds."

Rancor just shrugged. Obviously, such a person wouldn't be him. He wasn't a meta. So he claimed, anyway. Yet Verd thought he detected something in the man's momentary scowl. Jealousy? Envy? Maybe a little anger? As much as Rancor was capable of loving anything, he had loved that bike. And Verd had just suggested he would not be the one to take her to the next dance.

Verdigris smiled, but only on the inside. *Good.* He lived for the feeling that he was successfully playing someone.

Verd decided it was time to move on, and Rancor followed. The lights went out behind them.

Verd displayed the many rooms of his first research facility like the fine gems they were, laying them out for Rancor's admiration. And, grudging though the admiration was, Rancor did deliver it. What was more, he was showing definite signs of desire. He wanted this place, Verd's first "home." He wanted it badly.

*Good.*

"I've saved the best for last," Verd said smugly. "I wanted to make sure you appreciated this place. I can't leave it to someone who won't use it properly."

Ah, there it was. That little glint in Rancor's eyes that said "Oh, I am your equal. And with what I do here, you will acknowledge that I am not your underling, I am your partner."

*Hmm hmm. Oh Rancor. That will never do.*

He opened the last door; this time, lulled by the rest of the tour, Rancor went in ahead.

Verd slammed and locked the door on him, and activated the intercom. He waited until the cursing stopped.

"Now, now. I told you this place will be yours, and it will. But you have to earn it first—just like you have to earn the Methusalah Virus. Yes, I know we were going after that together, but I've gotten a teeny bit ahead of you, and you know how I hate coming in second." Verd laughed. "But you can still have it, and you can still have this place."

He pushed the last button on the remote, activating all the traps. There was one thing to be said about going old school, in this "old school." C4 never let you down.

"You just have to earn it, Rancor," he repeated, stepping into the elevator.

He thumbed a few buttons on the remote. "She has a lot of life left in her, but you need to learn how she really ticks. Tick tick ticks. You need to romance before you can have her, and she is just so sensitive. You have to earn her."

"How do I do that?" Rancor's voice growled from the speaker.

Verd had just enough time to call out before the elevator carried him beyond the sound of anything—voices or explosions.

"Survive the next 30 minutes."

His first lair felt like going home, sure, and even like a first love—but he'd gotten over every girlfriend he'd killed just fine. This was just the prom date of supervillain lairs.

The sound of Verd's laughter echoed up the shaft, and then with the slam of a multi-ton door, was gone.

---

MERCEDES LACKEY was born in Chicago Illinois on June 24, 1950. The very next day, the Korean War was declared. It is hoped that there is no connection between the two events. In 1985, her first book was published. In 1990 she met artist Larry Dixon at a small Science Fiction convention in Meridian Mississippi, on a television interview organized by the convention. They moved to their current home, the "second weirdest house in Oklahoma" also in 1992. She has many pet parrots and "the house is never quiet." She has over eighty books in print, with four being published in 2010 alone, and some of her foreign editions can be found in Russian, German, Czech, Polish, French, Italian, Turkish, and Japanese. Another current addiction is role-playing gaming in the online game City of Heroes. From this collaboration with Dennis Lee, Cody Martin and Veronica Giguere came the Secret World Chronicle, www.secretworldchronicle.com, a five book series of which the first two: *Invasion!* and *World Divided* are available from Baen. The second book features villain Dominic Verdigris II, of this story

LARRY DIXON was educated at the North Carolina School of the Arts during high school, and then at the Savannah College of Art and Design; his story work became as popular as his artwork. He has been an uncredited co-plotter or co-writer for many popular properties, bringing jovial and energetic approaches to collaborative work. Many cover-credited novels have followed, too, including the ever-popular Gryphon series, the Winds, Storms, SERRAted Edge, and Owl books with the mighty Mercedes (Misty) Lackey. *Born to Run* has been hailed as a "romp with a conscience," and *The Black Gryphon* has been critically referred to as "a modern classic," and is in its nineteenth printing. As a birds-of-prey rehabilitation specialist, he and his wife Misty have gotten hawks, owls, falcons and corbies back into the wild from their home-based facilities in Oklahoma. Additionally, Larry is an accomplished race car driver, world traveler, aviculturist, model maker and Internet veteran.

# HOME AGAIN, HOME AGAIN

(Another Mid-Death Crisis)

## Chris A. Jackson

BRIMSTONE AND ASH VENT from the beast's nostrils as the darkly armored figure kicks its flanks. The creature—half horse, half demon and long dead—leaps into a gallop, heaving beneath its master with an ungainly lurch. The spires of Kaegengul Keep swim into view through the dust and ash of the undead army's passage, lit like a burning hell with the setting sun.

Kaegen looks upon the fell towers and his cold heart swells with longing. Home…

The Necromancer of Kaegengul kicks his mount ahead of the van of his army, spurring it toward the ancestral home of his forefathers. The black iron portcullis screeches in its tracks as he approaches, lifting from his path as the taskmasters' whips crack, flaying the backs of the slaves manning the winches. He jerks his mount to a halt, sparks and ash flying from its burning hooves and nostrils. He steps from the saddle and flings the reins toward the master of stables. He ascends the broad stair to the towering obsidian doors that defend all that he holds dear, all that he fights to protect in this wretched world. He flings them aside with a single word of power, doffing his fell helm as he passes the portal.

"Wipe your feet, for Hell's sake!"

Kaegen freezes in his tracks and looks down at his evil boots, and the track of dark smudges he's left on the silk rug. Ice water invades his veins, and he takes a hesitant step backward.

"No! Don't move! You've already fouled the carpet. Just hold still!" A tall, pale figure strides forward flanked by several cowering servants. Beautiful and cold, dark and smoldering, his wife, the Vampire Thotris, glares with eyes that glow dark crimson, her pale hands on her shapely hips. "Do you *know* how hard it is to remove entrail stains from a fine Trokarian rug?"

"Thotris…I…" Words catch in his throat like cinders. "I didn't think…"

"Of *course* you didn't think! You never *think*, Kaegen, you just conquer, and then you track home the refuse for everyone else to clean up." She glares at him for a short eternity, then snaps, "Servants! Take my lord Kaegen's boots, and his helm and cloak while you're at it. They all reek of death and carnage, and I won't have them in this keep until they've been cleaned."

"Yes, Mistress," the entourage of servants says in unison, skulking forward to aid the removal of their lord's evil accouterments.

Kaegen places his helm into the hands of one unfortunate wretch, and watches her skin blister beneath its foul touch. One of the servants falls to all fours behind him so that he can sit and have three others pull his evil boots from his evil feet. His evil socks, however, are not any more floral than the remnants of the enemies that cling to the heels of his boots. It has been a long, hard campaign, but a victorious one.

When he is free to stand again, he announces, "I have conquered all of Lower Mulavia!"

"And did you bring me anything?" Thotris asks, her undead eyes boring into his. "A piece of jewelry? An object de art, perhaps?" When he doesn't answer immediately, she continues, "A souvenir spoon, even?"

"I have brought fifty wains laden with the spoils of my conquest, dearest Thotris." He bows low, sweeping his evil gauntlet wide. "It is all for you, milady! And I have taken the head of their traitorous king, Saer Musalisku, to boot!"

"*Spoils...*" Thotris says the word as if describing something moldy she has discovered at the bottom of an icebox. She waves yet another servant forward, a tall, well-dressed youth bearing a silver slaver and a single cup. "That doesn't sound promising. And don't think for a moment that you're going to mount another smelly head on a plaque and hang it in your den."

"Well, I thought..." The young man proffers the cup. He is well-built, with wavy black hair and broad shoulders. His face is pale, and a bare hint of blood shows at the white collar of his dress shirt. Kaegen takes the cup and quaffs its contents without tasting it, then recognizes the man's vestments as those of the house butler. "What happened to Melvin?"

"Oh, he fell ill," Thotris says with a dismissive wave. "I had to send him away."

*Acute anemia, I'll wager,* he thinks as he returns the empty cup to the tray. The youth shows every sign of vampiric charm. Kaegen opens his mouth to comment that his dear wife seems to change butlers more often than he changes evil socks, but she beats him to the punch.

"Oh, and you're late! We have a dinner at the Zorkins' tonight! Or did you forget? Again..."

"But dearest Thotris, I just conquered all of Lower Mulavia! I can't possibly..."

He quails under her glare.

"Dinner?"

"Oh, you're hopeless, Kaegen! Just go up and get changed, and I'll get the children ready. Hurry now! The sun's already down!"

"Of course, dearest Thotris." He strides past her, trying to maintain some dignity as his evil socks swish-swish along the spotless carpet.

The last buckle of Kaegen's evil armor finally gives way, and he heaves a sigh of relief. It has been nearly a month since he's had the enchanted armor off, and he feels as if the weight of the world has been lifted from his shoulders. He steps into the cleansing chamber and summons a pillar of unholy fire to burn every last hint of filth, carnage and sweat from his body. His evil undergarments also go up in smoke and ashes, but that is no real loss. They weren't evil when he put them on.

He strides past a long mirror on the way to his dressing chamber, and pauses to gauge his reflection. *Not bad for three centuries old*, he thinks, pulling in his stomach and turning just so. He is still a powerful man, and a necromancer to boot. He can raise the dead with a wave of his hand, as his armies of undead minions are testament. He has taken a vampire to wife, and has sired two offspring from her undead womb. No man, living or dead, could call him less than virile. A slim smile graces his evil countenance, then falters with one shrill note.

"Oh, for the Devil's sake, put some clothes on!" Thotris storms into their chambers, averting her eyes as she passes. She didn't used to do that. "I'm slaving away to get the children ready for the evening and you're up here preening *naked* in front of a mirror! You think it's easy raising the undead, let alone getting them to wear decent clothes for dinner? Stop admiring yourself for two seconds, and hurry and get dressed already!"

"The children are only *half* undead," he says, hurrying to his dressing chamber. "And I wasn't admiring myself! I have not seen my likeness in more than two months, and I thought I might have developed a slouch from so much time in the saddle, that's all."

"Oh!" She vanishes into her own dressing chamber, sarcasm fairly oozing out beneath the door.

*You're just jealous*, he thinks, pausing only a moment to pick out a suitably dark vestment and cloak. *At least I have a reflection!* He dresses in haste and affixes a belt of enchanted basilisk hide around his waist. When he emerges, however, he is met once again with Thotris' smoldering disapproval.

"Oh, please, Kaegen, wear something besides black for once! This is a dinner, not a funeral."

He opens his mouth to deride her own choice of garments in kind, but it is impossible. She is, of course, flawless. In a snug crimson gown, she looks like a tall, slim goblet of blood, curvaceous and exuding all the alluring charm only a vampiress can.

"What," he asks with a courtly bow, "would you prefer, dearest?"

"Oh, stop it and just pick out something not black!" She waves him away and storms out, unimpressed by his acquiescence to her wishes.

He turns back to his dressing chamber and takes a moment to actually look upon the racks of cloaks, vestments and accoutrements. Dismay unknown throughout his centuries of conquest smites his evil heart.

She has bought him new clothes...

"New cloak, Kaegen?" Terian Zorkin asks, raising his glass in toast.

"Yes, as a matter of fact." Kaegen touches the rim of his glass to Terian's and quaffs half of its contents in one swallow. "Thotris had it made while I was away. This and a dozen others. She evidently has a new tailor, and keeps him busy."

"I'm sure she does," the other man quips with a slim smile, sipping his drink daintily. "Rather different look for you, isn't it?"

Kaegen brushes the pastel blue satin, plucks at the ruffled collar and gulps the remainder of his bloodwine, wondering if he can *accidentally* spill some of the dark red liquid down the front. It might even look like blood. "Yes, it is different." He leans into his host's ear, and says, "Bloody awful, isn't it?"

Terian sighs, "Well, we are all victims, are we not? Conquerors or peasants, we are all brought low in the end."

*The end*...he thinks, wondering if his existence has come to this. He waves to the waiter and takes another glass of bloodwine.

"So, Lower Mulavia!" Terian says with a grin. "Must be beautiful down there this time of year."

"It was, until I finished with it," Kaegan remarks, grinning at his host. "I left it a burning wasteland, unfit to support life for a century at least."

"That must have been...gratifying," Terian says. "Was it profitable?"

"Very," he replies with no small satisfaction. "I took a full fifty wains of—"

"No shop talk, now!" Thotris' lilting contralto cuts through their conversation like a knife through willing flesh. They both turn as she saunters over, their host's entourage in tow. Thotris is, of course, ravishing in her blood-red gown and glittering ruby jewelry. One of the advantages of being undead, he supposes, is never losing one's figure.

"My dear Thotris, you are positively lovely this evening!" Terian bends to kiss her pale hand and smiles. "I see you've met Bulavia, my most recent..." he winks sidelong at Kaegan, "conquest."

"I have! She's lovely! And oh so...charmed."

"A new look for you, isn't she?" Kaegen says, unable to resist the dig. Terian's wife is a beauty indeed, pale, tall, shapely and utterly charmed with her new husband. Literally charmed...he's a sorcerer, and she is his eleventh wife. She's got that glassy-eyed look.

"She is! It's been blonde after blonde, so I thought, how about a redhead for a change!" He holds out a hand and the woman goes to him like a moth to a flame. "I tell you, she makes me feel a hundred years younger!"

"She's lovely," Kaegen says, thinking, *I wonder if he would teach me that spell.* He dreams wistfully of a quiet, compliant wife as the conversation buzzes around him. He finishes his glass of bloodwine and calls for another.

Thotris glares. "That's your third, my lord. Perhaps you should wait until dinner is served to slake your seemingly unquenchable thirst."

"And perhaps you should—"

A throng of children go tearing through the sitting room, a dark-haired boy wielding a blunted (barely) sword behind a flock of girls squealing in mock (also barely) terror.

"Oh, how I do wish you would set a better role model for young Kaegen Junior," Thotris says in a tone she usually reserves for servants who have outlived their usefulness, except for their nutritional value. "Every time you come home from conquest he is utterly unbearable!"

"Like father like son!" Kaegan says proudly, though he has certain concerns about his son's capacity to uphold the family name. The boy loves violence like no one he has ever seen, but he has the mental capacity of a root vegetable. Still, he is Kaegen's namesake, and will inherit Kaegengul Keep when the time comes. "He'll be out conquering on his own before long!"

Thotris glares at him again, and he knows he will pay for this later.

Their daughter, Pwison, joins the group. She is the elder, but doomed to be married off to some lesser noble by the curse of her sex. Half-vampire, she shares her mother's alluring look, but is shrouded in utter darkness; skeletally thin and pale, her dress all black, hair black, eyes black, lips black. She stares at them all, and Kaegen feels a deliciously evil chill race down his spine.

With no greeting, she says, "Can we go now?"

Kaegen stifles a smirk—*She must have read my mind!*—but Thotris intercedes before he can say a word.

"No dear. Dawn is still *hours* away. Why don't you have something to drink? Bulavia tells me that all of their servants donated a pint for the evening." Thotris sips her glass of blood appreciatively.

"Drinking blood is *barbaric*, Mother!" Pwison says with a curled lip.

*No wonder she's so thin*, Kaegen thinks.

"Not, my dear, if you are a vampire, or a half vampire, as is your case." Thotris drains her goblet and licks her luscious lips. "You've got to take something, dear. You're starving yourself!"

"Oh, leave her alone, Thotris," Kaegen says before his brain can stop his mouth. "It's not like she can starve to *death*." This earns him another glare from his wife.

His daughter just looks at him and says, "That color is nauseating, Father."

He smiles, and cocks an eyebrow at his wife. "And I thought we didn't agree on *anything*, dear Pwison."

Thotris turns away in a huff, waving her empty goblet and shouting for a servant. Pwison turns away, but not before he sees the hint of a smile on her ebony lips.

"That's going to cost you, Kaegen," their host warns him. "You're really digging your own grave tonight, aren't you?"

"Wouldn't be the first time," he admits, emptying his glass and waving for another. "Last time she killed me, I didn't manage to crawl up out of the damned grave for a week!"

The carriage rolls into the courtyard of Kaegengul Keep as the first glow of dawn lightens the eastern sky. It rumbles to a halt, the six demon horses snorting fire in unison as the lich driver hauls on the burning reins. The door bursts open and Kaegen Junior leaps out, sword in hand.

"Can we stay up to watch the sunrise?"

"Absolutely not!" Thotris says, following him out of the coach. "It's not good for your eyes! Off to your coffins at once!"

Kaegen follows her out of the carriage and, on impulse, extends a hand for Pwison to take. "Oh, why not, Thotris? They're only half vampire. A few sunrises won't burn their eyes to cinders. And it's not like there's no such thing as regeneration spells."

"Yay!" Kaegen Junior thrusts his sword into the air. "Dad is so awesome! He lets us do stuff!"

"Fine!" Thotris throws her crimson shawl across her flawless shoulders and storms into the keep. "But don't come crying to me in fifty years when your eyes are nothing but lumps of coal!"

"You are so dead," Pwison says, placing her slim hand in his and stepping down from the carriage.

"Undead, actually," he says, smiling back. "Necromancer, to be precise."

"I'll loan you a shovel," Pwison says, ascending the steps into the keep without a backward glance.

"Why do you insist on subverting my authority?" Thotris rages at him as he enters their bedchamber. She has divested herself of her evening gown and wears a slinky black...thing that is far too alluring for her tempestuous mood.

"I'm not subverting anything. I am merely trying to enjoy my children while I'm home." He removes his powder blue cloak and vestments, and dons a simple black robe.

"Oh, you get to enjoy them, and I get to be the evil mother." She is in rare form, her eyes flashing with crimson fire. "I get to make the rules and you get to let them break them!"

"I come home after months of conquering and I don't even get a 'welcome home' or a 'nice to see you.' All I get is accusations of subversion."

"Well, if either were true, I'd have said them!" She sweeps into his wardrobe and comes out with his recently cleaned battle-cloak. "What is this?"

"What is what?"

"This!" she says, poking one nail through a burn hole in the collar.

"It's a burn," he explains. "I was at war. Burns happen."

"You've been consorting with succubi again, haven't you?" She casts the cloak aside. "Admit it!

"No, I have not. Saer Musalisku was hurling pots of burning pitch from the battlements of his keep. I got burned."

"Oh?" She obviously won't believe him, despite the fact that, for once in his long, evil life, he is speaking the truth.

"Yes, I did. I might ask about our new butler, though. I did notice your mark on him."

"How else am I supposed to keep the servants in line, Kaegen?" Her pale visage goes a faint shade paler, and he knows he has scored. "You think I take *pleasure* in sucking the blood from peasants, just so we can have decent servants?"

"We could *pay* someone," he suggests. "It's not like we're destitute. I did bring back the spoils of an entire kingdom, you know."

"Money! Just throw money around, that's your answer to everything, isn't it?"

"Money never seemed to bother you before, Thotris. It bought that gown, and this castle, and the kids' clothes, and all your jewelry."

She glares at him, eyes blazing crimson fire as the first rays of morning invade their room. She shrieks as her hair begins to smolder, and flings herself into her coffin, slamming the lid.

He stares at the ornate box, thinking of nailing it shut. He sighs, leaves the room and climbs the tower to his den.

The select plunder of Lower Mulavia is arrayed there for him, gold, jewels, weapons, armor and the startled-looking head of Saer Musalisku on a nice oak plaque.

"Lucky bastard," he mutters, going to the sideboard for a glass of bloodwine. He drinks and stares out the window into the rising sun, looking out over his domain. *His* domain…

*What's it all about?* he wonders, not for the first time in his long, evil existence. *What's it all for? All the conquering, all the war, the plundering, the murder*...It wasn't about money or security or even something as trite as ego. Thotris had sucked that out of him centuries ago.

Why?

Why conquer?

"I'm good at it," he realizes. But he knows there is more to it than that. When he is out conquering, he is lord. He is in command. He makes the decisions and survives or perishes by them. It makes him feel...alive.

Every decision he makes here, good or bad, earns him nothing but one of Thotris' hissing fang fits. He quaffs the rest of his bloodwine and glares to the east.

"Daddy?"

He turns to find his daughter standing at the door to his den, still clad in her black. She hasn't called him that in many, many years, and instantly he is wary.

"Can I come in?"

"Of course, Pwison." He goes to the sideboard to fill his glass, and on impulse pours another. "Here."

"Really?" she asks, a surprised look on her deathly pale features.

"Sure. It'll put color in your cheeks." He hands her the glass. "Careful, though. Your mother's probably poisoned it."

She makes a face, takes the glass and sips, and a flush of crimson touches her features.

"Like it?"

"Yes!" she says, sipping again. She turns to the window and walks into the light of the sunrise. Her hair sparkles, and her skin shows a sheen of iridescence.

"Doesn't that sting?" he asks, moving to her side. He's not about to tell her not to stand in the sunlight. She's old enough to make her own decisions.

"A little," she says, taking another sip of bloodwine. They stare into the rising sun for a while. He can smell her smoldering hair, see her skin darkening under the sun's rays.

With a wave he summons a protective spell, and the sun's harmful spectrum is blocked.

She looks at him in surprise. "How..."

"Simple magic." He sips his wine. "Feel better?"

"Yes." She looks at the sun, then back at him. "Can you teach me that?"

"Sure." He sips again, then has a horrible thought. "Just don't teach your mother. If she knew how to block the sun, I'd never have a moment's peace."

"Don't worry. I won't." She looks back at the rising sun, and finally asks, "Can I come with you?"

"Come with me where?" His heart is in his throat, actually beating, he can feel it. He can't remember the last time he felt it like this.

"When you go on conquest again." She looks at him. "I don't like it here, and Mother...she's..." The bloodwine ripples in her glass. She takes a less-than-careful sip and says, "Do you have any *idea* what she's like when you're gone? She's like Bitch Queen from Hell every night! She doesn't let us do *anything*! She sucks all the fun out of being undead!"

"Well, she's—"

"She's...She's making vampires, you know. She's...*cheating* on you."

He sighs, wondering why the news doesn't surprise him. "Well, she *is* evil, Pwison. She can't help herself."

"I still don't like it," she says. "I want to come with you. I've learned some magic. I wouldn't be *totally* useless. I just can't STAND her anymore!" The glass shatters in her hand, and he realizes just how serious she is.

He hands her a handkerchief. "Don't bleed on the rug. Your mother will have a fit."

"She's *always* having a fit, Daddy!" She picks the broken glass out of her hand and flicks the pieces out the window one by one. "She's nothing but one...big...undead...vampire...fit, waiting to happen! I swear, if you don't get me out of this castle, I'll hammer a wooden stake through my heart!"

The thought of driving Thotris to another hissing tantrum poses less of a deterrent than it should. He looks at Pwison, imagining her in battle armor astride her own fire-breathing undead demon horse. Oh...Thotris would have a fit to rival the very fires of Hell...

He retrieves the carafe of bloodwine from the sideboard, fills his glass, and a new one for her. He returns to the window, hands her the glass with an evil smile, and raises his in a toast. "There *is* still *Upper* Mulavia."

---

The first three of CHRIS A. JACKSON's Scimitar Seas novels won sequential ForeWord Book of the Year Gold Medals in Fantasy in 2009, 2010 and 2011. His novel *Weapon of Flesh* won the USA Book News, Best Books Awards 2005 for best Fantasy and Science Fiction novel. His current project is a Pathfinder Tales novel for Paizo Publishing, due out in April 2013. Read and enjoy chapters of all his books at www.jaxbooks.com. Chris and his wife are currently sailing and writing somewhere in the Caribbean.

# THE BEST LAID PLANS

## *Steve Bornstein*

HE HIT THE GROUND off-balance, hooves stumbling in the soft sand as he caught himself against a thick tent pole and raised a hand to shield his eyes from Asmara's burning desert sun. Through the portal, the fortress-outpost burned white-hot. The cries of the soldiers mixed with the screams of those still trapped inside the structure. The few people he could still see through the portal were stumbling in the deep snow, running around and frantically trying to save what they could. Good. With a snarl he waved his hand, dismissing the gate and wiping the glowing ring from existence. They wouldn't be following him that way.

The sounds and smells of Asmara suddenly caught up with him. Asmara, the crossroads of Navarr, the place where all trade routes came together to create a great shifting bazaar. For once he didn't curse the luck of a random gating. All manner of people and goods came through Asmara. From here he could go anywhere and disappear, disguised and anonymous, but only if he moved before the dragons homed in on the telltale signs of his passage. Such massive expenditures of magery sent shockwaves through the mana stream. The dragons were one of the few races sensitive enough to actually track it—and through it, him. Time to move.

First, a disguise. His slender pointed ears would mark him as one of the Kin but his glowing eyes, talons, and inky hide would reveal him as anything but. The portal had opened in a dead space between several large tents; he was still hidden from the merchants and travelers filling the paths and lanes around him, but that could change as quickly as a wandering child or lost shopper stumbling past a closed tent flap. He grabbed a discarded bucket and squinted, fingers and lips moving silently as he spun *Change* into it. As soon as his fingers twisted the last knot in the air he upended the bucket over his head. A stray bit of sand spilled out and blew away in the wind but the magery hit its mark, flowing over him like an invisible liquid, changing powerful talons and hooves to graceful hands and feet, glowing coals to cerulean eyes, oily black hide to smooth alabaster skin, and a midnight blue mane to flowing blond locks. He tossed the bucket away and looked down at himself to check his handiwork. Now he looked like Kin, and with another quick sketch of his fingers through the air he spun mana into appropriately ornate robes and boots with a purse to match. Ready, he pushed his way between a pair of tents and emerged into the crowd.

It was well into the afternoon, judging by the sun. Draconic forces would be arriving shortly, searching for him, but a quick glance up and down the lane showed no phalanxes moving through the crowd just yet. He turned left on a whim and calmly strolled down the crowded street. It was past the hottest part of the day and the residents of Asmara, shielded by bright robes and white tents, were out in force, but those near him gave him room, all the same. He was a head taller than most; his robe's hood served as a flag, warning people from his path. Kin were powerful, politically and otherwise. Being Kin had its privileges.

Random gating wasn't truly random—inevitably, one ended up where the Fates would have one go—so he strolled through Asmara to learn what They had in store for him today. He hoped he wouldn't have to start a fight here. Asmara was more useful to him intact than laid waste, and he had no quarrel with most of its people. Better to lure the dragons out into the wastes and fight them there, give the good folk a fireshow in the dead of night.

He found himself stopped by a crowd at the great stone plinth of the aerostat tower in the center of town. He paused, looking up and around. Something was off, and it took him a moment to realize what it was. There were Kin everywhere, dozens of them, a thick knot all gathered in front of the ticket agents. Kin moved about in the world but were an insular race, preferring their own company above others. To see so many in public in one place was almost unheard of, and the throng milling about watching them was proof. The crowd parted, giving him a path through. Kin were being moved quickly through the ticketing lines as the human attendants gave them priority, and he caught the eye of a woman coming his way.

"Returning to the Homelands for Conclave, sah?" Her tone said that she already knew the answer; her stylus was readied.

The question struck him squarely between the eyes. Conclave. So this was what the Fates had in mind. His luck had taken a turn for the better after all, and he fought down the demonic urge inside him that threatened to bring yet another unwelcome memory to the fore. "Of course," he answered with the haughty tone the woman would expect from Kin, suppressing the gleeful smile that threatened to spread across his face as he reached into his pouch for coin for the fare.

Conclave meant that the mage-king of the Kin was dying. He wouldn't miss it for all the worlds.

He gave the attendant a throwaway name. In short order, he had his ticket and berth and was moving to the stone tower's lift. Three aerostats were docked, offering brief respites from the late afternoon sun with their sleek shadows. The line waiting for the lift naturally bent along the darker ground. The Kin here would occupy one complete airship, and squinting up at the vessels he could see the crew of one preparing for its guests. An elderly Kin, hair greying, stumbled on the hem of her robe and caught herself on his shoulder. "Oh! Pardon me, Brother," she said, patting his back.

He fought down the bile and rage at her familial greeting. He visualized tearing her head from her shoulders and hurling it away, his talons slick with her arrogant blood, and briefly felt them prick against the palm of his closed hand. "Of course, Sister," he replied through barely-clenched teeth, offering her a curt nod before putting some distance between them. If he was going to see this through without being discovered, he needed to minimize his contact with other Kin lest his control falter.

He arrived at his stateroom and ducked inside, closing the door behind him and latching the bolt. It was posh almost to the point of flamboyance, with an overstuffed chair, ornate rugs, and a bed with a mattress three hands thick. He could have done with far less, but he'd paid for the best with counterfeit coin because it amused him to think of another Kin doing with less during the overnight voyage. He unclasped his robes as he strode across a hundred-year-old rug, letting them slide from his shoulders and puddle on the floor. The deck moved gently under his boots and he could hear the faraway shouts of the crew as the aero rose into the sky and turned to depart. He stopped at the window and looked down, watching Asmara wheel below him. Soon the subsonic hum of the vessel's propulsion ramped up and they were on their way.

When the last tent had disappeared from view, he closed the shutters and stepped away. He fell into the chair and leaned back, letting the thick padding accept and mold to him as he kicked off his boots. The rest of the Kin aboard would be gathering and socializing now, but he would not join them. Just thinking about them laying about smoking, gossiping, and preening threatened to provoke him again; at the very least, he was certain they wouldn't appreciate hearing what he'd been engaged in prior to arriving in Asmara.

His memories frothed and rose; they didn't control him directly, but they were a force all their own, as they had been since the day Rhaedon had finished with him. Left suppressed too long, they could turn his motivations against him. The incident with the old matron had shown him that his tolerance for them was even lower than he'd thought. He would need his wits about him if he was to see this through. Given the task he'd embarked upon, he could guess at what he was about to relive.

In the quiet darkness of his cabin, as the aerostat droned its way northward, the Scourge of Navarr closed his eyes and remembered.

*The bright sun of a spring day, the scent of the renewed woods thick in his nose. The forest waking around him, readying itself for the long run to autumn. The softly glowing string of his bow taut in his fingers, holding it at the ready for his prey, stalking for a kill. These are his last good memories.*

*Waking dizzy. Hard stone under him. Cold iron manacles connecting him to the walls of the damp cell. Calling for help, for anyone. Waiting. Calling again. Then Rhaedon, the mad dragon wizard, answering.*

*He is a test subject, an experiment, a thing to be jabbed and prodded and twisted. The pain comes quickly and never leaves. Indignities are heaped upon indignities. He suffers like none should. Escape is impossible. The hours stretch to days stretch to weeks, months, years until time becomes an abstract concept, a myth he vaguely recalls from childhood. Yet still his heart remains pure, untouched by Rhaedon's insanity, infuriating the wizard. He wishes he could give in and let the wizard succeed even at the cost of his soul, but he can't change his basic nature. He wishes he would just die, and fails at that as well.*

*Rhaedon escalates again and again until he dabbles in raw, primal evil. Only then does the wizard succeed, and then beyond his wildest dreams.*

*He breaks free, kills Rhaedon in one blow, and consumes him. Power fills him, a reservoir of strength so wide and deep as to have been dug by the pain and suffering he's endured, but he can only sip at the surface of it.*

*He escapes Rhaedon's keep to find it buried in the dead of winter. The Homelands are far but he travels the snowbound distance in the space of a day, awkward in his new power like a freshly-hatched chick stumbling about its nest. He somehow knows the way instinctively and tries to not question it. He arrives in the dead of night, weeping on a hilltop at the sight of lands he thought he'd never see again.*

*He is found by his brother, patrolling in the dark. A cloud slides over the moon, deepening the gloom. He expects help but finds none. "I have been sent," he is told, his brother's voice a hiss in the night. "You are unclean and an abomination, and not welcome in the Homelands. You are banished, and if you return I will kill you myself. You are forgotten." He cannot believe it. He begs, sobs, pleads for relief, but he is answered with silence.*

*He is alone, truly alone, but the cold emptiness left in the pit of his soul is warmed in short order by the rage in his heart. Dragons did this to him, and dragons will pay for it.*

*He returns to Rhaedon's keep. By day he inhabits the dead wizard's library, learning to harness the foul power now bound to him. By night he curses the countryside and its people, tearing his sustenance from their bones and testing his new skills. The few heroes who dare to pose a challenge expect to find Rhaedon but find him instead. They are excellent practice. Almost a decade passes before he is ready.*

*His first dragon kill is almost too easy. The beast doesn't know what to make of him and certainly doesn't take him seriously, and it dies with surprise in its eyes and a hole large enough to walk through in its heart.*

*More dragons fall to his vengeance and soon they abandon their solitary lifestyle in favor of survival in numbers. He taps more of his power, rising to their challenge. They gain allies in their fight and he takes his war to them as well, killing and destroying with surgical accuracy and horrific violence, appearing without warning and denying the dragons any hope of safe harbor. He targets all who would stand with them and soon the whole of Navarr knows him. He is the Scourge.*

He stepped off the aerostat tower's gantry arm and slid out of the line of Kin making their way to the ground, stopping at the railing and letting the breeze blow through his hair. Below him was Tin'tean, the largest city in the Homelands and its capitol, marble buildings carved in organic shapes placed among ancient trees in perfect harmony. Beyond the city lay the whole of the Homelands, the Kin's ancestral home. At the horizon he could see the purple snowcapped peaks of the Shield Range, the barrier between the Kin's lush lands and the burning wastes of the Barrens. "From here to the Crown of the World," as the saying went, the Kin's ancient claim and oath.

He'd not seen this in decades, and it suddenly struck him how the aerostat tower had been placed for the greatest spectacle. Any outsiders arriving would be presented with this grand display of Kin power and wealth. He suppressed a sneer at the thought. His eyes naturally fell on the broad expanse of the Avenue of the Host as it wound through the city, following it all the way to its terminus at the Citadel, the seat of Kin power, six tall obelisks marking the wall surrounding the central taller spire. The Avenue was teeming with Kin, as was the whole city. In the distance he could see the line snaking into the Citadel, Kin queued up to pay their respects to their dying king.

Conclave was a time for all Kin to come together and celebrate the King Who Was and the King Who Will Be, and they were streaming in from all over Navarr to this place as fast as they could. Already the aero that had delivered him was making ready to depart and free its berth for another arrival. Inns would surely be full by now; citizens were likely opening their homes to their brethren. He would have a hard time finding suitable lodging, but he wasn't planning on staying long enough to need it. Just long enough to see the old king's eyes, and know he would soon be gone.

He made his way down the tower's spiraling ramp and onto street level, face set in a thoughtful frown to avoid casual conversation. The Avenue was crowded but he weaved his way through without much incident. A few of the more jolly folk tried to speak to him anyway, but the poisonous glare he shot them was enough to turn them away. Those standing in the queue were considerably less boisterous. The line moved slowly but steadily, gradually drawing him inside the Citadel's walls. He could see a storm brewing in the distance as the sun began to set. He was patient. He had all the time in the worlds.

The line passed through a soaring entrance hall and down an echoing marble corridor a hundred hands wide. Ahead would be the reception hall where the king and royal family would receive their subjects; the king laying on a raised lounge of spun goldsilk, the Herald Queen with her staff standing on one side and the prince regent, the King Who Will Be, standing on the other.

The corridor sloped upwards toward the hall and as the line moved forward suddenly he could see them. Pure, clean anger instantly seized him when they came into view. He was rooted to the spot for a moment, fighting his immediate inclination to start slaughtering his way to them. The queen and prince solemnly greeted each Kin as they approached. The old king did his best to do likewise but for some he simply lay there, trying to conserve his strength and prolong his stay on this world.

No, he wouldn't give them the pleasure of knowing he had been here. Old voices from a hilltop whispered in the back of his mind, but the gentle friendly tap at his shoulder from the Kin behind him shook him from his reverie and got him moving again. The hallway, the reception hall, the somber line of Kin and the royal guard arrayed around them all shrank away but for those three at its apex. His dead heart thundered in his chest with anticipation.

The queen and prince bowed to him as he stepped forward, dipping their heads in unison. He only saw them peripherally; his eyes were fixed on King Aifeal's prone form. Already the first wisps of Ascension were rising from his frail body, tenuous strands of mana twisting into the air as his physical form began to lose coherency and evaporate. The old bastard had maybe two days left. He'd gotten here just in time.

He bowed, a politely grim smile on his face. The king's eyes rolled to meet his and froze, then widened. The old mage seemed to deflate with a sigh—a *relieved* sigh. "You've come back after all," he whispered.

The Scourge froze. Impossible. His disguise was impenetrable. He looked up in alarm to see the queen and prince looking back at him, as confused as he was shocked.

The queen saw it first, her teal eyes growing as realization dawned. "Alc—"

He was faster than she. "Don't," he spat at her through clenched teeth. "Say that name and I'll burn you down where you stand." His brother the prince took a step forward, hand flashing to the hilt of his saber.

"No," the king murmured, raising thin fingers. The prince stopped, one step shy of drawing his blade and ensuring his own death. Aifeal turned his head carefully to his wife, who still gazed in horrified amazement at her disguised son. "Clear the hall," he said. "I will speak with him."

That brought her back to the present. She shook her head. "Aifeal, no…" The Scourge locked eyes with his brother and felt his muscles ripple with the promise of imminent violence.

The king nodded once. "I will. Have the guard seal the hall until I am finished." The queen looked back at the Scourge, then the prince regent, then finally at the rest of the hall. Deviation from protocol was strange enough, but whatever had caused the prince to nearly attack this random Kin had gotten the attention of the royal guard and the other Kin still waiting in line. Aifeal had spoken and it was her duty to pass the word. She hesitated only a second before pressing her lips together and nodding once. She turned, gesturing for the prince to follow. He reluctantly fell into step behind her, finally taking his eyes from his brother and stepping from the dais.

This was all highly unusual, but after a moment the guard followed orders and began herding everyone from the hall. The Scourge waited, watching his dying father as if daring the king to attack him. The king simply lay on his lounge and stared up through the skylight at the darkening sky. When the tall marble doors finally boomed shut, he returned his gaze to his son. "Did you really think I wouldn't be able to sense my own flesh and blood?" he asked with a tired smile.

That answered his first question. He wasn't in the mood for games. "And yet you stopped Eadmhar from drawing his sword? You've gotten soft in your old age, Father," he said bitterly, beginning to pace. "I didn't come here for a reunion, you old fool. I came to watch you die."

The king sighed again, his breath visible in the air despite the hall's warmth. His eyes drifted shut. "I owe you an apology—"

The Scourge whirled on him, the silver tips of his boots ringing on the marble as he stormed to the king's bedside. "An apology?" he shouted, burning blood pounding in his ears. "Do you think that could possibly undo what you did? Do you think it would change the past somehow and set things to right? By all means then, Father, please apologize to me." He stood back, arms thrown wide.

"And an explanation," the king continued patiently after his son's outburst. "I am sorry for what happened to you, and for what I did. Not since the decree passed my lips has a sun risen without my regret to greet it. You, my beloved firstborn, you were my heir and the best of us."

"And yet you banished me! I fought to survive, to endure, to escape, to return to the Homelands, and with it in my sight you sent your new heir to turn me away? Tell me, Father," he yelled, beating his chest. "Tell me how much you regret turning away another Kin in need, tell me how much you regret denying your son."

"I had no choice," the king moaned, fingers tangling weakly in the lounge's sheet. "The Council divined what had happened to you once Rhaedon was slain. They wanted to kill you before you could harness your power and become a danger, and because—" He choked to a stop, clenching his jaw, trying to will the words to come. He looked to the barred doors, unable to look at his looming son. "Because your corruption was proof that none of us was worthy of our claims. Better you never return and your disappearance stay a secret forever than have to face that."

The Scourge seethed, furious, hands clenched in fists, waiting. He could feel his grip on his temper slipping, one strand at a time.

The king's words came quicker now as his story spilled out. "I bargained for your life. I convinced them to spare you in exchange for banishment, in the hopes that you would go on to live a full life in peace, safe from the fears of ill-advised old fools." Aifeal's glimmering eyes rose again to meet his son's. "I banished you so you could live, because I loved you. I could not bear otherwise."

"And do you think I've lived up to my promise, Father?" The Scourge laughed. "Oh yes, I've achieved so much! Thank you for the opportunity, I hate to think what wouldn't have gotten done in my absence." He gave him a mock bow, far too deep to be serious.

"No," the king whispered, closing his eyes and shaking his head. "I don't regret saving your life, but you must stop your campaign against the dragons."

The Scourge snapped upright, nostrils flaring. "You dare?" he whispered, then shouted, "You dare tell me what to do? You've disowned me, dear Father. Better than that, you've banished me from the Kin." He stalked back toward the king, body trembling, and jabbed a finger at him. "The dragons think they know what's best, that they can just meddle with those they consider their lessers."

"As you have done with them?" the king asked.

"They brought this upon themselves, and I will not stop until they have all learned that the price of their arrogance is very high indeed!"

The king patiently met his son's eyes. "Are you so blinded by your revenge that you cannot see what you've done? The dragons were isolated. Powerful, yes, but unorganized. They couldn't muster any sort of real power in Navarr because they never saw the merits of it. Until you came along. Until you started slaying them with impunity. You are the one who united them. You are the reason they brought the lesser races under their wing, the better to protect them from your eventual predation, and when they joined the Draconic Combine you only proved them right. You woke them to the influence they always had but never knew. Their reign over Navarr is your doing, as surely as if you'd drawn the borders yourself."

The Scourge slammed to a halt, physically and mentally. "No," he said, eyes empty, but he knew it for the truth. It was perfectly clear to him now. How could he have missed it all? How had he not seen the signs? His mind whirled, his thoughts tumbling about without traction. In his campaign to show the dragons the folly of their ways, he had embarked on the very same path as they, and in the process ensured their rise to power.

The king paused as his son floundered, then whispered, "You must stop it, Alcre—"

*You are forgotten*, his memory whispered in his ear.

"NO!" The Scourge's fury blasted *Change* from him. Blond hair and perfect skin flashed to vapor, talons reaching out as he grew taller and stronger with his anger. The shockwave hammered the walls of the reception hall, shaking ancient dust from the tops of the pillars. Shouts started outside the closed doors and the Scourge turned to his father, pointing a too-long finger toward the entrance. "I am the Scourge," he hissed, leaning down until the king could see nothing past him. "It is my charge to put the arrogant in their place and I can see now that I've been lax in my duties." He grinned a smile full of teeth that had no place on a Kin's face. "I believe I will correct that."

The doors flew open and the royal guard charged in with spears at the ready, but stopped when they saw the monster with their king. "Impossible," gasped one. The queen stood by a door, watching with horrified eyes as the prince regent raced past, pulling his sword from its scabbard and roaring a battle cry.

"Excellent," the Scourge hissed, still grinning, as he stepped away from the king to face his brother's charge. His arms moved in quick, practiced movements as he began to spin *The Fist That Pierces*.

"*STOP*." It wasn't a shout, but a thought—a base urge triggered deep inside everyone's minds. Eadmhar stumbled to a halt, his blade clattering from boneless fingers. The Scourge froze where he was, one hand raised in an electric blue glow, ready to split his brother in half. King Aifeal lifted from his bed to stand in the air above it. Ethereal fog rippled and poured from him like steam from a boiling pot. He was sublimating completely from the effort. The Scourge was the last to turn and see it, and even he lowered his arm in awe at the sight, his hand still glowing with primed death.

"I cannot change the past, but I can change the future." It wasn't the voice of the elderly king, weakened and waiting for Ascension. It was the voice of his childhood, the voice of his father, good and strong and clear. "Pass the words of this, my final decree." Kin gasped from the doorway and the queen shook herself and strode forward to perform her last duty, crystal staff in hand. The king turned to his firstborn. "My son suffered a grave injury, and I have compounded it with my foolish shortsightedness. He is

Kin, as he should always have been. Never again will Kin be driven from Kin. The true nature of the Scourge will remain the secret burden of us all, from now until the worlds wind down."

The Scourge felt his hand unclench and the power captive in it leach back into the mana stream. He hadn't sobbed since a dark hilltop decades ago, but now his eyes began to burn as the King Who Was gazed down at him, smiling, calm and at peace as he dissolved into nothingness. "I love you, and I am sorry," he whispered. And then King Aifeal, 38th in the Line of the Kin, was gone.

The Scourge turned, numb, and slowly walked from the dais where his father once lay, the echo of his hooves the only sound in the hall. The guards and the crowd behind them parted to let him through, watching as he passed. Behind him he heard a soft sob and then the sharp ring of crystal on marble, followed by his mother's quivering voice. "Pass the word from Kin to Kin, from here to the Crown of the World. The Scourge is Kin, as he should always have been. Never again will Kin be driven from Kin. The true nature of the Scourge will remain the secret burden of us all, from now until the worlds wind down."

He heard the Herald Staff come down again and the decree was sent, a brilliant ring of light that flashed past him as it carried its message to every Kin. As he left the Citadel, Kin stopped to turn and watch, to see the legendary nightmare now among them as he should always have been. Behind him, bells began to toll the passing of the King Who Was, fading into the distance as he walked into the night, hooves carrying him away from Tin'tean and deep into the forest. Thunder rumbled, and when the rain had finally soaked him through, Alcreagh stopped, turned, and spun open a gate.

---

STEVE BORNSTEIN has been in the military, travelled to distant lands, and held the sorts of jobs you watch shows about on the Discovery Channel. His villainous inspirations include Snidely Whiplash, Ming the Merciless, and Walter Bishop. He lives in Central Texas with his wife, where they pay daily tribute to their feline overlords.

# ABOUT THE EDITORS

ED GREENWOOD is a Canadian writer and librarian best known as the creator of the Forgotten Realms® fantasy world setting. He's also an award-winning game designer and New York Times bestselling author, once hailed as "the Canadian author of the great American novel," whose fantasy novels have sold millions of copies worldwide in more than thirty languages. Ed shares a farmhouse with his wife, a reigning cat, and over 80,000 books. He's currently busy scripting a monthly Forgotten Realms® comic book from IDW, and writing his usual three novels at once. His most recent novel is *Elminster Enraged* from Wizards of the Coast.

GABRIELLE HARBOWY is an award-nominated writer and editor of fantasy and science fiction. She copyedits for Pyr, Seven Realms Publishing and Lambda Literary Review, and is Managing Editor at Dragon Moon Press. She has worked with first-time authors, New York Times Bestsellers, and Hugo Award winners, and has acquired books that have gone on to become finalists and winners of ForeWord Magazine's Book of the Year, the Bram Stoker Award, the Prix Aurora, and the Lambda Literary Award, to name a few. As a writer, her short fiction appears in print and podcast anthologies. She is based in San Francisco in the real world, and can be found on the web at www.gabrielle-edits.com, and on Twitter as @gabrielle_h.

Made in the USA
Lexington, KY
07 December 2012